WWP
2/18

2-

I10385231

THE PERFECT MURDER

Also by BRENDA NOVAK

THE PERFECT LIAR
THE PERFECT COUPLE
WATCH ME
STOP ME
TRUST ME
DEAD RIGHT
DEAD GIVEAWAY
DEAD SILENCE
COLD FEET
TAKING THE HEAT
EVERY WAKING MOMENT

BRENDA NOVAK

THE PERFECT MURDER

MIRA®

MIRA®

ISBN-13: 978-1-61523-274-1

THE PERFECT MURDER

Copyright © 2009 by Brenda Novak.

All rights reserved. Except for use in any review, the reproduction or
utilization of this work in whole or in part in any form by any electronic,
mechanical or other means, now known or hereafter invented, including
xerography, photocopying and recording, or in any information storage or
retrieval system, is forbidden without the written permission of the publisher,
MIRA Books, 225 Duncan Mill Road, Don Mills, Ontario, Canada M3B 3K9.

This is a work of fiction. Names, characters, places and incidents are
either the product of the author's imagination or are used fictitiously, and
any resemblance to actual persons, living or dead, business establishments,
events or locales is entirely coincidental.

MIRA and the Star Colophon are trademarks used under license and registered
in Australia, New Zealand, Philippines, United States Patent and Trademark
Office and in other countries.

Printed in U.S.A.

To my Aunt Judy and all her "ladies"—
I love hearing how you swap my books at the salon.
Here's hoping you enjoy the latest!

Dear Reader,

I was so excited about writing this book—even more than usual—probably because I knew I'd be using Jane Burke as the heroine. Jane was a secondary character in *Trust Me* (the wife of the villain), but with her experiences and background, I found her very worthy as a lead. In this story she's back on her feet and actually working at The Last Stand fighting crime along with Skye Kellerman, the woman who saved her life five years ago. But it isn't smooth sailing for Jane quite yet. Not when she gets involved in a case that puts danger front and center in her life once again.

It's hard to believe that I've already completed six books in this series—*Trust Me, Stop Me, Watch Me, The Perfect Couple, The Perfect Liar* and this one. While these books are only loosely connected and you certainly don't have to read one to enjoy the others, you might enjoy spending a little more time with some of the continuing characters.

Please visit me on the Web at www.brendanovak.com. There you can enter my many contests and giveaways, read interviews with various professionals in the criminal justice world, download free 3-D screen savers, take a virtual tour of the Last Stand offices, read a short prequel to the whole series, and more. If you sign up for my mailing list, you'll be invited to my annual cyber-Christmas party, which is a blast. Also at my Web site you can learn more about my annual online auction for diabetes research, an event I sponsor every May (my youngest son suffers from this disease). Together with my fans, friends, fellow authors and publishing associates, I've managed to raise over $700,000 to date. Don't miss the auction in 2010. It's going to be amazing!

For a free pair of 3-D glasses, send an S.A.S.E. to Brenda Novak at P.O. Box 3781, Citrus Heights, CA 95611.

Stay safe!

Brenda Novak

That I may tell pale-hearted fear it lies,
And sleep in spite of thunder.

—William Shakespeare

Prologue

These men who killed their wives...they didn't have a clue how to do it right, how to get away with it.

Malcolm Turner frowned in disgust as the credits appeared at the end of the true-crime show he'd just watched on TV. It had featured a male nurse who'd murdered his mouthy, blonde wife. As far as Malcolm was concerned, she'd deserved what she got—she'd been a straight-up bitch. But what kind of idiot talks about succinyl chloride right before using it to end a life?

"Punk," Malcolm muttered and glanced over at his wife, asleep in bed next to him. When he killed her and her teenage son, no one would question a thing. They'd believe exactly what he wanted them to believe because he knew what the hell he was doing.

He should—he'd been in law enforcement for fifteen years.

One

Mary looked good. Better than she had in high school. There were more curves to her body, a new sophistication to her face, and her smile seemed to have more meaning behind it. But Malcolm could tell she was weary. The divorce had taken a heavy toll. And she did a lot for her two boys.

He shifted, ducking when he heard an engine in the street. He was partly shielded by a large poplar tree and, judging by the volume of the music emanating from what appeared to be a muscle car, the driver was probably a teenage boy who was as oblivious and self-absorbed as he used to be at that age. But it wouldn't do to have someone see him peeking in Mary's windows.

The car, bass pounding through its speakers, passed without slowing. Then the beat and the motor dimmed, and the neighborhood returned to sleep mode. This was Malcolm's favorite time to watch Mary—although he sometimes came when the sun was up, too, if he thought she'd be home from work. Now that he was unemployed it was hard to fill all the hours in a day. His new life hadn't turned out remotely the way he'd imagined when he'd planned to start over. He missed the people he'd known before, wanted to contact some of them— but they thought he was dead and they had to go on thinking that.

Maybe that was why, after so many years, he'd looked up his high-school sweetheart and followed her to California. The compulsion to reconnect didn't make much sense otherwise. He'd moved on without her quite easily twenty years ago. Married twice, divorced once and…

He didn't want to think about what he'd done to his second wife. He didn't regret killing her or her son. As far as he was concerned, they deserved what they got. But ever since he'd gambled away most of the insurance settlement he'd taken when he left Jersey, he'd been forced to live in dumpy rental houses out in the boon-docks where the smell of cow shit was so strong it sometimes felt as if he was standing in it. Tough to find something better when the only jobs he could get were at two-bit security companies that paid a buck or two over minimum wage.

With a silent curse, he remembered the last job he'd held. It wasn't the meager pay that bothered him so much as the lack of respect. He couldn't take it; not after being a real cop.

Fingering the badge he still carried everywhere, he slid to the next window so he could have a better view of Mary checking her computer. She was probably expecting to hear from him. Claiming to be someone she'd once met briefly, he'd contacted her through her jewelry-making Web site and managed to strike up a relationship.

But hiding behind an alias and a computer screen wasn't satisfying him tonight. He was bored, restless....

After only a few minutes at the computer, Mary stood and started turning off the lights. With the kids in school and her job at the hospital, she was pretty damned predictable. From here, she'd go into her bedroom, pull the blinds and the show would be over.

Unless she didn't bother with the blinds. In the months he'd been watching her, she'd forgotten only once, but that gave him hope.

Creeping around to the other side of the house, he squatted in the shrubbery and waited for her to enter her bedroom.

She came in, turned on the TV, put away some clothes that were folded and sitting on a chair. Then she approached the window. They were only inches apart, so close he could see the mascara smudges that told him she'd been rubbing her eyes—

Then the blind went down.

Shit. Malcolm sank lower on his haunches. What now? Should he head to the Indian casinos and while away a few hours?

No. He needed something more visceral, something more exciting, something to remind him of the power he'd once enjoyed.

He toyed with the idea of slipping into the house, exploring the empty rooms, touching Mary's things, stealing a pair of her panties. Maybe even watching her sleep. The temptation to do so was growing stronger every day. He certainly thought about it a lot. But he was afraid he'd get caught and screw up the possibility of having a real relationship with her once he could trust her enough to reveal his true identity. He'd come too far to blow all that by being impatient....

He had to leave. But that didn't mean he had to call it a night. Thinking of the Kojak light he kept in his van, he felt his mood improve. Playing cop wouldn't put him in Mary's bed tonight, but it would give him the adrenaline rush he craved—and maybe a few sexual favors to go with it.

Three weeks later...

Jane Burke recognized an opportunity when she saw one. Ever since she'd started working at The Last Stand, she'd been waiting for her chance, hoping a case would come along that would allow her to prove herself.

She was pretty sure it had just walked through the door.

"The man who let me in said you might be able to help me." A short cannonball of a woman stood uncertainly in the entryway of Jane's office, swiping at tear-filled eyes.

Motioning for her to come farther into the room, Jane brought over a box of tissues. "I'll do my best," she promised. "But first I need to learn more about why you're here."

The young woman's obesity made it difficult to guess her age, but Jane pegged her at twenty-four or twenty-five. Gerald, the volunteer who'd admitted her, had told Jane she had two siblings who'd recently gone missing. So far, that was all Jane knew. If it'd been on the news, she hadn't seen it or heard about it. But that wasn't too surprising. She'd been so busy she hadn't even turned on the TV. "What's your name?"

In an attempt to control her emotions, the woman took two tissues and blew her nose. "Gloria. Gloria Rickman."

"Gloria, I'm Jane Burke. Please sit down so we can talk." Jane returned the tissue box to its generally ignored corner, then pulled a chair away from the wall, placing it in front of the desk, where it would've been if she'd been in the habit of taking her own cases. She was still in training, had been since she'd started six months ago, which meant she did all the tedious record searches, time-consuming court runs and boring clerical work for the three partners who were the backbone of the victims' charity. But she had a feeling the criminal justice courses she'd been taking, and everything she'd learned on the job, was about to pay off. With Skye Willis and Ava Trussell in South America on a rare job-for-hire, tracking a father who'd stolen his child from his ex-wife, and Sheridan Granger out on maternity leave, Jane had been left in charge of the office. This was the perfect time to tackle her first case. Other than the three volunteers who came in to stuff envelopes or solicit donations, she was the only person here.

"Let me get a notebook. Then I want you to tell me what's upset you so much."

The chair creaked as the woman settled into it. Rolls of flesh spilled over the wooden frame, but Jane didn't care about her excess weight. She'd once been heavy herself. Maybe not quite to this degree, but definitely frumpy. If not for the counseling, daily workout sessions and self-defense classes that'd become her routine—all a product in one way or another of her friendship with Skye—she'd probably still be the disillusioned, over-weight, hard-edged smoker she'd been four years ago.

Now she ran an hour a day, weighed a trim one hundred and ten pounds, and had stopped trying to kill herself with cigarettes. Only her smoker's voice remained. And the scars from that period of her life, of course. They'd never go away entirely—especially the ones on the inside.

"I'm here 'bout my two sisters," Gloria said. "They went missin' three weeks ago."

"Three *weeks* ago?" Jane echoed, unable to hide her shock.

Tears welled up again. "Three weeks ago las' Saturday."

It was Monday morning. That added another day, almost two.

"Why haven't I heard about this?"

"I don't know. There were articles in the paper. I reported it to the police the same afternoon it happened," she said, "but the detective who called me ain't found nothin' yet. He's been tryin', but...no one's got any idea where my sisters are an'...I'm so scared. That's why I'm here. I have to do somethin' more. I can't jus' sit around an' wait. I'm all they have. I'm all they ever had."

"Where're your parents?"

"We have different fathers, but none of 'em are any good," she said. "Our mother didn't hang with the best crowd, you hear what I'm sayin'? She died of a drug overdose when I was twenty-three. I was the oldest and had my own place, so I moved my sisters in with me. Latisha, the youngest, wasn't even in high school yet."

Jane could easily identify with being raised by another member of the family. Her parents had been killed in a car accident when she was six, leaving her to be raised by an aging aunt who'd stayed single her entire life and had since died, as well. "Where do you live?"

"In a one-bedroom apartment on Marconi. We been there since they came to live with me. It's a small place, but we make it work. I won't uproot 'em again and again and again, like what my mama did to me."

"It's wonderful that you've been able to provide some stability," Jane said. "How long ago did you assume responsibility for them?"

"It's been 'bout three years now. They eighteen and seventeen. They both graduated this last June," she stated proudly. "Marcie got her GED, but Latisha, she was put up a grade on account of she's so smart. She graduated with honors and won a scholarship to Sac State."

So the missing sisters were, for the most part, adults. That was probably why this case hadn't become a major focus for the media. That and the fact that there'd been nothing more to report. "Did you have an argument with them? Try to punish them? Anything that might've made them angry enough to leave?"

"We argue all the time, but that ain't what's wrong, Ms.—"

"Jane. You can call me Jane."

"They ain't never left before. They know I yell 'cause I want 'em to be more and have more than our mother. They gotta go to college. They keep tryin' to drop out so they can help me keep a roof over our heads. It's tough to earn a livin' workin' at a convenience store. I put in a good sixty, seventy hours a week. But I got Marcie's tuition at ARC to pay for, in addition to all the other bills. They're what make it worth doin'—knowin' they'll have a better life if I keep goin'. I can't lose 'em." More tears streaked her bronze cheeks. "We been through too much. It can't end like this."

Already Jane feared she might be in over her head. *Be careful what you wish for,* she silently chided herself. She'd been bugging Skye to let her start taking on her own cases, and Skye kept saying she wasn't ready. But if she didn't get involved now, Gloria would have to wait for Skye and Ava to return. Depending on what happened in South America, that could take a week to ten days, maybe longer. With the economy the way it was, donations were down by a significant margin. Skye and Ava needed to finish this job in order to keep the charity's doors open. That was the only reason Skye's husband had agreed to her going so far away. He was the one who'd insisted Ava go with her, since he couldn't take the time off work. They wouldn't be back until the woman who'd contracted them had her child back. And Sheridan, their other partner, was planning to spend the next three or four months at home with her new baby.

"Have you been in touch with all their friends?" Jane asked. "Do you have any other family in the area?"

"I talked to everybody. I been on the phone night an' day. Ain't nobody seen 'em."

"When's the last time you had contact?"

"That same Saturday. Latisha was sleepin' when I had Marcie take me to work. Latisha had to wait tables at noon and Marcie had to be at the Rancho Cordova Marriott at three. She's a maid." She leaned forward, as if taking Jane into her confidence. "I let 'em work part-time if they're keepin' up with their schoolwork and all." She rocked back. "Anyway, Latisha never showed up at the restaurant. I didn't know 'cause nobody called me. But when Marcie didn't go to work like she always does, the hotel wanted to know what was what. I tried her cell, but it kept goin' to voice mail."

"So you're thinking they disappeared from your apartment?"

"No. As soon as I could get someone to cover the store, I took the bus home and foun' the house Jus' fine, locked up an' everythin'. But the car was gone. We have a little Honda Civic."

Jane made a note of this information. "Is there any chance your sisters could be into drugs, Gloria?"

"Oh, no! You think I'd let *that* happen after I watched my mama kill herself with that shit? After all I done to raise 'em up good? They wouldn't dare. They know I'd kick their asses clear to kingdom come."

Jane believed she would, too. "Where do you think they might've driven?"

Gloria's double chin wagged as she shook her head. "With the price of gas, they had no business goin' nowhere. We gotta pinch pennies jus' to survive. Mosta the time, we take the bus. But maybe Marcie decided to buy some doughnuts and a paper. She been talkin' 'bout gettin' a new job, a better one. That's my best guess, since the car was found near Hank's Donuts. Hank's is our favorite."

Jane quickly tried to assemble the scenario in her mind. Car abandoned; girls missing. Both sisters were going to school and working. They were also living in an environment that wasn't easy by any stretch of the imagination, but it was very apparent that they were at least loved. What could've gone wrong?

"What condition was the car in? Did it have a flat, a breakdown?" she asked.

"That car has one problem after another. It ain't worth but a few hundred bucks. But the police found it parked on a residential street off Franklin Boulevard, a few blocks from the doughnut place, like I said. And it was runnin' jus' fine."

"Was there anything inside to indicate where your sisters had been that morning—some napkins from Hank's? A grocery sack? A Starbucks cup?"

"Jus' the books and stuff they leave in there all the time. I keep tellin' 'em not to leave their backpacks in the car. It don't even lock right. But sometimes they do. You know what kids are like these days."

This woman was only in her twenties, but she acted a lot closer to Jane's forty-six. With so much responsibility thrust on her at such a young age, she probably *felt* at least forty. "What about cell phones? Have the police checked to see if they've been used since Latisha and Marcie disappeared?"

"Their phones were in the car." Covering her face, Gloria broke into sobs but spoke through them. "That's another way I knew they didn't walk off. They wouldn't leave their phones behind. We got no money for two extra cell phones but they'd rather go without food."

This wasn't sounding very hopeful. Jane forced a pleasant expression to cover her concern. "Do you have the phones? We'll need to check all incoming and outgoing calls. It's possible they know someone you didn't realize they know. Maybe that person's seen them since you have."

"The police have the phones. A detective's goin' through their recent calls."

"Which detective is that?"

"They gave the case to a white guy named Willis. He a handsome man. But he wearin' a weddin' ring. I checked."

Jane might've been tempted to laugh at Gloria's aside, but she was too distracted by the name. "Did you say Willis?"

"Yes, ma'am, I did."

Too bad. Willis was Skye's husband. That would be tricky if Jane wanted to hide her involvement from her bosses, who wouldn't be happy to hear she'd dived in without permission.

On the other hand, having David on the case was fortuitous, too, since he was cooperative and sympathetic to what they were trying to accomplish at The Last Stand. Not all members of the department were friendly. They believed the mere existence of TLS sent a message to the community that the police weren't being effective. Some of the unflattering comments Skye, Ava and Sheridan occasionally made to the media didn't help. "Your husband's the cop, not you!" someone had yelled at Skye a few weeks ago.

Jane wasn't a cop, either. She wasn't even a full caseworker. Not yet. But if she'd learned anything in the past six months it was that drive, determination and sheer hard work could make up for a lot in an investigation.

Gloria was explaining the situation in greater detail. Taking a deep breath, Jane refocused.

"I guess Detective Willis worked them cases down by the American River a few years back." She wiped her nose. *"Murders.* They think this might be related."

Jane felt her eyebrows slide up. If those cases were the ones that sprang immediately to *her* mind, this wasn't related. It couldn't be. Jane knew the perpetrator. She'd been living with him at the time. Oliver Burke was dead. But the memory of what he'd done in the years she'd been married to him still made her shudder. He'd been so good at compartmentalizing, at playing whatever part he needed to play in order to avoid detection. He'd fooled even her, right up until the end.

That was what she had to offer The Last Stand that none of the others could, she reminded herself. She knew how a psychopath thought, how he behaved, how manipulative he could be. Not only had she shared a decade of her life with Oliver, she had a child by him— and was nearly murdered by him, too.

"I'll give Detective Willis a call," she told Gloria. "I know him. He's a friend."

The chair groaned as Gloria shifted. "You don't think my sisters are dead, do you? I can't even imagine what I'd do if they was dead."

Jane wanted to promise that they weren't. But Latisha and Marcie had been gone for three weeks. They'd left their car and their cell phones behind, and there'd been no trace of them. What were the chances that they weren't lying lifeless in the woods somewhere? The only thing they had going for them was the fact that they'd been together. That was better than disappearing alone. Unless the worst had happened. Then Gloria would lose both sisters at once.

"We'll find them, one way or another," she said. "Can you get me some photographs?"

"I got 'em right here." She took several pictures from a large purse, as well as a crudely made flyer. "I been postin' that flyer everywhere I can."

Jane accepted these items, stared into the faces of the missing girls and felt a renewed sense of urgency as they became real to her. One had a distinctly darker complexion than the other, cornrows and a nose piercing. The name *Marcie* was written at the bottom. The other, Latisha, had almond-shaped eyes, a wide smile and an attractive bob. "Good idea," she said. "I'll do what I can from here."

"Thank you." Gloria dabbed at her wet cheeks. "I— I got no money, but I'll do whatever I—"

"Don't worry about fees," Jane hurried to interject, setting the pictures and the flyer, which had the word *MISSING* written in large block letters across the top, on the edge of her desk. "Our services are free to those who need them."

Relief eased some of the tension in the other woman's bearing. "Hallelujah! Thank you, God."

"I might require some insight or answers as we go along, however," Jane continued. "Can you give me your contact information?"

Gloria complied with an address, work number and cell phone number.

"What about their fathers, and your father?" Jane asked. "Can you tell me how to reach these men?"

"What would you want with *my* no-good father?"

"I'm just being thorough."

"I don't want him callin' me again." She sank lower

in her seat. "But...I'll do anything if it'll help. His name's Timothy Huff. I don't have a number for him, but you can find him down at the pool hall on Florin Road most Fridays, drunker'n a skunk."

That was loose contact information indeed. "And Marcie's dad?"

"He call every once in a while from prison."

At least they could rule him out. "What's he in for?"

"Possession."

"That leaves Latisha's dad."

Gloria shook her head. "You don't wanna bother Luther Wilson. He got a' anger management problem. We call him Lucifer, but we do it behind his back. That's how bad he is."

"Does he know his daughter's missing?"

"I haven't told him," she said. "What's the use? He don' care 'bout her. He never has."

Jane dropped her pen and steepled her fingers. "How'd your mother meet these men?"

"Turnin' tricks."

"You're saying she was a prostitute?"

"She had to pay for her drugs somehow."

That explained a lot. "What's so scary about Lucifer—I mean, Luther?" she corrected.

"He was her pimp, and he beat the hell out of her."

Now Jane *knew* she was in over her head. She liked to believe a bottle of bleach and a couple of tattoos made her look tough. But at five foot four she was no match for an angry pimp. "I'll keep that in mind." Standing, she managed a smile. "Thanks for coming in. I'll call you when I've had a chance to do some checking."

When Jane walked her to the door, Gloria said, "Thank you. Thank you so much."

Jane wasn't prepared for the embrace that accompanied those words, but as Gloria's shoulders shook beneath her arms, she felt a renewed determination. She wanted to help, but could she handle this case?

Pimps. Prostitutes. Drugs. She'd never been part of that world. She'd lived with a psychopath, but Oliver was dead, and she was safe. She'd been safe for nearly five years....

Jumping into this was asking for trouble. Most people were kidnapped or killed by a family member or friend, which meant she *had* to contact Latisha's father. She had to talk to everyone associated with the missing girls. That was one of the cardinal rules of a good investigation.

But if Luther had anything to do with what had happened to his daughter and her sister, he certainly wouldn't want her snooping around....

Two

Sebastian Costas held the slip of paper the ATM had just spit out closer to his face. This wasn't a pleasant way to start the week. Was the damn machine running out of ink? Because the figure he saw had to be missing a zero. He knew he was getting low on funds. It'd been more than a year since he'd worked. In addition to the payments on his Manhattan flat and vehicles—not to mention parking for those vehicles—he'd spent a fortune on private investigators, skip tracers, airfare, hotels and rental cars. But…

"Shit, I must've thought the money would last forever." Apparently, he'd gotten too used to being able to buy whatever he wanted.

What now? he asked himself. He couldn't keep on like this.

"Excuse me. Are you finished?"

A woman stood behind him, waiting to use the ATM. He hadn't heard her approach, hadn't sensed her presence. He'd been too absorbed in considering what the paltry figure on that receipt signified.

Muttering an apology, he crumpled the paper and tossed it in the garbage on his way to the car. Nearing the end of his money meant he was almost out of time. He had a month, max. Then he'd be absolutely broke and the effort he'd put into his search would be wasted because all progress would grind to a halt.

He couldn't let that happen. He was closer now than he'd ever been.

His cell phone rang. Caller ID showed it was Constance, the woman he'd been dating when he left New York two months ago. They'd been together since before Emily and Colton were killed. But she was growing impatient with his lengthy absence and the intensity of his preoccupation.

He almost silenced the ringer and let it go to voice mail. He didn't want to talk to her right now. But ignoring her call could very easily mean the end of their relationship. He was already hanging on to her by a very thin thread. Did he want his life to be in *total* ruins after the nightmare he'd been living was over?

No. He needed to fight for her, fight for what was left of his former existence. "Hello?"

She didn't bother with a greeting. "Have you thought about it?" she demanded.

"Thought about what?" He knew exactly what she meant, but he was stalling for time. Although he'd had all morning to think about it, he wasn't any closer to making a decision now than when she'd delivered her ultimatum late last night.

"About coming home! Will you give up this…this obsession, Sebastian?"

Obsession? Was that what it'd become? He supposed

so. A man didn't abandon the kind of life he'd led for less. He'd been making more than half a million a year as one of the best investment bankers in NYC—until his ex-wife and son were murdered. After that, all he'd cared about was finding the man responsible.

Of course, given what the market had done since he'd taken leave from his job, he probably wouldn't have continued to make that amount even if he'd kept on working.

He unlocked the Lexus he'd rented. "Why the sudden rush, Constance?"

"Rush?" she echoed with incredulity. "I've waited eighteen *months* for our lives to return to normal."

"I've only been gone two."

"Are you kidding me? In the past year and a half, you've traveled all over the country, talking to various people, researching leads. Even when you were home, you shut yourself up in your condo and worked like some kind of mad scientist. This case is all you've been able to think about since the night it happened. We haven't made love in four months, haven't had a decent conversation since you turned into Dick Tracy."

He'd loved her, would've married her if murder hadn't disrupted his whole world. But what used to be didn't matter. Colton and Emily were dead and Emily's money was gone. Why? He couldn't give up the quest to uncover the truth. He was Emily and Colton's last hope—the only person, besides his own mother perhaps, who truly believed Malcolm Turner was still alive.

"I can't blame you for being disappointed." He slid behind the wheel and cranked the engine. A Sacramento winter wasn't nearly as cold as a New York winter, but it was chilly enough to require a heater.

"Then what are you going to do about it?"

She was far more direct now than she'd been before, which made him assume she might've met someone else. He'd expected it to happen a lot sooner, couldn't blame her for being ready to move on. A model-turned-stock-analyst, she was intelligent, successful, beautiful.

And yet, every day he widened the chasm between them. He couldn't promise to fly back to New York because he knew he'd break that promise. When he and other family members had gone through the house and boxed up Colton's and Emily's belongings, they hadn't found several things they should have. One was evidence of where the money had gone, money Emily had mentioned to him a week before her death. She'd said there was a safety-deposit box containing the five-hundred-thousand-dollar insurance settlement she'd received for being hit by a drunk driver. She'd said she was keeping it liquid, saving it for a new life, one without Malcolm in it, and showed him where he could find the key in case something should ever happen to her.

Planning to donate it to NYU—where Colton had hoped to go to school—Sebastian had attempted to claim it. The key was there. But the box was empty. And there was no indication of where the money had been moved.

Malcolm had not only killed Emily and Colton, he'd profited from it. Sebastian was sure of that.

"Malcolm didn't die in the crash, Constance."

"Oh, God, here we go again!"

It was beginning to rain. The windshield wipers came on automatically—a minor luxury he wouldn't be able to afford much longer. Considering his financial situation, he'd have to get a cheaper rental car.

"And what evidence do you have?" she went on. "That insurance settlement you're always talking about? You told me yourself Malcolm liked to gamble on football games, basketball games, any kind of sporting event. Did it ever occur to you that he paid off his debts with that money?"

"If he paid off his debts, why didn't he pay off his credit cards, some of which were at almost thirty-percent interest?" Sebastian had seen the bills when he cleaned out the house. Emily's parents had died in a plane crash just after he and Emily had divorced, so even her stuff had fallen to him.

"Maybe they weren't as good at financial planning as you are. Or maybe they paid off things you know nothing about," Constance responded. "Maybe they helped a family member who was about to lose his house. You weren't still married to Emily, Sebastian. Malcolm was her husband. For all you know, they invested it and lost everything."

He shook his head, even though she couldn't see him. "There would've been proof of any investments."

"You want to talk proof?" she nearly shouted. "The police have DNA evidence! Do you know what DNA evidence means? It's irrefutable. It means the body found in that car was Malcolm Turner's!"

Clenching his jaw, Sebastian struggled to control the urge to lash out. These days she always seemed to get under his skin. "It wasn't much of a body. It was mostly ashes. And he wouldn't kill himself, Connie."

"He would if prison was his only other alternative. You know what they do to cops in prison."

Sebastian pictured the man he'd been chasing for a

year. The buzzed red hair; the freckles that covered his face and arms; the blue eyes and long, effeminate gold eyelashes; the stubborn jaw; the short but stocky-bordering-on-overweight build. "He was too arrogant to give up that easily."

"Arrogant," she repeated in disgust. "That's what has you turning over every rock between here and the Pacific? Sebastian, we've been through this dozens of times. It's no secret that Emily and Malcolm were having problems. Emily told several people she wanted a divorce. She probably tried to act on it and, being the control freak he was, Malcolm snapped and killed her and Colton. Then he realized what he'd done and killed himself."

"Maybe that scenario would be easier to accept if it was your son and not mine," he said.

She didn't have any children, but it was still a cheap shot. The pain he felt at Colton's loss ate at him like acid, made him act in ways he'd never guessed he would. Some of that was because he felt partially responsible for Emily's helplessness. She'd had no family to rely on. He should've done more to help her.

"Screw you," she said. "I'm tired of being sensitive. I've done all I can to support you. And now—"

"And now that I'm really finding something, you're giving up. Malcolm's in Sacramento. He tracked down his high-school girlfriend and moved here to be close to her. And he's living on the money he stole from Emily."

"Or you're more involved with his ex-girlfriend than you want to admit," she said.

He rolled his eyes. There'd never been anything between him and the woman who'd placed the call that had brought him to the west coast. They'd only met face-to-face twice, and that was in a coffee shop. "We're *friends,* Constance. I'm here because Malcolm's here. You've seen the transcripts of their chats. I've faxed them to you."

"Who's Your Daddy could be anyone! He claims to be someone named Wesley Boss who lives in L.A., and for all we know that's true."

"It's Turner, Connie. Mary should know. She dated him for two years."

"Why'd she have to call you?" she muttered.

Because he'd tracked her down first, her and anyone else Malcolm had ever known, and asked them to call if they ever heard from him. He'd also told them why. "Are you kidding? She was an angel to do it. Judging by some of the things this Wesley Boss has said, he's far more familiar with Northern California than Southern California. I don't believe he's in L.A. I believe he's right here in Sacramento."

"That's it," she said. "I can't do this anymore. I now realize I've been hanging on to a dream, to the memory of a man who no longer exists."

Closing his eyes, Sebastian let his head fall back. She'd just accused him of being interested in someone else, but it was probably the other way around. "What's his name?" he asked.

No answer.

"Constance?"

"Stop it. This isn't about another man. This is about me being unable to cope with the person you've become. It's over between us," she snapped and hung up.

Panic, caused by the finality in her voice, tempted Sebastian to call her back. But he didn't. They'd never

agree. Besides, she was better off without him. All he
could think about was finding answers to the questions
that'd been burning inside him since that hot summer
day last year. That was when Emily's neighbor had
gone over to see why Emily hadn't shown up to carpool
for basketball practice and stumbled upon two bodies.
They'd been murdered the night before.

Opening his eyes, he focused on the transcripts in the
seat next to him. Whoever sent those instant messages
and e-mails to Mary claimed to be someone she'd met
in the past, someone named Wesley Boss as Constance
said, but Mary didn't remember a Wesley Boss. Their
first contact had come through a Web site she used to
sell jewelry she made as a hobby, so it could've been
anyone. After several months of "talking" to this person
online, she'd come to the conclusion that it had to be
her high-school sweetheart—Malcolm Turner. He knew
too much about her to be anyone else.

Sebastian had flown to Sacramento, hoping that
the alias Malcolm was using would be enough to find
him, but it hadn't been so far. He'd managed to track
down only four men in California named Wesley
Boss, three in L.A. and one in Bakersfield. One was
an old priest who didn't even have a computer, one
was happily married with five kids, one was a ten-
year-old, and the other, the one from Bakersfield,
was dying of cancer. Mary had been trying to get Sebastian an address almost from the moment she'd
figured out who she was really dealing with, but
Malcolm was too cautious. A man with his background knew how risky it was to contact someone
from his former life. That made him traceable, if

anyone was bothering to look. And Sebastian was doing more than looking—he was scrutinizing every possibility. He'd even hired a private investigator to see if he could trace through whatever means—legal or not—where the e-mails were coming from. But Malcolm was using a remote server. He'd thought of everything.

Popping the transmission into reverse, he backed out of the parking space. Regardless of the cost, he couldn't give up. Mary was his conduit to the bastard who'd killed Emily and Colton and, right or wrong, he'd keep the promise he made while bearing their coffins to the grave.

Jane had decided to interview Luther on her way home from work, the first task on her list of actions in the missing-girls case. But Oak Park was the most dangerous neighborhood in Sacramento, and Jane was fully aware of it.

The metal of her gun pressed into her waist as she crossed the weed-infested postage stamp of dirt that comprised Luther's front yard. In the early months after Oliver's funeral, she'd learned how to shoot— Skye had seen to that—but this was nothing like a visit to the range. She'd never carried her Glock to someone's house, never approached anyone with the thought that she might have to use it. Until now. Although she was currently undergoing the months-long application process, she didn't yet have a license to carry a concealed weapon. She was breaking the law. But she hadn't been able to reach David, and for the sake of the missing girls she couldn't wait. She was far less afraid of the police than she was of

Luther. She had a daughter at home, a twelve-year-old who'd lost enough already. No way would Jane orphan Kate altogether.

Taking a breath to calm the butterflies swirling in her belly, she raised a hand to knock on a door that looked as if the hounds of hell had attempted to scratch it open. It was barely five o'clock, but darkness seemed to creep up on this part of the city much more quickly than the Watt Avenue area, where she worked.

Expecting to hear dogs the size of horses, she wasn't surprised by the cacophony of barking that rose to her ears as she stood at the very edge of the concrete stoop.

Ro-of. Thump! Roof! Scratch. Ro-of! Roof! Thump.

Unnerved by the ferocity, Jane decided that perhaps this was something she should put off until tomorrow. Maybe Jonathan, the private investigator who donated so much of his time to TLS, would be available then. Or David. She was about to head back to her car when a man's voice cut through the racket.

"Shut the hell up!"

The dogs fell silent.

Hands clammy with sweat, Jane watched uncertainly as the knob turned and the door opened.

It was darker inside than out, which made it difficult to see anything except the whites of the man's eyes. "I don't know who the hell you are," he said, "but you don't belong here."

Three pit bulls growled at his feet. They weren't nearly as large as they sounded, but they looked as if they'd tear her limb from limb, given half a chance. Fortunately, they knew better than to attack without permission. They didn't even push their muzzles into the opening, the way so many dogs did.

The man was definitely in charge. They weren't about to disobey him…she hoped.

"I'm—" When her voice squeaked, Jane cleared her throat and tried again. "I'm Jane Burke with The Last Stand."

"Whatever you're sellin', I'm not interested," he said and slammed the door.

The bang almost caused her to fall off the stoop. She glanced longingly at her Toyota Camry, parked at the curb, but the vision of Gloria, crying at the office, prompted her to knock again. She couldn't fold that easily; her client was counting on her.

One dog dared to bark—but ceased abruptly with a high-pitched whine.

Certain the dog had just been kicked, Jane bolted for her car but forced herself to stop midway when the door reopened.

This time the man stepped out onto the porch, where she could see him. But seeing him didn't make her feel any safer. At least six feet four inches tall, he weighed close to three hundred and fifty pounds and had the thick neck and huge biceps of a hulking lineman.

"This better be good," he said. Behind him, the dogs crouched, baring their teeth in a threatening snarl.

Clasping her trembling hands in front of her, Jane pulled her gaze away from them. "Are you Luther Wilson?"

"That's none of your damn business." His eyes narrowed. "But…suppose I was. What would you want?"

She edged a step closer. Standing in the middle of

the front yard as if she was afraid to come within reach made her appear weak, and she knew it. "I'm looking for your daughter."

"She not home."

"I'm talking about Latisha."

"Latisha don't live with me. Never has."

He pivoted, but now that she'd gotten this far Jane couldn't leave, not without the information she needed. What kind of caseworker would that make her? A coward of a caseworker—certainly no one Skye or Sheridan could trust. Ava didn't think she had what the job required and hadn't agreed with hiring her in the first place. If she walked away now, she'd only prove Ava right.

She hurried to speak before Luther could close the door. "She's gone missing, Mr. Wilson. So has Marcie. It's been three weeks since anyone's seen them. The police are investigating. Gloria's frantic."

At her rapid-fire explanation, he swung around to face her. "What're you sayin'? Someone kidnapped Latisha? Someone kidnapped her *and* Marcie?"

"We don't know. But it's possible. It's also possible they've run away, or been injured and are lost." The pervasive chill of deepening dusk in mid-January seemed to seep into her bones. "Murder is, of course, another possibility."

Although he didn't actually speak, his eyes revealed plenty. He hadn't known his daughter was gone. He wasn't sure how to react to the information, but he wasn't as shocked as a lot of men would be. Living in this neighborhood, he'd probably seen too much to gasp at the word *murder*. "Why would anyone wanna kill her?" he asked at length. "She a good kid."

"That's what I'm trying to find out. You haven't seen or heard from her in the past three weeks, have you?" she asked.

"No. But I never hear from her. She's a straight-A student, too damn good for her father." His wide shoulders seemed to hunch forward. "But maybe that's 'cause I ain't been much of a father."

Jane made an effort to conceal her surprise at his honesty and regret. "Do you know if she had any involvement with gangs or—"

"I told you. She a good kid. She's no gangbanger." He ran a hand over his bald head. "What does Gloria say?"

"That she and Marcie are gone. That's all. Even the police can't locate them."

Stepping back, he looked her up and down. "If you ain't with the police, who are you? Gloria ain't got money for no P.I."

TLS was well-known in some circles. Skye and the others who'd founded the charity had solved several high-profile cases. As a result, they'd been popular with the media. But there was no doubt a large segment of Sacramento's one million residents had never heard of them or hadn't paid more than passing attention. "I'm a victims' advocate. I work for a charity that's been operating in the area for about seven years. Gloria came to ask for my help."

He fingered his clean-shaven chin. "So you came down here out of the goodness of your heart?"

She ignored his skepticism. "I make a nominal salary, if that's what you mean."

"Whatever they payin' you ain't enough," he said. "You have no business in this neighborhood. I suggest you don't come back." Eager to gain its freedom, or rip out her throat, one pit bull crawled forward. His toenails clicked on the metal weather stripping across the opening, but Luther growled a quick "Get inside," and the dog did exactly that—with its tail between its legs.

"I'll ask around," he said to her, "see what I can find out about Latisha and give you a call."

She fumbled in her purse for a card. He must've recognized the shape of the gun handle beneath her sweater as her coat parted because he made a *tsking* sound and shook his head, "Don't ever bring a weapon to a man's house unless you're prepared to use it."

He thought she was a joke, the gun some sort of accessory—like earrings or fake nails.

"Excuse me?" she said.

"You heard me. That's askin' for trouble. Folks 'round here got no respect for poseurs, no matter how fine they look."

Jane locked eyes with him. Now that she'd met "Lucifer"—now that he was standing directly in front of her—she realized there wasn't much about him that intimidated her. Not after what she'd been through. Despite his size, he wasn't half as frightening as Oliver had been. Jane didn't think *anyone* could be as frightening as her slight, soft-spoken and coldly calculating spouse.

"My husband was a serial killer, Mr. Wilson. He murdered four people by stabbing them to death and he nearly killed me in the same way." She raised her chin to reveal the scar where he'd slit her throat. "I survived by the narrowest of margins. But I did survive. And I promise you I'm prepared to shoot anyone who tries to hurt me again." She smiled and stuck out her card.

"Please call me if you come up with anything on Latisha. I'm determined to find her and Marcie."

The condescending air that'd bothered her so much evaporated, but it wasn't replaced with anything more positive. "Yeah, well, we'll see," he said.

Three

"Are you sure you want to get involved in this?"

Detective Willis's voice came over the phone as Jane stood at her stove, stirring the homemade broccoli-and-cheddar-cheese soup she was making for Kate's dinner. She'd grabbed a chicken salad as a late lunch and didn't plan on eating much more today. Now that she was thin again, there was no way she'd let herself gain weight. She wanted nothing to do with the woman she'd been during the Oliver years. Her status as a wealthy socialite before Oliver went to prison; her subsequent fall from grace and expulsion from the tennis-club set; her downward spiral, driven by desperation and despair; her illicit affair with Oliver's brother; even her job as a two-bit hairstylist. That wasn't who she was anymore. Taking this case was part of her transformation. "I'm positive."

"I'm doing all I can, Jane," he said. "I've gone to Luther Wilson's house three different times. He's never home or he won't answer, I don't know which. I've left my card, but he never calls."

"He opened the door to me."

"Probably because you're a woman and quite obviously a civilian. He didn't feel threatened."

"So? I got to talk to him. That helps, doesn't it?"

"Of course it helps, but you don't have the experience to—"

"How will I get any experience if I never have my own cases? I mean, come on—you have so much to do. With Skye and Ava out of town, and Sheridan on maternity leave, I have time. I can focus on this. Why not let me do some of the legwork?"

"Because I'm not thrilled about you going into Oak Park like you did this evening. Who knows what other risks you might take?"

She'd known in advance that it might be unsafe. She'd brought her gun, hadn't she? When she'd married Oliver, she'd had no idea of the monster that raged behind his pleasant face…. "Are you telling me I did something Skye wouldn't have?" she challenged.

There was a slight pause. "No. The fact that she's in South America right now should tell you that. I'm certainly not happy about it."

"Exactly. I did what I needed to do, and I handled the situation just fine. I believe Luther Wilson will look around, like he said, and call us if he comes up with anything."

"What if this case really heats up, gets dangerous?"

His mention of heat reminded Jane to lower the temperature on the burner so she wouldn't burn the soup. "If every person in law enforcement thought only of the danger, the bad guys would win every time. Then no one would be safe." What if Skye hadn't taken the risks she

did? Jane wouldn't be around. "Anyway, in this instance, I think the chances of any danger, at least to me,
are minimal. These poor girls are probably dead." Jane
hated to acknowledge that, but it was true. And if she
wanted to be good at her new job, her new life, she had
to deal in the truth. Deal *with* the truth. When this was
over, she'd be lucky to be able to tell Gloria what'd
happened to her sisters.

"You could handle that?" he asked. "You could handle getting a call tomorrow saying their bodies have
been found?"

"Stop protecting me," she said. "That kind of loss
is hard, but it's part of what we do. I'm tired of all
the coddling. Skye's protected me for too long. I've
been at the charity for six months. I'm eager to take
my own cases."

He blew out an audible sigh. "Then what can I say?"

"Say you'll welcome my help." Kate entered the
kitchen, dropped a kiss on her cheek and grabbed
some of the bread Jane had set out for dinner. "Hi,
babe," she murmured before returning to her conversation. "David?"

"Okay, you can help."

"Good. Is there anything you've uncovered that
you'd like to share with me?"

"I wish there was," he said. "I've spent three weeks
on this case and have almost nothing to show for it."

"Have you had a chance to talk to Timothy Huff?"

"Gloria's father? Don't worry about him. He has an
airtight alibi. He was in Arkansas when the girls went
missing, staying with a cousin. As a matter of fact, he's
still there."

So she wouldn't have to visit the pool hall this coming Friday. "What about the car?"

"We processed it from bumper to bumper and found nothing suspicious. No blood. No foreign strands of hair or other trace evidence. No unusual objects. No receipts. Nothing. I'm guessing whoever kidnapped these girls didn't have to drag them from the car."

"You're saying they got out willingly?"

"It appears that way."

"So maybe a fellow motorist flagged them down to ask for help? Or waved for them to get off the road because something was wrong with the car?"

"Or they saw someone they knew and trusted," David added. "A guy one of them had met at a dance place. A friend from work."

"That opens up a lot of possibilities."

"This won't be an easy problem to solve, Jane."

She nudged Kate's fingers away from the fruit salad she'd made for dessert. "What about the media?" she asked David. "Could they be of some help?"

"I've been in regular contact with them. They're running the story again tonight."

She'd have to record the news. "Maybe that'll stir up some leads."

"It always does—but I can't promise they'll be viable."

"You've already interviewed all the girls' neighbors, coworkers, friends?"

"Of course."

"Can I get a copy of your file?"

"I don't see why not. Just don't mention that I passed it along."

"I won't." She switched off the burner. The soup was ready. "Where are you now?"

"Home with the kids. But I have the file with me and I have a fax machine in the back room. You want it tonight?"

"If you wouldn't mind."

"I don't mind."

She laid the spoon she'd been using in the sink. "Fax it to TLS and I'll pick it up after I get Kate fed."

"Pick what up, Mommy?" Kate asked as Jane disconnected.

Setting her cell phone on the counter, she turned to her daughter, who seemed to be maturing more and more every day. "Some paperwork on my new case."

"*Your* new case? You have your own case?"

"Yep. I got my first one this morning."

Kate smiled brightly. Her wide dark eyes, thick brown hair and creamy skin—as well as the curves that were just becoming noticeable—promised great beauty. Her face reminded Jane of a young Brooke Shields, but she had little chance of being very tall, not with a mother who was only five foot four and a father who was five foot nine.

"So what's your case about?" she asked as she slathered butter on her bread.

Oliver had gone to prison when Kate was three and had been killed shortly after he came out when she was seven, so losing him hadn't affected her as much as knowing what he'd done. But it was hard to live in the shadow of such evil. Jane preferred to shield her daughter from the uglier details of the cases they tackled at TLS. "I'm trying to find two girls, possibly runaways."

"How old are they?"

"Seventeen and eighteen," she said, dishing up the soup.

"Why did they run away?"

"We're not sure."

She swallowed the bread in her mouth. "I hope you find them."

Jane smiled. Maybe she'd been shortchanged in the husband arena, but having such a great daughter made up for it. For the most part, anyway. There were times Jane lay awake at night, remembering what it'd been like to love Oliver's brother, Noah. Despite the betrayal that'd caused her so much anguish, he'd been a good man, the exact opposite of Oliver. Tall, handsome, strong, honest, giving. He'd owned her heart.

"What's wrong, Mommy?"

Quickly pulling herself out of the melancholy that threatened whenever she thought of Noah—their love, their mistakes, her heartbreak, his murder—she summoned another smile. "Nothing, why?"

"You had such a sad look on your face." Her daughter's lip came out in a pout.

Jane carried Kate's soup to the table. "I'm not sad. We have a comfortable home, we're both safe and healthy, I like my job and you're doing well in school. You even get to spend every other weekend with Grandma and Grandpa Burke. What more could we ask?"

Again, the image of Noah drawing her into his arms, of their lips meeting, appeared in Jane's mind. Not only did she miss his lovemaking, Jane missed his laugh, his conversation, his support. He'd been her life the entire time Oliver was in prison.

But so what if she no longer had the companionship she craved? If, after nearly five years of celibacy, her body hungered for a man's touch? She didn't have a boyfriend. And a casual encounter was completely out of the question. She was too afraid of what lurked beneath the smiles of the men she met. She'd once believed she'd married so well. Oliver had been a successful dentist. So pleasant. So friendly. So smart.

And an absolute sociopath.

Remaining single was far safer than seeking another relationship. She knew from experience that there were worse things than loneliness.

Malcolm was pretty sure he'd made a tactical error. He'd thought it would break up the terrible monotony to grab a couple of slaves, make them do his laundry, cook his meals and clean his house. He missed that aspect of being married more than any other. Emily had always kept a fine house.

But the free labor wasn't worth the effort required to feed the girls and keep an eye on them. Since he'd taken them captive, they'd severely hampered his ability to live as he'd grown accustomed to living. He couldn't go to Mary's house and watch her, couldn't gamble at the Indian casinos, couldn't drive around with his police light pretending to be an undercover cop. It'd been difficult to get the chains he'd needed to restrict the girls' movements, but he'd simply used handcuffs and rope until he could get to the hardware store. He was set up now—he'd even gotten them some old secondhand clothing—but he was so damned bored. And he hated not being able to move around with ease.

At least he could call his bookie and place a few bets here and there. And, fortunately, he lived in Turlock out in the sparsely populated boondocks among the dairies, orchards and tomato farms south of Sacramento. Otherwise, it would've been even harder to leave his victims unattended while he ran errands.

Still, he worried whenever he had to take that chance. He was leaving one of the girls alone right now. The other he had with him. He'd finally decided that if he had to run an errand, it was safest to take one along so he'd always have the other as leverage. That way, they couldn't scheme together. They'd proven to be a lot smarter than he'd expected. Yesterday, they'd somehow freed themselves and almost slipped out the back door. If it hadn't been so unnaturally quiet, if he hadn't gone to check on them when he did, they would've been long gone.

But putting a captive in the vehicle meant traveling at night and staying in remote areas. It was a pain in the ass.

"You try anything while I'm in that store, I'll kill you," he warned the one named Marcie. He had her in the back of his van, gagged, hands cuffed to the sliding door, feet tied together with a rope. The supermarket was ready to close, so there weren't many customers. But he parked around back just to be safe. He needed to buy some milk and eggs and bread or they'd go hungry tomorrow....

"If you're gone when I get back, I'll cut your sister up into tiny pieces before disappearing myself," he told her. "I'll be out of here, and your sister will be dead. Do you understand? Do anything, *anything at all,* to piss me off, and you'll be signing her death warrant.

"Do you get it?" he snapped when she gave no sign of comprehension.

This time she made a frightened grunt.

"Good." He tossed a ratty old blanket over her for added security. "I'm not sure how long I'll be willing to put up with you, so I suggest you stay on your best behavior."

She acknowledged this with another grunt, and he slid the door closed and hurried away.

His mind completely occupied with collecting groceries as fast as possible, he didn't realize he'd forgotten his cell phone until he was standing in line at the checkout register. He usually placed it in the seat next to him as soon as he got in the van so it could sync with his Bluetooth. In California, it was illegal to talk on a cell phone while driving, and he couldn't afford to get pulled over for something stupid. But leaving his cell behind with Marcie in the van was about as stupid a mistake as he could imagine.

"Son of a bitch!"

The woman behind him must've heard the curse. She frowned in disapproval, but he didn't care whether he'd offended her or not. He'd left his damn cell phone in the car! He'd told Marcie not to try anything. Then he'd put temptation only two feet away.

Shoving his cart to the side, he abandoned his groceries so he could hurry to the exit.

His breaths were short, foggy puffs as he jogged around the building. At first glance, everything looked normal. Chances were she was exactly as he'd left her. He'd warned her, hadn't he?

But as he crept up on the front bumper and peered through the windshield, he knew he'd had good reason to be worried. She'd managed to get her hands free, just as he'd feared. Her gag was down, too. He could tell because the lit screen on his phone bathed her face in an eerie glow—she was in the middle of placing a call.

If it was 9-1-1, they could trace the phone's location using the federal government's Global Position System satellites. Even if it wasn't 9-1-1, the location of any phone could be traced by the signal it sent to the closest cell phone towers.

Jerking open the sliding door, he leaned in and wrenched the phone away. Then he turned it off, used his T-shirt to wipe it clean and chucked it as hard as he could into the field behind the grocery store.

Marcie had one hand still cuffed to the door handle. The other was bleeding because she'd forced it through the metal circle of the other cuff. But that didn't stop her from pushing her legs through the opening and trying to get out.

Without warning, he slammed the door on her legs. When she arched back and cried out, he widened the gap enough that she could yank her legs in. Then he closed it tightly.

"I didn't call anyone important," she sobbed as he climbed behind the wheel.

If he'd had the time, he would've punched her in the face. "You lying bitch!"

"No, I swear," she said. "I jus' wanted to tell our older sister we're okay. She don't know where we're at. I don't even know…"

"You're dead," he promised but, careful to do nothing that would attract attention, he backed up, swung around and turned out of the driveway at normal speed. He had to get away from the supermarket before his vehicle could be spotted by whatever police unit had been dispatched. And he had to do it without creating a witness to his flight.

Four

The jangle of her phone came to Jane in a dream. She heard it ringing, but it had no relevance to her. It was someone else's phone. Distant. Removed. Then silence—until a much more subtle disturbance woke her.

Opening her eyes to total darkness, she blinked. For months after Oliver had left her lying in her own blood, she'd dreamt she heard him in the hallway, coming to finish what he'd started. He always had a knife in his hand and the look of murder in his eyes. She knew that look because she was one of the few who'd seen it and lived to tell about it. The nightmare was so vivid she could smell him, feel the warmth of his body as he drew close, his fingernails biting into her arm as he dragged her up against him—

"Mom?"

Jane gasped. She could breathe. It wasn't real. Oliver was dead. The noise that'd awakened her had been Kate. Her daughter was standing in the doorway. "Wh-what?" she said, willing her heart to slow its pounding.

Kate came to the side of the bed. "Didn't you hear me? Someone's on the phone for you. And she sounds like she's crying."

Who would call her in the middle of the night crying? Sheridan? Skye? Had there been an accident?

Alarmed, she threw off the covers and sat up. Then the memory of the day's events snapped into place, along with the news snippet she'd watched before bed, and she realized that her caller could be someone else.

"Thanks, babe." The time on her clock radio indicated it wasn't the middle of the night as Jane had thought. It was only ten-thirty. She'd been asleep for half an hour. "Go back to bed," she told Kate, but her daughter didn't leave. Understandably curious—they didn't receive many calls like this—she sat on the edge of the bed as Jane brought the receiver to her ear. "Hello?"

"Ms. Burke—Jane?"

It wasn't Skye or Sheridan. It was Gloria, as she'd suspected. "Yes?"

"They jus' called me," she blurted, so breathless she could hardly speak.

Jane cleared her throat to eliminate the rasp of sleep. "*Who* just called you? Latisha and Marcie?"

"Marcie, I think. I couldn't tell for sure. She was talkin' so low I could barely hear her."

The mind-numbing fatigue fell away like a cast-off shirt. "What'd she say?"

"She say, 'Gloria, you gotta help us.' I say, 'Where are you? Tell me where you're at an' I'll be there.' An' she say, 'I don't know.' So I told her to hang up and call 9-1-1. But she say she already tried that an' they put her on hold while they sent a cruiser."

"A cruiser's good."

"I know, but she was so terrified she panicked. She hung up and called me. I told her, 'Give me some clue, baby. Help me find you.' But she was cryin' so hard she couldn't talk. All she could say is, 'Oh, God, he's here!' Then the line went dead."

Jane's blood seemed to freeze in her veins. The girls were alive. But where? In what condition? And who had them?

"Someone has 'em both," Gloria was saying. "She said *us*. I heard that much. They're alive, but I don't know for how long. We gotta find 'em!"

Jane clutched the phone tighter. If they were alive, they needed someone better than her. Just hearing about Marcie's call—*Oh, God, he's here*—made Jane's own past rush up on her like a wave surging from behind. She tried to beat back the fear, but with little success. She'd already broken into a cold sweat.

"Hello?" Gloria cried when she didn't speak.

Drawing a deep breath, Jane forced a calm she didn't feel. She had to pretend she was everything Gloria thought she was, had to act as if she knew what she was doing or she'd be letting her client down. What good would it do to add to the poor woman's panic? "Have you contacted Detective Willis?" she asked.

"I called the number on his card, but it went straight to voice mail."

Of course it did. Jane hadn't been thinking when she'd asked that question. Detectives were basically on call twenty-four hours a day, but that didn't make them available to the general public. "I can reach him at home," she said. "Did your phone show the number Marcie called from?"

"It did. It wasn't blocked. I got it right here, on my list of incoming calls. But I already dialed it at least a dozen times, and I can't get anyone to pick up. A recording comes on, saying the voice-mail box hasn't been set up yet."

Jane wished Gloria hadn't done that. The ring might've alerted Marcie's captor to the fact that she'd made a call. But she didn't want to make Gloria feel bad for doing what anyone would want to do under the circumstances. "Give me the number. If we're lucky, I can find the owner via a reverse directory. Or maybe David can get the information from the phone company."

Gloria's voice shook as she dictated each digit, but she was careful to enunciate.

"I'll call David and get back to you," Jane promised.

Throughout the conversation, Gloria had held up admirably, but now she broke into tears, as she had in Jane's office. "Can you find 'em? You gotta find 'em. Right away. I can't live without 'em. They all I got."

And you're counting on me? Jane was hoping that aborted call to 9-1-1 had been more helpful than it appeared. Maybe it was just a matter of time before they heard from the police. Maybe the cruiser dispatched by the emergency operator had arrived....

Maybe she'd be able to believe that if whoever had taken Marcie and her sister hadn't appeared while Marcie was using the phone.

"I know. I'll talk to you in a few minutes," she said, and hung up.

Movement from across the bed startled her. She'd

become so engrossed in the conversation, she'd forgotten her daughter was in the room.

"What is it, Mommy?" Kate asked, creeping closer.

"Someone needs help." Jane took her daughter's hand. As usual, having Kate beside her made her grateful that they were alive and together. The situation five years ago could've ended very differently. But after Gloria's call, even Kate's reassuring presence couldn't keep the doubt that plagued Jane from striking deep.

Maybe Ava's right about me. Maybe Oliver put me through too much, and now I don't have the nerve to do this job. She felt physically ill at the thought of what might be happening to Latisha and Marcie. Somehow she couldn't imagine Skye or Sheridan or Ava taking it *this* personally. They all seemed to face every challenge with cool resolve.

Kate snuggled closer. "Those girls who ran away? Are they the ones who need help?"

"Yes."

"They didn't run away?"

"No."

"Are you going to rescue them?"

Jane rubbed the back of her daughter's hand against her cheek. "Do you think I'm capable of rescuing someone?"

Kate reached up to kiss her cheek. "You saved me, didn't you?" she said. "You can do anything."

A lump rose in Jane's throat. "I'll do my best," she said. Then she sent her daughter off to bed and called David.

Hey, you there? He wrote me again tonight. Around dinnertime. But I had to rush off to a meeting for a school fundraiser and this is my first chance to get back online.

Hello?

You said to let you know.

Sebastian had just stepped out of the shower when he spotted Mary McCoy's instant messages on his laptop. According to the time indicated on those messages, she'd tried to reach him twenty minutes ago, right after he'd gone into the bathroom.

Had she already signed off?

Afraid he was too late, he sat down wearing a towel and typed a quick response.

I'm here. What'd he say?

There was no immediate reply. A single mom, Mary was often up late. She'd told him it was the only time she could carve out of the day for herself. But—he glanced at the radio alarm by the bed—it was nearly midnight, and she had to go to the hospital where she worked bright and early in the morning. Maybe she'd gone to bed.

"Come on, come on." He tapped his fingers on the desk. She'd given him her phone number, but he couldn't call her at this hour, and he couldn't drive over there, either. He stayed away from her place in case Malcolm was closer than they thought. Letting Malcolm see him would blow everything.

Mary? he typed, as if he was speaking and not merely sending another message.

Nothing. *Damn.* He'd missed her.

Shoving his wet hair out of his face to keep it from

dripping into his eyes, he slumped in his chair, momentarily distracted by his reflection in the mirror hanging on the wall. God, he hardly recognized himself anymore. His hair, as thick and black as that of his Greek ancestors, was getting so long it curled around his ears and nape. His coal-black eyes were hollow and slightly sunken, so the sharp angles of his cheekbones protruded in an exaggerated fashion. Dark stubble covered a jaw and chin that, like his cheekbones, now seemed more pronounced. He'd once been so meticulous about his appearance and grooming. A haircut at Lucio's every six weeks, standing appointment. A close shave twice a day to combat an unrelenting five-o'clock shadow. Italian shoes. Designer suits. Gold cuff links. A Rolex watch. Now he wore mostly jeans and T-shirts and a brown leather bomber jacket, rarely cut his hair and shaved every three days. The only personal maintenance he hadn't abandoned besides regular hygiene was a stringent fitness routine. He pushed himself to lift and run more each day, but not because he gave a damn about improving his physique. It was all about coping with his frustration—and being ready to exact retribution.

In the same reflection, he could see his handgun sitting on the nightstand behind him. He'd spent a lot of time learning how to use it. Sometimes he even craved the feel of that smooth handle in his palm.

What have you become? he asked himself. Was he allowing what had happened to Colton to change more than his appearance and habits? Was he allowing it to twist his heart?

Constance certainly thought so. But he couldn't seem to escape the compulsion driving him. It was like some kind of centripetal force that'd sucked him in and held him fast.

Let it go and move on, Connie always said. *Come back to me. Don't let Malcolm cost you any more than he already has.*

For a moment, he grabbed at the hope in those words. Maybe it wasn't too late. Maybe he could go back to New York, to her.

He scooped his phone off the desk to see if she'd called again, but didn't bother checking when he noticed a change on his computer screen. A reply from Mary McCoy had popped up.

BrownEyedGirl: I'm here.

Relieved, Sebastian tossed his phone on the bed so he could type.

S.Costas: What'd our friend have to say tonight?

BrownEyedGirl: Not a lot. It was mostly me, doing what you said to do. I told him I'd like to hook up, suggested I drive down to L.A. this weekend to see him.

With luck, she was leading Malcolm right where he wanted to go. Considering all the time he'd put into re-establishing the relationship, he had to be secretly hoping to see her. Otherwise, there wouldn't be much of a payoff to their lengthy and sometimes sexual Internet discussions.

But would that desire be enough to tempt Malcolm into revealing his true identity? That was the big question.

S.Costas: Did he agree?

BrownEyedGirl: He didn't *disagree*. But he didn't make a commitment, either. I asked for his address. I said I wanted to see how far he lived from Sacramento. He said L.A. was about 400 miles. So I said maybe I should fly and he should pick me up at the airport, but he said he had a lot going on this weekend and we should plan it for another time.

He was dodging them, playing it safe.

S.Costas: Did he say when?

BrownEyedGirl: No. He said he'd have to check his schedule. Then he got off.

Shit. Sebastian hoped they hadn't spooked him.

S.Costas: Did he seem nervous or suspicious?

BrownEyedGirl: Not really. Just a little cagey. Maybe he'll get back to me, like he said.

He obviously wanted some contact with her or he wouldn't have gotten in touch. And Malcolm was cocky enough to think he could get away with anything. The killings had occurred in Newark, New Jersey, Malcolm and Mary had gone to high school in San Antonio, Texas, and Mary now lived in Sacramento. Perhaps he believed she was sufficiently removed from the situation. If Sebastian hadn't found that old shoebox in the storage above Malcolm's garage, the one that contained Mary's old letters and pictures, he wouldn't have realized they'd once been so close, and Mary might not have learned about the tragedy in New Jersey. She'd been completely surprised—stunned—when he'd told her. The news had brought her to tears. It wasn't until five months later that she'd dug Sebastian's card out of her desk and called him to say she was receiving some rather mysterious e-mails—e-mails that reminded her of someone they both knew quite well.

S.Costas: Don't mention seeing him again, not for the next few days. We have to be careful or we'll blow this.

BrownEyedGirl: If it *is* Malcolm, I can't imagine he'll really agree to get together, not after telling me he's someone else. How will he explain that?

S.Costas: Easy enough.

BrownEyedGirl: How?

S.Costas: By saying he's in the witness protection program or something.

Knowing Malcolm, and his desire to come across as a big shot, that was exactly the line he'd use.

BrownEyedGirl: I didn't think of that.

S.Costas: He wants to see you or he wouldn't be writing you so much.

BrownEyedGirl: He acts like it, but he won't ever commit.

S.Costas: He will someday.

BrownEyedGirl: And if he does...how will that work? If you show up instead of me, he could pull out a gun and shoot you. He won't let you take him to the police. Not after everything he's done to escape.

S.Costas: It would be best to arrange a meeting in a public place, a restaurant or a bar, if possible.

BrownEyedGirl: Maybe I should continue to pretend we're rekindling the romance and invite him here for a drink. I could get some of his DNA on a glass or something. The police will have to listen if you can prove he's alive, right?

Sebastian was no longer sure he wanted the authorities involved. He'd begun to dream of taking care of Malcolm on his own. It seemed so much simpler, more efficient. The police had done nothing so far except give him the runaround.

S.Costas: No way. He's a *murderer*. Do whatever you can to avoid letting him get that close. You haven't given him your address, have you?

BrownEyedGirl: No, but he asked for it.

Sebastian didn't like the sound of that.

S.Costas: You didn't give it to him, did you?

BrownEyedGirl: Of course not. I told him I don't share that information over the Internet.

S.Costas: If he doesn't want to get together, why'd he ask for it?

BrownEyedGirl: He claimed he was going to send me some flowers.

S.Costas: Cunning.

BrownEyedGirl: Actually, I think it's a telling coincidence.

S.Costas: What do you mean?

BrownEyedGirl: Tomorrow is the anniversary of the day he asked me to be his girlfriend. We celebrated the 19th every month for the two years we were together.

Interesting…

S.Costas: Mention of flowers was some sort of hint?

BrownEyedGirl: Could be.

S.Costas: How'd he respond when you wouldn't give him an address?

BrownEyedGirl: He said he could get it if he really wanted it.

That was true. She was listed; anyone could find her. But Malcolm probably had her address long ago. Sebastian believed Mary was the reason he'd come to California in the first place. They both knew he'd run into a mutual friend in New York City —months before the murders—who'd mentioned that she was now living in Sacramento. That friend had contacted her to say she'd seen him.

BrownEyedGirl: He said something else I think you'll be interested to hear.

S.Costas: What 's that?

BrownEyedGirl: He told me he used to be a cop.

This raised the hair on the back of Sebastian's neck. If he'd needed further proof, he had the coincidence of the anniversary and now this. Wesley was Malcolm. They had him on the hook; they just needed to reel him in. But was it safe to allow Mary to go on with this fishing expedition? If Malcolm figured out what she was doing…

S.Costas: This could get dangerous.

And because he'd been the one encouraging her to

communicate with Malcolm, he'd feel responsible if something happened to her. He had to be careful.

BrownEyedGirl: He has no reason to hurt me. I don't have any money.

Maybe she didn't have money, but Malcolm had contacted her for a reason. Was she simply someone to brag to? Was he bored? Lonely? In love with her? Hoping to meet for a sexual rendezvous?

Or did he sincerely regret having passed her up in his younger days? He'd divorced his first wife and murdered his second. He didn't seem very easy to please when it came to women, but there was no way to tell what was going on in his mind.

BrownEyedGirl: Isn't that why he murdered your ex-wife? For her money?

S.Costas: That was part of it, but there could be other reasons.

Exactly what those reasons might be Sebastian hadn't yet deciphered. Emily had asked that they meet for lunch. She'd been upset when she called him. But she'd scheduled the meeting for a week away, when Malcolm would be on a trip to Vegas with his brother, and been killed before that day could come.

S.Costas: Did he give you anything new to go on today besides letting you know that he was a cop— and that he remembers your anniversary?

BrownEyedGirl: Just more of the same.

S.Costas: The same what?

BrownEyedGirl: Flirting. Compliments. What you've read before. He tells me he wishes we'd gotten together. That his life would've been different if we had. His comments are getting more and more explicit, of course, and— Oh boy, *he just signed on!!!!!*

Sebastian sat up straighter.

S.Costas: Malcolm?

BrownEyedGirl: Yes! He's sending me a message. It says, 'Hey, you still up?' Should I respond?

Would it be smarter to play hard to get? Probably. But Sebastian was getting low on patience. And money. He had to press forward before circumstances forced him to give up.

S.Costas: Definitely. He might be ready to suggest a time and place.

BrownEyedGirl: I have to tell you, I'm beginning to have second thoughts about setting up a meeting.

S.Costas: Why?

BrownEyedGirl: Because I'm afraid of what you

might do if you have the chance. I'd hate to see you shoot him and then spend the rest of your life in prison.

S.Costas: Don't worry about me.

Only three years younger than he was, Mary was lonely after her divorce. But, contrary to what Constance believed, their relationship had never even bordered on the romantic.

S.Costas: Just see what he wants.

She didn't get back to him right away.
Anxious to learn what was going on, he got up and paced until the words It's no good appeared on his screen.
What did that mean?

S.Costas: He won't meet?

BrownEyedGirl: No. He says he's had one hell of a night and he'll be busy the next few weekends.

Son of a bitch.

S.Costas: Okay. Then I need you to do one more thing for me.

BrownEyedGirl: What's that?

S.Costas: Let me take over from here.

BrownEyedGirl: What do you mean?

S.Costas: I want to be the one communicating with him. There's no need for you to have anything more to do with this. It's not safe.

And it was too frustrating working through a third party. They were *so* close and yet they couldn't pin him down.

BrownEyedGirl: How do I let you take over?

S.Costas: Simple. Give me access to your account. I'll be you for the next week or two, see if there's anything I can do to convince this bastard to trust me.

BrownEyedGirl: You're crazy. He'll be able to tell you're not me. You don't write like a girl.

S.Costas: I can fake it.

Sebastian had read the transcripts of their instant-message sessions. At least the ones Mary had saved. If he wasn't sure how to respond to a certain question, he could look back through the pages she'd given him to see how the subject had been handled before. Or he could contact her. If he couldn't reach her in time, he'd sign off and blame it on a faulty connection. Already convinced he was in contact with his ex-girlfriend, Malcolm wouldn't suspect a thing—provided Sebastian didn't say something obvious or stupid.

BrownEyedGirl: But this is my only e-mail address.

S.Costas: I'll open another account for you, and I'll forward anything that comes in on this one that isn't related.

BrownEyedGirl: You don't understand. E-mail is my life right now. With two little kids, I can't get out of the house to meet people.

She was purposely ignoring the solution he'd offered, didn't want to be cut out of the loop. This was the one thing that kept her occupied at night—hearing from Malcolm and then reporting on it. Sebastian actually called her some nights and they formulated her responses together.

S.Costas: I shouldn't need it for very long. Like I said, I'll forward anything that's unrelated. AND I'll pay you $1000 for the inconvenience.

Thinking of his nearly empty bank account, Sebastian grimaced, but he knew if anything would smooth the way, this would. She lived on a very tight budget.

BrownEyedGirl: You don't have to pay me. You know I'd do it just because we're friends.

S.Costas: You could use the money, and I'm happy to help.

He didn't think it would be difficult to persuade her to accept. She thought he was rich.

BrownEyedGirl: If that's what you want. But you

have to keep me up-to-date, okay? I'd like to know what's going on. I've nursed this thing along for weeks and want to see the end.

Sebastian could certainly understand that. Okay, he said, and she gave him her password.

Five

Several hours later, Sebastian was still up, keeping an eye on Mary's buddy list while rereading the transcripts of her and Malcolm's previous online sessions. If he had the opportunity, he wanted to be sure he could pick up the conversation with full knowledge of everything that'd been said before.

He'd put on a pair of boxers and a T-shirt, but hadn't been able to relax enough to sleep. Malcolm was signed on. He'd been on for most of the night. Sebastian imagined him chatting with other women, stringing them along with compliments and promises of flowers, just like Mary.

How could he bring this bastard out of hiding?

Sebastian was dying to initiate a conversation, to see what he could do now that he had control. But it was nearly four in the morning and Malcolm knew Mary had children she had to get off to school. She also worked, which meant she was rarely up *this* late.

"Don't break the pattern," he warned himself. But he

couldn't continue to nudge Malcolm along at a leisurely pace; he needed to draw him out, make him commit.

Ignoring caution, Sebastian clicked on the *WhosYourDaddy* screen name. Brandon just woke up with the flu. Poor kid, he typed.

No, *kid* should be *baby*. *Baby* would sound more feminine. Using the backspace key, he made the change. And now I can't go back to sleep.

He sent it, but there was no response. "Come on," he murmured. "Forget whatever porn site you're on and take the bait. Don't you care about poor little Brandon?"

Sebastian adjusted his chair so he could stretch his legs. He'd been sitting too long. "Of course you don't care about Brandon," he said, settling in again. "You don't care about anyone but yourself."

After another five minutes, he made a second attempt. I keep thinking about you. Maybe that's the real reason I can't sleep. I get so lonely at night.

He waited…and waited. No response.

With a curse, he turned to the transcripts and skimmed through the exchanges he hadn't reread. A lot of these conversations had taken place last September before Mary realized she was dealing with someone other than *WhosYourDaddy* represented himself to be, but they offered insight to the man's psyche.

WhosYourDaddy: Are you as hot as you were when you were sixteen?

BrownEyedGirl: You don't know?

WhosYourDaddy: I haven't seen you for years.

BrownEyedGirl: I've sent you pictures. You're the one who hasn't sent me any pics. Where are they, by the way?

WhosYourDaddy: I lost my camera. I'll get one taken soon, though.

Sebastian paged through to find the Xeroxed picture Malcolm had eventually sent. It was of a man handsome enough to be appealing but regular enough to be believable—a smart choice, and probably no one Malcolm even knew. Sebastian's guess was that Malcolm had taken a snapshot of some random guy and used the picture to satisfy Mary's curiosity. Or he'd bought a stock photo.

Setting it aside, he went back to reading.

BrownEyedGirl: Do it tomorrow. I want to see who I'm talking to.

WhosYourDaddy: You know who you're talking to.

BrownEyedGirl: No, I don't. I still can't remember meeting you at Joe's party.

WhosYourDaddy: You really know how to hurt a guy's ego. I guess I didn't stand out.

BrownEyedGirl: There were, like...two hundred kids at Joe's house that night. And I had a boyfriend, so I wasn't paying much attention.

WhosYourDaddy: I remember your boyfriend. What was his name again?

BrownEyedGirl: Malcolm Turner.

WhosYourDaddy: That's right. You were really into him.

BrownEyedGirl: No joke. I was head over heels.

WhosYourDaddy: Lucky guy.

BrownEyedGirl: ☺

WhosYourDaddy: Have you seen him lately?

BrownEyedGirl: No. We lost touch when we graduated.

WhosYourDaddy: Do you know what became of him?

BrownEyedGirl: No idea.

WhosYourDaddy: You think about him sometimes, though, don't you?

BrownEyedGirl: Sometimes.

WhosYourDaddy: If you'd married him, maybe you'd still be married. Maybe your kids would be his.

BrownEyedGirl: I doubt we would've made it. He cheated on me with Sherry Stewart. I caught them together in the bedroom at Dennis Marchant's house. Broke my heart.

WhosYourDaddy: Only an idiot would cheat on someone as beautiful as you.

"Were you that idiot?" Sebastian asked and turned the page.

BrownEyedGirl: They got together after I broke up with him, but it didn't last long.

WhosYourDaddy: I met her once. She wasn't half as pretty as you.

BrownEyedGirl: Thanks. I never could understand what he saw in her.

WhosYourDaddy: She was a slut, and at that age, a guy thinks with his dick. He's dealing with too many hormones to know when he's got a good thing.

BrownEyedGirl: Does that ever really change? LOL

WhosYourDaddy: I'd never risk losing someone like you, that's for sure. Were you giving it up to Malcolm?

"You already know, don't you?" Sebastian said. "You just like thinking about it, talking about it."

BrownEyedGirl: You can guess the answer to that question.

WhosYourDaddy: You did.

BrownEyedGirl: It's not like I was easy. We were together for two years.

WhosYourDaddy: Would you make me wait that long before you let me touch you?

BrownEyedGirl: That depends.

WhosYourDaddy: On what?

BrownEyedGirl: On my level of trust.

WhosYourDaddy: You can trust me, babe.

BrownEyedGirl: I'd like to think so.

WhosYourDaddy: Do you ever talk to Sherry Stewart?

Sebastian checked his computer screen. Still no response from Malcolm.

BrownEyedGirl: Never. Not since that night.

WhosYourDaddy: What about your other friends from high school?

"Wondering what she's heard about you?" Sebastian asked. *WhosYourDaddy* was always probing. Sometimes it was just more subtle than at other times.

BrownEyedGirl: Not really. My best friend died of cancer while we were in college. That's when I realized I wanted something deeper than most of the people I'd hung out with in high school seemed to want. They were still partying on the weekends and screwing around. It was time for me to get serious about life. That's when I met Jimmy.

WhosYourDaddy: At UC Berkeley?

BrownEyedGirl: Yep.

WhosYourDaddy: Did you go back to San Antonio after college?

BrownEyedGirl: No, we stayed in California to be near his family.

WhosYourDaddy: So you haven't been to Texas in how long?

BrownEyedGirl: Years. My parents moved to Portland while I was at Berkeley, so there's never been any reason to go back.

Fortunately, that was all true, so they didn't have to worry about Malcolm learning otherwise.

WhosYourDaddy: Don't you want to see Malcolm?

BrownEyedGirl: I don't even know if he's still there. Last I heard, his family was, but he'd moved on.

WhosYourDaddy: What if you were to hear from him? How would you react?

Sebastian had highlighted this part. It showed Malcolm throwing out more feelers, seeing how he might be received if he ever decided to reveal himself.

BrownEyedGirl: Not sure. That would depend on why he was contacting me in the first place. I still haven't completely forgiven him. I've never been hurt like that, even by my ex-husband.

WhosYourDaddy: Maybe he's changed, grown up.

BrownEyedGirl: And maybe he hasn't. Once a cheater, always a cheater. That's what I say.

WhosYourDaddy: You don't know that.

BrownEyedGirl: I don't think I could trust him again.

Unfortunately, this conversation preceded Mary's realization that she could be talking to Malcolm or she would've answered differently.

WhosYourDaddy: Poor Malcolm. He's missing out on so much.

BrownEyedGirl: Don't give me that. He brought it on himself. I might be divorced but I'm not desperate.

WhosYourDaddy: I'd treat you better.

"Than you used to?" Sebastian murmured.

BrownEyedGirl: I'd like to believe that.

Sebastian grimaced. "If you're smart you won't."

WhosYourDaddy: I'll prove it to you.

BrownEyedGirl: Have you ever cheated?

WhosYourDaddy: I'd never cheat on someone as beautiful as you.

BrownEyedGirl: So you *have* cheated.

WhosYourDaddy: Not on my first wife.

BrownEyedGirl: How many wives have you had?

WhosYourDaddy: Two.

So had Malcolm.

BrownEyedGirl: You went out on your second wife?

WhosYourDaddy: She went out on me first. I think she was sleeping with her ex the whole time we were married. I know she never got over him. She was always throwing him in my face.

BrownEyedGirl: What was his name?

WhosYourDaddy: Prick, at least to me. LOL

Sebastian hesitated here. Malcolm was talking about him and Emily, but he couldn't be more wrong. There'd been times when Sebastian had felt a spark between him and his ex. He couldn't deny that. They'd cared about each other, cared for their son. But they'd never slept together, not after the divorce. If Emily hadn't married Malcolm, they might've reconciled, but she had, and then Sebastian met Constance and everything changed.

Trying to imagine what it would've been like if they'd managed to reunite their family, he closed his eyes. Emily and Colton would both be alive, and Colton would have the complete family he'd always dreamed about....

It was Malcolm who'd removed that possibility. First, when he convinced Emily to marry him by pretending to be a better man than he was. Then, when he'd assumed, without any proof, that Emily was cheating on him and killed her.

Or was his unfounded accusation just an excuse to get rid of her and take the money?

His eyes too bleary to continue reading, Sebastian put the transcripts aside and reached over to turn off his computer. Before he could press the off button, however, the response he'd been waiting for finally appeared on the screen.

WhosYourDaddy: You up? Sorry, I didn't see your message.

The exhaustion that'd been dragging at him fell away as Sebastian considered how to reply. He didn't want this session to be more inane chitchat, leading nowhere. He wasn't here to entertain Malcolm while Malcolm fantasized about getting it on with his ex-girlfriend.

After stretching his neck to loosen the tense muscles, he typed.

BrownEyedGirl: I'm up, all right, wishing you were here to hold me.

WhosYourDaddy: We'll be together someday.

BrownEyedGirl: I'd like that. You make me feel special—like more than a tired soccer mom. LOL

WhosYourDaddy: Because you *are* special.

BrownEyedGirl: Do you mean that? Or is it just a bunch of writing on a screen?

WhosYourDaddy: Touch yourself for me. Be my hands. I'll tell you what to do.

Sebastian rolled his eyes. Internet sex? "Mary" couldn't settle for that.

BrownEyedGirl: No, it's not the same.

WhosYourDaddy: It's the next best thing. I can't be there, babe, but I can do my part from here.

BrownEyedGirl: Why won't you agree to meet? L.A. isn't that far.

WhosYourDaddy: I can't.

BrownEyedGirl: Even if I come to you? I already told you I would. Let's get together and see if what we're feeling is as real as it seems.

There was a short delay.

WhosYourDaddy: My life is complicated right now, Mary.

BrownEyedGirl: You're not married, are you? You haven't been leading me on while you have a wife sleeping in the next room!

WhosYourDaddy: No, nothing like that. I swear it.

BrownEyedGirl: Then what?

WhosYourDaddy: I'm just…having some trouble with my roommates. It's been a rough night.

BrownEyedGirl: You've never mentioned any roommates.

WhosYourDaddy: They didn't have a place to stay. I was nice enough to take them in.

BrownEyedGirl: When?

WhosYourDaddy: A few weeks ago.

BrownEyedGirl: Are they male or female?

WhosYourDaddy: Female. Sisters. But there's nothing going on between us. They're not my type. I thought they could help out with the cooking and cleaning, that's all.

BrownEyedGirl: Right.

WhosYourDaddy: What's that supposed to mean?

Sebastian didn't respond

WhosYourDaddy: I can tell what you're thinking. But stop it. I told you, I'm not sleeping with these girls.

BrownEyedGirl: Then why don't you want to see me?

WhosYourDaddy: I do. I've wanted to be with you for years.

BrownEyedGirl: And yet all you do is chat. There's got to be a reason. You've got to be hiding a wife or a girlfriend.

WhosYourDaddy: I'm not! I'm just taking it slow, like you asked me to. Don't pick a fight. We were doing fine.

BrownEyedGirl: Having no physical contact is fine? Making empty promises through a computer is fine? You say I met you at a party, but I can't even remember what you look like.

WhosYourDaddy: I sent you a picture.

BrownEyedGirl: It's not enough.

When this brought no answer, Sebastian got up and opened a beer from the courtesy bar. He had so much adrenaline pumping through him he couldn't stay seated. Was he being too aggressive? Maybe. But this Internet relationship could go on indefinitely. He had to trick Malcolm into blowing his cover.

At last Malcolm's response appeared.

WhosYourDaddy: Someday, like I said. I promise. I think about you all the time.

Sebastian studied those words. Should he give up for tonight? Back off? He decided to at least change his approach. Sitting down again, he wrote back.

BrownEyedGirl: Forget I said anything.

WhosYourDaddy: No, it's okay to want to see me. I like that. I want to see you, too.

BrownEyedGirl: Then why don't you pick a place to meet? Harris Ranch is between L.A. and Sacramento. We could meet there.

WhosYourDaddy: I don't understand why you're

suddenly in such a rush. You're the one who wanted to take this slow, remember?

BrownEyedGirl: But it's as if I know you already. I mean, more than just a brief acquaintance. There's a kinship here I haven't felt with anyone in a long time. Am I crazy?

WhosYourDaddy: Not at all.

BrownEyedGirl: I think it's because you remind me of someone I used to care about.

WhosYourDaddy: Who?

Sebastian waited, hoping his delay would make Malcolm believe "Mary" was reluctant to respond.

WhosYourDaddy: Are you going to tell me?

BrownEyedGirl: No.

WhosYourDaddy: Why not?

BrownEyedGirl: Because it doesn't matter. It's not like I'll ever see him again.

WhosYourDaddy: Tell me!

The real Mary had made it sound as if she was still bitter over Malcolm's betrayal. Sebastian needed to spin that into something more appealing. If he played it smart, maybe he could make Malcolm so eager to reclaim Mary's adulation, the adulation he remembered from his glory days, that he couldn't help but step forward.

BrownEyedGirl: Just someone I once knew.

WhosYourDaddy: That's all the info I get?

BrownEyedGirl: You know him, okay? You've mentioned him to me before.

WhosYourDaddy: Are we talking about your ex-husband?

BrownEyedGirl: No.

WhosYourDaddy: Someone you met before that?

BrownEyedGirl: Yes.

WhosYourDaddy: This is driving me nuts, Mary. Tell me who you're thinking about.

BrownEyedGirl: Tomorrow would've been our anniversary.

WhosYourDaddy: Is it Malcolm Turner?

Bingo. He knew about the anniversary.

WhosYourDaddy: I'm right, aren't I? It's Malcolm.

BrownEyedGirl: Maybe.

WhosYourDaddy: I am.

BrownEyedGirl: Okay, I'll admit it. But if you talk to him or anyone who knows him, please don't say anything. He's no good for me. Even if he's single, I'm determined to leave him in the past.

Sebastian hoped he wasn't being *too* obvious. Malcolm wasn't stupid. But he was vain and arrogant enough to believe he could cheat on a girl, break her heart and have her pining for him fifteen years later.

WhosYourDaddy: You're telling me you're still in love with Malcolm?

BrownEyedGirl: I don't know what I'm saying. It's late, and I'm not making sense.

WhosYourDaddy: It makes sense to me.

BrownEyedGirl: It does?

WhosYourDaddy: There's someone I can't forget, either.

BrownEyedGirl: Who?

WhosYourDaddy: You.

BrownEyedGirl: So what about this weekend?

WhosYourDaddy: I'll let you know.

BrownEyedGirl: When?

One minute turned into two, which turned into five. Sebastian was afraid he'd lost him, for tonight, anyway. He knew he should sign off and go to bed; he could hardly keep his eyes open. But he tried to stay awake, just in case…and ended up falling asleep at the desk.

Six

Should he write back? Or wait for the night to pass and hope Mary would be less demanding the next time they talked?

Malcolm spent another twenty minutes in front of the computer on the kitchen table he'd rented along with the other furniture, trying to decide. He didn't want her to be as indifferent as she'd been before. Their recent conversations had been far more stimulating; he liked that she'd revealed her feelings for him. Despite her anger over what he'd done with Sherry Stewart, he'd known the chemistry between them was still there. But he wasn't sure where to take the relationship now that Mary was responding as he'd hoped. He hated to walk away, but he couldn't let her see him.

Being torn between what he wanted and what he knew he should do made him angry.

Damn it! He should never have started this. If he'd been able to go to the casinos, or patrol using his cop light and badge to generate a little excitement, or even go to a damn movie, it might not have gathered such momentum. But ever since he'd acquired Latisha and Marcie, he'd spent far too much time on the computer with Mary.

There was no use lamenting it, he told himself. Their relationship would've come to this eventually. Mary wasn't merely a diversion. He'd visited her place at least twice a week for months. He'd seen her kids playing out front and he'd stood in her yard, watching her move through the house. He'd thought about her a lot over the years, especially after he'd severed his past. She'd been the perfect fit, the one he shouldn't have let go. If he'd stuck with her, his life never would've become what it was now. They should've married and raised a family. Splitting up hadn't worked for either of them.

What a mess. With the incentive of half a million dollars and a fresh start, he'd imagined being able to walk away from his family and friends without a backward glance. He'd actually been eager to do so, had felt a sort of triumph in exiting with such a finale. He'd shocked and hurt them all, and they'd deserved it—especially his immediate family. Nothing he did pleased his parents, but it was the opposite for his older brother. And their baby sister had been absolutely worshipped.

But those people were part of the very fabric of his life. He couldn't seem to excise them without losing part of his own identity. And he'd discovered that his friends and acquaintances were just as hard to abandon. When he was planning to break away, he'd thought he'd mourn the loss of his career more than anything else. But hanging on to his badge and his gun had softened that blow. When he went out driving at night, he got to enjoy the perks of power without having to answer to anybody. It was the people he missed. That was why he'd reached out to Mary.

It'd been pure luck that he'd been able to find her so easily. Had he not run into Francine, the girlfriend she'd hung out with in high school, he would've had a much harder time of it. But, thanks to seeing Francine in New York City while he was vacationing there with Emily, he'd learned about Mary's jewelry hobby and her Web site, even the city where she lived. That was all it took.

Locating her had given him such a sense of excitement. He'd felt alive again, hopeful that he'd be able to re-create a normal life.

But keeping his identity a secret was no longer satisfying. It was a hindrance. She missed him, wanted him, and he couldn't go to her. She wouldn't put up with this situation forever. Another man would come along and she'd fall in love with him instead.

So what could he do? She'd turn him in if he told her the truth. She wouldn't understand how cornered, how trapped, he'd been, that the path he'd chosen had been the only way out with the debts he'd racked up and a pending divorce. Only something that extreme would allow him to start over.

Would a lie work any better?

He couldn't see how. Maybe he could present a different version of the past and get her to buy it, but he couldn't stop her from talking to her family and friends. She'd tell her mom or sister that she was back in a relationship with him, and word would spread until the news reached friends in San Antonio. Before long, someone would say, "I heard he was dead. I heard he killed his wife and stepson, then committed suicide in New Jersey." And that was all it would take to unravel the perfect murder.

The sound of movement in the extra bedroom brought Malcolm's head up, his ears tuned for trouble. What was that? He'd thought the sisters were asleep. He'd punished Marcie so severely, he couldn't believe either of them would dare breathe, let alone move. But something was going on.

With a curse, he shoved away from the table and crossed the hall.

"What the hell are you doing?" he hollered as he turned on the light.

Marcie screamed and curled into a ball. Latisha scrambled into the corner, her ankle chain rattling as she drew her knees to her chest. The mattresses he'd thrown down for them when he first brought them home had been tossed into the backyard. He was making them sleep on the hard floor, punishing them both, even though it was Marcie who'd disobeyed.

"I asked you a question!" he bellowed.

"We're not doing anything. Her—her mouth's bleeding." Squinting against the light, Latisha pointed at her sister. "I was just trying to stop the bleeding."

"She's bleeding because she didn't obey. If you don't lie down and quit shuffling around, you're going to be bleeding, too. Your sister's damn lucky I didn't kill her!" Lord knows he'd been tempted. If he hadn't had to concentrate on his driving he probably would have.

"You try to escape again and I'll do it. You understand? It's pointless to run. There's nowhere to go out here. We don't have any neighbors, no one close enough to help you."

Tears trickled down Latisha's face. "Please let us go," she said, her voice falling to a whisper. "We won't tell anyone about you. We swear it. We won't talk to the police. We just want to go home."

She sounded sincere. But Malcolm knew she'd change her mind once she was safe. He wasn't stupid enough to believe he could ever set them free. He also wasn't stupid enough to let them know it. They'd be a lot easier to control if they thought there was a chance.

"I'll tell you what," he said. "You be on your best behavior and work hard like you should and in another week or so I'll see what I can do. Okay?"

Latisha exchanged a glance with her sister, then nodded. "Yes, sir. We—we'll do whatever you say. Won't we, Marcie?"

Marcie seemed less willing to agree.

"*Won't we,* Marcie!" Latisha prodded.

"Yes, *sir.*"

Malcolm ignored the sullenness of her reply. "I'm glad we finally understand each other."

He managed a smile but let it fade as soon as he stomped out of the room. "Stupid bitches," he muttered under his breath. Most women weren't good for any-thing except...

The image that appeared caused a rush of testoster-one so powerful it brought him to an abrupt halt. He'd always taken full advantage of the "badge bunnies" who threw themselves at any man wearing a uniform. But he hadn't touched Latisha and Marcie. He'd told himself he wouldn't stoop that low. The officers he used to work with held sex offenders in the highest contempt. He didn't want to know they'd think of him in the same way.

But he'd never see his former coworkers again. So who would know? Besides, it was because of Latisha and Marcie that he couldn't go to Franklin Boulevard to pick up a prostitute.

After all the teasing and flirting he'd done with Mary, he wanted a woman. Badly. And there were two right here. Two who had nothing better to do. Two who were ripe for the taking.

They were just black women. What would it hurt?

Come on. Go for it. Maybe if he relieved some of his sexual tension, he'd be able to concentrate, make a decision about Mary. Then he might not be so influenced by the desire to get in her pants....

Returning to the bedroom, Malcolm flipped on the light. Both girls shrank away from him, but his gaze lingered on Latisha. His father had taught him from the time he was just a boy that minorities weren't worth his attention. But the younger of the two...she was quite pretty, if he let himself look at her that way. She had large tits, an itty-bitty waist and nice round hips. And she didn't have the welts, freshly swollen lip and black eye he'd given Marcie when he'd dragged her into the house from the van.

"I know how you can guarantee your ticket home," he said.

Latisha's eyes widened and grew wary at the same time. She'd noticed the change in his voice and manner, but the promise of his words proved too difficult to resist. "H-how?"

"Spend half an hour with me in the bedroom, doing whatever I ask, and I'll let you go. I promise."

"In the bedroom?" she repeated, looking as if she was about to be sick.

"What's thirty minutes?" he asked, trying to make it more appealing. "Thirty minutes for the sake of freedom."

"Will you let my sister go, too?"

"Sure," he said. "But that'll cost the whole night."

Marcie struggled to scoot closer to Latisha. "Don't do it," she warned. "He's lyin'. He'll drag you outta here and you won't be comin' back, and not 'cause he took you home. He's gonna kill us both. That's what he's gonna do."

Malcolm felt his hands curl into fists. Marcie was right. He had no choice. But it angered him that she wouldn't at least hope for the best. "Shut up! I'm not talking to you, you crackhead bitch!"

"Please, don' do this to her," Marcie begged. "It's me you're mad at. She ain't done nothin'."

"But she's the one I want. So stay out of it." He nudged Latisha's knee with his foot. "Take off your clothes."

Latisha whimpered but didn't act.

"Come on," he persisted. "Your sister's the one who's lying. I might kill her before we're through, but I won't hurt you, not if you've been good to me."

Tears slipped from her eyes, but it was Marcie who began to plead. "Please. She's my baby sister. She's a good girl. She ain't never been with a man. Take me. I can make it fun. It's me you want to punish."

This was the most respectful Marcie had been, but Malcolm knew how deeply she hated him. It was all an act to save her sister's sorry ass. "You've got to be kidding me," he responded. "Look at you!"

"You won't be able to tell what I look like in the dark. Jus' take me outta here, so she don't gotta hear it, and I'll make it worth your while. I promise."

She'd try to kill him, more likely. He didn't find her appealing. And because of her, he had to go to the trouble of getting a new phone, which meant he needed another alias. He preferred Latisha. But he'd never forced a woman before. He'd spent fifteen years as a cop, believing that rapists were the worst kind of scum, second only to pedophiles. Did he really want to become one of them?

Even prison inmates had no respect for a rapist. He remembered wondering why they didn't have enough pride to use some self-restraint, and here he was, facing the same temptation. It showed how much he'd changed, but he didn't want to think about that.

Attempting to ignore the part of him that still balked at what he was about to do, he stepped forward. He'd unchain Latisha and drag her ass out of here if he had to.

But Marcie got in front of her. "No!" she cried. "You won't take her! Let her be!"

The stupid bitch was willing to take another beating. He'd probably have to fight them both. And if it got too violent, he wasn't sure he could get it up.

"Shut your ugly mouth and go to sleep," he snapped and walked out. He didn't want Marcie or Latisha. He wanted Mary. And he was going to have her.

He just needed to figure out how.

Jane was getting out of the shower when the doorbell rang. She wrapped a towel around her head and pulled on her robe before peeking through the blinds in the kitchen. It was David.

"Hi," she breathed as she let him into her condo. She'd managed to fall asleep a couple of hours after searching every reverse directory available to her, without any success. Then she'd gotten up and worked out before taking Kate to school in her sweats, like she did every day. But David looked as if he'd been up since she called him. Wearing a sport jacket, a tie and some chinos, he'd tried to smooth down his hair, but it stood up in back. Apparently, he hadn't showered or shaved, but it didn't hurt his appearance. With short dark hair, light green eyes and a rugged face, he was handsome despite being a little frayed around the edges. Jane had always thought so, even when she hated him all those years ago.

"Where's Kate?" He glanced toward the kitchen.

"School. She likes to go early on Tuesdays. There's a ceramics teacher who allows the kids to make things." She plucked at his lapel. "You didn't have to dress up just for me," she teased.

He indicated her robe. "I could say the same."

"You could've called first."

"I was in the neighborhood. Anyway, I had to dress for the entire day. Who knows when I'll have the chance to go home again. This past week's been crazy. Fortunately, Jeremy's nearly thirteen, old enough to be some help with Chase and Jessica. And they love their sitter. But with Skye gone and the hours I'm pullin'…" He sighed. "I'll be glad when she's home."

David worked too hard. Jane had heard Skye say it, had experienced it firsthand when she'd been married to one of his most sought-after suspects. "Would you like a cup of coffee?"

"No." He dropped onto her soft leather couch. "I have a caffeine buzz already."

"How about breakfast? I can get dressed, make you some eggs."

"No, I don't have much time. I stopped by to tell you I went to the station first thing and used the databases there. The number you gave me didn't match any records."

"So you need to get a search warrant?"

"I already did." He straightened the bear sculpture on her coffee table. "I faxed it to the various cellular companies before I came here."

"How long will it take to get a response?"

"So far I've heard from two. No luck. I'm waiting on the others. Any word from Gloria?"

"I called her when I got out of bed this morning. She's still planning to go to work today. She said she'd only drive herself crazy if she didn't."

He shook his head in sympathy. "The rent has to be paid. That kind of thing stops for no one."

"I can't imagine what's happened to Marcie and Latisha, David."

"Me, neither," he said. "There was no sign of a struggle. That's what's got me. They simply disappeared—together and in broad daylight."

"How often does that occur?" she asked.

"Not once since I've been on the force."

Jane tightened the belt on her robe. She was close enough to David and Skye that it wasn't any big deal for him to see her like this, but she would've felt more comfortable in her clothes. "Gloria told me that someone downtown thought this case might be related to the murders along the American River."

He made a face. "No, you and I both know who committed those murders."

"Exactly. So what gives?"

"I've never been able to prove it was Oliver. That means that technically they remain unsolved."

"Are you still *trying* to prove it?"

"There's no point in spending any more time. I've already dug up all there is to find. Claiming this case might be related was just an excuse to dump it on my desk. Everyone's so busy." Closing his eyes, he let his head fall onto the back of the couch. "We really need more help."

"That's why you're letting me get involved," she said.

He opened one eye. "No, you're involved because I knew there was no way to stop you. I'm intimately familiar with the diehard who trained you, remember?"

She offered him a coy smile. "Have you talked to Skye?"

"Last night before bed."

"Did you tell her I'm working my own case?"

"I left that out—rather conveniently, I admit." The tenor of his voice changed, grew more serious. "I figure she has enough to worry about."

He was the one doing the worrying. That was obvious. He didn't like his wife taking some of the cases she did. This time Skye wasn't chasing anyone accused of a violent crime, but South America was too far away for David to feel comfortable about her absence. Even though Ava was there, too. Every once in a while, he nearly talked her into quitting her job. But she couldn't give up on The Last Stand, couldn't walk out on what she'd created.

"I'll get dressed and make you some breakfast."

"No, I'm leaving," he said and stood. "I'll catch up with you later."

She followed him to the door. "So you'll be in touch if—"

David's cell phone went off. She stopped, hoping whoever was on the other end might be calling about the warrant.

"Hello?" He cocked his head, listening. "Just a sec, let me grab a pen." He patted his jacket pockets and found a pad as Jane brought him a pen from a drawer in the kitchen. "Go ahead."

He scribbled something down, thanked whoever had called and hung up.

"Well?" she asked expectantly.

"That was Verizon. The number belongs to a guy named Wesley Boss."

"Do you have an address?"

"At this point, just a P.O. box. I'll head to the post office as soon as I have time and see if I can get a street address."

"Let me know when you have it."

He muttered Boss's name under his breath. "Wesley Boss...Wesley Boss."

"What is it?" she asked.

"That name sounds familiar."

"Why would it?"

"I've heard it before. Recently. Or maybe not." He stepped onto the stoop. "Wait, I remember now. Some guy from New York came to the station a few weeks ago, asking about a Wesley Boss. He said Boss loves police work, forensic shows, ambulance chasing. He wanted to know if he'd been a nuisance or tried to befriend any of the officers."

Jane hid behind the door to spare the other people in her complex the sight of her in her bathrobe. "Why was he looking for Boss?"

David didn't answer. His mind was elsewhere. "What was the name of that guy?" He squeezed his eyes closed. "It was Greek, I know that. Coast? That's close. Hang on." He hit a speed-dial button on his phone and asked someone on the other end to check his desk for a business card with a Greek last name beginning with the letter C. "It should be in my top drawer," he told whoever it was.

While he tried to come up with the information, Jane took the towel off and started patting her head dry. Her hair was short and choppy these days. She needed to style it, before it dried.

"No…no…no… There's a New York address… That's it," she heard David say. "What's the name?… Give me the number, too."

He still had her pen. He wrote the information on his pad, then tore out the sheet and handed it to her. "Call this guy and see if he ever found his man."

"You're willing to let me do this?" she asked in surprise.

"A homicide case I've been working for the past two months just went into fast-forward."

So the safety of Gloria Rickman's sisters wasn't the only thing keeping him up at night. "I'll take care of it," she said.

He tossed her a tired smile. "I'll get to the post office once I handle this."

"Okay." Jane read the name on the paper. *Sebastian*

Costas. "What's his connection to Boss? Why's he looking for him?" she called after David.

He paused midway to his car. "He claims Boss is an alias for a man named Malcolm Turner, an ex-cop from Jersey."

"And?"

"He believes Turner killed his wife and stepson, then faked his own death."

"So Costas is a cop himself? Or a private investigator?"

"He's the father of the boy who was murdered."

Her thoughts immediately reverted to Kate and how easily she could've lost her five years ago, when Oliver went on his killing rampage. "Ouch."

"He might not be thinking clearly."

"Is there any chance he could be right? About Boss?"

"I placed a call to New Jersey. They're convinced Turner is dead. They have DNA to prove it."

"So this Costas is crazy or desperate or both."

David seemed to consider the question. "What he says is highly unlikely. But…one thing I've learned in law enforcement—anything's possible."

"True. I'll talk to you later." She watched him drive away, then stared at the note he'd handed her. Maybe Sebastian Costas was out of his mind with grief or maybe he refused to believe that the man who'd killed his son was dead because he needed a target. Both were plausible scenarios. But Marcie's phone call had originated from a number owned by a Wesley Boss, and it was awfully coincidental that Mr. Costas was searching for a man with the same name.

Something was up with Mr. Boss. Whether he was actually Mr. Turner remained to be seen.

Seven

The ring of his cell phone woke Sebastian. Patting the desk, he managed to locate it without opening his eyes. "Hello?"

"You won't believe this," a female voice announced.

Biting back a groan occasioned by the crick in his neck, he sat up. "Mary?"

"Did I wake you?"

Still groggy, he checked the clock. It was after eight. He'd spent the night in front of the computer. "Looks like it's time to get up, anyway. What's going on?" He couldn't imagine she'd heard from Malcolm since she'd given up her screen name. He jiggled his mouse to dissolve his screen saver. She hadn't signed on from an alternate location. He was still actively connected, and his was the last message in the conversation.

"He sent me flowers!" she said.

"Malcolm?"

"Yeah. A dozen red roses. They arrived a few minutes ago. The card says, 'Happy Anniversary.'"

Sebastian came to his feet. "How did he sign it?"

"He didn't. That's all there is. Just 'Happy Anniversary.' But...aren't you excited? They have to be from him. He's letting me know his true identity! Malcolm's falling for it!"

Sebastian raked his fingers through his hair. "The anniversary may not be the giveaway you think it is."

"Why not?"

Wishing he had some aspirin, he rolled his shoulders. "I mentioned it to him last night."

"Oh."

As he passed the foot of the bed, he caught his reflection in that same damn mirror and turned away. He didn't need to see his raggedy-ass appearance. He needed coffee, even more than aspirin. "I was using anything I could to make him show his hand," he explained.

"But one guy would never send flowers to commemorate a competitor's anniversary."

"True. I guess that makes it a bigger step forward than I initially thought."

"He's getting closer and closer to revealing who he really is."

The scent of coffee granules rose to Sebastian's nostrils as he tore open the packet of gourmet roast that had been sandwiched between the coffeemaker and the bathroom wall. "Maybe. But I'm concerned about one thing."

"What's that?"

Apparently, she was so pleased by their progress she wasn't thinking of the risks. "He has your exact address."

Silence. Then she said, "Do you think he sent the flowers just to show that he can find me?"

He poured the grounds into the filter. "Knowing Malcolm? Probably. He told you he could get the information and this is his way of proving it."

"Sometimes it's hard for me to see him as the bastard you say he is," she admitted.

Sebastian's hand hovered over the start button. "Seriously?"

"He cheated on me, but we were kids. I never dreamed the boy I knew, the boy I slept with, would grow up to become a cold-blooded *murderer.* To be so dangerous. He had his moments, like everyone else, but he could be really sweet, too."

Sebastian started the coffeemaker, then wandered back into the room and pulled open the heavy drapes on the window. "Even Ted Bundy was once a kid. Did you call the Jersey police and check out my story, like I asked you to?"

"I did. I wanted more details. I thought it might help me absorb the shock. The man I spoke to said Malcolm killed his wife and stepson. But he also said Malcolm killed himself."

A thin fog and slight drizzle made Sebastian less than eager to head outside. From what he'd heard, Sacramento had perfect weather nine months out of the year. Just his luck to be here during their three-month rainy season. "That's the part that isn't true and you know it. You've been communicating with him for months."

"It's weird, that's all."

"You need to accept it. He's getting more committed to your relationship." The flowers signified as much. They also signified that he'd act soon. Now that he really thought about it, "Happy Anniversary" *was* a commitment of sorts, a milestone. He just hoped Malcolm acted the way they wanted him to. That was where the gamble came in.

"You don't think he'd surprise me by coming here," she said.

Now she was beginning to consider the possibilities. "He could."

"Oh, God. What would I do?"

From his second-story window, Sebastian could see people wearing business suits, getting into cars parked on the shiny pavement below. "You'd play along, buy whatever story he's selling. If he tells you he's been hiding behind an alias because he's in the witness protection program, or he's in the CIA, or the Feds are after him because he claims to have seen a UFO— whatever he says—act as if you believe it. Your life could depend on it."

A nervous laugh preceded her response. "That sounds ominous."

For her, their little fishing expedition had been all fun and games. Until now. These flowers made it real. The fact that Malcolm could get Mary's home address so easily, the fact that he already had it and was probably far closer to Sacramento than he'd let on, made anything possible. "You okay?" he asked.

"Of course. It's just…I've got kids." Her voice took on a beseeching quality. "He wouldn't hurt either of them, would he?"

Sebastian couldn't say what Malcolm would do. Malcolm had no conscience, nothing to inhibit his behavior, or he could never have planned and executed the deaths of Emily and Colton. Sebastian was sure only of Malcolm's self-interest. Narcissism was his most consistent trait. "He won't have any reason to hurt you as long as he doesn't find out about me."

"So if he shows up here, should I slip away and call you?"

"Only slip away if you're positive he won't catch you. Dial 9-1-1, *then* call me. Your safety comes before anything else."

"My *safety?* Now you're really scaring me."

Sebastian couldn't tell her to relax. She *needed* to be on guard. Last night, when he was exchanging messages with "Wesley Boss," he'd represented her as more interested in her old flame than she really was. He'd been hoping to achieve the meeting he was after—not this. What if Malcolm appeared on her doorstep expecting her to fall into his arms, but she refused to sleep with him? He might regret revealing himself and decide to tie up loose ends.

"I'll send him a message thanking him for the flowers and push for a rendezvous so he won't feel like he needs to come to your house," he said.

"Shouldn't *I* send that message?" she asked.

"Why?"

"I don't like not knowing what's going on. It makes me uneasy. You talked to him last night and today I received flowers for the first time."

The aroma of brewing coffee drew Sebastian back to the motel bathroom. "I'll tell you everything you need to know. Just keep your head down."

"So I don't get caught in the cross fire."

He wished he could frame his request in a more positive light, but his conscience demanded he not downplay the seriousness of the situation to meet his own goals. "More or less."

She released an audible sigh. "Wow. This sucks."

A beep signaled an incoming call.

"It should be over soon," he promised and held his phone so he could see caller ID. It showed a local number, one he didn't recognize. "I've got to go. I'll check in with you later."

"Okay," she said, but he could tell she wasn't happy to get off the phone. She'd gone along with his plans to ensnare Malcolm partly because of the friendship that'd developed between them, and Sebastian felt guilty for taking advantage of her. But they'd come too far. Malcolm was interested in her, already knew her address. There was no way out.

"Take care," he said and switched to the other line.

"Hello?"

The voice was deep, masculine and far more confident than Jane had expected. "Mr. Costas?"

"Yes?"

Although Jane was ready for work, she hadn't left the house yet. "My name is Jane Burke. I'm a caseworker at The Last Stand—"

"How'd you get my number?" he interrupted.

"Detective Willis with the Sacramento Police Department passed it to me. He said you visited the station a few weeks ago, inquiring about a man named Wesley Boss."

"And you're somehow related to the Sacramento police?"

Sebastian certainly didn't seem like some revenge-crazed lunatic. He sounded brisk, impatient—someone who thought fast and expected others to keep up or go away.

"Loosely." Dressed in an Ann Taylor sweater and slacks, she was just sliding her feet into a pair of pumps that'd cost her far too much. She'd developed expensive tastes when she was a wealthy dentist's wife. It'd been a long time since she could afford the kind of wardrobe she'd once enjoyed, but she'd splurged on this outfit the day she hit her goal weight a year ago. Now she was even more slender. "As I was saying, I'm with The Last Stand, a victims' charity here in Sacramento, and I'm currently involved in an investigation in which Boss's name has surfaced. I was wondering if we could get together. I have a few questions I'd like to ask you."

"What sort of investigation are you talking about?"

Jane packed her briefcase while she talked. "An abduction. Two African-American teens were taken three weeks ago."

"That doesn't sound like the man I'm looking for."

She dropped the file folder she'd grabbed and straightened. She'd expected him to immediately agree. Wasn't *he* the one who'd shown up in Sacramento, asking for help—asking for answers? "How many men named Wesley Boss are there in this area?" she asked.

"In Northern California? None that I've been able to find."

"My point exactly. And I'm telling you I've come up with one."

"I've already got a lead on the man I've been searching for, and I have a big day ahead of me, Ms....what did you say your name was?"

"Burke. Jane Burke." She folded her arms. "You don't think there's any chance they could be one and the same?"

"No way. My Wesley Boss is the biggest racist I've ever known."

"He's white?"

"He's white. And he'd never touch a woman who wasn't."

"You know him that well?"

"I should. He was my son's stepfather. I heard what he said when Colton took a Japanese girl to Homecoming."

"Maybe Wesley Boss has changed his M.O."

"I highly doubt it. Besides, kidnapping could compromise what he's already accomplished."

"Which is…"

"Getting away with murder."

"Maybe he thinks he can get away with this, too."

The silence stretched, and Jane wondered if Sebastian was considering her response. "I need another cup of coffee," he finally muttered.

Still feeling the effects of her strenuous morning workout, she sat in a kitchen chair. "What?"

"Just a minute." He was gone for several seconds. When he came back, he asked, "What do you have on your Wesley Boss? Do you have an address?"

"Do you have a few minutes to meet?" she countered.

"Ms. Burke, as I've mentioned, I have a busy day ahead of me. Someone else could be hurt if I don't find this SOB."

"I certainly don't want to see anyone hurt, Mr. Costas. That's why I owe it to these sisters to—"

"Did you say *sisters?*" he cut in.

Jane stood and scooped her purse off the counter. "Yes."

"The teens who were abducted were sisters?"

"*Yes.*" She looked inside her purse for her keys and managed to dig them out from beneath her wallet.

"Malcolm's having trouble with some roommates," he said. "He told me they were sisters."

"What are you talking about?" she asked.

"I'll explain later. Where should we meet?"

"Now you're willing?" she asked in surprise.

"Now I think we might be after the same person."

"Our offices are on Watt Avenue, not far from El Camino. Can you come there?"

"Give me an hour."

"See you at nine-thirty." She provided the address and hung up. Mr. Costas was articulate. And direct. She wondered if he could somehow be right about Malcolm Turner.

After a glance at her wall clock, she picked up her pace. Time was getting away from her.

Grabbing her phone, she dialed Gloria's number on her way out. "We have the name of the man who owns the cell your sister used last night," she announced as soon as Gloria answered.

"What is it?" she asked.

"Wesley Boss. Have you heard of him?"

"Never."

"We're working on getting his address and we'll check him out. I just wanted to give you an update." Her car chirped as she pressed the button on her key chain to unlock it.

"Luther came by las' night and put a note on my door," Gloria told her. "I found it when I lef' for work this mornin'."

Jane tossed her briefcase on the passenger seat. "What did it say?"

"'You think that skinny white bitch who came to see me cares any more than the cops do what happens to people like us? You should've come to me. I'll find Latisha. Lucifer.'"

Skinny white bitch? Jane knew she should be offended, but she'd worked so hard to lose weight that the *skinny* part was almost a compliment. "I thought Lucifer was a name you only used behind his back," she said.

"He musta heard it. I guess he ain't offended. I guess he likes it."

Yikes. Anyone who purposely adopted a name like that had to be dangerous. "He's wrong, you know. We do care. We're doing all we can." She didn't add that David had to deal with a homicide today. She figured the realities of police work would appear to support Luther's side of the argument. Those waiting for news of a loved one didn't want to face the fact that police officers had a lot of different cases, a lot of people to help, and that they also had to eat and sleep and look after their own families.

"I appreciate that you're tryin'," Gloria said.

It would've been difficult to miss the reticence in those words. "But..."

"If Latisha's dad can finally do somethin' for the poor chil', I'm grateful for that, too."

Oh, hell. Now they had a three-hundred-pound pimp with killer pit bulls on the case. "Gloria, don't share any of the information I give you with Luther, okay?"

"Why not?" she asked.

Because Jane had no idea what he might do with it. "His methods could be a little sketchy."

"He mean business."

"It's the way he does business that worries me. He could hurt somebody. He might even hurt the wrong somebody. You need to trust the police. And me," she said, hoping it wasn't quite so apparent than she had little faith in herself.

"I jus' want my sisters back."

Jane opened her mouth to try and convince her to give them more time before allowing Luther to get involved. But she knew it wouldn't help. It was too late. Gloria saw Luther as power. She wanted action, results, not more talk. Despite a concerted effort, the police hadn't been able to offer her even a hint of relief in three weeks. At this point, she'd take any shortcut. And Jane couldn't blame her. She knew she'd probably do the same thing if she were in Gloria's shoes. "You won't listen to me, will you."

"Like I said, I jus' want my sisters back."

"Then heaven help Wesley Boss if Luther gets to him before we do," she said and disconnected.

The man who walked into Jane's office at precisely nine-thirty stood over six feet and weighed about two hundred and fifteen pounds. Somewhere in his mid-forties, he was wearing expensive jeans, a rugby shirt and a brown leather bomber jacket, but even dressed so casually he looked like a yacht owner or executive on holiday. Maybe it was his autocratic bearing—or his staggering good looks. He had an abundance of dark hair, currently on the long side, an olive complexion, brown eyes with thick sweeping lashes and the kind of muscular build that would've made the stylists in Jane's last salon drool.

Hoping he hadn't noticed her jaw hit the floor, she struggled to ignore his physical assets so she could concentrate on the purpose of his visit. "Thank you for coming, Mr. Costas." She put out her hand and experienced a firm grip as his warm, dry palm met hers.

"Ms. Burke."

Lisa, the volunteer who'd let him in, hadn't left. She stood behind him, mouthing, "Oh my God!" while fanning herself.

"That will be all, Lisa," Jane said, her smile pointed.

Blushing when he turned to look at her, Lisa ducked her head and moved on.

Jane motioned to the chair she'd placed across from her desk for Gloria yesterday and stepped back. She felt as if she was acting again, pretending to be a professional victims' advocate instead of a mere trainee. But she instinctively knew Costas was the type of man who'd assume she didn't deserve his respect if she didn't demand it. "Please, have a seat."

His lithe movements graceful yet extremely masculine, he did as she directed.

Jane cleared her throat. "Thanks for coming."

"Hopefully, we'll both be glad of this meeting," he said. "What do you have on Wesley Boss?"

Jane didn't sit down. She felt more in control standing. "Not much. Yet."

"You said you have an address?"

"I have a P.O. box. Detective Willis is working on a street address."

"Have you met Boss? Can you tell me what he looks like?"

"No. At this point, he's only a name to me."

He studied her so intently she felt the blood rush to her face. "How did he come up in connection with the two missing African-American girls?"

"One of them made a call last night using a cell phone that corresponds to his name."

Costas folded his hands in his lap. "Interesting."

"We think so, too." Jane realized that standing might make her seem nervous, so she took her seat and tried to appear more at ease. "Tell me what you know about Boss."

"As I explained to Willis, he's really Malcolm Turner, the man who killed my ex-wife and son in New Jersey, then faked his own death."

"Was he married to your ex-wife at the time of the murders?"

"Yes."

Jane couldn't help sympathizing. She also couldn't help wondering if he'd remarried. She didn't think so; he wasn't wearing a ring. "I'm sorry. I know that must've been hard for you." She could tell it was hard for him even now. "But what makes you believe Wesley is Malcolm?"

"In a roundabout way, I've been in touch with him via the Internet for nearly three months."

"You...chat with him?"

"After setting up his new life, he sent an instant message to Mary McCoy, a former girlfriend who lives here in town. He claimed to be Wesley Boss, but some of the things he said reminded her of Malcolm, so she gave me a call. They've been e-mailing, with me sort of listening in, ever since."

"How did she know to contact you?"

"After the murders, I spent months visiting every friend, family member and acquaintance Malcolm

Turner's ever had. They all know to contact me if they hear from him."

"I see." She straightened the objects on her desk. "You're very thorough."

"I'm determined to achieve justice for Emily and Colton," he said.

"So you've made contact with Mr. Boss but don't know where he lives?"

"Not yet. He's getting more and more interested in Mary, though, and he has her address. That's why I've got to find him, fast."

"You think he might go to her house? That he might hurt her?"

"He's a murderer, Ms. Burke. There's no telling what he'll do."

Jane was afraid her inexperience was showing. "What did you mean on the phone, when you mentioned roommates?" she asked.

"Last night Mary gave me the password to her e-mail account and I posed as her while chatting with 'Wesley.' I wanted to press him for his location, or get him to identify himself as Malcolm. He didn't do either, but he seemed more distracted than usual and blamed two roommates."

The phone interrupted. Jane ignored its ringing because she knew one of the volunteers would pick up. "And?"

"He mentioned they were girls, as opposed to women. He even said they were sisters."

Excitement and hope shot through Jane. "My kidnap victims."

"Possibly."

"He talked as if they were still alive?"

"Yes."

Jane had no idea what shape they'd be in but, given the odds, this was welcome news. "So if Wesley Boss is Malcolm Turner, and Malcolm's such a racist, why did he take them? Why these two? Why not two white girls?"

"I'm guessing it was a crime of opportunity."

"Earlier you said he was having trouble with them."

"He made it sound that way."

"What kind of trouble?"

"He didn't specify. But if he has these girls with him, it would certainly explain why he's been so reluctant to see Mary."

Crossing her legs, Jane toyed with a ballpoint pen. "She's willing to meet with him?"

"I'll be the one doing that."

"Oh, right. Of course."

The intercom buzzed. "Jane?" It was Lisa, the volunteer who'd shown Sebastian into the room.

Jane hit the button that would let her respond. "Yes?"

"Detective Willis on line one."

"Thank you." Standing, because she had too much energy to remain seated, no matter how much more relaxed it made her seem, she picked up line one. "David?"

"Jane, I've only got a second. I'm on my way to perform a search. But I had someone else get the address associated with Wesley Boss's P.O. box. Are you ready?"

Her eyes connected with Sebastian's; then she grabbed a piece of paper from the holder on her desk. "Ready."

He rattled off an address in Ione, a small town in Amador County about forty-five minutes away.

"Got it," she said.

"I've already called the sheriff's department. A

deputy will join you there, but I'm betting he's closer than you are, so you'd better hurry."

"I understand. Thanks for letting me know." She hung up and grabbed her purse from under the desk. "We've got to go," she said.

Sebastian came to his feet. "You know where he is?"

"I have an address. What we'll find when we get there is anyone's guess."

Eight

Could it really be over? After all the time he'd spent searching?

Sebastian almost didn't dare hope. But as he drove Jane Burke to Ione—her car didn't have GPS and he hadn't yet sacrificed his Lexus—he called to share the news with Mary. He doubted he'd be able to reach her this early. She was at the hospital working in admissions until four. But he could leave a message she might get on her break. With those flowers showing up at her house this morning, he wanted to alleviate her fears as soon as possible.

The voice-mail recording he'd expected came on. He waited for the beep. "Mary, this is Sebastian. I think we have him. Don't worry about anything, okay? I'll be back in touch when I know more."

As he hung up, he felt Jane watching him and glanced over. He wasn't quite sure what to think of her. She seemed like such a contradiction. She dressed like a typical professional, in conservative business casual, but her hair—dark at the roots and jagged and bleached on the ends—was anything but conservative. Her low-pitched, raspy voice suggested she smoked and yet she was obviously in great physical shape. Then there were the tattoos. She had one on her breast. The V of her sweater came up too high for him to see what it was, but when she moved, he occasionally glimpsed the edge of it. The other was the word *survivor* written on the curve between the thumb and finger on her left hand.

The fact that she was working at a victims' charity led him to believe that tattoo had nothing to do with being a fan of the popular reality show.

What had she been through?

The scar on her neck, noticeable when she turned her head, posed some frightening possibilities....

"You really think we'll find Malcolm Turner?" she asked, shifting her gaze to a point outside the car, as if uncomfortable with his perusal.

"If this is the right Wesley Boss, I do." Sebastian signaled so he could make a left onto Jackson Road. They were heading toward a string of historic gold-rush towns in the Sierra Nevada foothills. Since coming to Sacramento, Sebastian had studied the whole area. According to what he'd read, Ione wasn't a mining town, but it had been a staging and agricultural center for the mining towns around it.

Jane braced herself with a hand against the door as he took the corner a little too fast. "DNA evidence is pretty reliable."

"I know. Malcolm's certainly been able to rely on it." He passed the vehicle in front of him. They'd only left the office fifteen minutes ago, but his impatience made the drive seem interminable. "He was a cop. He knew the men who'd be taking the samples, how they'd go about it, where they'd store them after they were collected, where they'd be tested."

"You think he traded them out or something?"

When she stated it that way, it sounded far-fetched, even to him. But stranger things had happened. He'd once read about a UCI professor who found that DNA evidence as evaluated by a certain police lab had resulted in a young man's wrongful conviction of rape. Sloppiness, sample corruption, dishonesty, human error, overstatement of the odds—all of it could potentially "prove" the wrong thing. "He could have. They were bone-marrow samples. But it might not have been necessary to go that far. He had half a mil to buy the help he needed."

She whistled softly. "I can see why the police might not have bought your accusations. If what you say is true, they have a bigger problem than one bad cop."

"Definitely not a possibility they want to consider. I would've been happy just to convince them to take a new sample. But by the time I realized something wasn't right, it was too late. Malcolm's family had already cremated the remains of whoever was in that car."

"Do you have any idea who that person was?"

"No."

"No one else in the area suddenly went missing."

"No. I'm guessing it was a homeless person or a corpse he dug up. Or he paid off some mortician who had a body awaiting cremation." That was part of the reason the police were so convinced by the DNA match. There'd been no corresponding missing-persons report or disturbance of a cemetery plot—at least, that had come to their attention. They hadn't bothered to look very carefully. Sebastian had tried, but he'd come up empty.

"So what tipped you off?" she asked. "How'd you figure it out?"

The Prius ahead of them was traveling more slowly than Sebastian would've liked, but it was only a two-lane highway and traffic streaming in the opposite direction wouldn't let him pass at the moment. "There were too many unanswered questions."

"Such as?"

"Why didn't he shoot himself? He used his firearm to kill Emily and Colton. He could easily have turned it on himself and ended his life right there in the house with them. Instead, he ran his car off a steep embankment, after which it burst into flames."

"Making it impossible to visually identify the body."

Finding an opening in the traffic, he floored the accelerator. "Convenient, don't you think?"

"What about dental records?" she asked.

He eased back into the right-hand lane. "What about them?"

"They're often used to identify burn victims."

"Not in this case. The police didn't see any reason to go to the extra trouble. As far as they were concerned, they already had a positive ID. The car they found was Turner's. They had a bone-marrow sample. They even had a suicide note he'd e-mailed to his sergeant saying that he'd lost a huge sum of money in an investment and his wife was having an affair with her ex."

She held on to her seat belt as he swung out to pass again, but she didn't complain about the aggressiveness of his driving. He suspected she was too preoccupied. "Wait, *you're* the ex."

"I'm the ex."

"Was it true? Were you involved with Emily?"

He'd faced that question a million times. Just because he and his ex-wife had been able to maintain some mutual respect, a friendship, everyone assumed they were intimate. "She was very important to me—she was the mother of my kid. But I wasn't sleeping with her. Malcolm's claims were merely an excuse, a way to garner sympathy."

They flew past an SUV before Sebastian had to move over to avoid a head-on collision with a Dodge truck. "You'll get a speeding ticket if you don't slow down," she warned. "And getting pulled over will waste more time than you'll save by going so fast."

Evidently, she was paying more attention than he'd thought. And she was right. Grudgingly, he let up on the gas.

"What does Malcolm look like?" she asked as they slowed.

"Average. Five foot nine, hundred and seventy-five pounds. Irish background. Red hair. Blue eyes. Why?"

"Just curious."

She might be seeing him in a few minutes. Until then, Sebastian had a picture he could show her. Leaning across the seat, he opened the jockey box and fished around inside, eventually coming up with the photograph he'd been using in his search. "That's him," he said, handing it to her. "Emily and Colton, too. It's what they sent in their last Christmas card."

She studied the photograph.

"So?" he prompted. "Have you ever seen him before?"

"No."

"Is he what you expected?"

"Not really. He's losing his hair."

"You can tell in *that* picture?" he asked, surprised.

"I used to be a hairstylist." She held the photograph closer. "He seems to have a nice physique, though."

"Classic short man's complex, trying to compensate with muscle mass for what he lacks in height."

She didn't respond to his comment. "Emily is beautiful."

Bitterness overwhelmed him. "*Was* beautiful," he corrected.

Jane hadn't said anything about Colton, but Sebastian guessed she was studying the similarities between them. His son had looked so much like him, except he'd had his mother's light-colored eyes.

Grabbing the photograph before she could mention it, Sebastian shoved it back in the jockey box. He didn't want to talk about Colton. Not with a virtual stranger. And not with anyone who was close to him, either. That was the real reason Constance was moving on. He hadn't been able to include her in what he was suffering. He'd withdrawn.

Fortunately, Jane said nothing. She watched the green rolling hills between Sacramento and Ione fly past her window—or stared at nothing, he couldn't tell which—but she gave him some space and for that he was grateful.

Several minutes later, she resumed the conversation, and her question had nothing to do with the photograph he'd shown her. "What about the five hundred thousand dollars you mentioned? Where'd that come from?"

The money he could talk about. He'd been talking about it since Malcolm's escape. It was the strongest proof that Malcolm was still alive. "That was Emily's. She'd gotten an insurance settlement a few months before and cashed the check. She was saving it to build a new life for her and Colton. At least, that's what she told me. But after the funerals were over and we went to clean the house, the key to the safety-deposit box was there but the money wasn't."

"Maybe she moved it."

"Where? There was no record of it ever going into any of their accounts. And if she was ready to invest it, she would've asked for my help. I'm an investment banker. She mentioned doing something with it once, but Malcolm put a quick stop to my involvement. He said he didn't trust me, and he accused us of having an affair."

"More smoke and mirrors?"

"A way to make sure the money wasn't tied up when he made his getaway."

"Malcolm traded his profession, his family, *his whole life* for an amount that might last him five years—if he lives modestly?"

"People have killed for much less," Sebastian said quietly.

"Usually those people are on drugs or looking for the money to get high. They're not thinking straight. This was planned. Was he in debt?"

For someone who'd seemed a little out of her element when they were at the office, Jane was actually pretty savvy. She came across as sort of tough, certainly more streetwise than the typical middle-class white woman. Sebastian respected that.

"Deeply. He probably wanted her to bail him out, but she wouldn't do it. As I said, she planned to use her money to leave him and start over. Not only would he lose her, he'd have no insurance settlement to avoid financial ruin."

"A major embarrassment, to say the least."

"Exactly. But if he killed his wife and stepson and faked his own death, he could take the money, escape punishment *and* evade his creditors without ever having to face the people he'd hurt."

"A good plan, provided you're a monster," she said. "So what kind of debts did he have?"

According to GPS, they'd already driven eighteen miles on CA-14. Sebastian slowed, looking for Ione Road. "His credit cards were maxed out, and he'd pulled all the equity from their house so it was way overmortgaged. He'd borrowed from his parents, his brother, his best friend. He'd even drained his retirement account."

"Where was the money going?"

"Sports gambling. That's all I can figure. I'm guessing he kept chasing his losses. I think he was even placing bets online."

"Online gambling's illegal, isn't it?"

"Depends on the state. There's only been one guy I'm aware of who's been prosecuted for placing bets online. He paid a five-hundred-dollar fine, but his winnings were over one hundred thousand dollars, so I doubt he minded too much."

"Did you tell the police about Malcolm's financial situation?"

"Since he admitted to having financial problems in his suicide note, they weren't overly concerned." He shot her a glance. "But they didn't meet the shady character who showed up at the house one night while I was there."

"A loan shark?"

Sebastian found their turn. According to GPS they had another five miles before the next one. "He claimed to be a friend, said Malcolm owed him money. Apparently, he'd missed the piece in the paper announcing the death of the whole family. Or he was coming by to pick the bones."

"What was his name?"

"Johnny DiMiglio. At least, that's the name he gave me."

"Did you tell him you thought Malcolm was alive?"

"I did. I was hoping he'd go after him. It would've saved me a lot of time and trouble."

"But that didn't happen."

"I haven't seen or heard from DiMiglio since. He probably figured he'd spend more to find Malcolm than he'd lose by letting it go." Lord knows Sebastian had lost enough.

"Bottom line, Malcolm thought he had nothing to lose by murdering Emily and Colton and everything to gain."

"That's my guess."

She adjusted her seat belt. "Now I know why you're doing what you're doing."

He felt his eyebrows go up.

"I'd be doing the same thing," she said.

There was no time to respond. They'd reached their destination.

Jane's stomach muscles tightened with trepidation as Sebastian pulled to the side of the road, next to a canal, a good distance from the lonely rambler that matched the address Detective Willis had given her. They'd already driven by the house twice. Located at the edge of town, it sat on a large square lot that was mostly mud, thanks to a lack of landscaping and plenty of rainy weather. A dated Volkswagen Beetle, dented and rusted with a flat tire, took refuge beneath the attached metal carport.

The place wasn't much to look at. If Wesley Boss was Malcolm Turner, he certainly hadn't spent much of Emily's insurance settlement on lodging. But Ione encompassed such a hodgepodge of housing styles that such a dilapidated ranch house didn't surprise Jane. The thousand or so households in the area straddled a wide range of styles and incomes—everything from broken-down trailers to a handful of high-end mansions overlooking Lake Comanche.

"What I don't understand is why there's no deputy around," she said. "We couldn't have beaten him here. We had to drive all the way from Sacramento."

That was the second time she'd mentioned it, and the second time Sebastian ignored her. Reaching under his seat, he retrieved a handgun and got out of the car. He didn't seem to care about the deputy. He cared only about finding his man. But what would happen then? He couldn't arrest Wesley Boss or Malcolm Turner or whoever the guy was.

"This can't be good," she breathed. She had her 9mm in her purse. She'd taken it out of her bottom desk drawer before leaving the office, but she was still very conscious of the fact that she hadn't received her license to carry concealed. And Sebastian was from New York. Even if he had a license, California law didn't recognize CCW licenses issued in other states.

"One way or another, we're going to get into trouble. Where's the damn sheriff's deputy?" she asked again, only this time she was talking to herself. Sebastian was halfway to the house, keeping low to the ground and using every tree or bush he could for cover.

Briefly, Jane acknowledged that he looked good using the SWAT approach, like a professional. But she had more important things to worry about than admiring his athleticism and technique—like trying to stop him from taking the law into his own hands.

"Sebastian!" she hissed, standing on the triangle of soggy earth outside her car door. "This isn't safe. Someone could get hurt."

She knew he'd heard her when he looked back. But he wasn't happy she'd broken the silence. With a dark scowl, he waved for her to get back in the car and shut up.

Obviously, he was going in whether she liked it or not. She could call David and try to find out where the deputy was, or she could follow him.

It would definitely be safer to stay in the car. But if Malcolm Turner was in that house and he was as dangerous as Sebastian thought, she should probably try to help. And what about Latisha and Marcie? They could be inside, too. Jane definitely didn't want them to get hurt in whatever was about to happen.

With a curse, she stepped around the car door and closed it so softly it didn't actually latch. Then she copied Sebastian's SWAT performance. She was positive she didn't look as good doing it, but there were no neighbors to witness her behavior—and she preferred to take any precautions she could to avoid getting shot.

"This is crazy," she told herself over and over.

Sebastian was on the porch before she reached the front yard. He glanced in her direction, then did a double take. Pointing, he motioned for her to return the way she'd come, but she shook her head resolutely and continued forward, forcing him to wait for her.

Once they were close enough to speak without alerting anyone inside, she whispered, "I'll go around the house, in case anyone comes out the back door."

He'd been about to complain, or order her back to the car, even though he had no authority to do that. He had no authority to do anything, but he wasn't asking permission, and she could tell by the crease in his forehead that he didn't care if she had complaints.

Her plan must've made sense to him, however—or else he was pacified by the fact that she had a gun and could defend herself if necessary, thus removing the burden from him. Either way, his annoyed expression dissolved into the determination that'd been there before.

"Okay," he said, his voice barely audible. "But make sure you have some sort of cover at all times. Do you understand?"

Ignoring the "Do you understand?"—who put him in charge, anyway?—she slipped around to the side yard. Fortunately, she didn't have to worry about running into any unfriendly dogs. There was no fence around the property. She could see that the backyard held nothing except a weather-beaten shed, some old tires and more mud.

"This is going to ruin my nice shoes," she grumbled and did her best to hug the concrete foundation of the house—to avoid their destruction as much as her own.

It started to sprinkle as she took her position behind

the shed. Although she was farther from the house than she would've liked, she couldn't find better cover. The tires were lying flat on the ground, and there wasn't so much as a tree between her and the back door.

Nothing seemed to be happening, anyway. Where was Sebastian? Had he knocked? He hadn't fired; she would've heard that.

The wind whistled through the cracks of the shed, but there were no voices, no evidence of movement.

"Come on, come on." Peering around the corner, she saw the same static view she'd seen before and wished it was all over. Her teeth chattered from the cold and rain. She'd been so concerned that a man she'd met an hour ago was approaching the house with a loaded firearm that she'd left the car without her coat.

A sudden noise—a loud crack—made her knees go weak. She was just reassuring herself that it hadn't been a gunshot when Sebastian called out to her. "It's safe. There's no one here."

Thank God. Leaning her head back to gulp for breath, she dropped her gun to her side.

"Hey, Burke!" he called when she didn't answer. "You there? You okay?"

Burke? She hated going by Oliver's last name. She would've changed it except that she would've had to change Kate's, too, which would have hurt Oliver's parents even more. They were good people. They didn't deserve the pain he'd caused them.

"Burke!"

She leaned over to see him standing under the small covering that sheltered the back porch. The crack had been the wind wresting the door from his grasp and slamming it against the exterior wall. She could tell by the way he was hanging on to it.

"Name's Jane," she said. "And I'm fine."

"You planning to stay out in the rain all day?" he asked when she didn't budge.

With her free hand, Jane rubbed the wetness from her face. So many things could've happened in the past few minutes. She could've been shot in a gunfight—or shot someone else. Innocent victims might have been injured or killed. She could've been apprehended by the police and lost her weapon and any hope she had of obtaining a permit. Any of which would've cost her the job she needed in order to support her daughter.

All because of Sebastian Costas.

A surge of anger lent Jane's legs fresh strength. Too furious to worry about damaging her shoes, she marched across the muddy yard, sinking a few inches with every step. "What did you think you were doing?" she demanded. "Trying to get us both killed? You're not a cop! You don't have a license to carry that gun in California! And no one put you in charge!"

"Calm down," he said. "Everything's okay."

"Only because there was no one around for you to shoot!"

Obviously not intimidated by her, he looked her up and down as she came closer. "That isn't strictly true, now is it?"

Jane narrowed her eyes. "Are you threatening me?"

Irritation carved another crease in his forehead. "Of course not. I'm just telling you to stop being such a pain in the ass."

"*I'm* the pain?" she shouted. "I trusted you when I

brought you here." She ignored the fact that he'd driven, because she'd provided the address. "And then you pull out a loaded weapon and approach this house as if you've got the right to storm anyplace you want. What was going through your head? For all you knew, there were children inside!"

"Malcolm Turner is dangerous."

"He doesn't even live here anymore. What if someone else had moved in?"

His face an implacable mask, he shrugged. "Then I would've put the gun away."

Blowing out a sigh, she shook her head. "If I report this, you could be brought up on charges. At a minimum, your firearm would be confiscated. You realize that?"

"Nothing happened," he reiterated and walked inside.

Unwilling to be left in the rain, Jane followed. "You're making me wonder who's more dangerous— you or Wesley Boss," she yelled at his back.

He didn't respond. He went into the entry hall and checked the coat closet. Then he went into the garage.

She remained in the empty living room, staring down at her feet. Sebastian was to blame for her soggy shoes, too. But haranguing him about it wasn't going to change anything.

After her blood pressure returned to normal, she began to look around herself. Obviously, whoever had lived here had packed up and moved on. There was some old furniture—just the bare necessities—but no signs of habitation. That had to be why the deputy wasn't around when they arrived. He'd already come and gone.

Avoiding the kitchen because Sebastian had just gone in there, she walked from room to room. Brown shag carpet, matted from wear, covered the floors, except for a small patch of tile at the front door. There were three bedrooms, two baths, the standard kitchen and dining room combo with a large family room. Jane didn't see any evidence that Latisha or Marcie had ever been here. But she didn't see any evidence that Wesley Boss had been here, either.

When she returned from her quick tour, Sebastian was still in the kitchen, going through the cupboards and drawers. She wasn't sure she wanted to speak to him, but now that her anger had dissipated, there didn't seem to be any point in holding a grudge. Not if sharing information could help them both. Maybe he was reckless, but he seemed to be very capable. His approach to the house had been breathtaking in its confident precision.

"I smell only cleaning chemicals and room deodorizer," she said, leaning against the doorway. "Makes the place feel as if it's been vacant for a while."

He looked up at her, met her eyes, then moved to a different drawer. "I think it has been. I'm guessing whoever lived here moved away months before the girls were abducted."

"I'll have to contact the owner to see for sure," Jane said. "Maybe he can provide a forwarding address. Someone obviously went to some trouble to salvage his security deposit."

"I'm guessing the only address the owner will have is the P.O. box connected to the phone," he said.

"I could always do surveillance on the post office where that box is located. See if Malcolm shows up."

"Problem is, you could be sitting there for a while. He could go days, weeks, even months without checking it."

"It might be the best lead we have."

The slam of another cupboard resounded in the empty house. "Not if I can convince him to meet me."

Via their Internet chats. That did seem a lot less random. "What do you think the chances are?"

"Tough to say, but…" His words fell off. He'd found a drawer with something in it. From what Jane could see, they were manuals for the various kitchen appliances. She expected him to close that drawer like every other, but he didn't. He riffled through it. A minute later, he pulled out the dishwasher manual and began to read some words that'd been written on the back.

"What is it?" Jane took a step toward him, but he tore off the cover and slipped it inside his coat.

"Nothing. Let's go."

Nine

"So now you're shutting me out?"

Sebastian glanced over to see Jane watching him with narrowed eyes. They were on their way back to Sacramento, but she hadn't spoken for the first thirty minutes of the trip. He'd cranked up the radio and the heat to fill the void.

"I'm not shutting you out," he said.

She turned down the radio until the squeak of the windshield wipers, beating frantically against a fresh onslaught of rain, was the only sound. "You found something at that house. What was it?"

He scowled at the gray sky. The constant damp made the car feel more like a cocoon. "It's nothing, like I said."

"Then why'd you take it?"

Realizing she wouldn't let the subject go, he pulled the cover of the dishwasher manual out of his coat and handed it to her.

She read it, then frowned at him. "This is directions to an Indian casino."

"See what I mean?"

"No, I don't. Why do you want it?"

He adjusted the heat coming into the car. "It's written by hand."

Understanding dawned in her eyes. "You think Malcolm Turner wrote this?"

"I think he *could've* written it. The gambling would appeal to him. That's what caught my attention."

"I doubt handwriting evidence would ever trump DNA evidence," she said, but she spoke slowly, as if she was still considering his find, wondering about its value. "But I guess if the handwriting matched, it would show us that your Wesley Boss and my Wesley Boss are indeed the same man. Right now, all we have to connect the murders and the kidnappings is the name and those cryptic comments your Wesley Boss made about the 'sisters.'"

"Handwriting is unique to each individual. And handwriting evidence is more than I've got now, which is just a pile of missing money, along with a missing gun, badge and police uniform."

She put the torn-off cover on the dash. "The gun concerns me."

"It should. He definitely knows how to use it."

"What would you have done if Malcolm had been there?" she asked.

He wanted to believe he would've called the police. But Malcolm knew how to work the system, was a product of it. If he had sufficient ID to "prove" he was Wesley Boss, they'd start by questioning him about the kidnappings, and he'd know how to play that. If they couldn't get anything on him, they'd release him

pending further investigation—and he'd be gone long
before they ever got around to identifying who he really
was. It wasn't as if they'd send him back to New Jersey
on Sebastian's word, or get a court order compelling him
to provide a DNA sample. They had certain procedures
they had to work through. Police involvement equaled
bureaucracy, and bureaucracy was never efficient.

But what did that mean? Did it mean Sebastian
would've shot him?

Maybe. He might not have been able to stop himself.

"Do you plan to answer me?" she asked.

He turned the radio back up. "He wasn't there."

Jane hesitated as she stepped out of Sebastian's
Lexus. Unless the landlord of that house could provide
a new address, he was suddenly in a much better
position to find Wesley Boss than she was. He was in
contact with him, wasn't he?

That meant she needed to continue working with
him, enlist his help, regardless of how she felt about the
way he'd handled the situation in Ione. "So you'll call
me? You'll let me know if you arrange a meeting with
Boss?" she asked.

Sebastian leaned forward until she could see his face.
"I'll think about it."

She didn't like his attitude. "I shared my information with *you*."

"Your information turned out to be a bust."

"Not a complete bust," she argued. "You got directions to that Indian casino."

"Which might mean nothing more than an enjoyable
night of craps."

She adjusted her purse. The gun inside made it unusually heavy. "What about my kidnap victims? Surely you're not so consumed with revenge that you don't care what happens to them."

He scowled. "That isn't it at all."

"Then what is?"

"I don't see how bringing you along will help save them."

His arrogance irritated her. "Oh, really? Who backed you up in Ione, even though you had no business doing what you did?"

The barest hint of a smile curved his lips. "I wish I could've caught that on tape."

Jane stiffened. "What?"

"You, trying not to get your shoes muddy while hurrying toward me with that gun."

She hadn't realized he'd paid enough attention to notice. "Little good it did me," she grumbled. "My shoes are ruined."

He sobered. "Could've been worse."

"I think that was *my* argument." Besides, it was easy for him to say. He was obviously used to having money. No one she knew rented a Lexus. At least, no one she knew *these* days. "Point is, I could've stayed warm and dry in the car," she said. "So will you cooperate with me or not?"

Wearing a scowl, he stared off into the distance.

"Sebastian?"

His gaze moved her way, and he studied her as if seeing her for the first time. She might've been flattered, except there was a calculating air to the appraisal that told her he wasn't necessarily admiring her figure. "Maybe there'd be some benefit to having you involved."

"Meaning…"

"Maybe you could provide a woman's perspective."

"Considering I *am* a woman, that shouldn't be too difficult," she said dryly.

Another flash of his pearly whites told her he understood why she was a little piqued. "Good. Mary works until four. Then she does homework with her kids and takes them to various sports practices. Most nights she doesn't get on the computer until eight. I need to stick with the same pattern as much as possible, so I'll sign on with her screen name about that time. If you want to be part of this, come to my motel room at seven-thirty."

Kate would be home then, but Jane knew she could take her daughter to her in-laws' for the night. Kate would be excited about staying with Grandma and Grandpa. When Oliver was in jail, she stayed there often, but now Jane rarely allowed it on a school night. "Where's your motel?"

"The Raleigh Pete, off Cal Expo. Room 213."

That wasn't far from her Howe Avenue condo. "I'll be there." She started to shut the door, but he spoke again.

"If I gave you fifty dollars, is there any chance you'd bring dinner?"

Jane wasn't sure she'd heard correctly. *"What?"*

"I hardly ever get a home-cooked meal," he admitted, as if that was reason enough to make her agree.

Austin, an intern from Del Campo High School who was working at TLS in order to get credit for a sociology class, had just parked in the lot. Jane said hello and waited for him to go inside before responding. Then she said, "You want me to make you dinner?"

"I'll pay for it, like I said. Is some pot roast or meat loaf too much to ask?"

"How do you know I can cook?"

"You've got a kitchen, don't you?" He pulled out his wallet and handed her a fifty-dollar bill. "I've been on the road since forever. Anything's got to be better than what I've been eating."

As Jane accepted the money, she couldn't help feeling some measure of sympathy. Maybe Sebastian wasn't the humblest person she'd ever met. But he'd been traveling a long time and no one knew the impact of violence like she did. "I've got to cook for Kate, anyway," she said.

"Kate?"

"My daughter."

"I didn't realize you had a child. How old is she?"

"Twelve."

"What will you do with her?"

"She'll go to her grandparents' for the night."

His gaze fell to the tattoo on her hand. "What happened to you, Jane?"

Survivor. That word had reminded her of who she was during the difficult months when she'd fought to recover from being attacked by her own husband. Skye had been with her when she'd visited Express Yourself Ink. They'd both gotten the same tattoo. Skye's was on her shoulder blade, which she usually kept covered, but Jane had needed hers in plain sight.

"Maybe we'll talk about it later," she said and closed the door.

* * *

The room smelled like clean male. So many of Jane's memories of Oliver were negative that she'd forgotten this more appealing aspect of the opposite sex. Afraid she'd never experience that scent again, at least not in such an intimate setting, she paused to appreciate it before the aroma of the food she carried in her picnic basket could overpower it.

"Come on in." Sebastian was standing at the door, wearing faded jeans and a burnt orange long-sleeved thermal shirt.

A second later, that male scent was gone, replaced by the sausage in her homemade lasagna and the garlic butter on the bread.

"That smells good," he said, taking the basket from her as she passed him.

She smiled—she'd just been thinking the same thing but about a completely different scent.

Moving into the room, she purposely turned her attention to the furnishings, which were beige and green and fairly standard, so she wouldn't be tempted to stare. If she'd thought Sebastian was handsome before, he looked even better without his coat. That shirt fit his upper body like a second skin, revealing the contour of every muscle—and there were plenty of muscles to admire.

Even at his best, Oliver had never been built like that. Jane had been attracted by his sweetness, his harmlessness, his earnestness, his intelligence. And the fact that she'd felt safe with him....

"Is something funny?" Sebastian asked.

Sobering, she shook her head. "No, I was just…remembering."

He'd been about to dive into the hamper, but at this he paused. "Remembering what?"

"What it was like," she said.

"To…"

"Be innocent."

He gave her an odd look. "In what way?"

She shrugged. "In every way, I guess." She could never go back, never be the person she'd been before. That made her sad. But trusting the one man who was supposed to love her above all else had nearly gotten her killed. Wasn't it better to be wise than innocent?

Her eyes swept over the bed. Experience, at least the kind of experience she'd endured, changed everything, even the simplest of life's pleasures….

The stillness in the room told her Sebastian wasn't digging into the food as she'd expected. She turned to find him watching her, his expression tinged with surprise and curiosity.

"Is there a Mr. Burke?" he asked.

The tone of his voice told her he knew she'd been thinking about sex, knew she was hungry in a way that had nothing to do with food. But, regardless of the promise inherent in such a perfect body, there was nothing he could do to satisfy her. She wouldn't let him, or anyone else. She couldn't. She was incapable of lowering her guard to the degree making love would require, especially with a stranger.

"I'm a widow," she said. "But I might as well be married."

"You're seeing someone, then?"

"No." She didn't bother to explain.

He put the picnic basket on the dresser next to a flat-screen TV and waved toward a bottle of white zinfandel on his nightstand. "Would you like a glass of wine?"

"No, thank you."

Undaunted, he uncorked the bottle and poured himself a glass. "I'm sorry to hear about your husband's death." He took a sip. "How long ago was it?"

She regretted turning down the wine. Maybe it would help settle her nerves, take the edge off. "It's been nearly five years."

"And…you're still in love with him?"

She chuckled without mirth. "God, no."

His eyebrows knotted as he walked toward her with his wine. "What happened?"

When she didn't answer, he set his glass down and took her hand, rubbing his thumb lightly over her *survivor* tattoo. "Did he have anything to do with this?"

Like an old heater with a pilot light that'd gone out years ago, she didn't think she'd ever get warm again. But his touch sent a spark through her that somehow made her shaky.

Surprised, she jerked her hand away and stepped back, but in just half a foot she came up against the bed.

"Whoa, I didn't mean to scare you." She was still within his reach, but he didn't attempt to touch her again. He held out his hands, palms up, as if to show her he had no intention of hurting her.

The last time Oliver had made love to her had been a cruel experience, one of the worst in her life. In some ways, it had hurt her more than the violence that'd followed because it involved hate disguised as love.

But Jane knew it was her past—and nothing Sebastian was doing—that had her so rattled.

Overriding her panic, which seemed to come out of nowhere, she forced herself to stand where she was, instead of edging farther away. "I'm not scared."

He seemed unconvinced but didn't argue. "Did he do this to you?" He pointed to his own neck, but she understood that he was talking about her scar.

"Yes."

He lowered his voice. "How'd he die?"

From the deference in his tone, she knew he was guessing she'd killed Oliver in self-defense. She'd often wondered if that would've made her recovery easier— or more difficult. "After he left me for dead, lying beside his murdered brother, he attacked a woman he'd attacked once before, a woman by the name of Skye Kellerman."

"The woman who started The Last Stand."

"You've been doing your homework."

"I pulled up the Web site."

"Skye knew he'd be coming for her eventually." She shrugged. "She was ready for him when he did."

"She killed him."

"Yes."

"It didn't say that on the Web site."

"No. She doesn't talk about it, either. But she was prepared to do what had to be done. She had the benefit of knowing what he really was. I didn't."

Sebastian shoved his hands in his pockets. "What was he exactly?"

"A serial rapist and murderer, masquerading as a dentist, a husband, a father." Her voice dropped involuntarily. "My lover."

He whistled. "How did you survive such a brutal injury?"

"His knife missed my jugular by a fraction of an inch. Skye brought the authorities to my house before I could bleed out."

"This Skye sounds like an impressive woman."

"She is. That's partly why I work for her." Jane motioned to the picnic basket. "You'd better eat. The food's getting cold."

He spoke over his shoulder while reclaiming the basket. "You're not planning to eat with me?"

She had been. She'd fed Kate, then loaded her daughter and the food in the car and raced to her in-laws' place, thinking she'd have dinner at the motel. But she felt too jittery for food right now. She wasn't sure why Sebastian's touch had affected her so deeply. She'd been alone with men plenty of times since Oliver's death—at work, at home, in the car. She'd been fine.

But she'd never been this attracted to any of them. That had to be the difference—that and the fact that they were standing next to a bed.

"I've already had dinner," she lied and tilted the screen of his computer so she could avoid the glare of the lamp. "Wesley Boss isn't *WhosYourDaddy,* is he?"

Sebastian decided to make Malcolm wait. He didn't want to come across as too eager, didn't want it to seem as if Mary was always online, hoping to hear from him. The role he was playing would be more believable if Malcolm had to work for the attention he craved. Earlier,

Sebastian had sent an e-mail from Mary, thanking him for the flowers. That would suffice until after dinner.

Jane sat at the desk, sipping the glass of wine she'd finally accepted when he was halfway through his meal. "I don't think I've ever seen a human being eat so much in one sitting," she mused as he polished off a second gigantic piece of lasagna and yet another slice of garlic bread.

"I was lucky. I grew up in a home where my mother cooked. I miss that."

She swiveled in the office chair, back and forth. The nervous energy in that motion told him she wasn't quite as comfortable as she was hoping to seem. "Where's your mother now?"

"Upstate New York."

"Is she still with your father?"

Full at last, he put his plate aside. When he'd asked her for dinner, he'd assumed she could cook, and he'd been right. "No, he passed away a decade ago."

"I'm sorry."

"It was a blessing in the end," he said, remembering those difficult days.

"What happened?" He doubted she would've asked had he not been so direct with her.

"After being perfectly healthy his whole life, he woke up one morning and started convulsing. Then he went into a coma. My mother got him to the hospital right away, but when he came to—" he shook his head "—when he came to, it became obvious that he'd suffered quite a bit of brain damage."

Concern softened the hint of suspicion with which she seemed to view him. "What caused the convulsions?"

"A rare infection that'd gone straight to his brain. There was no warning, nothing we could've done to stop it."

"How terrible!"

It had been terrible. Although Sebastian was grateful for the time they'd had at the end, he and his mother had spent three long years looking after Angelo, knowing he'd never recover, knowing how much he'd hate being so helpless. It was during that dark time that Emily had married Malcolm. Sebastian had been far too preoccupied with his job, his father and taking his turn as a custodial parent to pay attention to the kind of man she was dating. He wasn't sure he would've been able to spot trouble even if he *had* paid attention. Malcolm was a cop, and cops were supposed to be safe. "As I said, it was a blessing in the end. I think he wanted to go."

"Your mother hasn't remarried?"

He pictured his trim, attractive mother. She looked twenty years younger than her age, but she didn't seem interested in the men who asked her out. "No."

Jane crossed her legs. "What does she think about you chasing after Malcolm?"

"I think she'd prefer it if I gave up and came home."

"But you can't."

After what he'd learned about Jane, he was sure she understood why. "No."

"So you have to hire strangers to cook for you and then you eat a meal for ten all at once."

He refilled her wineglass. "When you leave, the food goes with you, right?"

"I'd let you keep it, but it doesn't look as if there's a fridge in this room."

"There's not." He poured himself more wine. "You see my dilemma."

Apparently pleased that he liked the food, she smiled as she sipped from her glass. It was a pretty smile, one that contrasted with the caution in her eyes.

He didn't know exactly what had changed, but her coming to his room had somehow altered the chemistry between them. He'd realized she was attractive when they'd first met. He couldn't miss that. But the two of them sitting here alone made him far too aware of her on a physical level, far too aware of the possibilities.

As if to avoid the awkwardness that sprang up with any silence, she turned to his computer. "Looks like Malcolm's getting impatient."

"What's he saying?"

"'Hey, where are you?'" she read.

"Tell him you had to get the kids to bed."

"You're kidding, right?"

He couldn't imagine why she'd think so. "No."

"That'll only remind him that Mary's an exhausted mother. What's sexy about that?"

"It might not be sexy, but it's believable. It's something the real Mary might say."

"He won't care if what we say is believable. People who have online relationships are usually trying to fulfill a fantasy."

Again, the bed seemed to take up all the space behind them. "Are you talking from experience?"

"No. I can't afford to have fantasies."

"Everyone has fantasies, Jane."

"Okay, then I could never afford to fulfill mine, especially with someone I couldn't see. There are a lot of perverts on the Internet. There's no way I'd expose my daughter to another man who could be like her father."

This brought up a subject Sebastian had been curious about. "Did your husband ever hurt Kate?"

"That depends on what you mean by hurt," she said. "He didn't physically molest her, but he killed her uncle and hurt those she loved most. Living with that knowledge isn't easy. And there's always the genetic factor, you know? The question you'd ask yourself late at night—am I even remotely like him? Kate sees this scar on my neck every day, and she knows who put it there."

He pulled the cushioned chair from the corner and placed it beside her so he could see the screen. "Is she in counseling?"

"She was. We both were for a while."

"Did it make a difference for you?"

"It did. But doing what I do at The Last Stand has made a bigger difference."

"Fighting back."

She nodded. "What about you?"

"What about me?"

"Are you getting any counseling?"

"No."

"You should. It might help."

"Seeing Malcolm go to prison for the rest of his life will help more." He motioned toward the computer monitor. "So Mary can't talk about her kids. What do you suggest she say?"

She typed: Thinking about you. Then she raised her eyebrows, asking his permission to send it.

"Go ahead." He'd tried a similar approach last night and it hadn't gotten him anywhere, but it was a start.

The response came almost immediately.

WhosYourDaddy: You can't think while we talk?

Jane began to type again. I'm afraid talking will only make me more confused.

"Where are you going with this?" Sebastian asked.

"You'll see," she said and sent it.

WhosYourDaddy: I've confused you? About what?

I think I'm falling in love with you. Jane looked over at Sebastian. "Is it too much?"

"Judging from past transcripts, I'd say so, but…"

"He wants to conquer her, wants to feel safe, as if there's no way she'd reject him," she said. "Let's give him that."

He had to try *something* different; he was getting desperate. He nodded, and she hit the enter key. Again, Malcolm's answer popped immediately onto the screen.

WhosYourDaddy: I'm already in love. I've been in love with you for years.

Jane had been right. Malcolm was going for it. But Sebastian was a little uncomfortable that there hadn't been much transition between his and Mary's more cautious chats and this. Were the flowers enough to explain it? Sebastian didn't want to tip Malcolm off….

Just in case, he took over the keyboard and typed: All from meeting me at one party?

WhosYourDaddy: From making love to you so many times in my mind.

"Things are heating up," Jane breathed and typed the next entry.

BrownEyedGirl: When will you do it for real?

Sebastian caught her before she could hit Enter. "He's got Mary's address."

"We have to draw him into the open. Until then, he'll be a threat to her regardless. And Latisha and Marcie don't have forever."

She had a point. They needed to put an end to this.... "Okay."

Jane sent it and they waited.

WhosYourDaddy: You want me in your bed?

Sebastian deferred to Jane, who responded.

BrownEyedGirl: Now. I can't wait any longer. I dream about your hands on my body, about feeling you move inside me.

Sebastian tried to separate Malcolm's fantasy world from his own reality, but it wasn't easy when he was sitting in a motel room with an attractive woman who'd looked at him the way Jane had earlier.

WhosYourDaddy: Sometimes that's all I think about.

BrownEyedGirl: The thought of it makes me wet.

Shifting to ease the tightening in his groin, Sebastian told himself to ignore the deluge of testosterone. But images of making love to Jane filled his head.

WhosYourDaddy: I should've sent you roses ages ago.

BrownEyedGirl: I'm going to Fresno this weekend. Meet me there.

"Fresno?" Sebastian said, even though she'd already sent it. "Fresno isn't the most romantic place."
"Do you have a better idea?" she asked. "It's about halfway between here and L.A., not too far to drive. And it would allow him to see me and keep pretending he lives down south."
"Once you know who he really is, the L.A. part won't matter."
"But it does now."
His nerves taut with hope and fear, Sebastian held his breath as he awaited Malcolm's response. Would he fall for it, or would he shut them down?

WhosYourDaddy: I told you, this is a bad weekend for me.

BrownEyedGirl: I'm going, anyway. I'll be at the

Motel 6. If you want me like you say you do, you'll be there.

"Are you sure about this?" Sebastian asked, catching her before she could send it.

"It'll work," she replied. "I can feel it."

He nodded, and she hit Enter.

WhosYourDaddy: Are you serious?

BrownEyedGirl: You'll see.

WhosYourDaddy: But I'm in a mess right now.

BrownEyedGirl: Then I guess you'll miss out.

WhosYourDaddy: You're killing me!

BrownEyedGirl: Wait till you see what I bought to wear for you.

Fleetingly, Sebastian imagined kissing Jane's throat, imagined moving lower until he reached the soft curve of her breast and removed her sweater to see that tattoo....

WhosYourDaddy: What about your kids?

Jane looked at Sebastian. "Mary's ex helps out with the kids, doesn't he?"

"Every other weekend." In an effort to conceal his arousal, he scowled in concentration. "But I don't think it's his turn next weekend."

That news didn't deter her. "Fortunately, we can make an exception," she said and started typing.

BrownEyedGirl: Their dad's taking them. He has something special going on, so I agreed. That's why I'm coming to you. It's the perfect opportunity.

WhosYourDaddy: You don't know how bad I want this.

BrownEyedGirl: Then take it. I'll be wearing my stockings and garter belt and nothing else. Imagine me on the bed, waiting for you....

The same picture popped into Sebastian's mind.

WhosYourDaddy: Should I bring some wine?

BrownEyedGirl: Yes. And condoms. Lots of condoms. ☺

WhosYourDaddy: You have me so hard I'll never be able to sleep tonight.

BrownEyedGirl: I'll take care of you when I get there....

WhosYourDaddy: Talk me through it now.

Jane started to type, but Sebastian took over again. He knew he couldn't bear letting this get any more explicit.

BrownEyedGirl: Sorry, you'll have to wait. I'm not interested in anything but the real thing.

WhosYourDaddy: I want you bad.

BrownEyedGirl: You can have me—this weekend.

WhosYourDaddy: But can I trust you?

Eyebrows arched, Jane glanced over. "Uh-oh."

"Answer right away," Sebastian murmured. "You can't seem hesitant."

Her chest rose as she drew a deep breath.

BrownEyedGirl: What's that supposed to mean?

WhosYourDaddy: Nothing.

BrownEyedGirl: I've got to go.

WhosYourDaddy: No, not yet.

BrownEyedGirl: Don't worry. We'll talk again before Friday.

With that, Jane signed off.

Sebastian sat next to her in silence, his thoughts returning to the way she'd reacted when he touched her. That simple brushing of their hands had been an experiment to see how she'd respond to physical contact. He'd assumed it was what she wanted—he'd noticed the way she glanced at his body when she thought he wasn't paying attention, how her gaze fell to his lips when he was talking, how she blushed when their eyes met. He'd been with enough women to recognize the signs of attraction.

But what Jane wanted and what she'd permit herself were two different things. Considering her past, he understood, but he was reluctant to leave it at that. He hated to see such a pretty, vibrant woman so determined to deny herself any chance of getting beyond what her bastard husband had done.

"I'd better go," she said.

"You have to pick up your daughter?"

"No, she's staying overnight, but I should get some stuff done before bed."

He wanted to stall her if he could. Her actions were opposite to the way she wanted to act—opposite to what he wanted, too. "Like…"

"Laundry, housecleaning."

"Sounds exciting."

"Not exciting, but necessary."

She was making herself seem as asexual as possible. It was the reverse of what he'd just seen her do online. Suspecting that was because she felt the same desire he did and was trying to put some distance between them, he decided to be honest with her. "You know you're going to have to get over it eventually, don't you?"

A deeper wariness entered her expression as she packed up the food. "Get over what?"

"Your fear of men."

"I'm not afraid of men."

"You nearly jumped out of your skin when I touched you."

"You startled me—that's all." She lifted her chin. "I don't react that way with every man."

"Only me."

She didn't seem comfortable agreeing or disagreeing. "It's probably the setting," she hedged.

"That and the fact that you haven't made love since your husband's attack. Five years is a long time."

Her throat muscles moved as if she had trouble swallowing. "How do you know I haven't made love since then?"

"It shows. When you look at me, you start remembering what it was like." He lowered his voice. "I'm guessing you want to be touched. That you want to feel alive, carefree."

She slung her purse over her shoulder. "That's a nice illusion. But I can't be carefree," she said with a brittle laugh. "Not anymore."

He put his wineglass on the desk and stood. "You don't have to give up that easily, Jane."

"Give up?"

"You could fight for what you want—decide to recover in this way, too."

She shook her head. "You…you're wrong. I'm fully recovered."

"You don't miss the feel of a man's hands on your body? His mouth on your breast? His—"

"Stop it! I don't know why you're doing this. I don't miss anything."

It was a lie. She'd spoken too loud, too rapidly. "Then what are you thinking about right now?" he asked.

"Nothing."

"Those wide eyes of yours tell another story."

Her attention drifted to the bed, but she edged away from it. "I'd better go."

No matter how much she denied it, she'd rather stay. He could sense it. If only he could convince her to trust him. "I don't have any condoms, Jane. I haven't been with anyone in months. But I could get some."

"I appreciate your including me in your investigation," she said and grabbed the hamper.

That was a *no*. He wouldn't push her any further. "Fine." He took the basket so he could carry it to the door. "Thanks for the cooking."

"No problem." She stepped outside and grabbed the basket from his hands. At that point, he meant only to say good-night, so even he was surprised by the words that came out of his mouth.

"I'll be here if you decide to come back."

Ten

Jane parked at the convenience store but let her car idle. It was stupid to waste gas, but it was hard to care about such practicalities when all she could think about was the way her body had burned the moment she'd come into close contact with Sebastian. He was right; she missed having a sex life. She'd tried to cut that away, along with everything else that'd been part of her relationship with Oliver, but it was getting more difficult to ignore the natural cravings of a healthy body. She'd assumed that she bore too many scars from the past, that she couldn't take the risk. Now she was beginning to wonder if she just hadn't met anyone who tempted her enough.

Go back to his motel. When will you get another chance like this? She was certain Sebastian would be discreet. They knew only David in common. And Sebastian wouldn't be staying in Sacramento for long. He was living in a motel, for crying out loud. They'd enjoy a short interlude together, he'd leave and that would be it. No one would be the wiser.

Taking a deep breath, she called her in-laws to check on Kate.

"She's brushing her teeth. Do you want to talk to her?" Betty asked.

"No, I...I just wanted to be sure she was settled in for the night."

"She's ready for bed. Her homework's done. And I'll get her to school on time. Don't worry about that."

Her in-laws were reliable. Betty and Maurice had helped out a lot over the years, especially when Oliver was in prison and Jane had been struggling to make a living as a hairstylist.

"Thank you. You're so good to us."

"I love doing it. But...you won't mind being home alone tonight, will you?"

She heard the concern in her mother-in-law's voice. As illogical as they knew it was, the Burkes felt some measure of responsibility for Oliver. They'd created him, raised him; therefore, it was their mistakes that'd made him turn out as he had. "I won't mind."

"It's only nine-thirty, Jane. Why not go have a drink somewhere? See if you can meet someone?"

If her mother-in-law had any idea what she was contemplating... "I'm too tired for that," she lied. "I think I'll head straight home to bed."

"I wish—" Betty fell silent.

"What is it?" Jane asked, but she already knew what her mother-in-law wished. She wished they could all heal and forget.

"You must be lonely, Janey."

She and Noah's widow, Wendy, and the grandkids were all the Burkes had left. Wendy had grown as close to them as Jane had, but they weren't close to each other. Wendy still blamed Jane for Noah's death.

Jane took a deep breath. "Mom, stop worrying about me, okay?"

"I'll try, honey." There was another brief silence. "Do you need me to pick up Kate from school tomorrow?"

"No, I've got it."

"Call me if you change your mind."

Jane smiled at her willingness to pitch in, to be involved. The Burkes adored their grandchildren, clung to them even tighter now that they'd lost so much. "Will do. Love you," she said and disconnected.

A car pulled in alongside hers. Jane continued to let her car idle as the driver went into the store and came out with a six-pack.

Should she go back to Sebastian's room?

Why not? What was the big deal? It would be merely a temporary arrangement between two lonely people. Once she knew she could get beyond her fears of intimacy, maybe she'd be ready to start dating again.

Jane couldn't imagine that, but the idea of a trial run seemed logical. Wouldn't it be better to know if she was capable of letting go?

Her cell phone rang. She didn't welcome the diversion—she was too focused on her decision—but it was David, so she answered.

"How'd it go today?" he asked.

Jane got out of her car and walked through the aisles of the convenience store as she explained what had happened in Ione and at the motel with the instant messaging.

"So Sebastian seems normal?" David asked.

He was as "normal" as she was, but she knew she was using the term loosely. They were both damaged, both still fighting to build new lives from the ashes of their old ones. "Yeah, he's fine. We're lucky he's helping us. How'd your search go?"

"I found the gun."

"The murder weapon?"

"Yep."

"So you'll be able to close this homicide case?"

"I can only hope."

A bored-looking man in his late fifties stood behind the cash register. Every time Jane glanced up, she saw him watching her, so she purposely passed up the condoms and pretended to be examining the snacks.

"Tomorrow, I'll get hold of the owner of that house in Ione, see if Wesley Boss has a forwarding address," she told David.

"Let me know what you find."

"Of course."

He yawned loudly. "Thanks for your help, Jane. I'm so buried, I don't know what I would've done without you today."

"You're doing the best you can. Don't beat yourself up because you can't do more."

"I've gotta go. Sounds like one of the kids is up, and I need to get whoever it is back in bed. Have a good night."

"I will," she said and hung up.

Trying to assess her birth-control options while standing by the beef jerky, she eyed the condoms. One box touted "ultrathin for maximum sensation." Another said, "Appealing vanilla scent."

It'd been far too long since she'd been in the market for

such items. What a selection! Red, green, blue, thin, sheep-skin, ribbed, large, medium, scented. She had no idea what to buy. Would ultrathin provide enough protection?

Suddenly, none of them seemed to provide enough protection. So what if Sebastian was every woman's dream? So what if her heart pounded at the thought of touching him? She was a *mother;* she had responsibilities.

She walked out. But five minutes later she pulled into a drugstore and bought three different kinds—ribbed, sheepskin and vanilla-scented. If she was going to do this, she'd do it right. And why not? Why let Oliver cost her any more than he already had?

"This is for you," she told him and marched to the checkout register, where she dropped all three boxes on the counter as if daring the clerk to think anything of it.

Jane had gone home, showered, shaved and used scented lotion. She'd thought if she gave herself time, she might change her mind. But she hadn't. If anything, she'd become more determined. She would've considered buying some pretty lingerie, but the stores were closed and she didn't own any she could bring from home. In the past five years, she'd gotten far too practical to spend money on something she wasn't likely to use. Hoping to obliterate the memories, she'd thrown out everything she'd had from before. What a mess her life had been....

Since she didn't have anything more suitable, she'd opted for an attractive yet casual designer sweat suit, one she'd picked up on eBay for half the cost. She'd also put on her prettiest lace bra and some brown-and-beige panties. Now that she stood at Sebastian's door, however, she couldn't force herself to knock. Her underwear didn't really match her bra, and he had expensive tastes. Would he care about that?

No. He just wanted a quick one-night stand. At least, he'd wanted one when she left. Maybe she'd wasted too much time since then. She could hear the television through the door. But that didn't mean he hadn't changed his mind or nodded off....

Shivering more from nerves than the cool air of the open walkway, she checked the time on her phone. Ten-thirty. Not *too* late, but ten-thirty wasn't exactly early on a weeknight.

Knock! Don't just stand here like a big chicken.

She turned off her phone. Then she squeezed her eyes shut and raised her hand. She'd tap once. If he didn't answer, she'd leave and pretend she'd never returned. Tomorrow Kate would be home and she'd be Jane the Mother, Jane the Survivor, Jane the Victims' Advocate. Tonight she was giving herself permission to be Jane the Woman.

She wasn't sure she'd knocked at the door hard enough to be heard over the TV—until it opened.

Then he was there, wearing nothing but a pair of jeans, unbuttoned at the top as if he'd pulled them on just to be able to answer the door.

Oh, God... Jane's mouth went dry as their eyes met.

"Hey." He moved aside to let her in, but she couldn't make her feet move. She stood where she was, clinging to her purse and the sack from the drugstore. Finally, without a word, she charged back in the direction from which she'd come. She was about to break into a run when Sebastian caught her by the arm. He didn't grab very hard, but he managed to stop her.

"Whoa, you're not even going to say hello?"

She didn't have an answer and he didn't insist.

"Come on," he coaxed, leading her into his room.

"I—I just came to…" She let her words fall away. She'd been about to make up some silly excuse for her sudden appearance, something besides the obvious, but why pretend? He knew why she was here. Even if he didn't, he'd soon find out. She was holding a sack full of condoms.

"Jeez, your hands are cold." He covered them, his fingers curling around the fists she was making in order to hang on to everything, including her composure.

She swallowed hard. "It's chilly out."

"I can get you warm," he whispered and leaned in to kiss her neck.

"Is this crazy?" she breathed as his lips moved over her skin. "Because it feels crazy. I—I can hardly breathe. And my heart's pounding so hard…."

"It's not crazy."

Jane wanted to cast aside all her inhibition. She'd promised herself she would. What fun would this be if she held back the whole time? But as his mouth slid up toward hers, he paused ever so slightly on the scar that remained from Oliver's knife, and she was suddenly terrified she'd fail.

"Relax," he murmured. "I'm the one who's supposed to be stiff."

He was trying to tease her out of her discomfort. She knew that because he was smiling—but her self-esteem had suffered such a terrible blow the joke made her fear he'd find her inadequate.

"Are you?" she asked.

He guided her hand to the proof, and her heart pounded even harder.

"I won't push you to do more than you want," he whispered. "I promise. If you feel I'm being too aggressive, you just let me know."

She released her breath, but she didn't remove her hand. She couldn't. She was too curious, too captivated. On some level, she was actually surprised she could affect him to that degree.

With his knuckle, he tilted up her chin and stared into her eyes. "You're beautiful, you know that?"

No. She'd never been beautiful. At twenty or thirty pounds overweight, she'd been overlooked in high school. It wasn't until recently that she'd begun to turn heads. She would've loved the attention she received now when she was younger. At this point, she couldn't take it seriously. No matter how thin or toned she became, she saw herself as the pudgy girl with acne and a personality that was just a little too eager. "You don't have to say things like that," she said. "This will be easier for me if you're honest."

He seemed taken aback by her response. "I am being honest."

Was he? Or was he trying to create a fantasy? Maybe based on what she'd written as *BrownEyedGirl*. Was he playing into it?

"If you say so."

"You don't believe me."

She had no response. Her lack of confidence wasn't something she wanted to admit, and yet she couldn't deny it, either.

"Maybe it's time you started to," he said and touched his lips to hers. She expected him to use his tongue, to get right down to business. Her fingers were still tracing his erection through the denim of his jeans. But she couldn't imagine he'd want to waste much of his night with her. Wasn't this kind of hookup all about quick satisfaction?

If so, he didn't seem to be taking things very fast. He made that one touch very innocent and brief, and he didn't pull her into his arms. He stepped away, taking the sack she'd been carrying.

"What have you brought?"

Jane could feel the heat in her cheeks as he looked inside.

"Wow. Either you're planning to stay a few days or you're seriously overestimating my ability," he said with a laugh.

"Don't get the wrong idea. I know this is just a one-time gig. But I didn't know what to buy. I—" she shook her head "—I've never bought them before. Oliver always..." She couldn't finish the sentence.

"A selection is nice." He tossed them onto the night-stand. Then he rested his hands on her shoulders, demanding her undivided attention. "I'm glad you mentioned Oliver because I want to tell you something. I'm not him, Jane. I'm not anything like him. I will never intentionally hurt you."

Perhaps it was true, but as much as she'd changed in some respects, she hadn't escaped the conditioning she'd received at Oliver's hands. "I understand."

"Can I pour you a glass of wine?" It was another attempt to put her at ease. She appreciated the effort, but she wasn't sure even wine would work. Entering his room with a sack full of rubbers made her feel as if she'd just jumped out of an airplane—without a parachute.

Only she did have a parachute, she told herself. The fact that Sebastian was leaving town as soon as he'd solved the mystery of Malcolm Turner's faked death was her parachute. This wasn't a *relationship*. This didn't require the deep consideration a relationship would. Her future didn't figure into it, and neither did Kate's. Which meant she could relax. It was just for tonight.

"No, thank you."

He'd already picked up the bottle. "It might help," he said, lifting it higher.

"I'd rather not miss anything. The next hour might have to last me for a few years," she teased, but he didn't laugh at her words. Apparently, he knew it wasn't a joke.

He put down the bottle. "How about some music?" he said and turned the television to a music station. "Classical okay?"

She'd never made love to classical music, never listened to it at all, but the emotion surging through the piece appealed to her. She could relate to it. And she liked that it was different, that the music evoked no associations, no memories. "That's…good."

Draping an arm over the corner of the TV, he leaned against the dresser. "Is there anything I should know?"

She glanced nervously at the bed. Maybe *now* they were getting down to business. "Are you asking about STDs? Because I'm clean."

This evoked a smile. "I can't say I'm not happy to hear it. For the record, you don't have to worry about me in that area, either. But I was referring to phobias. Are you afraid of the dark? Afraid of feeling cornered? Afraid of being overpowered?"

Images from the last time she'd made love with Oliver

flashed through Jane's mind, but she threw up as much of a mental barricade as she could. "I want the lights off."

He reached around her for the switch and plunged the room into darkness. "Anything else?"

"Don't restrict my movement."

"In what way?"

"Don't tie me up—or hold me down."

"You don't have to worry about that. I'd rather be with someone who can respond." He stepped closer. She could sense the warmth of his body—but he didn't touch her. "I've got an idea," he said. "Why don't you take control? Why don't you make love to me?"

Thinking she'd be in charge made her feel safer. But it'd been so long. And she didn't know Sebastian very well. How did she initiate such intimacy? Did she simply...stand up on tiptoe and start kissing him?

"It's not difficult," he whispered as if she'd asked the question aloud. Bending his head, he met her mouth, but he didn't put his arms around her until she slipped her arms around him. And she was the first one to part her lips.

Sebastian would've preferred the lights on. Jane was far prettier than she realized; he wanted to see the athletic female body beneath that sweat suit. But he wasn't calling the shots. He had to remind himself of that over and over as habit and natural desire prompted him to take control. With every flick of her tongue against his neck, his nipple, his stomach, his desire increased.

And then she moved lower....

His muscles bunched as he struggled to keep himself in check. He longed to roll her onto her back, to use his mouth and hands until she was moaning and bucking against him, begging for the fulfillment he already craved. But he was afraid he'd frighten her. He'd known from the beginning that making love to Jane would be different, would require more restraint.

He'd expected to have no problem exercising that restraint, but it wasn't easy. It'd stopped being easy thirty minutes ago, when she'd taken off her clothes and her flesh had touched his. She'd been so tentative it was as if she was making love for the first time. There was a powerful eroticism in her rediscovery. Going so slowly wound him that much tighter.

"Jane." His voice was hoarse, almost unrecognizable even to him.

"What?" she breathed.

"I can't take any more."

She hesitated. "You want me to stop?"

"Will it freak you out if I get on top? I'll bear my own weight. It's just until we get settled. Then we'll switch."

"Okay."

Thank God. Shifting her onto her back, he held himself above her so she wouldn't feel trapped and lowered his body until he could rub his chest against hers. There was so much he wanted to do to her and with her, but she didn't know how to guide him to what she most enjoyed. Every time he thought he found something that pleased her, she stopped him. He couldn't insist for fear it would send her into a panic—she'd nearly bolted when she'd first arrived—but she seemed to be thwarting her own enjoyment. Why?

He guessed the man she'd married had used her terribly. It made him angry, but he couldn't undo all the damage in one night. And because she felt more comfortable touching him than letting him touch her, he was so far gone he'd blow it completely if he didn't salvage what he could.

"That's it." Just easing into her almost pushed him over the edge.

When her legs went around his waist, drawing him deeper, he wanted to thrust. But he'd promised her she could call the shots, so he rolled over and let her straddle him instead. "You okay?" he whispered.

"I'm okay," she said and began to rock against him.

Sebastian hung on for as long as he could, but it wasn't long enough. When it was over, he was pretty sure she hadn't experienced the same completion.

She lay beside him until she recovered her breath, then started to slide away. "That was nice," she said. "Thanks."

"You're leaving?" he asked in surprise. "It's barely eleven-thirty."

"I've got work in the morning."

He didn't want her to go, not like this. She was being polite about it, but he knew she had to be disappointed. "Stay. Next time will be better. I was afraid of scaring you. I was trying to be too gentle. Now that you know you don't have to worry about me, I can have more confidence in—"

"It's not you, it's me," she interrupted.

"Jane—"

"Good night." She gathered her things in the dark and he heard the door click as she went out.

Eleven

Tears streamed down Jane's face as she sat in the parking lot of the motel. She started the car so she could turn on the heat, but she didn't leave. She couldn't stop shaking and wasn't sure she could drive.

What the hell was wrong with her? How could she have thought sex with a total stranger would help anything?

She rested her forehead on the steering wheel. "Because I'm an idiot. I can never get anything right that has to do with men."

Sebastian had been the perfect gentleman. She had no complaints. But their session hadn't carried her away as she'd hoped. Not even for a moment. She hadn't been able to let go, to enjoy their lovemaking the way she'd imagined. Oliver had made that impossible. Just when she thought she'd be able to escape the past, he seemed to reach out from the grave....

"You bastard," she said. "You cruel, selfish bastard."

If only she'd never met Oliver. If only she'd been able to have Kate with someone else. But—her fingers sought the tattoo on her breast—Oliver wasn't all that was holding her back.

A knock on the window startled her. She grabbed her throat as if fending off Oliver's knife before she realized there was no threat.

"It's just me." Sebastian stepped back and held up something. "You left your wallet."

She looked more closely at the object he'd brought. It definitely was her wallet. How had she lost it?

Then she remembered. They'd made a mess of the bedding and knocked her purse to the floor. It must've fallen out.

Shit! If she'd dropped anything else, she would've told him to keep it. She didn't want to speak to him right now, didn't want to let him know she'd been crying. But her wallet contained all her money and credit cards, as well as her driver's license. She had to get it back, and the sooner the better.

Great way to top off the evening, Jane.

Lowering the window, she kept her face averted while he handed it to her. "Thank you," she said, but she knew her voice sounded far too polite. She added a "Sorry" that only made it worse as she began to roll the window back up. She wanted to get out of the lot before he noticed her tears. But a quick glance showed his stricken expression: it was already too late.

She wondered if she should try to explain. She would've tried, but she wasn't sure she could. He hadn't done anything wrong. These were *her* issues, issues she'd been dealing with for years. He couldn't take the blame for that. Anyway, she had no business crying. At least she was alive. At least she had Kate.

That was enough. Plenty of other victims weren't so lucky. She should be grateful, not wallowing in self-pity because she didn't know how to act like a normal human being anymore.

Determined to put this behind her, to forge ahead as she'd done since Oliver's death, she shifted into reverse. *Forget and move on.* That was the name of the game. *Don't look back.* Those who did never escaped.

"Jane, wait a minute! I'm sorry," he called after her, but she didn't stop. She backed out of the parking space and drove away.

Malcolm had given Marcie and Latisha some sleeping pills so he wouldn't have to hear from them tonight. It was a relief to know they'd be out for a good twelve hours, that they wouldn't wake and start scheming against him. Maybe kidnapping had taken the thrill of wielding his badge to greater heights—they'd done most everything he told them to with a "Yes, sir"—but he should've let them go after scaring them senseless. That was what he usually did. Playing cop made for an enjoyable evening. He could order people around, act like the Big Man, and no one ever questioned him. The prostitutes on Franklin Boulevard were especially impressed when he told them he was undercover, so impressed they often gave him whatever he wanted for free. *Officer Boss.* Hearing people call him that cracked Malcolm up, which was why he'd chosen the name.

But he'd taken things too far with Marcie and Latisha. Now that he'd have to kill them, it was no longer a game.

After lowering the volume on the TV, Malcolm dialed the cell phone number he'd kept in his wallet. It rang once before he got a recording: "Please enjoy the music while your party is reached."

A country song came on.

Trying to quell his impatience, Malcolm tapped the arm of the couch. He'd have some answers soon, he told himself. It was the middle of the night. Pam Wartle had to be home.

But Pam didn't pick up. From "You Look Good in My Shirt" he was transferred to voice mail.

With a curse, he hung up and dialed again. Not only was it late, it was during the work week and she had a family as well as a regular nine-to-five job. Where the hell was she?

Finally he heard a sleepy voice. "Hello?"

He tried to gauge whether he had the right person. It was definitely a female—but was it Pam or her daughter?

"Hello?"

Malcolm let his breath go. It was Pam. "Hey."

He could sense the tension in her breathing, even though she spoke only two words. "Hang on."

"Pam?"

Silence.

"Pam!"

At last she responded, but this time her voice was soft and low and he assumed she was hiding in a closet or a bathroom—somewhere her husband wouldn't be able to hear her. "This had better not be who I think it is," she hissed.

"If you're having an illicit affair, it's not your lover. Does that help?"

"No! What the hell are you doing calling me? You swore you'd never contact me again!"

He straightened his uniform. He rarely wore it out of the house—regular clothes and a Kojak light worked better since he no longer had a cop car—but he'd wanted to wear it tonight. It gave him a chance to relive the good times he'd had in the past, reminded him of the power he'd once legitimately held. "Calm down. I blocked my number."

"That's not enough!" she snapped. "I have a husband, kids. I don't want to be forced to explain to them why Mommy's getting phone calls in the middle of the night!"

"Tell them it's job-related. They'll believe you."

"Forensic technicians don't have job-related calls after midnight. That only happens in the movies."

Even on low, the noise from the television was irritating. Malcolm muted it. "Take it easy. I'll make this quick. I have a question."

"What could you possibly want from me? We concluded our business over a year ago."

"I need to know what's been going on since I left."

"What do you think? Nothing! It went down just the way we planned it. If something had gone wrong, you wouldn't be walking around a free man."

"I'm free for now, but I can't be sure it will last. I have no idea whether or not I should be looking over my shoulder."

"And I'm supposed to care?" she snarled.

"I can't help wondering what's happening back home."

"As you can tell, I don't give a shit. I've got to go. Don't *ever* call me again."

"Wait! Just one more question."

There was another long silence, but he didn't hear a

click, so he spoke up. "Have you heard of a man named Sebastian Costas?"

"You're kidding, right?"

Her response surprised him. "No. Why would I be kidding?"

"Anyone remotely associated with you has heard of Sebastian Costas."

He gripped the phone tighter. "He's contacted you?"

"He's contacted anyone and everyone who's ever known you. When you got me into this, you didn't tell me I'd have him on my ass every step of the way."

Malcolm didn't react to the accusation in that statement. He was too preoccupied with what her words signified. "He's looking for me, then." He'd been afraid of this. Sebastian had been a thorn in his side from day one....

"What'd you expect? That you could kill his son and he wouldn't mind? Why'd you have to do that, anyway? You didn't say anything about shooting the boy. You only mentioned Emily."

"What did you *think* would happen to Colton, Pam?"

"You could've left him alive. His father would've taken him."

"His father would've gone after the money."

"You mean like he's doing now? God, I wish I'd never met you."

"It's a little late for that, isn't it? You wanted twenty thousand dollars to pay off your credit cards before your husband found out you'd been shopping again, and I gave you the opportunity to earn it. Now you want to blame *me?*"

"I'm hanging up."

"Wait! So everyone knows I'm alive?"

"Sebastian knows. Or at least he's guessed. But the DNA evidence has everyone else convinced you were in that car—so unless he can prove otherwise you're fine."

Except that he was probably doing his damnedest...

"You're lucky your family cremated that body before he started raising hell," she added.

Thank goodness his mother had followed through. He'd laid the groundwork several weeks in advance by telling her he wanted to be cremated if anything ever happened to him. But until this moment, he hadn't been sure she'd acted on his request. He'd watched the papers online, but they'd never included this detail. Not even the obituary had mentioned it. And until now he hadn't dared contact Pam, who was the only person on earth who was supposed to know he wasn't dead. "You're even luckier than I am," he said.

Obviously uncertain how to take this statement, she didn't respond right away. When she did, her tone was wary. "What do you mean by that?"

"What we did saved your marriage, your family. Mine is gone."

"Don't cry on *my* shoulder. You're the reason they're gone. You wanted it. You could've spared the boy and you didn't."

Because he'd hated Colton almost as much as Colton's father. That boy was all Emily had lived for. "It was the only way our plan could work, and you know it."

"No. You could've taken the money just like you did. Chasing five hundred thousand dollars would be a lot less of a motivation than chasing your child's killer. You might've signed your own death warrant and mine, too."

"Oh, quit sniveling. You were able to pay your bills, weren't you?"

"And you paid for a new life. I hope you're happy with it."

"Up yours." He disconnected, then sat staring at the flickering TV. Damn Pam Wartle. And damn Sebastian Costas. Sebastian and Colton were all Emily could ever talk about. *Sebastian never would've treated me this way.... Sebastian will pay for it. He wants Colton to have whatever he needs.... I'll ask Sebastian for a list of stocks. Maybe he can help us with some investments.... You ever touch Colton like that again, and I'll tell Sebastian....*

She'd always acted as if Sebastian was tougher, smarter and more dependable than he was. She was proud her son was turning out so much like his father because she'd been in love with her ex. She'd probably been sleeping with him the whole time.

So why the hell hadn't he shot Sebastian, too? He could've called him up and had him come over to find Emily and Colton, then placed a slug in his head. The bastard deserved it.

Malcolm smiled as he imagined Sebastian's reaction had he been invited to that party—his shock and horror, his heartbreak when he saw his son lying in a pool of blood, his righteous but impotent anger as he faced the barrel of Malcolm's Glock.

But it was just a dream. Malcolm hadn't killed Emily's ex. He'd told himself it was smarter to work quickly and efficiently, smarter not to include anyone else. The fewer victims, the better his chances of pulling it off.

Too bad. Not killing Sebastian had been a mistake.

Now he had to worry, watch his back. And he couldn't have that if he planned to start a new life with Mary.

He needed a clean slate, no one chasing him from the past—which meant he had to deal with Sebastian once and for all.

"Where were you last night?"

Jane's hand froze, her coffee cup halfway to her mouth. The few hours she'd slept had been restless. Between the knowledge of what she'd done with Sebastian, skipping her workout routine and Kate's absence at the breakfast table, it had already been an odd morning. Getting a call from Jonathan made it even more unusual. They spoke at the office whenever they passed each other, but he'd never called her before. And he'd certainly never questioned her whereabouts.

Trying to play it cool, she put her mug down. She didn't want anyone at TLS to become aware of the fact that she'd slept with someone involved in her first case. Sleeping with Sebastian wasn't a conflict of interest, but it wasn't very professional. She was embarrassed by her own actions, and by the neediness that had caused them. "I went to bed early. Why?"

"At your place?"

His apparent confusion surprised her. She'd missed a call from him late last night, but she hadn't thought much about it. If he was on an important case, either one of his own or one for TLS, he worked around the clock. She'd figured she'd touch base with him when she got to the office. "Of course. Where else would I sleep?"

"I don't know, but you weren't at home."

"Yes, I was," she argued. "This morning I saw that I missed your call, but I had my phone turned off when you tried to reach me." At least that much was true.

His voice grew firmer. "Jane, I dropped by."

Damn! What was he doing coming to her house? He'd never done that before. "When?"

"Just after midnight."

"What was so important that you'd visit that late?"

"I was worried about you. I was at The Last Stand using the Internet because my laptop battery is on the blink. Then, out of nowhere, this guy showed up, asking for you. I said I was the only one there, but he demanded I tell him where you live or call you for him. He was angry that your business card doesn't have your cell phone number."

"Who was it?" she asked.

"Said his name was Luther. Wouldn't give a last name."

Latisha's father. As long as she wasn't facing his pit bulls, she could relax. "I know who he is."

"You do?"

"Of course. He's connected to my case."

"He wasn't too happy when he left. On the off-chance he managed to find you, I drove over to make sure you were safe. But you didn't answer the door."

"I must've been sleeping too deeply to hear the bell."

"Come on, Jane. Your car was gone. I was worried enough to cruise the lot several times."

She was making this worse by the second. Jonathan was a private investigator, someone trained to notice details. She should've known better than to bullshit him. She should just tell him the truth—or as much of the truth as she was comfortable revealing. "All right, I was with someone," she admitted. "But please, don't tell David or anyone at TLS. I don't want to deal with this at work."

There was a long silence. "Secrets make me uncomfortable, Jane."

"This isn't a secret. It's my private business. There's a difference."

"If you'd told me you were out with someone when I first brought it up, it would've ended there."

She rolled her eyes. "Jonathan, it's nothing, really. I lied because...because it's none of your concern. I can see whomever I want."

"Jane, that guy who came here last night was dangerous. I'm pretty sure he was on drugs, and I know he was packing a gun. You have to watch out for yourself, especially if you're coming home late."

"He doesn't know where I live. My number's unlisted, so he couldn't find me even if he wanted to."

"There are ways...."

"For people like you. We're talking about a pimp from Oak Park."

"Don't underestimate him," he said. "Maybe it isn't my concern, but if he's someone you met through The Last Stand...you should be cautious. The people we come into contact with aren't typically the type of people you'd want to date."

"I know. But some of them are worth risking a relationship. You met Zoë through TLS."

"True, but her child had been abducted. That's not the same."

"Of course it is," she said. "She has to rebuild her trust just like Skye and me and anyone else who's ever been violated. You think I don't know that I have to be careful? I understand the risks we face. That's the problem. That's why last night was the first time I've been with a man in five freakin' years!" Her voice was getting shrill but she couldn't seem to gain control of it. "Can't I shake off the past just once and spend the night with a guy simply because I want to? Can't I forget about danger for a few minutes and act as if I don't have to doubt every single person I meet?"

Finally, she caught herself. This wasn't what she wanted to tell Jonathan. This wasn't what she wanted to tell anyone. "I'm sorry," she said. "Ignore me. I...I made a mistake, that's all."

"Jane?"

"What?"

"You'll get beyond Oliver."

She didn't realize she was crying until the tears fell from her chin. Frustrated by her inability to stanch the emotions last night had churned up, she swiped an impatient hand across her wet cheeks and tried to swallow the lump that threatened to choke her. "Yeah, I will." She continued to backpedal, pretending to believe she'd eventually recover, but she had no idea if she really would. Relationships were complicated enough without throwing her background into the mix.

Jonathan's voice lightened, as if he hoped to tease her out of her current mood. "I hope it was fun, at least."

She wasn't even tempted to smile. "It should've been." She couldn't imagine he'd want to challenge that candid an answer, so she went right on. "I'll give Luther a call, see what he wanted."

"Whatever you do, keep your distance from him,"

Jonathan warned. "Meth, or whatever he's using, makes people crazy."

Loneliness could make people crazy, too, if last night was anything to judge by. "I will," she said, pouring her coffee down the sink. It was cold and she didn't have time for another cup. What did it matter that she'd slept with Sebastian? Or whether she'd enjoyed it? Latisha and Marcie were still missing. They were the ones with the real problem. She needed to get going, work harder to find them.

"And on that other issue, you know the cliché," Jonathan added.

From his tone she guessed he was referring to what she'd done with Sebastian. "What cliché?"

"You gotta get back on the, er, horse."

The metaphor brought a smile to Jane's lips. "Sometimes it's better not to ride at all. Sometimes it's smarter to stay out of the way of flying hooves."

"Depends on the horse." He disconnected, and she chuckled as she went in search of her purse.

Twelve

A clap of thunder woke Sebastian. After the initial boom, it rolled across the sky loudly enough to shake the whole building and was soon joined by an onslaught of wind and rain.

"What a morning," he grumbled. It was still early; he felt like going back to sleep. Especially when his first thought was of Jane—and the disappointment and frustration that had resulted from their lovemaking. He couldn't help feeling he'd let her down. She'd summoned the courage and trust to return to his room, and he hadn't been able to deliver what she wanted. She wasn't sexually liberated enough to take advantage of being in charge. Not after five years of celibacy. Not after what she'd been through. He should've thought of that, should've realized she actually needed him to take the lead. He would've slipped into that role if he hadn't been so afraid of spooking her.

What she needed was a happy medium between aggressiveness and restraint. He could see that now. But at the time, he'd been feeling his way through the experience, too. He'd never made love to a woman who'd been viciously attacked by a stranger, let alone by the man who was supposed to love her and protect her above all others.

He wondered how Emily would've reacted to the violence of having been shot had she survived....

When he considered it in those terms, he had to admit Jane was recovering quite well. She'd been attacked in a brutal, very personal fashion. Yet she was standing her ground, battling her fears. That alone told him she was a brave woman.

He wished last night had brought her some comfort, some satisfaction.

"Live and learn," he said aloud. Too gentle was almost as unfulfilling as too rough. He instinctively understood that, but he'd made an exception for Jane.

In an attempt to put her out of his head, he showered and checked his voice mail. But he didn't have any messages and his chores offered little distraction. While he was working, part of his brain kept replaying that moment when her tongue had first touched his and sent his heart racing. He hadn't been so aroused in ages....

The phone interrupted his thoughts. Halfway hoping it would be Jane, he picked up. "Hello?"

"Sebastian?"

It wasn't Jane; it was Constance. His disappointment surprised him—and confirmed that he wasn't himself anymore. Didn't he *want* to reconcile with his girlfriend? Maybe she didn't seem vital to him now, but she would at some point. At this rate, he'd have to rebuild every aspect of his life.

And yet he'd rather speak to a woman he'd met yesterday, a woman with whom he had no future, a woman who'd left him feeling off-balance.

"Yes?" he said into the phone.

"You haven't called."

He'd just sat down and booted up his computer, but at the sulkiness in her voice, he pushed away from the desk and stared at the rain sliding down the window.

"You told me it was over."

"And you were willing to leave it at that?"

"I thought it was what you wanted, what would make you happiest."

"I was angry."

"And now?"

"I'm still angry. But…I'm not sure I can give up on us."

Sebastian had no idea how he felt about their relationship anymore, how he felt about *her*. Was it fair to let her believe things would go back to the way they were before? He'd drifted so far from the man he used to be; he doubted she even knew him anymore. And what about last night? Once he told her he'd been intimate with another woman, they'd have more problems. Constance was nothing if not intensely jealous.

"Malcolm is within reach, Connie," he said. "I can feel it."

"I think you might be right."

Her sudden reversal surprised him. *"What?"*

"Someone called late last night, Sebastian, at about 2:00 a.m."

"Who?"

"A man. He wouldn't give his name."

He gazed out at the overcast sky. "What'd he say?"

"He asked for you."

Below, puddles formed in any depression, mirroring the gloom overhead. "Did you get the number he was calling from?"

"I couldn't. It was blocked."

"What'd you tell him?"

"I said we broke up, that you were at your condo. But I don't think he believed me."

"Why not?"

"He said, 'Then why the fuck doesn't he answer?' and hung up. He was...enraged. I could feel the hate coming through the phone. It was weird."

Trying to absorb what that call, and the emotion of the caller, could mean, Sebastian looked over at the parking space where he'd found Jane crying. He wished he could have last night to do over again.... "You think it was Malcolm?" he said.

When Constance replied her voice was softer than it had been in a long while. "Yes."

Sebastian had immediately considered the possibility, but he had Malcolm on his mind 24/7. He'd never expected Constance to suspect a man she believed was dead.

Or maybe she simply *wanted* to believe he was dead—so Sebastian would come home and they could get on with their lives.

"It sounded just like him," she went on with a degree of acceptance.

Lightning flashed in his peripheral vision before another crack of thunder rumbled overhead. "Are you sure? You only talked to Malcolm occasionally."

"I talked to him enough to recognize his voice! I picked up Colton for you several times. Or have you forgotten?"

He hadn't forgotten. He'd wanted her to get to know his son, to see how they'd interact. He'd been on the verge of asking her to marry him—they'd been that close—which was why he couldn't believe he felt so indifferent to her now.

"He always made it a point to answer the door and harass me," she was saying. "He'd clarify the time we'd be bringing Colton home, ask what we were planning to do with him   as if he had any right to approve or disapprove. He'd also inform me when Colton had homework so he wouldn't be 'saddled' with it. Or he'd say we needed to get Colton a physical for sports or have his teeth checked or whatever. Don't you remember? He passed off every chore he could, especially the ones that cost money, although you were already paying an exorbitant amount of child support."

As long as it was for Colton, Sebastian hadn't minded. His son had meant everything to him. Sometimes he'd even sent a little extra for Emily. He had no problem buying her a new dress or a meal out so she wouldn't have to account to Malcolm for the expense. Why would he? She was the mother of his child. The happier she was, the happier his son would be.

What he wouldn't give to have the option to overpay her again….

Clenching his teeth, he pressed his forehead to the cool glass. "He always had something to say." It hadn't been easy having another man tell him how to raise his son. That, more than anything, made Sebastian regret ever allowing his marriage to end. If only he hadn't been so caught up in work during those early years. He'd been far too driven. With the hours he'd spent at the office, it was almost inevitable that Emily would get involved with someone else. She needed love, attention. He'd neglected her, yet he'd felt so angry, so betrayed, that he hadn't been able to forgive her until it was too late.

"You hated it."

"I did. All of it." Because he'd been such a poor husband himself, his son had ended up living with a stepfather no one liked. And Emily had felt trapped. She didn't want to "fail" again. But she'd been afraid of Malcolm....

Sebastian wished he'd given those fears more credence. But his father had needed constant care during the years she was first with Malcolm, and once his dad had died and he'd managed to forgive her, he was accustomed to the situation. He'd passed along a few bucks to ease the financial strain, hoping that would help, but he'd never expected it to end the way it did. The fact that Malcolm was a cop—that he loved being a cop—had convinced Sebastian that Emily's husband was basically a good guy. Sebastian had thought he was just rigid and difficult to deal with on a personal level.

Even after so long, he was shocked by how wrong he'd been.

"So you finally agree that Malcolm is alive?" he asked.

"Now I do. It was him. Who else would be calling here in the middle of the night?"

Sebastian had no idea. But it was a relief to hear Constance acknowledge the possibility that Malcolm was still among the living. Until now, only his mother and, to a point, Mary—had believed him.

"Should I e-mail him? Let him know it was me?"

"You have his e-mail address?"

"It was on those transcripts you sent me."

"No. I can't afford to spook him. But why would he be looking for me?" he asked, but he could guess. Malcolm was tempted to see Mary this weekend, more tempted than he'd ever been to let someone from his former life know he was alive. But he was scared, too— scared enough to be searching for signs of trouble.

"Maybe he realizes you're on to him. Maybe he feels you're getting close."

Lightning illuminated a few souls determined to brave the weather. At nearly eight o'clock in the morning, it was still dark enough that they had to use their headlights. One pair flipped on, then another.

"It's possible," he said. It wasn't as if Sebastian had kept his search a secret. He'd flown all over the country tracking down everyone Malcolm had ever known, including Malcolm's first wife. If Malcolm had been in touch with any of them, he'd probably been told that Sebastian was asking questions. Malcolm had contacted Mary, hadn't he? Perhaps he'd contacted someone else, too—someone who'd heard what he'd done but didn't quite trust the news. Or someone who was willing to accept any denials Malcolm had to offer.

"Do you think he checked with the bank?" she asked.

"That would be my guess." Sebastian couldn't believe that Malcolm would call Constance first, that he'd let her hear his voice when there were easier ways to get information. Lincoln Hawke Financial, the bank where he worked, was holding his position open, despite the topsy-turvy economy. Had Malcolm called there, he might've been told that Sebastian was still an employee. Or, depending on whom he'd spoken to, he might've been told that Sebastian hadn't been in for more than a year.

What would Malcolm make of such a long absence?

"I'm nervous," Constance said. "If he's afraid you're on to him, there's no telling what he'll do."

Turning away from the window, Sebastian went back to his computer. "It'll blow the meeting this weekend, that's for sure."

"I'm not worried about the meeting—I'm worried about your safety!" she cried. "He's already killed two people and gotten away with it. If he thinks you're on to him, he might decide to get rid of *you!*"

"I'm prepared for that."

"How do you prepare for being shot?"

"By knowing how to shoot back. After all the time I've spent at the range, I'm not bad."

"But he could use this meeting with Mary to set you up. You might go there thinking you've got him, and it could be exactly the opposite."

Maybe, but he'd never been this close to catching the man who'd killed his son. This could be his only opportunity. "Then we'll see who outsmarts whom."

"You've got to be joking," she snapped. "*That's* your response? That cavalier attitude will get you killed!"

"You know I can't turn back now."

"Sebastian, you could stop this madness if you wanted to. How will it help Colton or Emily if you die, too? And what about me? Don't I matter at all?"

He logged in to his e-mail program. "I can't move on until I put this to rest," he said. "This is the only way."

"Sebastian?"

"What?"

"Do you love me?"

The question caught him off guard. He didn't know what to say, but he couldn't lie to her. That was one thing he'd promised himself he'd never do with any woman. Not after Emily had cheated on him, not after he'd learned how it felt to be on the receiving end of such lies. "I don't know anymore."

His admission met with a prolonged silence. "Then you won't be coming back, anyway, not to me," she said and hung up.

Exhaling, he tossed his phone aside and held his palms against his eyes. He'd just slipped even farther away from the woman he'd wanted to marry, away from everything he had left.

A knock sounded at the door. It was early for the maid, but Sebastian couldn't imagine who else it would be. "No housekeeping," he called.

"It's me."

Jane. He crossed to the door and opened it to find her standing in the hallway, shaking off an umbrella, which she propped against the wall. She was wearing a trench coat that fell open to reveal a fitted brown business suit with a narrow skirt and a turquoise blouse. Only her rock-star hair, that tattoo on her hand—the one on her breast was completely hidden today—and her large dangly earrings gave away the fact that she wasn't like other women who might wear this kind of tailored clothing.

"I got hold of the owner of that rental house we visited yesterday," she said.

Sebastian felt torn. He'd just broken up with Constance—and this time he was sure it was for good. That was probably a mistake. And yet he wanted to touch

Jane. He wanted a second chance to make it a pleasant experience for her.

But her starchy bearing told him she had no intention of letting that happen. She wasn't even going to acknowledge that they'd ever been intimate.

"And?" he prompted.

"Wesley Boss moved out three months ago."

"Any forwarding address?"

"Just the P.O. box we already have, as you expected."

He stepped back to let her in. She paused uncertainly, but when he cocked an eyebrow at her in challenge, she clutched her purse in front of her and marched past him in her sensible brown pumps.

"Did Malcolm put a phone number on the rental application?" he asked as the door swung shut.

"He did. It was the number of that cell phone my kidnap victim used. A phone that's disappeared from the network and can't be found, of course."

She had the smell of rain on her, mingled with the perfume he'd noticed the night before. "So it's a dead end."

"Yes."

He motioned to the desk chair. "Would you like to sit down?"

"No, I'm on my way to work. I just stopped by to see if you'd lend me that picture you have of Wesley Boss—or Malcolm Turner or whoever he is—so I can make a copy of it. It'll be a lot easier to find him if I can at least show people what he looks like."

"The one you saw yesterday is still in the car, but I've got another one." He crouched next to his briefcase—he'd opened it on the floor on the far side of the bed—

and riffled through the contents, eventually withdrawing a manila envelope containing an eight-by-ten of Malcolm. He'd taken it from a second photo that'd had Emily in it, too, until he'd cropped her out.

Jane avoided any incidental contact as she accepted it. "Thank you."

"No need to make a copy. I have a whole stack."

"Perfect."

"What about references?" he asked.

"References?" She'd obviously lost the thread of the conversation.

Following her line of sight, he realized she was looking at the condoms on the nightstand. Maybe she wanted to pretend last night had never happened, but she was as preoccupied with it as he was.

"On the rental application," he clarified.

She jerked her eyes back to his face. "Oh, right. They were all bogus."

"The landlord never bothered to check?"

"No. He was going negative trying to carry the mortgage every month so he was just grateful he had someone to move in and pay rent."

As Sebastian sat on the bed, images of their time together paraded across his mind in greater detail. The softness of her skin. The way her mouth had yielded beneath his. The sounds she'd made. He hadn't gotten nearly enough of her. He wished she'd let him redeem himself.

But he knew better than to try. She'd taken a giant step backward.

"That means we're down to the link we have through Mary," he said.

With a shrug, she perched on the edge of the office chair he'd offered her a moment earlier. "At this stage, it's our best hope."

But what if Malcolm had figured out that Mary was betraying him? That call to Constance signified *something*. "I think Malcolm's concerned about me."

She frowned. "What do you mean?"

"He called an old friend last night, asking for me."

"He knows your friends?"

"This one he does."

"How?"

"She picked Colton up for me on occasion."

"She?" Genuine confusion showed on Jane's face, but it cleared a second later. "Oh! You were with her."

"Yes."

Her voice dropped. "Is that still the case?"

"No."

"You're sure? Because I assumed…" She cleared her throat. "You're not wearing a ring."

"I'm not married, Jane. She's my *ex*-girlfriend." Did it matter that they'd broken up only a few minutes ago?

She spoke through a crash of thunder, but he could hear the relief in her voice. "What did he say to her?"

"He asked about me. He's poking around to see what I'm doing."

Jane held her purse primly in her lap. "If he connects you with Mary—"

"Best-case scenario, he takes off again and I'll be starting from scratch." Worst-case scenario, he killed Mary before disappearing. But Sebastian didn't want to think about the worst-case scenario, let alone state it.

"You wouldn't give up and go home?" she asked.

He shook his head. "Never." Although he had no idea how he'd continue to finance such efforts.

"Is there any chance he could find out you're in Sacramento?"

"I'm sure there is. My family and friends know I'm here. But my being here doesn't necessarily imply it was Mary who betrayed him."

Lightning flickered, preceding another *boom*. "Someone had to tip you off to come here."

"Or *something*. For all he knows, I traced him a different way."

Her eyes ranged over him as if she was matching what she saw to what she'd touched last night, and the tension between them ratcheted up. It was ugly outside, ugly everywhere else. He wanted to hole up in this room with her, show her that she could forget the past if only she'd trust him enough....

She shifted uncomfortably. "I still think he'd question her loyalty. I'd wonder about her if it were me. She could be in trouble, Sebastian. At some point, she might have to take her kids and go to a motel booked under a friend's name or something."

"I agree. But we can't uproot her too soon. It'll be too hard on her and the kids to be away from their regular lives for very long."

"What if we can get to him before this weekend?" she asked. "Before he has time to do much investigating of his own?"

While part of his brain was busy maintaining the conversation, the other part was remembering the feel of Jane's breasts against his chest....

He sat up so his body's reaction to that image would be less apparent. "How?"

"We could tell him that Mary's sending him a package, ask for an address."

"He'd provide the P.O. box we already have."

"Curiosity is a powerful motivator."

"You think he'd go there to pick it up?"

"I do. And we'd be waiting." She smiled, but when his gaze fell to her mouth, the smile faded and her tongue darted out to wet her lips.

"I'm not sure it'll work," he said. But he was sure *this* was working. God, he wanted to touch her....

"Why not?"

"He knows the police have the number for his cell phone, which means they also have his P.O. box."

"A lot of people come and go at any given post office. The idea of running in and picking up a package might be too tantalizing to resist."

He needed to get her to leave before he pulled her into his arms. But he couldn't bring himself to walk her to the door before she was ready to go. The torture of having her close but not close enough was bittersweet.... "It's worth a shot. I'll try to set it up tonight."

She nodded and got to her feet. "Let me know how it goes."

"You're not coming back?"

"I don't think we should be alone together."

"If you're afraid we might fall into bed, we already did."

"That doesn't mean we should make it a repeat performance."

When he stood, they were separated by only a few

inches. "Why not? Maybe if you let your guard down next time, you might actually enjoy it."

"You don't know what you're talking about," she said, but the scowl that accompanied those words was a mask. He saw the truth beneath it, knew he'd hit a nerve.

He ran a finger down her cheek. "You stopped me every time I did something you really liked. Why?"

Stepping back, she fastened her coat and tied the belt. "I was just trying to…trying to—"

"Sabotage your own pleasure?"

"No!" She headed for the door.

"I think that's exactly what you were doing," he called after her. "Then you could convince yourself that you're not really missing anything."

"Stop it! You…you're wrong." She reached for the door handle. He expected her to open it and leave, but she didn't. She turned back to face him as if she was going to argue some more—and met him in the middle of the room instead. Then she was kissing him as hungrily as he'd ever been kissed.

This time Sebastian swore he wouldn't treat her as though she might shatter. Pushing her against the wall, he claimed her mouth as he'd longed to claim it last night and knew it was okay when she clenched her hands in his hair, pulling him even closer, and moaned deep in her throat. At last she was letting go, allowing her body to do what came naturally.

"That's it," he murmured. "No need to hold back." Then he slid her skirt up to her waist.

Thirteen

A torrent of sensation began to roll through Jane, as powerful as the thunder shaking the sky outside. Only this time she embraced it, refused to acknowledge the hesitation, fear and worry that had inhibited her before. She didn't care what happened after this. With their bodies, she and Sebastian were fighting the memories and the pain—raging against the sorrows of the past.

Except for her panties, she had her clothes on, but she'd never felt more naked, more exposed, as she leaned against that wall. Sebastian was driving into her like the wind and rain beating at the window and touching her at the same time, touching her in a way that made her pleasure escalate until she could scarcely breathe. All her energy traveled into the very center of her body, and it encompassed every last nerve, every secret part of her, every unfulfilled desire, everything she'd lost....

"Jane..." There was a warning note in Sebastian's voice, but she was too caught up to heed it. She wouldn't let anything intrude, not this time.

"Don't stop!" she gasped and arched into him.

He forgot about whatever he was about to say and complied. When she cried out, he answered with a growl of masculine satisfaction, and Jane opened her eyes to witness his expression. For a split second, he watched her with feral intensity, then his eyelids slid closed....

It wasn't until he carried her to the bed and they both lay on it, exhausted, that it occurred to her—they hadn't used any birth control.

"Oh, no," she whispered as she stared at the boxes on the nightstand. Now she understood what he'd been trying to tell her during that brief hesitation.

"What's wrong?" He sounded as satiated as she was.

When she didn't answer, he rose up on his elbows. That was when his expression grew wary, alarmed. "Jane?"

She couldn't react immediately. Visions of the life she'd so carefully reconstructed swam before her. Kate. Her job. Her self-respect. Her in-laws. Her touchy relationship with her sister-in-law. If she got pregnant, she'd just confirm Wendy's belief that she hadn't changed at all....

Cool resolve suddenly masked Sebastian's panic. "Don't worry about it. It was my fault. I convinced you to let go," he said, but she knew he was only being a gentleman. He'd tried to stop before it was too late, and she'd said no. She'd been too carried away. She was finally enjoying herself, finally releasing her inhibitions, so he'd continued—because she'd asked him to.

Embarrassed by the frantic greed that'd taken hold of her, she covered her face. What if she got pregnant? At *forty-six?* Aside from all the other reasons a baby would be a catastrophe, at this age there were added risks involved with pregnancy, risks she didn't want to take.

"What's going through your mind?" he asked tentatively.

Sheer terror. But she told herself to relax. It was an isolated incident. Surely one irresponsible act in five years was nothing to worry about.

"Hello?" He snapped his fingers in front of her face. "You still with me?"

She dropped her hands to find him watching her closely. Even if she did get pregnant, she couldn't hold him responsible. She'd initiated this. Then she'd pushed him beyond the point of no return. "Nothing. I'm just...relaxing."

His gaze cut uncertainly between her and the condoms. "You don't *seem* too relaxed. Is the lack of birth control a potential problem?"

She curled her fingernails into her palms. "Only because it's not safe to...you know...be unprotected."

He grew very serious. "I told you, I'm clean. I swear it."

"Right." She attempted a smile. "Me, too."

"So...is there any chance?" he pressed.

Her hope that he'd had a vasectomy at some point in his life before meeting her was destroyed. "No. I had the doctors do something, uh, permanent after Kate was born."

It was a lie but apparently he bought it. Releasing his breath, he sagged in relief. "You scared the shit out of me," he said with a laugh.

She got off the bed to search for the panties he'd thrown aside, which was the perfect excuse to pretend she was focused on something else. "You hid it pretty believably."

He didn't respond to the comment. "God, that was great!" he said, his smile once again genuine.

"Yeah, it was fun." Standing around the corner, where he couldn't see her, she slipped her underwear back on. "But I'd better get to work."

He fixed his own clothes while watching her smooth her skirt into place and tighten her belt. "I'll call you," he said.

Immediately switching to business, as if that was the only reason he'd have to call her, she nodded. "Let me know if you get anywhere with Wesley. I'll be visiting the Indian casinos today, asking around. Maybe I'll get lucky and come up with someone who's seen him or knows when he usually comes in."

"Be careful."

"I will."

He walked her to the door, but she hurried out before he could touch her again. Muttering a soft "Bye" over her shoulder, she headed down the walkway. She didn't want to deal with that awkward moment—both of them wondering if they should embrace or kiss goodbye. It had been a furious coupling, nothing more. Now that she was emerging from her long hibernation, she was doing it with a vengeance, but she had to avoid confusing lust with love. Between Noah and Oliver, she'd already had more than her fair share of difficult relationships. No need to ask for another hard knock.

On the ground floor, she raised her umbrella and braced against the cold wind as she picked her way through the puddles in the parking lot. When she reached her car, she allowed herself a final glance at Sebastian's window—and saw him standing there, staring down at her. What was he thinking?

Managing another casual wave, she got behind the

wheel. At least he knew how to make love. That bone-melting moment when he'd brought her to the heights of pleasure had been unlike anything she'd ever experienced.

She thought of Jonathan's advice to "get back on the horse" and almost laughed aloud. She'd done exactly that. And it'd been worth the ride.

As long as she wasn't pregnant....

After tossing and turning for most of the night, suffering from another bout of heartburn and the anxiety created by what Pam Wartle had told him, Malcolm slept late. He was eventually awakened by Latisha and Marcie yelling to be let loose so they could go to the bathroom. But he wasn't willing to leave the comfort of his bed. Ignoring their pleas, he listened to the storm rage outside while going over his late-night conversation with the one person who'd made his escape from justice possible.

When Sebastian had stopped going to the brokerage house, Malcolm had assumed Colton's father just needed some "personal time." That was what he'd been told. The man at Lincoln Hawke Financial—the man he'd spoken to on the phone last summer—had said Sebastian was taking "a few months to deal with a personal tragedy." Malcolm had known what that personal tragedy was, had even taken pride in being the cause of it. Finally, he'd knocked the arrogant Sebastian Costas on his ass.

But it'd been more than a year since the shootings. Why wasn't Sebastian back at work? What the hell had he been doing for so long? Was he hurt and suffering—or was he angry and vengeful?

Probably both. And if he was tracking Malcolm, he had the wherewithal to do it. Judging by the cash that'd passed through Emily's hands whenever Colton had the simplest need, Sebastian had plenty of money.

The threat that Colton's father might come after him made Malcolm's esophagus burn again. Sebastian could be a stubborn son of a bitch. Why hadn't he accepted the DNA evidence, like everyone else? If Sebastian was convinced that the man who'd killed his son was alive, he wouldn't stop until he found what he was looking for....

"Wesley? Can you unchain us? Please?" It was Latisha, and the whine in her voice put his teeth on edge. "I gotta pee. I can't hold it."

"Didn't I tell you to shut up?" he yelled. "It hasn't been five freakin' minutes since you complained before. I'm tryin' to think in here!"

"But...it'll only take a second," she called back. "I don't want to go on the floor."

"You'll lick it up if you do," he hollered.

"Please? I'll make you breakfast if you'll let me use the toilet."

Damn it! They wouldn't give him a moment's peace. What did he care if they had to go to the bathroom?

Muttering a string of oaths, he rolled out of bed, once again lamenting the fact that he'd saddled himself with two young women—with *anyone*. What had started out as a thrill—and a potential convenience—had turned out to be a major mistake. He wasn't getting any work out of them. He couldn't unchain them long enough to get them to do anything. If he did, he had to release one at a time, then watch her like a hawk.

Instead of making his life easier, he'd ended up with a situation that prevented him from ever leaving the house. He hadn't been by Mary's in three weeks, hadn't gone to the casino in even longer. Forget cruising Stockton Boulevard. Being cooped up all the time was making him edgy. The only thing that might make him happy was something Marcie and Latisha wouldn't willingly give.

So what good were they? No good, just dead weight. He had to shoot them. Why not get it over with? There wasn't anyone around to hear the shots; the storm would cover it even if there was. He could bury them in the barn out back and at least he'd be free. He needed to be mobile. If Sebastian was after him, he might have to move fast.

"Wesley?"

"Shut the hell up!" This time he knew they'd heard the fury in his voice. They wouldn't call out again. But it was too late. He'd made up his mind.

Instead of putting on the shirt he'd grabbed off the floor, he stripped off the boxers he'd slept in. No need to soil his clothes. He hated to do laundry almost as much as he hated to cook his own meals.

The sound of Latisha and Marcie whispering made him even more determined. He was tired of wondering what the hell they were saying about him. He wasn't a bad guy. He'd just gotten himself into a mess. And now he was going to get himself out of it.

After pulling his gun from under the mattress, he walked down the hall and stood in the open doorway. Both girls stared at him, their mouths falling open. They didn't seem to notice that he was naked. Their eyes were riveted on the gun.

"Wh-what are you doing?" Latisha asked, her voice barely a whisper.

"Who wants to go first?" he said.

"Is there a reason you're smiling like the cat who ate the canary?"

Startled out of her thoughts, Jane looked up to see Jonathan standing in her office doorway. She'd called him a little while ago, hoping to talk him into canvassing the Indian casinos with her, but she'd gotten his voice mail. She hadn't expected him to show up so soon after she'd left her message.

"I was...thinking," she said, but she'd been reliving those few minutes in the motel with Sebastian and she suspected he could tell that she was lying to him again.

Sure enough, his lips curved into a devilish grin as he motioned toward the list she'd made. "You looked pretty distracted from whatever you're doing there."

She'd been using the Internet to search for all the Indian casinos in the area and hadn't even realized that her mind had drifted—until he'd called her on it. "I was remembering something cute Kate said to me."

"Oh, yeah? What was it?"

Suddenly, she couldn't recall a single example. "Nothing you'd enjoy."

"I'm guessing that's true."

She sat back. *"What?"*

"I doubt it has anything to do with Kate," he said. "I'm guessing it had to do with a naked man. Definitely *not* something I'd enjoy."

She couldn't believe he was on to her—again! She'd

heard he was a good P.I., but this was ridiculous. "How'd you know?"

His grin went crooked as he strolled in. "Do you really want me to tell you?"

She narrowed her eyes at his sheepish expression. "I do."

"I followed you to the Raleigh Pete."

Throwing down her pen, she pushed away from her desk. "You *what?*"

"David asked me to help you out with this case. He and another detective are canvassing the neighborhood where the car was found, trying for the second or third time to find someone who saw something that morning, but he's worried about the lack of leads. I just wrapped up a case for one of my own clients, so I've got some time. I was coming down your street when I saw you pull out of the driveway."

"So you followed me."

"When you didn't turn toward the office, I was curious."

"I went to the Raleigh Pete to get a picture of the man we're searching for." Knowing it was a bit late for this, she shoved the picture toward him. "See?"

He glanced at it. "This is all you got?"

Her cheeks blazed. "What, you weren't listening through the door?"

"Actually, I wanted you to be able to get that, er, *picture* in peace, so I went out for breakfast while I waited."

She glared at him. Then, with a sigh, she gave up the charade. What was the point? She'd already told him about last night. "If you tell Skye—"

"It's your business, like you said." He took a seat

across from her. "But I wish all my cases were as easy to figure out as what you've been up to this morning."

"Quit teasing me," she said with a scowl. "We have what could be a long day ahead of us. We should get going."

He bent his head, imitating a subservient bow. "I'm properly caffeinated and at your service."

She ripped off the piece of paper she'd been writing on and handed it to him.

"Damn, there must be thirteen casinos here," he said as he studied it. "I never dreamed there were so many in this area."

"They're pretty spread out. But I used MapQuest to determine the distances between them so we could chart the best route. I was numbering them when you came in." Grateful his attention had finally turned elsewhere, she got her purse. "We'll start with Cache Creek."

"Why not Thunder Valley? It's closer."

"Because we discovered handwritten directions to Cache Creek at Wesley Boss's last known address."

"This guy's a gambler?"

"He's a gambler, all right. And from what I've learned so far, no stakes are too high."

Jonathan sobered as he slipped the paper in his pocket. "We'll find these girls, Jane."

The conversation she'd just had with Gloria came back to her.

So you're meetin' him this weekend?

We hope so.

You can't make it sooner?

We can't tip him off.

But by then it might be too late!

Gloria was right.

"We have to do more than find them, Jon. We've got to find them *alive*," she said and walked out ahead of him.

The Internet provided an extensive list of handwriting experts. It took Sebastian some time to vet them, but there was a woman named Ritchie Lymond whose on-line biography impressed him. She'd done a lot of work for the FBI and other police agencies.

He clicked on the link, which took him to a Web site with her contact information.

Thinking he might be able to reach her more quickly by phone, he called the number listed on the site. The phone hadn't even started ringing on his end when he heard a woman say hello.

"Ms. Lymond?"

"Yes?"

He explained who he was and what he wanted.

"I sympathize with what you're trying to do, Mr. Costas," she said. "But I hate to see you throw any more money at this. Even if I could determine that the handwriting sample was written by the man who murdered your son, there's no way it could overturn DNA evidence. Handwriting analysis is ultimately subjective. It's becoming more widely accepted now that we can scan it into a computer and digitize the comparison process, but…it's not foolproof."

"I understand that. I just…I need to know what you think."

There was a long pause. "What do you have by way of exemplars?"

"Exemplars?"

"Samples to compare his writing to."

Sebastian had the entire contents of Emily's house in a series of storage units. He had that shoebox containing Mary's old letters, but if Malcolm had written back, he hadn't reclaimed those letters and Mary hadn't kept them. They'd already discussed the fact that she'd disposed of everything he'd ever given her when she got engaged to her husband. Sebastian also had a journal and some letters he'd found when packing up the Turners' home office, but all of that was primarily Emily's. Would he have enough of Malcolm's? Malcolm's own family had come for his things. The storage unit would yield only the scraps from the storage area above the garage or drawers Malcolm's family had overlooked. "I'm hoping I can get several. What would you like to see?"

"Letters, contracts, lists. The more you have the better. Are the directions to the casino written in both lower- and uppercase?"

"Yes."

"Then get something that has both. I can't compare lowercase letters against uppercase."

Before he'd called Ms. Lymond, he'd contacted his mother and asked her to go to the storage place to see what she could come up with. "If I can get what you need, I'll overnight it tomorrow or the next day."

"Okay, but even if you get the exemplars, don't set your hopes too high, Mr. Costas. I'll do what I can, but it's a long, tedious process, and there are a lot of variables."

If he could get the damn exemplars, what else stood in their way? "Like..."

"Someone who's been taking drugs, who's exhausted or ill or emotionally distraught, may write differently when in that state."

After what he'd seen on various forensic shows, he'd thought it would be easier. But ever since Colton and Emily had died, he'd realized that nothing about police work was easy. "I understand."

He hung up—and immediately started thinking about Jane again. How was she doing with the various Indian casinos? She hadn't called, but she hadn't been gone that long, either.

Should he act on her suggestion to tell Malcolm that Mary wanted to send him a package? Maybe if it came from Mary's work e-mail, it would lend him even more credibility. It would certainly build a more believable picture. And if he had Mary tell Malcolm she was shipping it via FedEx, they might be able to get an address out of him. Most people knew that FedEx and other couriers couldn't deliver to a P.O. box.

"You like to gamble, Malcolm? Let's roll the dice," he said and called to see if he could get hold of Mary.

It wasn't her first time. Marcie had been wrong about that. Latisha was on the pill. She'd been sleeping with a waiter she'd met at the restaurant. She just hadn't told her sister or anyone else. Although sex with Wesley Boss had been very different—merely physical, mechanical, an act of panic and desperation, not mutual attraction—Latisha couldn't regret it. She and her sister would both be dead if she hadn't done what she'd done.

As Wesley curled around her and began to doze off, she stared at the ceiling, trying to figure out how well she'd survived the experience. She certainly hadn't enjoyed herself, but it hadn't been as bad as she'd expected. She'd merely separated her mind from her body, closed her eyes and imagined she was swimming in a deep pool, submerged under water, where she could see only murky shapes and hear only muted sounds.

In less than fifteen minutes he was finished. And he hadn't been cruel or particularly rough. She would've been grateful for that, except she was pretty sure his "normal" approach was what had her so confused. This was rape, or a form of it, yet there'd been no violence. She'd always associated rape with brute force.

Movement in the next room told her Marcie was as agitated now as she'd been when she fought to keep Latisha from going with Wesley. Because her sister had received a quick kick to the face for her efforts, Marcie was more badly hurt than Latisha. But Latisha knew the physical injuries Marcie had sustained—so far—would heal. She was more worried about the psychological damage. Her sister was already so angry at the world. Their mother, her father, certain schoolteachers and various peers had let her down so terribly. Marcie didn't need another reason to hate....

Resisting the urge to grab her clothes, Latisha drew a careful breath so she wouldn't disturb Wesley. She and her sister were alive. For now that was all that mattered.

"Am I too heavy on you?" he muttered.

She froze. He wasn't asleep, after all. And that was something her boyfriend might've said to her. "No."

"That was freakin' amazing," he gushed. "You did great."

How did she respond to such praise? She hadn't done anything at all except lie still and let him use her.

"It wasn't that bad, was it?" He rose up to see her face, and the entreaty in his expression surprised her. "No big deal, right?"

She could tell he wanted to believe it. He preferred not to acknowledge that what he'd done was one of the worst crimes imaginable.

She resisted the temptation to make him aware of what his actions made him. No self-respecting cop would've done this, yet he prided himself on his police background more than anything. But she was afraid he'd get rid of her that much sooner if she did. The memory of him standing in the doorway with that gun, which he'd since unloaded and hidden under the mattress, was too clear in her mind. She had to outsmart him, had to play him better than that. Chances were she'd gain more by winning his friendship. Someday maybe she'd be able to get a bullet or two from his pocket, where he'd dumped them, and load that gun he'd put under the mattress....

"You said if I slept with you, you'd let us go," she whispered.

"You rejected that offer."

She swallowed hard. "But...I came in here with you last night."

"Only to save your skin. That's not the same."

"So...will you ever let us go?"

He was lying down again. When he didn't answer, she tilted her head to look at him and found him watching her. "Of course. Someday," he said.

But he didn't mean it. He hadn't asked if she was on the pill, hadn't bothered with any birth control. That alone told her he didn't expect her to be around long enough to worry about getting her pregnant. Marcie had been right from the very beginning. He had no intention of letting them go. Their only chance was the one Latisha was taking. If she could make him want her, make him like her, he might keep her around and, in time, maybe she'd be able to create an opportunity for escape.

Or an opportunity to put a bullet in his chest.

"Are you ready to do it again?" she asked.

He raised his head. "You want more?"

Her muscles tensed with revulsion. "Why not?"

"There you go, girl. Doesn't hurt a damn thing, does it." He smiled eagerly. "Give me a few minutes to rest."

When he eventually rolled on top of her, she hummed silently to herself, swimming in that same deep imaginary pool where she could feel nothing but the water swirling around her limbs. She and Marcie would get away. Wesley was human.

That meant he had weaknesses.

Fourteen

The pressure Jane felt to work fast made their day at the casinos seem interminable. She knew from what she'd witnessed at TLS that real investigations weren't like what she saw in the movies. They could be tedious. But this was her first experience feeling such intense personal responsibility to see that the case moved faster.

"We're getting nowhere," she complained to Jonathan after they'd spent several hours asking dealers and waitresses at each casino about the picture Sebastian had given her. Some said they'd never seen the man, others said they couldn't be positive—too many people passed through a casino to remember them all.

"You ready to give up?" he asked.

"I'm not sure what to do." She stood amid the flashing lights and clattering slot machines of Thunder Valley, gazing down at the photograph. "Maybe Sebastian's Wesley Boss isn't *my* Wesley Boss. Maybe I'm using the wrong man's photograph."

"Or maybe we're asking the wrong dealers."

"You think we should wait until later?"

"We don't know when he gambles. If it's at night, it makes sense to ask the dealers who work that shift."

She'd already thought of that, but waiting meant they'd lose even more time. Marcie had been alive when she called. Was she still alive? What about Latisha? "If I need to come back, Kate will have to stay at my in-laws' again," she mused.

"I'd offer to make the rounds for you but I promised Zoë I wouldn't work tonight," he said. "My hours have been crazy lately."

"I can do it," she told him. "Kate loves it at the Burkes'."

A security guard gave them a funny look, as if he suspected them of trying to do something wrong. What, exactly, that might be, Jane couldn't figure out. They weren't even gambling. Maybe he'd seen her flashing that picture around and didn't like it. She always felt so *watched* in a casino. It made her uncomfortable. But the fact that they'd caught this guy's interest gave her an idea.

Stepping around Jonathan, she approached him. "Sir, could you help me?"

Bushy salt-and-pepper eyebrows like those of an old-time sea captain jerked together above murky gray eyes. "With what?"

After introducing herself and Jonathan, she explained their purpose. "Have you seen this man?" she asked once he understood.

He studied the photograph, but ultimately shook his head. "No, I'm afraid not."

"Is there any way we could view the security tapes to see if he's been in?"

"I'm not the one who can give permission for that. I'm guessing you'd need to contact the police and have them get in touch with management."

"There's already a detective on the case. I could talk to him, see what he can do," she said. But this was such a long shot. Would there be probable cause to get a court order, if one was necessary? And was it the best place to spend their time, anyway?

"Although…" Security considered the picture again. "I suppose I could check the tapes myself."

Jane exchanged a glance with Jonathan. "Would you mind?"

"How far back do you want me to go?"

"Would six weeks be too long?" Jonathan asked.

"Nah." He clicked his tongue. "But I'd have to do this on my own time, so it could take a while."

More discouraging news. Maybe David could shorten that time frame by gaining access to the tapes, but he'd have to work it out with the tribal council. Jane assumed they had jurisdiction. "We'd appreciate whatever you can do." At least it was a start.

"No problem."

She handed him the picture, along with her business card. "You can reach me here if you find anything."

"Will do."

Jane's cell phone rang as they walked out of the casino. "It's Skye," she told Jonathan in disbelief.

He seemed just as surprised as she was. "Calling from South America?"

"Must be."

When she hesitated instead of answering, he stopped. "Aren't you going to take it?"

Jane wasn't sure she wanted to. So much had changed since her friend and boss had left. She was searching for two kidnap victims, had made love with someone she'd just met—and she might be pregnant. She didn't want Skye to know about these things, did she? How much could she tell her?

"Jane?" Jonathan prompted.

"Of course." She punched the talk button before the call could transfer to voice mail. "Hello?"

"How's it going?" Skye asked.

Jane tried to put a smile in her voice. "Fine. What about you?"

"Could be better. We still haven't found the child we've been looking for. It's so difficult when you don't speak much of the language."

To escape the noise, Jane stepped away from the automatic doors but remained under the overhang to avoid the rain. The worst of the storm had passed, but it continued to drizzle. "How much longer do you think it will take?"

"Who knows. We've got some good leads, some extended family members who are sympathetic and asking around on our behalf, but there's no way to tell for sure. I'm hoping it won't be more than a week. I really miss David and the kids."

"They miss you, too."

"I hope I never have to take another job like this."

"You didn't have to take this one," Jane reminded her.

"Yes, I did. We need the money. Besides, someone's got to help out in situations like this. It's more of a problem than people realize."

Someone spoke in the background.

"Was that Ava?" Jane asked.

"Yes, she said these are tough cases."

There were plenty of tough cases at home. Jane was working on one—not that Ava would be happy to hear it. "No kidding."

"What's been happening at the office?"

Biting her lip, she turned away from Jonathan. She didn't want to see his reaction when she lied. "Nothing much, why?"

"Just wanted to make sure you were managing okay without us. It must be weird being the only one there."

"Jonathan's been in and out. And there are the volunteers to keep me company."

"So you're okay."

The smell of someone's cigarette wafted toward Jane, making her crave a smoke. "Of course. I'm fine."

"Good. Thanks for looking after TLS while we're gone."

She glanced around to find the person who was smoking, spotted the security guard and smiled enviously. She knew she'd never light up again, but that didn't always stem the desire. "Anytime. Be safe, and I hope to see you soon," she told Skye.

Jonathan frowned when she hung up. "Don't you think you should've told her?"

"Why? It's over already. I'm not going to sleep with him again."

A crooked smile curved his lips. "I was talking about the case."

Sebastian was at the gym when his mother called. He fished his BlackBerry out of the pouch of his sweatshirt, which he'd tossed on the floor beside him, and relaxed on the seat of the bench press he'd been using.

"I've got Malcolm's signature on stacks and stacks of checks. Will that work?" she said the moment he answered.

"No, a signature isn't what we need. It doesn't include enough letters. And signatures can be different from regular writing." He mopped the sweat on his forehead with the towel draped around his neck. "We have to have a letter of some kind. The more writing, the better."

"I don't think I'll be able to find it. Most men don't write letters anymore, Sebastian, at least not very often. If they do, it's on a computer."

"What about a greeting card?"

"You and I both know that Malcolm wasn't the type to give Emily cards."

"There could be more practical things."

"Like to-do lists and grocery lists? They get thrown away. Why would anyone keep them? If I had to provide a sample of *your* handwriting, I'm not sure I'd have any more luck, unless I could use some of your old schoolwork."

She had a point. He tended to call her or e-mail her. He didn't write letters—or lists—unless it was on his computer or BlackBerry. But that wasn't the answer he wanted. "You've gone through every box?"

"Not every box. There are a lot here. Some are stacked too high or they're buried behind the furniture and are difficult to reach. But I've gone through the ones that I can get to without tearing the whole place apart." A change in tone indicated tears. "I found Emily's journal. Seeing that, reading parts of it…was heart-breaking. And I'm finding plenty of Colton's school-work. The poor kid…." she said on a sob.

Sebastian steeled himself against a similar onslaught of emotion. "Nothing from Malcolm?"

She sniffed. "Nothing from Malcolm."

Resting his elbows on his knees, Sebastian hung his head. This couldn't be easy on his mother. He didn't think he'd be able to go through that stuff himself. Even after all these months, the pain was too raw. "I'm sorry, Mom."

"I want to help you," she said. "I want to see Malcolm behind bars as much as you do. I'd like it if you could come home and live a normal life. But I doubt we'll get the handwriting samples you need. Not from this collection of miscellaneous odds and ends."

Sebastian closed his eyes. There had to be some of Malcolm's writing somewhere. Maybe Colton's stepfa-ther hadn't kept a journal or written any letters that were with Emily's stuff, but surely the Turner family would have *something*.

Question was…did he have the nerve to ask them to look? They weren't too happy with his views on the suicide. They didn't want to face the possibility that Malcolm might've turned his back on them.

Suddenly it occurred to him. He had a sample of Malcolm's writing at his condo in New York. It was a sheet of spiteful complaints Malcolm had left on the windshield of the Porsche Sebastian had owned back then. One day, Sebastian, Constance and Colton had been out in the BMW; Colton had sustained a sports injury, and they'd taken him to the hospital, but Malcolm didn't get the word. He'd gone to pick up Colton without taking his cell phone. Then he'd been furious that the misunderstanding might make him late for his weekly poker game.

Sebastian had kept the hateful note in case he ever decided to sue for custody. He wanted to be able to prove that Colton's stepdad had a dark side—a temper disproportionate to whatever trigger set it off.

If only he'd known how dark Malcolm could be....

"Mom, forget about the storage," he said.

"You want me to stop searching?" She sounded relieved.

"Yes. I know where we can find what we need." In that note, Malcolm had used almost every foul word in the book. But now Sebastian was glad Emily's husband had put his thoughts on paper.

"Where?" she asked.

He told his mother where to look; then he smiled as he hung up. "You won't get away with it," he said to an imaginary Malcolm, setting his phone aside so he could finish lifting weights. He needed to get back to the motel and call the florist. It wasn't likely that they'd have an address other than the P.O. box Malcolm put on everything else.

But Sebastian planned to check, just in case.

Malcolm admired Latisha as she moved around the kitchen, preparing dinner. She made a damn pretty sight wearing nothing but his T-shirt. He would never have guessed he could be so attracted to a black woman. He'd purposely kidnapped these girls because he thought they'd pose less of a temptation sexually. But now that he was being a little more open-minded, he had to acknowledge that Latisha was as fine as any young woman he'd ever seen.

Damned if he'd admit that to another white person, though.

The image of his father, his face contorted with disgust, appeared in Malcolm's mind, but he quickly shut it out. He no longer had to worry about pleasing that racist asshole. Warren Turner didn't even know that his youngest son was alive.

Latisha must've felt him watching her because she sent him a tentative smile.

Maybe kidnapping her hadn't been a mistake. Besides making life more enjoyable in other respects, she'd been cooking and cleaning all day.

But her sister. God, Marcie was a different story. When he'd gone into the bedroom to tell her he hadn't hurt Latisha one tiny bit, she'd called him a rapist devil and spit in his face. If she ever got free, she'd be dangerous. She was the type who might come after him. He should kill her and get it over with, but he couldn't do it quite yet. It hardly seemed fair to go back on his word so soon after Latisha had made him happy.

"I'm not a rapist," he said aloud.

Latisha stood at the stove. "What?"

"I said I'm not a rapist. I didn't force you. You offered, I accepted, and you enjoyed yourself as much as I did, right?" Heck, she was the one who'd asked for more.

The answer came so softly, he could hardly hear it. "Right."

"What?"

After clearing her throat, she spoke louder. "I said 'right.'"

"You need to tell your sister because no matter what she says, I'm nothing like the men I used to put behind bars. I've met them. I've seen the crime-scene photos. I know what they're like. You don't have a single bruise on you."

"I'll tell her." Her voice was low again, but at least he could make out her words.

"Good. Otherwise, I might have to kill her."

Latisha whipped around, wearing a stricken expression. "You promised me you wouldn't! You promised me you wouldn't hurt either one of us!"

"I won't put up with her bullshit. I just want you to know that."

"You promised," she said again.

He scowled. "I don't *want* to hurt you or anyone else, but…you'd better tell her not to provoke me. Okay?"

With a curt nod, she went back to cooking, and he fantasized about how peaceful and pleasant it would be if he had Latisha all to himself and didn't have to worry about her nasty sister. It wasn't as if he could marry Latisha—how would that look? He had *some* pride. But, for the time being, she was better than nothing.

He thought of Mary McCoy. His ex-girlfriend was the woman he *really* wanted. But that relationship was riddled with risk. If they were going to have a chance, he'd have to convince her to cut all ties with her past. If he could make her believe a friendlier version of what had happened the night Emily and Colton died, it was possible. He could say Colton was playing with his gun, accidentally killed his mother and then freaked out and shot himself. He could claim to have staged the crash because he knew the authorities would look at him before anyone else, and he didn't have an alibi.

But even if she bought that, letting go of her family

and friends wouldn't be easy. He should know—it'd been difficult even for him. And after what Pam Wartle had told him, he was beginning to wonder if he *could* trust Mary. Whenever he brought up his real name, she didn't indicate that she'd heard about the deaths of his wife and stepson. Yet Pam had told him that his nemesis had dogged anyone and everyone he'd ever known.

Had Sebastian contacted Mary? If so, why hadn't she mentioned it during their discussion of Malcolm Turner? It was natural that she would, wasn't it? Anyone would...

Opening his laptop, he logged on and checked his buddy list. Mary wasn't online. But she'd sent him an e-mail.

You on for this weekend? I can't wait.

I have a surprise for you. A sample of what you can look forward to. I want to overnight it so you get it immediately. Where should I send it?

Love, Mary

"'Where should I send it?'" he muttered.

"What?" Latisha asked.

He waved her off. Mary's question seemed innocuous. But was it really? Why would she be so interested in couriering him a package if she was planning to see him this weekend?

What is it? he wrote, then deleted the message before sending it and sat there brooding. How could he determine whether or not she was telling him the truth, whether or not she was trustworthy? There had to be a way....

He chewed his fingernails while he tried to think. He could call her work, ask the nurses if she'd ever mentioned Sebastian. But he doubted they'd open up to a total stranger. He could call the house and pretend to be Sebastian, see how she reacted, but she might recognize his voice....

Then, Malcolm had it—the perfect plan. He'd send her an e-mail from Sebastian, see if they'd been in touch. He knew Sebastian's e-mail address, didn't he? They'd exchanged a few messages when Emily and Colton were alive. He couldn't use that exact account because he didn't have the password, but lots of people had more than one e-mail address. After dinner, he'd create a new account using a variant of Sebastian's name—with the same server, if possible—and send her a message as if they'd already spoken. Something like, "Hey, any word from Malcolm?" That generic a question could mean today, yesterday, in the many months since contact had first been made. In this situation, less was definitely more.

If she wrote back demanding to know who he was and how he knew Malcolm, he'd trust her. And if she didn't, if she wrote back and said, "I haven't heard since asking for his address," Malcolm would set up the meeting she'd been angling for—and kill them both.

Fifteen

The florist turned out to be a bust. Pretending to be Wesley Boss wanting to double-check the billing address he'd provided with his credit card, Sebastian had spoken with Love in Blooms. But the manager there merely confirmed the P.O. box.

As he ate some more of the Chinese takeout he'd picked up for dinner, he tried to come up with other ways to track Malcolm and, as usual, thought about the charred body. It'd been found in Malcolm's car, which was discovered the day after Emily and Colton were murdered. Did Malcolm kill a drifter, whose corpse he used for that purpose? Did he "borrow" a freshly buried body from some remote cemetery? Or did he pay off a mortician? If Sebastian could turn up a lead on that body, he might be able to tie it to Malcolm. But he'd spent the first two months of his investigation working that angle and had found nothing.

The murders had been carefully choreographed. That was probably what bothered Sebastian the most. While eating and sleeping in the same house as Emily and Colton, while playing the part of caring husband and stepfather, he'd been taking steps to end their lives. He'd *slept* with Emily, knowing he was going to kill her.

Maybe Sebastian hadn't liked Malcolm. But even after all this time it was hard to imagine the man he'd known, *any* man with a regular upbringing and a regular job, as that cold-blooded. Especially a cop.

How could Malcolm live with himself? Did he realize what he'd done? Or care about the people he'd hurt? Look at the humiliation he'd brought his own family....

The telephone jolted Sebastian out of his thoughts. Dumping what was left of his dinner in the trash, he got his cell phone from the desk. He'd already heard from Mary while he was at the restaurant, waiting for his food. She'd called to let him know she'd sent the e-mail from her work account notifying Malcolm of the package and requesting his address.

This was her again. "Hello?"

"How's it going?"

"Not bad," he said, but he was feeling restless. He suspected it was because of Jane. He'd been thinking about her all day, fixating on the fact that he'd made love to her twice and still hadn't seen the tattoo on her breast. "Have you received a response?"

"Not yet. That's what I'm calling to tell you. I just got home from taking the boys to their hockey lessons and checked my work account. Nothing."

"It probably won't come until later this evening."

"I won't be around. I'm heading out. Some of the girls at work are getting together for dinner and a movie."

This was unusual. Mary was such a dedicated mother

she didn't allow herself to leave the boys very often. "I'm sure you could use the break. Do you have someone to watch Brandon and Curtis?"

"I've got a sitter lined up."

"Sounds like you're all set."

"I am, but…I'll check in with you when I get back, okay?"

They'd developed such a routine it was difficult for her to pull away. She acted as if she felt almost as responsible to him as she did to her kids. But now that he could communicate with Malcolm directly, he didn't need her to be in contact as much as before. "Don't worry about it. Go have fun. You can e-mail me when you get home, and if I'm awake, we'll talk. Otherwise, we'll catch up tomorrow."

"What are you planning to say to him tonight?"

"The usual."

"Should I expect more flowers?"

"Who knows what to expect from Malcolm? That's the problem." He said goodbye and disconnected, but before he could put down his phone, his mother called. She'd found Malcolm's hateful note in his home office and would overnight it to the handwriting expert in the morning.

Sebastian wasn't sure this would have a big payoff, but some proof was better than none. He'd collect whatever he could. "Thanks, Mom."

"Sebastian?"

He brought the phone back to his ear. "Yes?"

"What would Malcolm want with two teenage girls?"

The rain had stopped but the chilly air and early darkness made it seem later than it was. Sebastian had kept his coat on while he ate, but was finally warm enough to take it off. "I'm afraid to guess."

"If he's raped them or...or tortured them, he can't let them go. He'd know the value of a witness."

Sebastian regretted telling her about Gloria Rickman's sisters. He talked with Christa often, shared most things with her, but the kidnapping had upset her so much he should've left that out. Knowing Malcolm had already killed two people made the possibility of more murders all too plausible.

Fortunately, he hadn't told Mary, or he doubted she'd want to go out tonight. "I'll find him," he said.

"Now you don't have any choice," she responded. Then she was gone.

Releasing a deep sigh, Sebastian threw his phone on the bed and signed on to the Internet as Mary. It was time to strike up another conversation with Malcolm, see if he could get him to talk a little more about his new "roommates." But Malcolm wasn't on and Jane called a few minutes later.

"I'm going back to the casinos to talk to the dealers who work the night shift, so I need another picture. I gave the one I had to an employee who promised to go over the security tapes for us."

"You don't have to stay home with your daughter tonight?" he asked in surprise.

"She went back to my in-laws'. I felt it was best. I've already spoken to the dealers who work the day shift. I figured I should check with the night-shift staff, and the sooner the better."

"Of course. You want to stop by to get another picture on your way?"

"Unless you'd like to come along," she said.

"Where are you planning to start?"

"Thunder Valley. I want to hit Cache Creek later, once the nightlife really gets rolling, since it's our best bet."

He didn't need the promise of her tattoo to tempt him. Wanting to find Malcolm was enough. But Sebastian knew he'd be lying to himself if he pretended, even for a moment, that he didn't think of that tattoo whenever he thought of Jane. "I'm in," he said. "Where do you live? I'll pick you up."

It was nearly midnight when Mary got home. Fortunately, she'd caravanned with a friend who gave her babysitter a lift so she wouldn't need to drag her kids out of bed. That was nice. These days, Mary found herself grateful for the slightest kindness. She'd never dreamed being a single mom would be so hard.

Her boys were safe and sleeping soundly. That was a relief. But it was also a relief to get a break from the drudgery of daily life. She needed to have more fun. The movie had been a chick flick, the perfect let-it-all-out-and-cry movie, and she'd done just that. Her eyes felt swollen, which made her eager to take off her makeup. But she was even more eager to see if anything had happened with Malcolm and Sebastian in her absence.

She hesitated as she walked past the flowers on her dining room table. Should she throw them out? She didn't want flowers from a man who'd murdered his wife and stepson. But she left them where they were. They didn't commemorate reconnecting. They were more like funeral flowers, marking the death of the positive image she'd once had of her first real boyfriend.

Saddened by the memories of holding hands while walking down the hallway of their old school, attending prom together and cruising down Main Street, not to mention their more intimate moments, she muttered, "How could you?" and sat down in the kids' homework room to sign on to the computer.

She checked her work account first. She wanted to be able to tell Sebastian whether or not Malcolm had responded.

Sure enough, Malcolm—or "Wesley"—had sent her a brief note. He didn't provide his address but he seemed to be intrigued. Give me a hint. What are you sending?

She didn't answer right away. She switched over to her regular account—it wasn't currently in use or she wouldn't have been able to sign on—and saw a message from Sebastian. It came from a different account, not his regular one, but he'd just set her up with a new account so she figured he'd created a new one for himself, too. This one included his full name: *Sebastian.Costas@yahoo.com.*

With a click, she opened it. Hey, any word from Malcolm?

Hoping he was still up, she tried to instant message him at both addresses, but he wasn't online so she decided to reply to his e-mail and go to bed. They could talk more tomorrow.

Malcolm responded, she wrote. He wants to know what's in the package, but he didn't leave an address. I'll reply, see if I can get it out of him, okay?

Sleep tight. I'm glad you got to bed early for once.
Mary

Yawning, she sent it, then went back to her work account and replied to "Wesley."

It's something you gave me a long time ago. Interested?
Love and hugs—Mary

Maybe if he thought those flowers had given him away, that she was beginning to realize who he really was, he'd drop the charade and agree to meet.

It was impossible to be with Sebastian and not think about what'd happened between them earlier. Jane had known that their previous intimacy would be a problem, but she didn't want to be alone all night, driving from casino to casino. Latisha's father had been leaving hateful messages on her voice mail, claiming she couldn't be working hard enough if she hadn't found Latisha by now. In the last message, he'd even accused her of giving priority to the white victims she was trying to help.

Jane didn't know how to respond to that. She wanted to find Latisha and Marcie as much as he did, but the color of her skin had convinced him otherwise. And part of her *did* feel guilty—not because she wasn't doing her best but because she didn't know how to do any better.

"It's nearly one o'clock. How are you holding up?" Sebastian asked as they pulled out of the parking lot at Red Hawk.

Since they hadn't come across anyone who recognized Malcolm's picture, not particularly well. The fatigue dragging at her heels made it difficult to keep going. She and Sebastian hadn't gotten much sleep last

night, and she'd been on her feet all day. But she *had*
to finish canvassing the casinos. She wasn't about to
call Gloria or Luther and tell them she had no more to
go on now than she did yesterday. Besides, there was
only one more place to visit, and it was the one that
mattered most.

"Knowing Malcolm Turner, when would you
expect him to gamble? During the day, in the afternoon, or at night?"

"I have no idea. This Malcolm Turner isn't the
Malcolm Turner I thought I knew. Even if he wasn't the
nicest guy, I believed he cared about Emily and Colton.
I believed he hated me, but that he'd do the right thing
because he was a cop." He shook his head helplessly.
"This person—this man who could kill with impunity—
he's as much a stranger to me as he is to you."

He adjusted the heater while she stared at Malcolm's
picture. "It'd be nice to finally catch a break, wouldn't it?"

"We're doing everything we can, Jane. You're going
to have to accept that this might not happen fast or
you'll run yourself into the ground."

He should know. He'd been searching for more than
a year. But it really wasn't the long hours that were
getting to her. It was the *what if* questions that chased
each other around and around in her mind. *What if* she
wasn't a good enough investigator to be handling this
case? *What if* she or the police didn't get to Latisha and
Marcie in time? How would she deal with that? *What
if* she was pregnant? How would she tell her friends and
in-laws—and Kate? Would she ever tell Sebastian? It
hardly seemed fair to burden him with her mistake. But
it didn't seem fair to make his decisions for him, either.

Then, as she grew more tired, there was another *what if* question that kept presenting itself. *What if* she went home with him tonight? *What if* she allowed their relationship to turn into a full-blown affair for the duration of his stay in Sacramento?

But she had no business even *considering* that, much less acting on it. She'd told Sebastian she couldn't get pregnant, which meant she couldn't let him touch her again. If there was a next time, he'd see no reason to use a condom, and a repeat performance would significantly increase the risk of destroying everything she'd created—her new life, her sense of security.

She must have dozed off as they drove because the next thing she knew, Sebastian was gently shaking her shoulder. "We're at Cache Creek, Jane. I'm going to go in. You wait here."

Maybe he liked being large and in charge, but she had to admit he was always willing to carry the heavy end, always willing to do more than his share. Oliver had been so different, more like an indulged little boy who expected her to make all the sacrifices.

When Sebastian covered her with his coat, she wanted to close her eyes and drift away again. But letting him take care of her somehow weakened her resistance to him.

Forcing herself to return his coat, she sat up. "No, it'll be quicker if we both go. You must be tired, too."

"Jane—"

"I'm fine," she insisted. "You've got your copy of Malcolm's picture?"

"Listen to me. Running yourself ragged isn't going to help."

She arched her eyebrows at him. "I can do it if you can."

His lips were compressed in a straight, unhappy line. "Suit yourself."

As soon as they passed into the casino, Jane looked for the security guard she'd met earlier, but she couldn't find him. No doubt his shift had ended.

Sebastian touched her arm. "You take that side, I'll take this one."

Hoping she was doing it subtly enough, she stepped out of reach. The attraction she felt grew stronger when they stood close together. "Okay."

"Maybe you should get a cup of coffee first."

"Are you kidding? Then I'll be up for the rest of the night. This won't take long."

She strode purposefully off, but when she glanced over her shoulder to see if he'd done the same, he was still standing there, watching her. "What?"

"Nothing," he muttered and disappeared into the crowd.

Covering a yawn, Jane headed to the closest table, which turned out to be a blackjack table. She'd been to so many casinos and spoken to so many people, she expected another negative response. But this time when she flashed Malcolm's picture, she saw immediate recognition on the dealer's face.

"Yeah, I know him," he said while someone cut the deck. "He used to come in all the time."

Like magic, her exhaustion disappeared. "Have you seen him tonight?"

"No, not for a while. Several weeks."

"When does he normally come in?"

Obviously feeling some pressure to get back to work,

he looked uncomfortably at the people waiting for him to deal. "He done something wrong?"

He had only a few seconds. She had to convince him to reveal what he knew before he brushed her off. "He might've kidnapped two teenage girls."

The dealer whistled and shrugged off his hesitation. "Comes in late, usually on the weekends when it's crowded."

"Do you know his name, where he lives?"

He dealt the next hand. "No."

The man on the left was already asking for a hit, and the pit boss was coming to see why she was interrupting business, but Jane had to ask one more question. "Does he have any friends here? Anyone who might be able to tell me more about him?"

She realized from his manner that the dealer knew his boss was on the way. He kept his eyes on the cards. "Not that I'm aware of," he said. "Keeps mostly to himself."

"Thank you." Before the man with the microphone in his ear could shoo her away, she walked over by the slot machines to call Sebastian.

"I just talked to someone who's seen him," she announced.

"So did I. Apparently he's a regular. But he hasn't been in tonight."

"The dealer I spoke to hasn't seen him in weeks."

"I'm guessing he's had other things on his mind."

She bit her lip. "Latisha and Marcie?"

"Something's been keeping him busy."

"Maybe he's been looking for you, trying to figure out what you've got on him."

"He could be doing that, too," he said. "Let's get out of here."

But instead of going to the exit, she perched on a stool. "I'd rather stay. Maybe he'll come in tonight."

There was a long pause. "I have a better idea," he said when he spoke again. "Meet me at the door."

Sixteen

"Do you think that security guard you just paid will really call us if Malcolm comes in?" Jane asked.

Sebastian signaled before taking the Howe Avenue exit off Highway 50. "I do."

"He's already got your money. How do you know he won't forget?"

"Because I promised him more money if he remembers."

"How much more?"

The money he'd offered might make him appear far wealthier than he was at the moment. But he didn't want to make a bigger issue of it by refusing to answer. "Five thousand."

"Dollars?"

"I tried pesos, but...no go."

She wouldn't be diverted by his flip remark. "Five thousand dollars just for making a call."

"No. Malcolm has to be there when we arrive. I have to get a glimpse of him."

She adjusted her seat belt so she could turn toward him. "You don't mind throwing away that kind of money?"

His bank account couldn't hold out much longer. He figured he might as well use what he had left to full advantage. "If this works, it'll be the best money I've ever spent, don't you think?"

"Saving Marcie and Latisha is worth any amount. It just seems like a lot to pay someone who's already on the clock," she said. "I bet he would've done it for less."

Maybe that was true, but Sebastian wasn't taking any chances. "We want to give him enough incentive."

"At that price he'll study every face."

"That's the point. Now we can go to bed with some confidence that he'll do his job."

"True," she murmured. "And I'm tired again."

He pulled into her condominium complex and parked. "I'll walk you to the door." He didn't ask. He stated it as if she didn't have a choice. Because there was no way he'd let her walk up there without knowing she got in safely.

Fortunately, she didn't argue. She actually surprised him by asking him to check inside, too. He thought it was her background that had her spooked until she explained that she'd been getting some harassing phone calls from Latisha's father, someone she called both Luther and Lucifer.

Jane had left the kitchen light on, but the rest of the apartment was dark. They flipped switches as they walked from room to room. Sebastian had expected to see a fairly standard condo, furnished in a fairly standard fashion, but there was art everywhere—sculptures, paintings, handmade pottery, blown glass, metal objects. One painting, in particular, caught his eye. It was hanging on the wall in her bedroom and showed the outline of a man and a woman in a naked embrace. There were no details—no eyes or ears or specific body parts—just shape and color, but it brought the image vividly to mind.

"You like art," he said.

She'd followed him into the room to watch him look in the closet, the bathroom and under the bed. "Yes. But it's actually a fairly new passion for me. I never really thought about it or noticed it much before, but since Oliver...I don't know. It helps me cope with the ugliness of the past."

"This is nice," he said, gesturing at the painting. "What is it, watercolor?"

"Yes."

"You have excellent taste."

"I'm no expert," she said with a self-deprecating laugh. "I just buy what I like."

"I don't recognize any of the artists."

"Because it's all new talent. I can't afford the more established painters and I don't want replicas."

"Only the real thing."

"For me, it has to be original."

"Then I'm especially impressed you were able to spot such gems."

"I like helping new artists get started," she mused. "As far as I'm concerned, they make the world a better place. Art is another way to fight back, to fill the world with beauty and inspiration instead of hatred and anger. Don't you think?"

"I've never thought of it in that way, but I guess

you're right." He turned to face her. "Where do you find new pieces?"

"I visit galleries wherever I go. I check eBay. Lots of places, really. I love the discovery process. You could say it's become my hobby—my only hobby now that I'm working so much."

He indicated a blown-glass piece on her dresser. "That looks expensive."

"It was about three hundred dollars. Not bad, considering how much it'll be worth someday." She smiled. "If the artist makes it big, of course."

He jerked his head toward the watercolor. "This painting had to cost more."

"It did. I used my tax refund to buy it. I should've been more conservative and put the money into savings, but…I just had to have it."

He could see why it appealed to her. The painting depicted two halves coming together to make a perfect whole.

"The blues suggest peace and tranquility," she said.

The painting suggested a lot of things. But, at this moment, it was the sensuality of those figures that struck Sebastian most deeply. He wanted to make love to Jane in her own bed. "Is Kate at your in-laws'?" he asked, instead of commenting on the colors.

"Yes." She was no longer at the door; she was standing right beside him. Within reach.

He turned to watch her expression while she gazed at the painting and found her watching him instead. Caught up in the artist's vision and the energy that crackled between them, they stared at each other for several seconds without speaking.

Demanding honesty of himself, Sebastian refused to mask what he was feeling. He wanted her again, but this time he planned to make love to her tenderly—to take all night, if necessary. He wanted her to relax and to trust him.

But just as he was leaning forward to kiss her, she stepped back and shoved a self-conscious hand through her short hair. "Thanks for checking the place. I—I know I shouldn't let Lucifer rattle me, but it's a bit unnerving."

It took so much effort to put those barriers up again. He didn't understand why she bothered. What was she fighting?

Instead of filling the silence, he waited, hoping she'd change her mind. When she gave no indication that she might reconsider, he was disappointed, but he didn't push. It wouldn't be what he wanted if he had to pressure her into it. "Will you do me one favor?" he asked.

She seemed hesitant to commit herself. "What's that?"

"Will you tell me what the tattoo is on your breast so I can sleep tonight?" He grinned by way of enticement.

"My tattoo? It was dark when...in your motel room. How'd you see it?"

"I didn't see it then. I saw the edge of it above the neck of your sweater when we were in the car yesterday."

Her chest rose as if she'd just taken a deep breath. "I—it's nothing. Hard to explain."

His eyes riveted to hers. "Then why don't you show me?"

He expected her to refuse, but she didn't. She gave him the kind of smile that said she'd take that dare and unfastened her blouse, parting it so he could see the portion of the tattoo that extended above her bra.

Suddenly he understood why she hadn't been able

to explain. It wasn't a rose or a character or a butterfly. It was a beautiful, artistic decoration—so ornate that he almost didn't see the letter *R* scrolled among the curving loops and lines.

When he did, he lifted his hand and, encouraged when she didn't step away, ran a finger over it. "A lover's name?"

"No." She wouldn't meet his eye.

Taking it one step further, he lowered the lace of her bra far enough to see the rest. The *R* wasn't the only letter. There was an *I* and a *P*. "Rest in peace," he said. "This is for Oliver?"

Her breathing had gone shallow. He wanted to kiss her—but she chose that moment to move out of reach. "No. Someone else. Someone who wouldn't be dead if I hadn't been stupid and lonely and weak." She'd said it with finality, as if she wouldn't elaborate, but her words triggered a memory, a snatch of something she'd told him before. *He left me for dead, lying beside his murdered brother.*

"Another member of the family?" he asked.

She started to button her blouse. Her fingers worked quickly as if she'd exposed too much—of her body and her pain.

He took her hands, which were ice cold. The fact that she was trembling suggested there was more to the story. "What happened, Jane?"

She shook her head. "Like I said, I was stupid."

"Oliver thought you were having an affair with his brother?" Was that why he'd tried to kill her?

Tears swam in her eyes.

"Jane?"

"Yes."

Yes, he thought it? Or, yes, it was true? "Was he right?"

"I was so lonely," she whispered miserably.

That was another *yes*. Sebastian wasn't sure how he felt about this revelation. It certainly wasn't what he wanted to hear, wasn't what anybody would *want* to hear. "How?"

She pulled away to finish buttoning her blouse. She had to feel for the buttons with her fingers because she kept her head high, almost challenging him to see the monster she believed herself to be. "Oliver came from a wonderful family. He had a brother, Noah, who was everything Oliver seemed to be but wasn't."

Her eyes glazed over. He could tell she was remembering and hating herself for what those memories brought to life. Seeing her emotions made Sebastian regret asking. The subject was too close, too private. He didn't even plan on staying in Sacramento. He had no right to pry into her pain. "Jane, I'm sorry. This is none of my business—"

She held up a hand. "No, now that you've asked, now that you know this much, you might as well see how terrible I am."

He could barely hear the last two words. "Jane—"

"Let me finish," she said.

Realizing it was too late, he deferred with a slight nod.

"None of us really knew Oliver wasn't what he appeared to be. He could make you believe he was Santa Claus, if he wanted." She wiped a tear that rolled down her cheek and blinked away the rest. At that point he could almost hear her backbone snap into place. She was approaching this as one might approach a firing squad—determined to face her executioners with some dignity. "After he attacked Skye the first time, he was convicted of attempted rape."

"Did he go to prison?"

She buttoned her top button, the one she usually kept open. "For over three years."

There was a photograph on her dresser next to that glass sculpture—a young girl who had to be her daughter, Kate. "That left you and Kate where?"

"Adrift, mostly. I'd let myself depend on him and on our lifestyle so much that it felt as if I'd lost everything. I'd been out of the workforce for several years—and I'd never made much money when I *was* working. I had a cosmetology license but not a college degree, and I was rusty even at cutting hair. I guess you could say I'd grown spoiled. Lazy."

"So it was a financial shock, in addition to everything else?"

She sat on the bed, which was covered with a large blue-and-green comforter and lots of pillows. "It wasn't a smooth transition. I had no choice but to go back to cutting hair. But it'd been so long since I'd worked I didn't have a clientele. None of the nicer shops would have me—my skills were out-of-date. I was also an emotional wreck. So angry and bitter, so sure Oliver had been wrongly accused and Skye had deprived me of my husband, my child's father, our breadwinner, my fancy house, my high-class friends. Even my membership to the country club," she added with a disgusted laugh. "And I thought she'd done it all out of spite."

Sebastian shoved his hands in his pockets. "Was there much proof that he was guilty?"

"He admitted being in her house. He had to admit

that. They had his DNA, his blood on her bed. But he claimed she invited him over for consensual sex, then freaked out because she was on drugs. He said she tried to stab him."

"So, as far as you knew, he cheated on you first."

"That's no excuse."

"I'm not excusing you. I'm trying to figure out how it all happened. Did you know Skye at the time?"

"I'd never heard of her before in my life. It was all so confusing. I couldn't understand why she'd point a finger at *my* husband. There was no way he could be what she claimed. I would know, wouldn't I? That's what I kept telling myself. I lived with him, loved him, *went to church* with him...."

He whistled under his breath. "Those accusations couldn't have been easy to hear."

"Believing adultery to be the worst of his sins was easier than accepting the truth," she said. "I was determined to forgive him and reclaim what we'd had together."

She would've been better off divorcing him while he was in prison. Then maybe she could've gotten away before he attacked her and left that scar on her neck. "So you believed your husband."

"He said he loved me." She was no longer looking at him—or seeing him, at any rate. Her voice had fallen to a whisper, as if she was talking to herself.

"Maybe he did, in his own way."

She shook her head. "No, Oliver never loved anyone. He was incapable of it. But his brother was different."

A twinge of jealousy surprised Sebastian. "How'd you get involved with Noah?"

"He started coming over to help out, to make sure

Kate and I had everything we needed—fix up the place,
hang drapes, get us moved, whatever."

Sebastian could easily imagine the situation. At least
Noah had been trying to do right by his sister-in-law.
Or maybe it was just hard for Sebastian to blame Noah
because he felt the same attraction to Jane. "And it
turned out to be a little too much time alone?"

"I was so needy…" He saw shame, even anguish, in
her body language. She was shouldering all the guilt,
but this Noah deserved some of it, too, didn't he?

"It takes two," he reminded her.

She managed a wobbly smile. "He didn't mean for
it to happen."

"Did *you?*" Sebastian countered.

"Of course not, but—"

"People make mistakes, Jane." Sebastian suspected
there were some who'd hold this against her. But he'd
been through a similar situation with Emily and he
knew that even good people sometimes got involved in
relationships they shouldn't. Besides, how could
anyone say what he or she would've done in the same
circumstances? Although he'd never cheated, he had his
own regrets. Some bad decisions were easier to correct
than others.

"This was more than a *mistake,*" she said. "Noah is
dead because of me. He left a wife and three children."

In light of what she'd told him, the painting on her
wall took on greater significance. Did the colors repre-
sent the peace *she* longed for but couldn't quite achieve?
Her emotional burden was so heavy, he was astonished
that she'd been able to carry it for the past five years.

Knowing what he knew now, Sebastian could understand why she hadn't been able to heal. She wouldn't let herself. She was still berating herself, still paying penance. That explained why she hadn't met someone else and moved on, why she hadn't made love since the attack. It even explained why she wouldn't allow herself to enjoy making love with him last night. This morning, human need had won out—briefly—but she was already back to self-denial.

He sat on the bed next to her. "How did Oliver find out about the two of you?"

"Once he got out of prison, and he and I were trying to make another go of it, Noah's conscience got the better of him. It was never as if I was trying to *steal* Noah from his wife and kids, I swear. I knew all along that our...relationship couldn't continue. I cared about the entire family. I didn't want to see them hurt."

"How'd his wife take the news?"

"To this day, she won't really speak to me. She thinks I'm the worst kind of... Well, you can imagine the names she reserves for me. And I can't blame her."

Although she'd long since closed her blouse, Sebastian glanced toward the tattoo he'd seen on her breast. "You had that tattoo placed right over your heart."

She seemed confused by the statement. "So?"

"I think that's significant."

"How?"

"What are you mourning, Jane? Noah's death or your own?"

She stood. "I don't know what you mean."

"Sure you do. You've cut yourself off from any chance at love. You say you've gone through counseling, but you won't forgive yourself. What good is the counseling you've had if you're going to continue punishing yourself?"

She watched him in the mirror but said nothing.

"Maybe Skye saved you from Oliver, but who's going to save you from yourself?"

Rubbing her chest as if the tattoo suddenly burned, she faced him. "I don't deserve any more than I have. As long as I have Kate, that's all I need, all I ask for."

"You're settling."

"No, I'm not."

"Yes, you are. You stock your house with inanimate objects that portray the love and completeness you won't allow yourself." He motioned toward the painting as a case in point. "But life doesn't have to be so lonely!"

She raised a skeptical eyebrow at him. "Are you saying you're the man I should trust?"

She had him and she knew it. He wasn't any more whole than she was. "No," he admitted. "I'm not."

Although he could tell she'd been expecting his admission, the tightening of her mouth told him she was disappointed. "Then I guess we should say good-night," she said and walked him to the door.

Malcolm had never gone inside Mary's house. Not until now. In the past, he'd contented himself with skulking about the shrubberies and peeking in the windows. He hadn't wanted to blow his cover until he felt sure he'd be welcomed. He'd stuck to the plan, and the plan was to woo her back, to set up their future together.

But now that he knew she was working with Sebastian, and probably had been from the beginning, plans had changed. She'd found out he was still alive. And she couldn't be trusted.

It was time they met, time they came to terms with the past and the present, and who did what to whom. He'd thought he'd be able to wait for the meeting Sebastian and Mary had been trying to arrange. Turning the tables so perfectly really appealed to him. He'd imagined the scene so often…. But then he'd realized that Mary wouldn't show up at any meeting. Sebastian would come alone. And they'd only schedule it for a public place, where he couldn't do anything because there'd be witnesses. He had to get to Mary while he could, in a setting he controlled—make her tell him where Sebastian was.

A noise from the street caused him to pause in the open doorway. What was that? He cocked his head to listen. He would've thought it was Marcie, screaming for help from inside his van, but he'd parked it three blocks away. And he'd gagged her to keep her quiet.

Several seconds passed and there was only silence. Satisfied that what he'd heard had been a neighbor's dog, a car backfiring on J Street half a block over, or some other irrelevant noise, he dropped the lock-picking tools he'd just used in their felt pouch and returned them to his coat pocket. Then he adjusted his surgical gloves and closed the door. He'd chosen to enter through the front because that was the way he'd always hoped to come over, as a guest at first—and then, eventually, the owner, the patriarch of the family, Mary's husband. He'd also chosen the front because it was the boldest approach, and he was making a statement here: Sebastian would never get the best of him.

The plastic bags he'd used to cover his shoes swished as he walked across the living room, but he wasn't worried about a little creak or rustle. This was an old home, the kind of place that made a lot of settling noises. Midtown wasn't the best neighborhood for kids, but the area had undergone a revival since downtown Sacramento had become a place to live as well as work. He could understand why Mary had kept the house after she and her husband split. It was small, but with its plaster walls, hardwood floors, arched doorway connecting the living room to the dining room, and steps that led from the dining room to a study alcove, all of which he'd seen many times through the window, the house possessed a cozy sort of Norman Rockwell charm. And it was practical. She worked at Sutter Hospital, only a few blocks away.

Tonight, it was too dark to see the details. A sliver of moon hung in the sky outside, but fog blocked even that. Afraid he'd betray his presence by bumping into the furniture or breaking something fragile, he turned on the flashlight he'd brought and angled it around the room.

This was a nice place, all right, certainly nicer than the dumps he'd lived in after blowing most of Emily's money.

"We could've shared this," he muttered. "But you traded it all away."

Was it because he'd been unfaithful to her when they were in high school? If so, what a hard-hearted bitch. He wouldn't want to get with anyone who could hold a grudge for that long, anyway. He'd already explained to her. He'd been a dumb kid, thinking with his dick instead of his brain, just like he'd said. And he'd paid the price for it, hadn't he? Although he and Mary had tried to get back together a few times afterward, things were never as good as before. Otherwise, they might've gone to the same college, as they'd once planned. And they might've gotten married. Then he wouldn't have married his first wife, who'd turned out to be the biggest shrew he'd ever met, always complaining about her emotional needs and how they weren't being met. That hadn't lasted long. He'd gotten out as soon as possible.

Spotting a family picture, Malcolm crossed to the buffet to take a better look. There was Mary with a tall dark man and her two boys. Her chestnut-colored hair was pulled back and she was smiling the same broad smile he remembered from high school. He loved her gorgeous smile. She really hadn't changed much. She still had the same clear skin, the big brown eyes, the upturned nose.

"How could you be so cruel?" he asked as he gazed down at her.

Had Sebastian purposely ingratiated himself? For some reason, women couldn't seem to resist Emily's ex. They didn't see how autocratic and overbearing he was. They didn't see the way he constantly challenged those around him.

He'd probably shown up here, talking slick and flashing his money. Mary was certainly the type to be impressed by some big spender from New York City. She'd told him how cheap her ex-husband was.

Snapping off the flashlight, Malcolm moved toward the back of the house. Now that he'd familiarized himself with the obstacles he might encounter, there was no need to press his luck by using the flashlight. But before he killed Mary, he wanted to see her boys, to look down at them in their beds as he might've done had he become their stepfather. He couldn't believe that while he'd been planning to become a good companion to her, she'd been trying to trick him—but it was right there, in almost every e-mail. She'd pressed him for his location, pretended she was still in love, even used his desire for her against him.

She'd made a fool of him, and nothing infuriated him more.

Judging by the number of doors branching off the hallway, there were two bedrooms and one bath in the house. A radio or a TV had been left on. He could hear the low rumble as he drew closer to the end of the hall. It helped to mask the creak of his footsteps.

The first bedroom wasn't the one with the TV. That room belonged to the boys. Even if a night-light hadn't revealed the children sleeping in twin beds that took up most of the space, Malcolm would've known it wasn't Mary's by the smell. Stale sweat from the sports jerseys, clothes, tennis shoes and cleats scattered on the floor competed with male cologne. The combination wasn't a stench so much as it was a distinctive, familiar odor. It reminded him of Colton. His room had smelled the same way—of boy.

Why had he even *considered* taking on the responsibility of raising two more kids. Stepparenting was a thankless job. Colton had hated him almost as much as Sebastian had. They constantly united against him. Even Emily had taken their side more often than not.

But he'd dealt with her. He'd deal with Mary, too. And then Sebastian. Heck, he had several hours until dawn. Why not kill the whole family? That would make her regret what she'd done, wouldn't it? That would hurt her as much as she'd hurt him. And then Sebastian would die knowing that his meddling had caused the loss of three lives, two of them children.

The older boy somehow had most of the younger boy's blankets. He was using two comforters while his brother was uncovered and curled into a ball to ward off the cold. *Typical,* Malcolm thought as he stood over the bed. The younger brother never had a chance. That was how it'd been in his family, too. Jack had taken more than his share of everything, especially their parents' love and attention.

Malcolm blew out a sigh. Mary cared more about these boys than she did about anyone or anything else. Should he march them into her room and kill them in front of her?

It'd be easier if he had his gun, he decided. Quick. Lethal. One shot and it would all be over, just like with Emily and Colton.

But he couldn't use a gun. It was too loud and the ballistics tests would reveal too much. He had to use a knife. Did he have the nerve to murder two children he'd never even met, especially with a knife? The rage he felt certainly tempted him. Malcolm responded. He wants to know what's in the package, but he didn't leave an address. I'll reply, see if I can get it out of him…. She'd taken away the one positive aspect of his life, the one thing that had kept him going over the past few months since the money ran out. After being fired from yet another job as a security guard for a large commercial complex in downtown Los Angeles, he'd come to Sacramento to start over—

again. Mary had been his promise that this time he'd finally build a new life, just as he'd planned ever since leaving Jersey.

But she'd ruined it for him. Sacramento wouldn't be the answer. He'd have to move elsewhere, try to get on with another crappy security company, assume another alias—but not until he'd finished his business here. Not until he'd put an end to Mary and Sebastian and knew for sure that there was no one left—other than Pam Wartle—who had any idea he was alive. Only then could he truly forget the past. Only then could he really move on.

He could kill the kids, he assured himself. He'd do it in front of Mary. But not until he'd had the chance to confront her….

Slipping out of the boys' room, he approached the door at the end of the hall and paused to listen to the TV droning behind it. Was she awake and watching a program as he liked to do? Or had she fallen asleep with the TV on?

He was about to find out, about to see the woman he'd loved since he was sixteen years old. Maybe he'd tell her she could save herself and her children by having sex with him. He'd threaten her, tell her not to make a sound while he forced her to deliver on all the false promises she'd made. She owed him that much, didn't she? Then he'd kill the children, saving her for last, clean up any evidence he might've left behind and slip away.

Too bad her first glimpse of him would include overalls, a hairnet, gloves and plastic bags over his feet. Dressed this way, he certainly couldn't compete with the stylish, debonair Sebastian Costas. But he couldn't compete with him, anyway.

At least Mary would be scared. She'd be terrified, and that was all that mattered.

He'd teach her that he was no fool, he thought, and went into her room.

Seventeen

Sebastian was so tired he almost fell into bed without checking to see if Malcolm was online. For once, he didn't want to get involved in a conversation. His time with Jane had left him even more unsettled than after she'd lowered her skirt and walked out this morning. Why? What was it about her? His feelings were so confused—a mix of commiseration, identification, admiration, lust. Even disgust for what she'd done with Oliver's brother. He knew it would be easier not to think about her if he could sink into unconsciousness for a few hours. After all the late nights, he needed a break.

But force of habit had him booting up his computer while he brushed his teeth.

He opened his own e-mail first. Mary had IMed him from her account around midnight. Hey, you there? You up?

He checked to see if she was still on and got no response, so he read his e-mails. His mother had sent him a message, letting him know she'd couriered the handwriting sample. His boss from Lincoln Hawke had also sent him a message.

When are you coming back? There's a great opportunity here for you, perfect for someone who wants to get away. It's in Hong Kong.

He was hearing from Bill Masters more and more often. His boss had been understanding to begin with, but now he was getting impatient. He didn't want to lose one of his most successful investment specialists, and had repeatedly said that Sebastian could make it even in today's banking environment. But Sebastian wasn't remotely tempted to accept an assignment in Hong Kong. He felt as if he'd been living in a foreign place ever since Malcolm killed Emily and Colton.

After rinsing out his mouth, he thanked his mother and wrote a polite response to Masters, telling him he needed a little more time. Then he logged into Mary's e-mail account. He didn't see a message from Malcolm, but he knew she'd been using the account earlier. She'd IMed him from it. So he opened the Old Mail file to see what had happened in his absence.

He found nothing from Malcolm, or Wesley as he called himself, in Old Mail, either. But something stood out that seemed very strange. Mary had received an e-mail from *Sebastian.Costas@yahoo.com*.

He didn't have an account at that address, and he doubted Mary knew someone else with his name and had failed to mention it.

What was going on? A trickle of fear ran through him as he read the message.

Hey, any word from Malcolm?

There was no signature, nothing but that one line.

The dread kicking up his heartbeat increased as he opened Mary's Sent folder and saw that she'd replied.

Malcolm responded. He wants to know what's in the package, but he didn't leave an address. I'll reply, see if I can get it out of him, okay?

Sleep tight. I'm glad you got to bed early for once.

Mary

Who'd sent the first message? *And who'd received the reply?*

Sebastian's muscles tensed as he realized who the likely culprit was. Malcolm was on to them. He had to be. The sneaky bastard had figured out a way to see if they were in communication with each other, and because they'd been out of touch tonight, it had worked.

His pulse racing, Sebastian checked the time on Mary's message. She'd sent it at 12:08 a.m., presumably right before she went to bed. Several hours had passed since then. It was after two when he and Jane had finished at the casinos. What time was it now?

His eyes flicked to the bottom right of his monitor—3:15.

With a curse, he called Mary's house. He had to find out if she was okay. And if she was, he needed to warn her that the jig was up. This changed everything....

The phone rang several times.

"Answer, please answer." He could hardly hear

above the rush of blood in his ears, but he was fairly sure the voice that finally came on wasn't a live one. A beep confirmed it. He'd reached her answering machine.

"Mary, take the kids and get out of the house! Immediately! Go somewhere safe. Malcolm knows you've been helping me. God, Mary, please pick up."

The machine beeped again, this time to signal the end of the tape. Then a dial tone sounded. Sebastian would've redialed, but he was in too big a hurry. After he hung up, he called the police. Then he grabbed his keys and his coat and dashed out the door.

The telephone was his first clue that something wasn't as it should be. When it rang, Malcolm didn't wake Mary, although he'd been about to. He shrank back, into her walk-in closet. There was a phone on her nightstand, but she didn't even stir. She probably didn't get many phone calls in the middle of the night and assumed it was the TV, which got louder whenever a commercial came on. Or maybe she'd taken a sleeping pill. He knew she didn't like living alone. She'd said so.

After what felt like an eternity, the ringing stopped. He could hear someone talking. An answering machine? It seemed to be coming from the middle of the house. But some guy selling exercise equipment on TV made it impossible to hear anything more than a low murmur.

What should he do? Get it over with? Or get out? Would lingering for another ten minutes get him caught?

The thought of prison terrified him. He knew what the inmates did to cops gone bad—even former cops. And what about his parents and siblings, and the men with whom he'd served on the force? They'd hear about it; they'd learn the truth.

Mary stirred as he left the closet. "Curtis?"

The phone had awakened her, after all. She believed the kids were up.

He hurried to the door and hustled down the hall.

"Brandon?" she called. She sounded more alert, almost frightened. Damn whoever had interrupted with that phone call! He'd been so close....

But he'd fix it, Malcolm told himself. He'd have another chance.

Afraid he might run into someone—like the police—if he went out the front, he darted into the laundry room and crossed to the back door. Without any streetlights, the yard was dark and provided more places to hide.

Opening the door as quietly as possible, he slipped into the yard and maneuvered through the shrubs. Then he hopped the fence, crouching in the corner of the neighbor's yard to watch and listen. If that random call turned out to be nothing, maybe he could still get to her, demand Sebastian's address before he killed her and disappear before dawn.

She'd heard movement. Mary was sure of it. Someone had been in her bedroom. She'd seen a large dark shape move quickly to the door just as she was coming awake. But both her boys were asleep and, when she roused them, they insisted they hadn't gotten out of bed even to go to the bathroom. What was going on?

A sense of foreboding gripped her as she walked through the house carrying her son's baseball bat. Looking in closets and peering around corners, she paused every few seconds to listen. But she heard nothing she didn't hear every night.

When she reached the study, a rush of cold air hit her. It seemed to be coming from the laundry room....

Taking a slight detour from her frightened trek to the living room, she poked her head into the laundry and flipped on the light.

The back door stood ajar. She'd been right. Someone—a man, judging by the size of the shape she'd seen—had been in her house.

Fear made her knees go weak as she gaped at the fog blanketing her yard. If he was still out there, she couldn't see him.

Her hands shook as she closed the door and drew the bolt. She hadn't left it open. She knew that much. She'd locked this door and every other before bed, checked them twice. So how had he gotten in? And what did he want?

Was it a robbery?

Gathering her courage, she turned on the rest of the lights in the house. As far as she could tell, nothing had been stolen or disturbed. And she'd already made sure the boys were safe. Whoever it was hadn't taken anything, but she figured it was best to report the incident. The police needed to be aware that there were burglars in the neighborhood.

She was about to call 9-1-1 when she heard a brisk knock at the front door. Parting the blinds on the closest window, she saw the flashing red lights of a squad car in her driveway. The police were already here. Someone else must've called them.

"Thank God," she muttered and raced to her bedroom for a robe.

A second knock rattled the front of the house as she reentered the living room. "Coming," she called. But she didn't need to unlock the door in order to open it. Because it was already unlocked.

Even more confused, she swung the door wide, expecting the young, clean-cut officers on her stoop to offer some sort of explanation.

"Hello, ma'am."

Now that she could make out their faces, she could tell that one was clearly older than the other. He was the one who spoke.

"I'm sorry to disturb you, but we received a call about a possible intruder at this address."

His words only created more questions. "You did?" she said. "I was about to place that call myself, but I haven't had a chance."

"Maybe it was your husband."

"I'm divorced. Maybe it was a neighbor. Please come in. I don't know what's going on, but something's up." She waved them toward the couch. Then she spotted the flowers on her dining room table and caught her breath. Had it been Malcolm? Sebastian had warned her that he might act now that he had her address.

The thought that her home, her safety and her children's safety might be compromised made her ill. She'd been through so much with the divorce, had just gotten on her feet again. She didn't think she could deal with another upset, not like this.

The officer who'd greeted her cleared his throat. Dimly, she realized that he'd asked her a question. "Excuse me?"

"How do you know something's going on?" he repeated.

She was about to explain when she heard the screech of tires. Someone else had arrived. Dropping the ends of the tie to her robe, which she'd been nervously fingering, she ran to the window to peek through the blinds again. Then she relaxed. This man she recognized.

Throwing open the front door, she waited for Sebastian to get out of his car and come charging up the walk. "Oh, my God, what's happening?" she cried.

He pulled her into his arms and squeezed her tightly. "Are you okay?"

The man she'd come to know over the past two months normally had an olive complexion. Tonight, he looked pale and drawn. "I'm fine, but—" she worried her lip "—is it Malcolm?"

He nodded. "He knows, Mary. He knows it was a trap."

She reached for the door frame to steady herself. "He was in my *bedroom,*" she whispered.

By the time Sebastian had dropped Mary's children off at her ex-husband's apartment and taken Mary to her mother's house, it was almost five o'clock in the morning. He was relieved that she and her children were safe. Last night could've ended so badly. But he still couldn't avoid an overwhelming sense of loss. Now that Malcolm knew they were on to him, they didn't stand a chance of catching him, of making him pay for his crimes. After all the careful plotting and planning and the interminable chase that had carried Sebastian through more than twelve months, he was back at square one.

It was too disappointing to even contemplate. Maybe the exhaustion that weighed on every muscle was part of the problem, made it that much more difficult to cope with such a setback. But Sebastian couldn't bring himself to return to his motel. He didn't want to see those same four walls, his computer on the desk, half his clothes in the bag he'd send out to have laundered and the other half hanging in a closet where he couldn't even remove the hangers.

All he wanted was to see Jane.

He'd parked in a visitor slot at her condominium complex almost before he realized where he was. Letting the engine idle, he tried to talk himself out of going in. Jane had enough to deal with. He wouldn't be doing her any favors by piling his frustrations on top of hers.

And yet, if anyone could understand the disillusion that threatened to consume him, it was Jane.

A truck turned in at the driveway. The newspaper delivery person. Sebastian watched as an older driver double-parked and had his teenage son run the paper to the various residences. The boy was about Colton's age....

Memories of taking his son to play racquetball, go dirt-bike riding or waterskiing at the lake—or even wash the cars—swept over him. *Why?* Why had Malcolm done what he'd done? Colton's death was so unnecessary. Malcolm must have known that Sebastian would've gladly finished raising him, must have known how badly it would hurt Sebastian to lose his only child.

That was the reason, Sebastian decided. Malcolm had *wanted* to hurt him, had refused to show even that much compassion.

A young boy murdered...

"You bastard," he said through gritted teeth.

Life could be fleeting, he thought. Sometimes you

didn't even know what you had until it was gone. So why spend the night alone?

Removing his keys from the ignition, he got out, slammed the door and locked it.

A knock at the door brought Jane to full consciousness. As usual, her thoughts reverted to Oliver. It'd been five years, but whenever she was startled, she automatically wondered whether she was really safe. She had to remind herself that he was gone. Then her pulse settled. But it was still odd that someone had come to her condo so early in the morning. Her alarm wouldn't go off for another two hours.

Praying there hadn't been some sort of emergency involving Kate, she got up, yanked on her robe and hurried to the living room. "Who is it?" she called through the door.

"Me."

Sebastian. Was he okay? She checked the peephole.

He appeared to be fine.

Throwing the bolt, she opened the door.

She thought he'd explain why he was on her doorstep at five-thirty in the morning, but he didn't. He just stood there, rumpled and exhausted and disheartened, and she realized he hadn't come to talk. He was looking for comfort.

A warning voice in her head told her not to invite him in. He was already the subject of every fantasy she had. But she couldn't see him so miserable and do nothing.

Taking his hand, she drew him inside.

As soon as she'd shut the door, his arms went around her, holding her close.

Jane held him in return, wishing she could somehow soothe away the pain that was obviously tearing him up. "Are you okay?" she whispered.

He didn't answer. He buried his face in her neck and, seconds later, she felt the moisture of tears.

When Jane woke, she was in her bed, naked, with Sebastian. They hadn't done anything before falling asleep except curl up together. But he was touching her now—intimately. With his chest to her back and his legs tucked up under her behind, he held her to him, cupping her breast as he kissed her neck.

This was the moment to stop him, before it was too late, she told herself. Even if she came clean about her possible ability to conceive, all the condoms she'd bought were at his motel. She couldn't make love with him.

"Sebastian…" She rolled over to face him so they could talk, but he simply brought her up against his chest and kissed her parted lips.

His kiss started out as more of a request, a soft, tempting lure, but the more she responded the more passionate it grew.

"Sebastian," she gasped when he moved to her neck. "We can't do this."

He didn't comment. Apparently, he wasn't any more interested in talking now than he'd been before—except, perhaps, with his hands. They let her know exactly what he thought they should be doing.

She tried to say *no* one more time, but his fingers had found the sensitive spot that'd brought her such pleasure the previous morning, and his name on her lips came out as a moan.

"Trust me," he whispered.

"I'm the one who can't be trusted," she told him, but he didn't take her seriously enough to stop. Slipping one arm beneath the small of her back, he lifted her slightly off the bed and covered her breast with his mouth. At that point, she knew she'd give almost anything to let him continue—anything except being as irresponsible as she had before. That was a line she couldn't cross again.

She was about to stop him, to blurt out the truth, if necessary. She had no choice. But then she remembered that her doctor had sent her home with a barrier device called a Lea's Shield at her last visit. She'd kept telling him she wasn't sexually active, but he'd pressed her to take one, even shown her how to use it, just in case.

Now she was incredibly glad.

"Sebastian?"

"Hmm?"

"I need a minute," she said and slipped away, into the bathroom.

She'd made love without being completely honest, but at least she'd used birth control. That made it okay, didn't it?

Still, Jane wasn't sure her conscience was *totally* clear....

How was it that she'd wound up in bed with Sebastian again? She'd said good-night, locked her door and gone to her room *alone*. Could she help it that he'd returned when she least expected? That he knew exactly how to break down her resistance?

Hearing him in the kitchen, she allowed herself a muffled groan of frustration as she rolled onto her side.

It wasn't his fault. Just the way he looked at her could demolish her defenses. She obviously hadn't changed as much as she wanted to believe. After spending five years proving to Wendy, and to herself, that she possessed some restraint, she'd once again been humbled by her own shortcomings.

"Hey, breakfast is ready." Sebastian poked his head into the room.

Jane was facing away from the door. "I'm not hungry."

She thought he'd gone back to eat until he spoke again. "We're both consenting adults, Jane. And neither one of us is in a committed relationship. We haven't hurt anyone."

He knew she was berating herself, but he didn't understand why.

Dragging the blankets with her, she sat up. "I've never had a tubal ligation, Sebastian."

He straightened. *"What?"*

"I could be fertile." How was that for dropping a bomb? "You mean this morning—"

She waved her hand. "I used a Shield this morning. I'm talking about last time."

Propping one shoulder against the door, he rubbed the beard growth on his chin. "Why'd you tell me otherwise?"

"Because it was too late to take back what we'd done, and I was the one who wouldn't let you stop. I figured it was my problem, so I'd pay the consequences. But I didn't think we'd... I never dreamed we'd be together again. I used birth control this morning, but we both know the barrier methods aren't as absolutely reliable as a tubal ligation. I feel like—" she raked her fingers through her hair "—it's not right for me to be making the decision to take that chance on my own."

He studied her. "For the record, I would've gone for it," he said.

"What does that mean?"

"It means that if you'd told me you hadn't had your tubes tied before we made love this morning, but said you had a Shield, I would've wanted to continue."

That was a nice thing to say, to take partial responsibility. She couldn't help being impressed. But did he truly realize that using a Shield this morning didn't change the fact that she might already be pregnant? Why wasn't he angry that she'd taken such a huge risk without warning him? "I'm sorry. I don't know what I was thinking. I *wasn't* thinking."

"I like it when you're not thinking," he said with a grin.

She smiled back. "So what's for breakfast?"

Eighteen

Wearing only his jeans, Sebastian held his coffee cup loosely. He was sitting at the breakfast table with Jane, trying to figure out why she made him feel better when Constance always made him feel worse. It made no sense. There'd been times over the past few months when his former girlfriend had wanted to make love and he'd had no interest, times she'd begged him to open up and talk and he'd been unable to do so.

But it was different with Jane. Was it because she understood what he felt without his having to explain? That was part of it, but he liked too much about her to pin his feelings exclusively on her understanding. Mary had kids. She understood, too. But he hadn't been attracted to her.

"So what are we going to do about Malcolm?" Jane asked.

He'd just told her about the e-mail Malcolm had sent Mary, Mary's response and the intruder she'd subsequently had at her house. "I don't know."

"I mean, Mary can't go back home."

Setting down his coffee cup, he leaned back and stretched out his legs. "No, not until we're sure Malcolm has moved on."

"What makes you think he'll move on?"

"Escape is his best option in terms of risk management."

"But killers don't necessarily think logically. You've chased him all over kingdom come. Maybe he's planning to put a stop to it here."

The fact that Malcolm had broken into Mary's house suggested he wasn't willing to let her betrayal go unpunished. But Malcolm was basically a coward. Sebastian had always believed it, and he believed it more than ever now. "You think he might try to get rid of me *and* Mary?"

She added some cream to her coffee. "That's what Oliver would do. He'd stay until he tied up the loose ends, then he'd move on."

Malcolm wasn't the same kind of killer. But he was definitely the kind of man who'd hold a grudge. And this was growing more personal by the day. "As long as he comes after me and not Mary, I wouldn't mind. I'd rather put an end to it, too."

"One way or another."

"It's not a death wish. I'm just tired of living like this."

The phone rang before she could comment. While she answered, Sebastian started clearing away the dishes.

"Don't make Grandma drive all the way over here," she said into the phone. "I'll bring it to school." She listened for a bit. "You want to what?"

Sebastian glanced over his shoulder and found her watching him. When their eyes met, she turned away.

"No, I'll bring it to you… Because you don't need to come home right now… I'll feed your hamster. I do that when you're gone on the weekends, don't I?… Kate, it'll make you late for school… I said I'll bring it, okay?… I love you… Bye."

"Kate forget something?" he asked as she hung up.

"Yeah, but it's not a problem. I can drop it off at the school."

He leaned against the counter. "You seem a little rattled."

She set the phone on the counter. "I'm just wondering what I would've done if they'd shown up here without calling first," she said with a nervous laugh. "Can you imagine? I haven't even gone on a *date* since her father was killed."

"Does she know Skye's the one who killed her father?"

"Yes."

"And she knows why?"

"Yes."

"If she can handle that, she can handle anything," he said. He was about to add, "There's nothing wrong with having a male friend," but didn't. He doubted it would be smart to categorize their relationship. At this stage, neither one of them really knew what they were to each other.

"But it's eight o'clock in the morning," she muttered.

"Maybe I stopped by because we're working together."

She arched her eyebrows at his state of half-dress. "Like that? It's not as if she would've waited for you to put on your shirt before barging in. She has a key. This is her home."

It would've been awkward. But he was too stubborn

to concede. He didn't want to feel he had to be hidden or segregated from her regular life. "Having a romantic interest isn't exactly unnatural, Jane."

"It's more complicated than that and you know it."

She started to slip away, probably so she could shower and dress, but he caught her elbow. "I'd like to meet Kate." If he could back up a little and include her daughter, maybe Jane would be able to relax, maybe she wouldn't view him as merely a guilty pleasure.

"Sure. Someday," she said.

"Today. Why don't I take you both to dinner?"

She pretended to consider the invitation, but he knew she wouldn't accept it. "I don't think so. There's no need to confuse her. You'll be going back to New York when this is all over, and then..."

He let go of her. He understood why she might be extraprotective, especially of Kate. But she had to get beyond that sometime. "And then she'll have a friend in a different state. So will you. How can that hurt?"

"There's just no point."

"Because..."

"Because this is a temporary fling."

That was how she justified getting involved in such a high-risk situation? "What if you're pregnant?"

Twin spots of color appeared high on her cheeks. "We'll deal with that if it happens."

"Wouldn't it be easier to explain if she'd at least met me? Maybe she's only twelve, but surely she knows it takes two to make a baby."

"I'm sorry," she said. "I can't handle even the possibility. Not now. I mean...I'm forty-six. I'm too old to be having another child."

Sebastian shrugged. "People are waiting longer these days."

"And if they wait this long, they face some serious risks."

"I realize that. But even when the mother's forty-six, most babies are healthy."

"So what are you saying?"

"I'm just not going to panic, that's all." He had no idea how they'd work out the details but, as crazy as he knew it was, a baby sort of made sense to him. Why he'd want to have that baby with a woman he'd only known for a few days, he couldn't say. Maybe it was because Constance had been so definite about not wanting children. It hadn't been a problem between them. When he'd made a commitment to her, he'd been satisfied with the one kid he had. Since the issue was already decided, he'd never reconsidered. But now...

He wouldn't be unhappy if it happened, he decided. Maybe another child would help fill the terrible void in his heart since Colton's murder. Maybe he'd have a little girl this time. Although no one could take the place of his son, it'd be nice to have a child he could love as much.

But having a baby with Jane would be a nightmare if she wasn't as pleased as he was. "Would you be too upset?" he asked.

She folded her arms in a protective manner. "I don't know if *upset* is the right word."

What would she do? A man had so little control. "Would you consider an abortion?"

"I can't even think about that. Not right now."

"Just so you know, if you are pregnant and you don't

want the baby, I'll take it," he said. "You could tell everyone you agreed to be a surrogate. It'll be an easy out."

Pressing a hand to her stomach, she said, "Don't you dare offer me money!"

He chuckled. She wouldn't worry about that if she knew his financial situation. "I wouldn't dream of it."

"Okay, then. Let's make sure there *is* a baby before we discuss it further. Deal?"

"Deal."

"I'm having a shower."

He reclaimed the dish towel. "I won't be here when you get out. I'm going over to check on Mary."

"I'll call you as soon as I get hold of David. I'm hoping one of Mary's neighbors jotted down Malcolm's license-plate number."

"Or at least noticed the make and model of his car."

"That would help."

They were finished with the conversation and had, essentially, said goodbye. But she didn't leave the kitchen. She stood there studying him.

"What is it?" he asked.

Her expression grew wistful. "Do you *really* want a baby?"

The thought triggered another smile. "What do you think?"

She shook her head. "It seems like it's never the man who wants a child."

"This time it is," he said.

"It'd be a change." With that understatement, she headed down the hall. But a frantic knock at the front door stopped her from getting in the shower.

* * *

Jane wasn't sure whether she should ask Sebastian to duck out of sight, or if she should answer the door while he was bare chested and drying dishes in her kitchen. She tried to check through the window but whoever it was stood too far to the right. Surely, Betty hadn't brought Kate home to get her phys ed clothes. Jane had been very clear with her daughter on the phone that she wasn't to come home right now....

A trickle of anxiety made her tense. "Who is it?" she called out to her visitor.

While she waited for a response, she half expected to hear a key in the lock. But it wasn't Kate.

"Jane? It's Bob."

She breathed out in relief. Bob lived in the unit at the far end of the building. She saw him out walking his dog occasionally. They exchanged pleasantries, but this was the first time he'd ever come to her door. "Um, I'm not quite up and ready for the day, Bob. What can I do for you?"

"There's a Lexus in visitor parking. Do you have any idea who it belongs to?"

Her eyes cut to Sebastian.

"Was I supposed to park somewhere else?" he whispered.

"I know the owner," she told Bob through the door. "He's a...a work associate."

"Who just might be the father of your baby," Sebastian teased.

She couldn't help smiling as she waved him off. "Stop it. Something's wrong."

"They'd better not have towed my car," he grumbled as he strode toward the bedroom.

"Can you have him come out here?" Bob asked.

"What's the matter?" Jane replied. "Do you need him to move his vehicle?"

"No. The police are in the lot. They want to talk to him."

At the word *police* Sebastian whipped around to face her before reaching her bedroom.

"What's going on?" she asked him.

Obviously as confused as she was, he shook his head, so she repeated the question more loudly, this time for Bob. "What's going on?"

"I'd rather not yell it through the door," he said.

Sebastian disappeared from the hallway. After running her hand self-consciously through her hair and making sure her robe covered any hint of nudity, she turned the dead bolt. "What is it?" she asked once she'd opened the door.

A bone-thin retired widower, her neighbor had on his typical polyester slacks, Windbreaker and comfortable shoes. "There's been a murder," he explained.

The words were so far from what she'd been expecting, it took her a moment to absorb their meaning. "A...*what?*"

Sebastian came up behind her, fully dressed.

"There's been a murder." Bob's eyes shifted to Sebastian. "Do you own the white Lexus in visitor parking?"

A muscle twitched in Sebastian's cheek. "I do."

"What does his car have to do with anything?" Jane asked.

"There's a body in the backseat."

Sebastian was already stepping around her. The

levity and excitement she'd seen in his face a few minutes earlier were gone. Now he was alert and intent on
finding out what had happened. But he stopped when
he saw her horrified expression.

"Jane?"

There was a strange numbness creeping up from her
toes. But she ignored his concern, keeping her focus on
Bob. He was the one with the information. "A *body?*" she
repeated. "Whose is it? Surely, no one in the complex."

"No." Her neighbor shoved his hands in his pockets
and jingled his change. "It's an African-American girl."

Terror clutched at Jane's chest. "How old?"

"Early twenties or so. Difficult to tell. I've never
seen her before. She's not from around here, if that's
what you're asking."

That wasn't what she was asking. She was afraid
this girl was one of the two she'd been hoping and
praying to save.

The floor began to spin. She grabbed for the door
handle and felt Sebastian haul her up against him before
she could even touch it. "Breathe," he murmured.

She nodded, swallowing hard. "I'm fine," she said,
but he didn't believe her. He forced her to sit down at
the kitchen table.

"You okay?" he asked and waited until she met his
eyes and he could tell that she was before he stalked off
and out the door.

Bob had followed her inside and was sitting next to
her. He was always a hard person to escape, even when
they were standing in the rain. Obviously shaken by
what he'd seen, he was more talkative than ever. "I was
out walking my dog when I saw that someone had

broken out the window of one of the cars in the lot," he explained. "So I went over to investigate." He leaned closer. "We've had some burglaries in the area," he told her as if she hadn't received the same notices he had. "You can't leave anything in your car."

"I know," Jane answered, as though this was no different from any other conversation they'd had in the past. It was the only reaction she could muster. She wanted to follow Sebastian to the parking lot, but her legs wouldn't hold her weight. Leaning her head against the back of the chair, she took several deep breaths.

"And when I looked inside, there she was," he went on. "I've never seen anything like it. There was so much blood. I couldn't tell if she'd been shot or stabbed." He massaged the back of his own neck. "But I knew she was dead."

Was the victim one of Gloria's sisters, as Jane feared? The color of the girl's skin, the placement of the body, the timing—it was too much to be a coincidence.

What did that say about the man Sebastian was chasing?

It said he hadn't fled Mary's house when he was nearly caught. He'd waited around and watched the activity. Then he'd brazenly followed Sebastian. How else could he have found Sebastian's car?

Had he killed Latisha—or Marcie? And did that mean he'd eventually kill Sebastian, too?

That was the thought that finally brought Jane to her feet. She was still in her robe, but she didn't care. Leaving her neighbor in the middle of another rambling sentence, she walked out the door and, as her strength returned, started to jog.

"I don't think you want to see that," Bob called after her. "I'd stay here, if I were you."

He wished he hadn't seen it. That was clear. But Jane was suddenly desperate to know if this was true, if this was *reality,* because it felt so much like one of her bad dreams.

"Jane?" He'd come to the door to yell, but she could tell he didn't intend to return to the scene. He stayed where he was, as if just the thought of going back evoked images he'd rather forget.

She didn't answer. She was already turning the corner, where she could see the activity previously blocked by the building. There were six cop cars surrounding the Lexus—and two men were photographing the body of a young black woman in the backseat.

Latisha had been tied up for so many hours, she could no longer feel her hands or feet. And the headache that had started last night had only grown worse, since she'd been forced to lie in one place. But when she heard the front door open and knew Wesley was finally back, she could think only of her sister. He'd dragged Marcie out of the room when he'd left last night.

"Wesley?" she called. "Is everything okay?"

He didn't respond, but he must have heard her. The house wasn't that big, and his footsteps traveled past her door several times. She would've shouted again, but she didn't dare. The last time she'd bothered him when he didn't answer he'd entered her room with a loaded gun.

The shower went on in the master bedroom. Closing her eyes, she counted to a thousand over and over again, trying to endure the aches and pains. Usually when he tied her up, she could at least sit—but that was when he shackled her to her own stake in the floor. Last night, he'd chained her feet to her stake *and* tied her hands. The added security measures suggested he had something big planned.

He finished showering and went outside. A few minutes later, she could smell smoke. Had he set the house on fire? Was he leaving her to die?

Helpless, she whimpered at the possibility. But although she strained to hear the crackle of wood or to see smoke creeping beneath her door, there was nothing.

The bang of the front door told her he hadn't left. She guessed from his movements that he'd gone into the kitchen. She heard the chime of the microwave, smelled coffee. He was making breakfast, which suggested he hadn't set the house on fire. So what *had* he done? Why didn't he come for her? Why hadn't he made her do the cooking?

And where was Marcie? That was the question that frightened Latisha the most. Was her sister still tied up in the van? If so, why didn't he bring her in? It didn't make sense that he'd leave her out there alone. He had to keep an eye on her, couldn't risk letting her get free. She was the one who'd almost escaped the last time he took her from the house....

Something was wrong. Latisha could feel it deep inside. This wasn't Wesley's normal behavior....

After what seemed like an hour, maybe two, Latisha couldn't take another minute of not knowing. Maybe he'd kill her for it, but she had to call out again, had to find out if Marcie was okay. "Wesley? You there?"

Finally, he approached. There was a click, then the

hinges of the door whined as he pushed it inward. "You awake?" he asked.

The lightness of his tone told her he was pretending he hadn't heard her yell before. Latisha could tell he had, but she didn't bring it up. She was still trying to figure out what had changed. He had thick razor stubble on his jaw and chin, and the lines around his eyes and mouth were more pronounced than usual. Obviously, he'd been up all night. But why?

Glad she'd caught him before he fell asleep and left her chained up even longer, she sent him a tentative smile. "My—my head's killing me. C-can you let me up?"

"Sure. Then I'll get you some painkillers." He bent immediately to release her.

Could he see the tracks of her tears? Latisha wondered. Did he care? Her pain had never mattered to him before. But he was different today, nicer....

"Where's Marcie?" she asked.

He smiled as he finished with her hands and turned his attention to her feet. "I let her go."

"You did?" Latisha could hardly believe it. Her hands were swollen. They burned as the blood flowed back into them, but she didn't care. Not if what he said was true. *"Really?"*

"I told you I would, didn't I?" he said proudly. "You gave me what I wanted, and I returned the favor."

Latisha studied him more closely. She *wanted* to believe him, but what he said just seemed so...odd. He'd been worried they'd get free. Why would he suddenly let Marcie go?

"How'd you do it?" she asked uncertainly.

He shrugged. "Just dumped her on a street corner. I imagine she's home by now."

Latisha grasped for some hope in his words. If her sister had escaped, then a part of her had, too. There was also the hope that Marcie would bring help. But if Wesley had let Marcie go, wouldn't he be scared that she'd tell? Wouldn't he at least act worried? Or maybe start packing up and moving them somewhere else?

"She doesn't know where this place is," he said as if he could read her mind. "It's not like she'd ever be able to lead anyone here."

The crazy thing was, for all his fear that they might expose him, that was probably true. The day he'd kidnapped them, he'd tossed them in his van and cuffed them to a bar welded onto the floor. They couldn't see anything, and they'd been completely overwhelmed and confused, wondering why a police officer, even an undercover officer, would be acting in such a bizarre way. Latisha knew they were out in the country somewhere, but that was all.

Could she trust that he'd really let Marcie go?

His smile promised she could. Now alone and more frightened than ever, she so wanted to trust him.

"I'll get you some Tylenol."

He brought her two tablets. Then he freed her from her makeshift prison to clean the house. Movement was difficult at first, but once the pain in her hands went away, she began to feel encouraged. Maybe she wasn't at home, but her sister was, she told herself. Picturing Marcie falling into Gloria's arms made her so happy....

But while she stood at the window in Wesley's room looking out at the backyard, she saw the barrel that'd been the source of that burning smell. There were still wisps of smoke rising from it.

Getting as close to the glass as possible, she tried to determine what, exactly, he'd destroyed. He'd never started a fire before. He must've had a reason. What was it?

It could be anything. He was sick, weird. But that was partly what concerned her so much.

Turning, she went back to cleaning his room. But it wasn't long before she came across the shoes he'd worn last night and concern turned to panic. She picked them up from where he'd kicked them off and was about to place them in his closet when she spotted several flecks of a dark brown substance spattered near the sole.

Licking her finger, she rubbed one of the droplets. It smeared into a red blur that looked just like—she gulped—*blood.*

Then it dawned on her what Wesley might have been burning in that barrel. Was it the clothes he'd worn last night? She didn't see them in the room. Maybe they were so soaked with blood he hadn't wanted her to see them—or hadn't wanted to deal with washing them.

But if he'd burned his clothes, why hadn't he burned his shoes?

Because he had fewer shoes. Because he liked this particular pair. Because he didn't see the blood or thought he could wash it off. There could be a lot of reasons. But if he'd really let Marcie go, why would he need to burn anything?

"You just about done in here?"

Trying to see through the blur of tears, she tossed his

shoes into the closet and leaned down to straighten the bedding so he wouldn't see her eyes. "Almost."

"I've decided to move you in here with me." He said it as if she should be happy about it. She wouldn't have minded so much if she thought Marcie was really at home with Gloria. But Marcie wasn't. She was dead, and Latisha knew that if she didn't do something to save herself, she'd be next.

Nineteen

Jane perched on the couch beside Gloria. With only one bedroom, one bathroom and a tiny kitchen and living room, the apartment was cramped. Bookshelves made of planks and cinder block, spray-painted light blue, took up one whole wall. Each piece of tattered furniture bumped up against another, and cheap knickknacks cluttered most horizontal surfaces. But overall it was more of an organized mess than a disorganized one.

The smell of grilled onions permeated the apartment. After the blood she'd seen in Sebastian's backseat, the thought of food made Jane nauseous. But it was easier to focus on the sights and scents surrounding her than on Gloria, who was crying in her embrace. It had been hard enough to tell her that Marcie was dead, but it was even worse to say that her body had been found in Sebastian's car and her own parking lot. Fortunately, that didn't seem to make her blame Jane, but she was still brokenhearted.

"I was afraid of this," she cried. "I been livin' in fear

for weeks. But I never really believed it.... *Why Marcie?* Why *my* sister?"

Jane continued to pat and rub her broad back. She had no answers. She only knew that Gloria's sisters had been in the wrong place at the wrong time and, despite her best efforts and those of the police, Marcie was dead.

She prayed that Latisha wouldn't meet the same fate but couldn't help wondering if she already had.

Regardless of what happened in the future, she'd see Malcolm Turner behind bars if she had to dedicate the rest of her life to it. For Marcie. For Latisha. For Gloria. For Sebastian, too. But also for herself. Finding Malcolm had become a way to banish Oliver's ghost. She finally had the chance to defeat a man who was just as bad as the one who'd nearly killed her. She'd strike back.

"I'm so sorry." Even as she said it, she realized that phrase was inadequate, but she had nothing better to offer. David was still processing the crime scene. He'd be arriving shortly, but they'd talked and decided it might be easier on Gloria if Jane visited ahead of him—to break the news. Sebastian was giving the police a statement. Since Marcie's body had been found in his rental car, they had some questions for him.

"I can't live without her," Gloria wailed. "I can't do it."

Using her free hand, Jane wiped the tears sliding down her own cheeks. "You can, and you will," she said. "I'll help you."

"And what about Latisha? She probably dead, too."

Jane couldn't promise otherwise. While she was searching for words that might comfort Gloria without giving false hope, the door swung open so hard it banged against the inside wall. Even Gloria jumped.

She calmed the minute she realized it was Luther, but Jane grew that much more uneasy.

"What do ya know." A gust of wind whipped into the apartment along with him. "It's the charity worker who's too good to return my calls."

Jane had meant to call him. She'd told Jonathan she would. But, reluctant to deal with the force of his personality, she'd put it off. "The messages you left for me didn't deserve a response," she said. She couldn't let him know he frightened her. That would only encourage him to continue behaving the way he was.

"Because I'm not some white dude in a suit? Because I don't have the money to make a donation to the cause?"

Letting her arm slide away from Gloria, Jane stood. "Because your messages were antagonistic and abusive."

"My *messages* were abusive?" he scoffed with a laugh. "Bitch, you don't know what the word means until you've lived in *my* world."

"Luther, stop." If Gloria was intimidated by Latisha's father, she didn't show it. But, at the moment, she probably didn't care a whole lot about her own welfare. She sounded fatalistic and just plain exhausted. "*She* ain't the problem. Marcie's *dead*. You hear what I'm sayin'? Dead. And you come in here cussin' at the one person tryin' to help us. What's the matter with you?"

Luther's bloodshot eyes had widened at the word *dead.* Jane was pretty sure his brain hadn't registered much beyond that. "What'd you say?"

"Marcie's dead," she repeated numbly. "They found her body this mornin'."

His nostrils flared. "What about Latisha?"

"She probably dead, too." Gloria began to rock back and forth. "They both gone. Oh, God! How could this happen?"

The news seemed to sap his strength as well as his anger. Slumping onto a kitchen chair that looked too small to hold him, he bowed his head. "It's a bad cop," he said to the floor. "I know it is. That's what I been tryin' to tell ya. It's a bad cop who done it."

Because of Luther's arrival, Jane had been hoping to make a quick exit. She'd been planning to grab her purse and her briefcase and go, but this gave her pause. She'd heard about Malcolm Turner's background, guessed that he might've used a cop light or something similar to pull the girls over, but she hadn't shared that information with Gloria, so Gloria couldn't have passed it along to Luther. "How do you know?" she asked.

"Word on the street."

"Which comes from where exactly?"

"Some of the hos on Stockton Boulevard."

"Prostitutes?"

He didn't answer.

"They're familiar with Wesley Boss?" she persisted. "They've seen him?"

"A man's been comin' 'round the past few months, flashin' a badge. Won't give a full name but says they can call him Officer Boss. Likes to rough 'em up a bit, make a few threats, but if they do him for free, he leaves 'em alone. Makes sense, doesn't it? Marcie and Latisha stopped because they thought they were gettin' pulled over."

She should've provided Luther with a photograph.

But she'd avoided him rather than including him. "Has anyone described to you what this man looks like?"

"Short, stocky and *white*," he said pointedly.

Ignoring his emphasis on race, Jane pulled Malcolm's photograph from her briefcase and handed it to him.

Gloria studied it while he did, but it was his rapt attention that held Jane's focus. She could sense his desire to make Malcolm Turner pay for what he'd done to Marcie. "This him?"

"That's him," she said. "Do you know when it was that the cop named Officer Boss was last seen?"

He didn't bother asking Gloria if she was finished looking before he folded the photograph and put it in his coat pocket. Jane had planned to give it to him but even if she hadn't, she wouldn't be getting it back. "Been a while, far as I can tell—more'n three weeks."

"He's been busy since he took Marcie and Latisha."

"Strange thing is, the girls on the street, they say he only like white women. He won't touch nothin' else." He pinned her with his angry eyes. "So what's he want with Latisha and Marcie?"

"Maybe it's not about sex."

"It's always about sex," he said. "What else a man want with a woman? You think he wants to put up with all that bitchin' and whinin' for nothin'?"

Jane was so offended by what he said that she almost told him to go to hell. But Gloria kept the conversation on track. "Then why would he take 'em?" she asked.

"For companionship, to feel powerful, because they were easy marks," Jane said. "Or maybe he has it in for minorities and is on some sort of power trip, trying to 'cleanse' the world of certain races. I can't say. Some people hate just for the sake of hating." She shifted her focus to Luther. He was one of those people, but she knew he didn't see himself that way. To him, it was everyone else who was at fault. "If he comes around again, you have to let me know."

His large hands dangled between his knees. "What makes you think he'll be back?"

"There's always a chance. I'm guessing it's what he does for entertainment." When he wasn't gambling, anyway. "He'll return when he gets lonely or bored."

"He come around again, I gonna kill 'em, and that's a promise." Luther got up and started for the door, but she grabbed his arm. When he jerked out of her grasp, she realized she should've kept her hands to herself, but she refused to cower at the threat he posed.

"If you kill him, we might never find Latisha," she said. "You *have* to call me so I can bring the police, or call the police directly, if you prefer."

"He *is* the police," he said and stalked out.

Now that he was thinking clearly, Malcolm wished he'd dumped Marcie's body somewhere else. He didn't regret killing her, but he regretted revealing the fact that he knew where Sebastian lived. But when he'd worked his way around to the front and seen Sebastian arrive at Mary's house, when he'd witnessed the man he hated more than any other sweep her into a hug, he'd grown so livid he could barely breathe. He'd had to strike back, especially when Sebastian disappeared before Malcolm could get close enough to see which condo was his. By then it was so close to daybreak, he couldn't search without considerably raising the chances of being seen.

Now, because of his own impetuous actions, Sebastian knew he had to keep his guard up. But there'd been no other way for Malcolm to vent his rage. At least he'd taken something for what had been stolen from him. At least he had the satisfaction of knowing how horrified Sebastian must've been to find an innocent young woman dead in the backseat of his fancy-ass car. Sebastian had to live with the knowledge that his involvement had cost another life—at any rate, he had to live with it until Malcolm killed him, too.

Malcolm booted up his computer and waited for it to run through its opening sequence. He wasn't in a bad position. The chance he'd taken hanging around long enough to follow Sebastian home had paid off. He knew where the bastard lived, didn't he? It was only a matter of finding the right opportunity.

"What do you want for dinner?"

Glancing up, he saw Latisha watching him from over by the sink and shoved away from the table. As eager as he was to check his e-mail—he hoped he'd receive *some* sort of response from Sebastian or Mary, some hint of Sebastian's devastation—he needed to give Latisha some attention first. Ever since he'd returned without her sister, she'd been acting more afraid of him than ever. He wasn't sure she believed he'd let Marcie go....

"I don't know. What do *you* want?" he asked.

Her gaze dropped to the floor. "We don't have a lot of groceries."

Because of her sister, he hadn't been able to shop when he needed to. That bitch had deserved to die. She'd been disgusting and vile, and he was glad to be rid of her. But he felt sorry for Latisha, who was sweet and willing to compromise. After putting a combination lock on his bedroom door, he'd pulled her into bed with him and slept for most of the day. When they woke up, she didn't even try to fight him when he wanted to make love, but she'd gotten sick right afterward. She'd been vomiting in the bathroom ever since. She claimed it was just a flu bug, but she flinched whenever he touched her.

Would he have to kill her, too? He hoped not. He'd rather kill Mary and Sebastian and take Latisha away with him. She provided a lot—housework, sex, companionship. And without Marcie to collaborate with her, she wouldn't be as much of a threat to him. Maybe, over time, she'd settle in and he wouldn't have to chain her up when he left the house. Hell, maybe he could even take her out with him. In law enforcement, he'd seen kidnap victims develop an affinity for their captors. It might be weird, but it was part of human beings' ability to adapt.

He just had to make sure she didn't see anything about her sister's murder on the news. He'd kept the TV off all day just in case.

"What's your favorite meal?" he asked, feeling generous.

"*My* favorite?" she echoed.

"Yeah, what would you eat if you could have any-thing?"

She shrugged.

"Come on, price doesn't matter," he told her. "I can give you whatever you want."

"I—I don't know," she mumbled.

She might be too sick to eat. But she'd need food later. She'd already gone twenty-four hours without a meal. No way did he want her losing any weight. Her body was just right—so perfect it had probably spoiled him for anyone older.

"You're so pretty," he said.

This brought no response, but he imagined how flattered she was by the compliment and motioned her toward him. "Come sit on my lap."

She perched on his knee and stared at the floor, so innocent and sweet. Taking her chin, he turned her face toward his. "I'm going to buy you a present," he said. "Do you want to know what it is?"

"The chance to go home?" she asked softly.

It bothered Malcolm that she was still bugging him about letting her go, but she didn't understand how much better it was going to be now that he'd decided to make the most of what he had. "No, you'll be staying with me from now on. But if I can trust you, it'll get easier. I promise." He studied her high cheekbones and almond-shaped eyes. "Maybe I'll even marry you," he said.

Confusion drew her eyebrows together. "Why would you do that?"

He winked at her. "Because I'm falling in love."

Her eyes filled with tears.

"Don't cry," he whispered and kissed her cheeks, her nose, her mouth.

She pulled back enough to meet his eyes. "Did you kill Marcie?" she asked.

He was tempted to tell her the truth and get it over with, but he knew he never could. It would only come between them if he did—like that one indiscretion when he'd cheated on Mary in high school. He had to make

Latisha believe he'd let Marcie go, and the only way to do that was to remain adamant. "Of course not. I wouldn't do that to you, sweetheart."

Pressing her head against his shoulder, he rocked her until she fell asleep in his arms. Then he carried her into the bedroom and returned to his computer.

There were no messages from Sebastian. But his bookie had written him three times. He'd lost the bet he'd placed on the Boston game last night, and now his bookie wanted him to pay up.

Shit. Where was he going to get the money?

Wendy's car was parked in the driveway.

Jane sat in her own vehicle at the curb of the Burkes' house, her eyes on her sister-in-law's minivan. Because of what had happened to Marcie, she'd asked Betty to get Kate from school so she could work longer, but it hadn't occurred to her she'd have to face Wendy when she came to pick her up.

"I hate this," she muttered. It had already been a terrible day. The memory of Marcie's blood in the backseat of Sebastian's car would be forever etched in her brain—along with the expression on Gloria's face when she heard the news. Now she knew why Skye and Sheridan made such an effort to shield her. Their work was *hard*. Besides her distress over today's sad event, Jane had no idea what Luther was going to do, whether or not he'd cooperate if he came across Malcolm. She was afraid he'd get himself killed. Luther was formidable, but Malcolm used to be a cop, and he was sneaky, like Oliver had been. As far as Jane was concerned, that made Malcolm more dangerous than an

angry pimp with pit bulls. He was certainly no one to
trifle with.

Cold air was seeping into the interior of the car. Jane
pulled her coat around her, but she knew there was no
point in delaying further. If she wanted her daughter, she
had to go in. "Just what I need," she grumbled and
scooped up her purse before getting out.

Her heels clicked on the pavement as she approached
the house. Seeing her father-in-law through the front
window, sitting in his favorite recliner, and her mother-
in-law bringing him a plate of food, reminded her of the
night Noah had called his family together, in that very
room, to air his confession. He hadn't even warned Jane
that he was about to expose her....

Oliver had soon joined that meeting, and he had not
been as forgiving as Noah had hoped.

The betrayal she'd experienced overwhelmed Jane
again. As much as she'd loved and admired Noah, as
much as he'd helped her get through those difficult years
when Oliver was in prison, he'd failed her in the end. But
he'd been under the false assumption that Oliver was
innocent. She'd been equally convinced, so convinced
she couldn't even hold it against Noah. Besides, maybe
it *was* all her fault, like Wendy believed. Maybe she'd purposely set out to seduce him. She didn't think so, but she'd
been so desperate, maybe she was capable of anything.

Cringing at the memories she usually avoided—and
her role in what had taken place—she threw back her
shoulders and let herself into the house. "Hi."

Her father-in-law twisted around to see who'd just
arrived. "Janey!" He didn't get up. He knew she'd come
over to give him a hug. "How's my girl?"

She was terrible, a wreck. She hadn't felt so on edge since the whole ordeal with Oliver. Maybe that was why she was thinking of her husband so often these days. Getting involved with Sebastian made her feel out of control. It also made her wonder if she was as bad as Wendy thought. She hadn't been able to deny herself the pleasure Sebastian promised. She'd gone to his motel room not once, but twice. She'd even welcomed him into her bed.

"I'm fine," she said with a smile.

Wendy entered the room, carrying a glass of soda for Maurice. Her step faltered when she saw Jane, but in less than a split second she continued as if Jane wasn't even there. "Here you go, Papa. It's the last of the ginger ale, but I can get you some more tomorrow."

"Don't worry about it," he said. "Betty and I need to do some shopping, anyway."

"Hello, Wendy," Jane said.

As usual, Wendy pretended not to have heard the greeting. Calling her children, she located her purse and got out her keys. "I'd better run. I'll call you tomorrow, Papa. Tell Mom I said goodbye."

Maurice scowled. "You're going already?"

Wendy shot Jane an accusatory glance. "I have stuff to do."

"But it's only been fifteen minutes since you got here," he argued. "And Janey's with us now."

Jane wished Maurice wouldn't try to convince her to stay. He knew she was leaving *because* "Janey" was here. She always left. But he couldn't accept it. He had to try and patch things up between them. Betty did the same.

"There's no need for you to go. I'll only be a second," Jane said.

Wendy wouldn't acknowledge this, either, but Jane felt Wendy had more of a right to be here than she did. She was exhausted, anyway. She needed to get home, grab a quick bite and fall into bed.

"You're going, too?" Maurice complained.

"It's been a long day," she said. "Where's Kate?"

"On the computer. She's researching stem cells for a science paper."

"Jane, is that you?" Betty poked her head out of the kitchen.

"Sorry, I'm late," Jane said. "Work was crazy."

"Everything okay?"

"Of course. Just more of the same." It was another lie, but she didn't want to go into detail, especially with Wendy in the room. Why give her sister-in-law the opportunity to gloat over her difficulties? Jane usually believed she deserved that, too, but she felt too raw inside to tolerate it tonight. "I might have more work to do before bed," she said. "I'm just here to get Kate."

"If you're that pressed for time, we could've brought her home," Betty said. "I thought maybe you'd let me warm you up some dinner."

Jane was tempted. Especially when Wendy kissed Betty goodbye and headed out the door. Her three children followed, all but the oldest mumbling hello and goodbye. Wendy had managed to poison Rusty against her. The accusation in his eyes sometimes hurt more than having Wendy ignore her.

"You've already been a big help," she told her mother-in-law. "And I really appreciate it."

Kate must've heard her voice because she came down the hall without having to be called. "Hi, Mom! You staying to eat or should I grab my backpack?"

"Unfortunately, we've got to go."

"Okay."

Jane smiled at Betty and Maurice as she waited. She could tell they had something on their minds, but she wasn't sure she wanted to discuss anything weighty. She felt too fragile.

"It wasn't your fault, you know," Betty murmured.

Jane didn't need to ask what she was talking about. Betty was referring to what had caused the rift between her and Wendy. "It *was* my fault," she said.

Her mother-in-law's eyes filled with sympathy. "You were going through so much. Can't you be a little easier on yourself, Jane?"

"I knew it was wrong." She just hadn't been able to stop herself. She'd needed to feel loved and protected, which wasn't bad in itself. It was putting those needs ahead of Noah's family that had been unforgivable.

"It's in the past, Jane."

She gave Betty a slight nod to acknowledge the kindness of that statement but said a silent prayer of relief at Kate's sudden reappearance. She was feeling guilty again because she hadn't done any better with Sebastian, even though she'd promised herself she'd keep her desires firmly in check. "You ready, kiddo?"

Kate slung her backpack over her shoulder. "All set."

"Thanks again," Jane told her in-laws.

She felt better once they reached the privacy of their own car. As usual, Kate was full of chatter about school, her girlfriends and her teachers—even the cute boy she liked in her second-period class. As Jane embraced their everyday routine, she all but forgot about her uncomfortable run-in with Wendy. But she tensed up again when she pulled into her parking lot and saw Sebastian, leaning against a new rental car—a Pontiac—while talking on his cell phone. She wasn't sure what he wanted, but she was fairly sure she wouldn't want to discuss it in front of Kate. She needed to keep her daughter separated from the ugliness that had overtaken her work.

Spotting her immediately, he finished his conversation and hung up. Then he walked over.

Twenty

With long dark hair and clear brown eyes, Kate was almost as pretty as her mother. Sebastian couldn't help smiling as she looked up at him, her expression tinged with surprise when she realized he wasn't just a friendly stranger.

Jane seemed less pleased to see him. Sebastian noted the way she stiffened, and understood that she preferred not to allow home and work to mix.

"Go on in, honey," she said to Kate as soon as he reached them. "I'll be right there."

Too curious to do what she'd been told, Kate hovered at her mother's side. "Can't I wait for you?"

"I have some business to take care of," Jane insisted. "Give us a minute."

Kate's narrow shoulders slumped in disappointment. "O-kay," she said and, with an exaggerated sigh, started past him, but Sebastian stuck out his hand.

"You must be Kate."

Her face brightened. "Yes."

"I'm Sebastian Costas, a friend of your mother's."

"A work associate," Jane clarified.

Kate placed her small hand in his. "Are you part of The Last Stand?"

"More or less. For the time being," he hedged.

"It's nice to meet you."

Impressed by the sweetness she put into a saying that'd become so trite, he winked at her. "It's nice to meet you, too." He'd been curious about this part of Jane's life, the part that meant more to her than anything else. "I can already tell you're going to be a beauty, like your mother."

Ducking her head, Kate blushed and mumbled a shy "Thank you."

"Go on now," Jane prompted.

Her feet dragging, Kate headed to the condo but threw one last glance over her shoulder.

The caution that lurked in Jane's eyes eased once her daughter was out of earshot.

"That wasn't so bad, was it?" he asked.

"I never said it would be *bad.* It was just...pointless."

He folded his arms. "I'll try not to be offended by that."

"I don't want her to know we...we're anything but what I told her."

"Work associates."

"That's right."

"Why?" he demanded.

"I told you, I haven't even been on a date since her father was killed. She might find it—I don't know—threatening. Frightening."

The man who'd found Marcie's body was out walking his dog. Hoping the sight of Jane wouldn't draw him over, he lowered his voice. "Unless you plan to spend the rest of your life alone, you've got to start somewhere."

"Yeah, well, jumping into bed with someone I barely know isn't the way to do it," she said. "I think we're both conscious of that."

It was true. Under the circumstances, they had no business getting so intimately involved. So why had he wanted to see her again this soon? "Every relationship begins in a different place," he said.

"It doesn't matter where we began. We both know where this will end."

He scowled. "We don't know anything. Life isn't something you can script, Jane. It's full of surprises, and those surprises can change everything." Look at what had happened to him. Never in a million years would he have guessed he'd walk away from his lucrative and rewarding career to chase down Emily's husband for killing her and Colton. Never had he thought he'd crave another child, especially with a woman he hardly knew. "Speaking of surprises that can change everything...would you like me to pick up one of those pregnancy tests?"

"No. I—I'll deal with it when I'm ready."

"It might be better to know."

"And it might not. If I miss my period, then we'll worry."

He nodded. "Okay, but I didn't actually come to talk about pregnancy tests. And, much as I liked getting to see Kate, I didn't come to meet her, either. I came because the two of you can't stay here, not by yourselves."

She shifted her briefcase to her other hand. "What are you talking about? I live here."

"Malcolm associates this place with me. He'll come back. And if he thinks I care about you, he'll…" He didn't finish. There was no need to spell it out. She knew what Malcolm was capable of. She'd witnessed it this morning.

"He'd be crazy to come back," she said.

"Why?"

"Because he could get caught!"

"You don't understand. He'll take those risks. This thing between him and me—" he shoved a hand through his hair " it's become very personal. He'll do whatever he can to get back at me."

"And that includes killing me."

"I'm not positive he even knows about you. You weren't in the car with me when I came here. But he'll watch this place, search for whatever he can find that might lead him to me."

"Why isn't he scared? Why doesn't he run, get out of here before he's arrested?"

She didn't know Malcolm the way he did. "He beat the system once. I'm sure he believes he can do it again."

"And you're relieved instead of worried."

"Like I said, I want to end this."

She glanced around the parking lot as if their surroundings had somehow changed, but she'd felt safe here and didn't want to let go of that. "How can you be so positive that's what he wants?"

With a sigh, Sebastian pulled out the e-mail message he'd printed an hour ago and handed it to her.

Jane set her briefcase on the pavement and unfolded the paper. "It's from M.T."

He nodded. "Malcolm Turner."

"'It's you or me, prick,'" she read, then glanced up at him. "He's calling you out?"

"He's telling me this won't be over until one of us is dead."

"Where did this come from? Can we have David trace it?"

"It would be a waste of time. I've already had the ones he sent to Mary traced. He's using a remote server."

She gave the paper back to him. "How is Mary?"

"Pretty shaken up, but I was able to convince her to take the boys and go to Phoenix for a week or two. They're staying with her aunt."

"He won't try to follow her there…."

"Not if I draw his fire, make myself an easier target."

"Target?" The blood drained from her face. "You don't have to do that, Sebastian. The police will handle this."

"Like they handled it before?" he asked.

"We're talking about David this time. He'll listen to us. As a matter of fact, I just talked to him. Someone else is going to finish the case that's been taking up so much of his time. This is now his only priority. Forensic technicians are already processing your car. And Marcie's body is scheduled to be autopsied tomorrow. Maybe they'll find some sort of evidence."

"They won't find anything. He was a cop, Jane. He knows what they'll be looking for." He scratched his face. "Besides, this will come to a head long before any of that can help."

She hugged herself against the cold. "So what do we do?"

"Tonight? Get some sleep. I think we might need it."

"Where?" she asked.

"At my motel. Unless you want me to stay here. I'm not leaving you alone."

Bowing her head, she nodded. "What do I tell her?"

"That I'm a coworker who's down on his luck and needs a place to stay."

"Just for tonight?"

"Until I feel comfortable that you're safe on your own."

"That could be a week or more!"

He grinned at her. "What's the matter? Afraid you won't be able to resist me for that long?" He was teasing, trying to cheer her up, but when she answered, he could tell she was absolutely serious.

"Yes."

Why hadn't he responded? Malcolm knew Sebastian *had* to have checked his e-mail, had to have received the message. He'd gone to the trouble of taking Latisha to that Internet café. The least Sebastian could do was acknowledge receipt. Malcolm wanted to know how it had affected him, what he'd felt when he found Marcie murdered in his backseat. The silence, not knowing, was driving him mad. He was tempted to cruise past Mary's house or Sebastian's condominium complex to see what was going on. But he couldn't; he had to lie low, until he could devise a way to get close without getting caught.

He glanced at the clock on his computer. It was after midnight, but he couldn't sleep. Not with his mind whirring away like this, and not after spending most of the day in bed, catching up on the sleep he'd missed last night.

Where was Sebastian? Did he live alone in that condo? How long had he been in Sacramento?

Malcolm had called Constance's office. She was still

in New York. So did that mean Sebastian was now with Mary? Was he making love to her this very minute?

The thought of them together made Malcolm clench his jaw. It was one thing to turn Mary against him, another to do it so completely that she became Sebastian's lover. After what he'd done to her in high school—*once a cheater, always a cheater*—she probably saw it as the ultimate irony to take this sort of revenge. But he didn't find it the least amusing.

Using a prepaid cell phone he'd picked up a few hours ago, he called Constance. It was three hours later in New York, which made it almost 3:25 a.m. She didn't answer, but he left a message. "Your lover boy is sleeping with my old girlfriend. Just thought you might like to know," he said and hung up. He enjoyed thinking that might hurt her, or get Sebastian in trouble if they were still together, but it wasn't enough. A few seconds later, he considered calling Sebastian directly. Chances were Sebastian hadn't changed his number. Why would he?

"Is something wrong?"

Latisha had come up behind him. He was allowing her as much freedom as possible tonight, partly to make up for what he'd done to her sister and partly to convince her how good it could be between them if he could trust her. Today he'd taken her to the mall, and bought her some clothes that actually fit and a ring. It wasn't an expensive ring, but she kept staring at the little diamond as if it was the most beautiful gift she'd ever received.

He'd told her that he hoped to marry her someday. Women loved that shit. If he could get her to care about him, even a little bit, he wouldn't have to worry about her trying to get away every second his back was turned. "Nothing's wrong," he said. "I just have a lot of nervous energy."

"Do you want me to make you something to eat?"

He pulled her onto his knee so he could fondle her breast. "I'm not hungry." He grinned at her. "Why don't we get some cooking oil and go back to the bedroom?"

"Cooking oil?" she echoed.

"I think it's time I gave you a massage."

"I've never had a massage."

"Then you're in for a treat."

She gazed at her ring. "Did you mean what you said earlier?"

"When I told you how I feel about you?"

She nodded.

"Of course." Letting go of her breast, he took her hand instead. "I know what I did was wrong, Latisha. I know I shouldn't have forced you and Marcie to come back here with me. And I'm sorry I didn't treat you right once I got you out here."

"So why'd you do it?" she murmured.

"I was lonely. Sometimes I get so…angry at the world. If you knew what'd happened to me, you'd understand." He bowed his head as if the weight of the past was too heavy to bear.

"Tell me," she said.

To give her the impression he could barely stand to talk about it, he pretended to choke up. "Someone killed my wife and kid when I was living back east."

Sympathy brought her eyebrows together as she bent her head to see into his face. *"How?"*

"It was a guy I put in prison, a guy named Sebastian

Costas. When he got out, he came for revenge. I've been hunting him ever since."

"I'm sorry," she whispered.

He rested his forehead on her shoulder. "So am I."

"Then you're not on the force anymore?"

"That's why I quit—to chase him down." He kissed the back of her hand. "And when I saw you and Marcie in that car, I guess I just...snapped. Other people are out there living normal lives, but here I am without the two people I loved more than anything. I decided to change my situation, to force it to be more like what I wanted."

"You can't force it," she said, but her words were more earnest than judgmental.

"I know, and I would've realized it if I hadn't been working on so little sleep. I'd been up all night, following another false lead and wasn't thinking straight. Then, after I'd taken you, I couldn't see how I could let you go without winding up in prison myself." He paused for impact before continuing. "It didn't seem fair, you know? That I could've made my life worse by trying to make it better." He shook his head. "Until recently, I was so depressed and angry at myself nothing else seemed to matter. I was actually thinking of killing us all. That's what I had in mind when I came to your room with that gun. But then—" he cupped the right side of her face with one hand "—then there was you."

"*Me?*"

"You brought me fresh hope, made me want to live a good life again."

She seemed confused. "But what about Marcie?"

"That's why I let her go, babe. I realized I had to do

it, no matter what happened to me. I couldn't bring myself to do anything else, mostly because it would hurt *you.*"

She stared at his fingers as he drew designs on her forearm. "Why didn't you let me go, too?"

"Because it would break my heart to lose you. You're the first person I've cared about since my wife."

She turned the ring he'd given her around and around on her slim finger. "Does that mean I can go— if I want to?"

This was a test. Malcolm recognized that immediately and dropped his hand so she'd feel no restraint. "I was hoping you'd stay long enough to let me prove what I'm really like. But if you want to go, I won't stop you."

She stood and glanced at the door.

Don't do it, he chanted in his head. If she did, he'd have to drag her back and force her to resume the way they'd been—or kill her. He preferred the more pleasant version of the life he'd begun to envision.

"You want me to stay?" she asked, fiddling with the hem of her T-shirt.

"You're my hope for the future. Once I catch the bastard who killed my family, I can provide everything a cop's wife deserves—a nice house, babies, anything you want. Give me two weeks. That's all I ask."

"Can I call home?"

"No. You know what Marcie would do. She hates me. She'd tell you to leave me. She'd try to get me in trouble."

"I just want to let my other sister know I'm okay."

He searched for an excuse and came up with a solution instead. "Does she have a computer?"

"It's an old hand-me-down her boss gave her, but she can do e-mail."

"Perfect." He slid his laptop over to her and watched as she logged in to an e-mail program and typed a brief message.

Gloria—
Don't worry about me. I'm safe. I'll be fine and will be in touch in two weeks. Until then, take care of yourself and be happy.
I love you—
Latisha

The tormented expression on her face made Malcolm fear she might change her mind. She was missing her sister, missing home.

"Just two weeks?" she said.

"Just two weeks," he promised. "That's nothing, right?"

She drew a deep breath. "Okay."

He squeezed her affectionately and nuzzled her neck. "And now it's time for that massage I promised you." Determined to win her over, he carried her into the bedroom.

While Jane was trying to convince her daughter to get ready for bed, Kate kept disappearing into the living room to take another peek at Sebastian. She loved the excitement of having male company and kept asking if Jane thought he was handsome.

Jane did her best to act indifferent, but she was even more aware of the man watching TV on her couch than Kate was.

When she finally managed to get her daughter into

bed, she carried out some blankets and a pillow for Sebastian and piled them on a side chair.

He muted the television. "How're you holding up?"

"I'm fine." He had his computer on his lap. She waved toward it. "Any word from Mary?"

"Not yet. She's probably getting settled in Phoenix. I doubt she'll write or call me until tomorrow."

"Are you worried about her?"

"I feel bad for disrupting her life by getting her involved in all this, but…I think she'll be okay."

"I wish I could have that kind of confidence when it comes to Latisha."

Looking more tired than she'd seen him, he covered a yawn. "Have you talked to Gloria?"

"Not since I was over there." Jane felt she should call, but she didn't know what else she could say. Taking a deep breath, she patted the blankets. "Here's what you'll need for the night."

"Thanks."

"You're welcome." Their eyes met and the intimacy they'd already shared seemed to draw them together again. For a second, Jane wished Kate was still at her in-laws'. Sebastian felt like the best thing ever to have happened to her. She craved his taste, his smell, his touch—craved *him*. But Kate wasn't at the Burkes'. She was just down the hall.

"Okay. I'll see you in the morning," she said.

"Yeah. See you then." The volume went back up a little as he returned his attention to the TV.

Clenching her hands in determined fists, Jane

marched over to her bedroom, closed the door and got into bed, where she lay wide awake for what seemed like hours.

Although Sebastian had dozed off, he'd done it without the blankets Jane had left him. He hadn't even put away his computer. He was still sitting there with the TV on when he woke up at two.

He made himself a bed but couldn't go back to sleep. The macabre images of the day kept intruding—countered only by the more positive knowledge that Jane was just a room away.

He considered going to her. He wanted to lose himself in her warmth, feel her melt against him the way she had last night. Kate was asleep; she'd never know…. But Jane had made her wishes clear.

He hoped a shower might relax him, so he got up and went to take one.

Leaving the light off, he stripped, turned the water to hot and stood beneath the pulsing spray. He was trying to blank his mind, to force Emily, Colton, Mary, Malcolm and Jane—especially Jane—out of his thoughts. He was pretty sure it was working, until he heard the door open.

He could smell Jane's perfume. He hadn't locked the door. That had been a conscious decision, one he'd made with exactly this hope in mind. But when the door closed again, a click told him it was locked now.

Twenty-One

She was addicted to him. That was all there was to it. She couldn't continue to lie in bed, aching with need. She had to have him. And somehow the resistance she'd tried to summon but couldn't made the experience all the more intoxicating. Giving in had never felt so sweet.

The scrape of the shower curtain against the rod told Jane that Sebastian had heard her come in. In some deep recess of her brain, she hoped he'd send her back to her bed. This had to end somewhere, didn't it? If she wanted to get out of this affair unscathed, the sooner it ended the better. But he didn't rebuff her. She could sense his anticipation, feel him waiting for her approach.

Biting her lip, she wondered what she'd do on the off chance that Kate woke up and discovered them both missing from their beds. She'd tell her daughter that Sebastian had left and let Kate think she was in the bathroom alone, she decided. If Kate was older, she might doubt that, but not at twelve. Not when Jane had never had another man over.

They had to be quiet, though. *Very* quiet...

Assured that she had a way to protect her daughter from knowing too much, she slipped off her nightgown and dropped it on the floor. Steam billowed through the open curtain, so thick it felt like a thousand hands reaching out to curl around her.

Sebastian found her as soon as she stepped toward him and drew her against his slick, hard body. "There you are," he breathed in her ear. "I've been waiting for this since you brought me those damn blankets. What took you so long?"

The memory of Wendy's scorn. The hope that it wasn't too late to atone for her mistakes. The determination to do what was best for her daughter.

Clearly, she wasn't up to those challenges. But she'd already made love with Sebastian several times over the past two days. What would one more night matter?

"I wanted to do the right thing," she told him.

"I can't think of anything that feels more right than this," he said. Then his lips met hers in a breathless, frenzied kiss spurred on by the urgency rising in them both.

"You've got the Shield?"

"I'm ready." Her thoughts were somewhere in the stratosphere, but she'd hung on to that much of her sanity.

He licked away the water dripping from her left breast. "Smart girl," he whispered.

Minutes later, he lifted her onto him and she could think of nothing except the rasp of his labored breathing, the contraction of his muscles as he held her against the tile wall and that moment of ultimate ecstasy when he covered her mouth with his to capture her moan.

She didn't hold back with him anymore. She couldn't. She gave him everything she had, physically and emotionally. She knew that was why making love with him was so much better, so different, than before.

But she also knew that what made it different could swing back the other way—and hurt her more deeply than ever.

The next morning, Sebastian sat at the breakfast table with Kate while Jane stood at the stove, dressed for work in tailored pants and a starched white blouse, frying eggs. Kate already had her meal and was somehow managing to fork up her food and find her mouth without ever looking down at her plate. She had eyes only for him. Every time he glanced up, he found her watching him with rapt attention. He was beginning to wonder if she'd somehow caught on to the fact that he'd had sex with her mother last night. Maybe his smile was giving it away, or the fact that he still felt so aware of Jane as she cooked behind him.

"Are you married, Mr. Costas?" Kate asked.

"Call me Sebastian," he said. "And no, I'm not married."

"Do you have any children?"

"Kate, you need to finish your breakfast," Jane interjected from the stove. Sebastian wasn't sure if she was trying to protect him from having to say he no longer had children, or if she was trying to stop Kate from getting to know him. Maybe both.

"No. No kids, either," he said to keep it simple. After what Kate had been through, he didn't want her to hear what had happened to him. She had to be traumatized enough already.

"Oh." She drank the rest of her milk. A white mustache covered her upper lip when she put the glass down, but she quickly grabbed a napkin to wipe it off. She was beginning to cross the boundary between child and young woman, and he liked that stage, admired the innocence of it.

Jane brought him three eggs and some toast. He thanked her and began to eat.

Kate continued to stare. "Do you like kids?" she asked as her mother cracked more eggs into the frying pan.

"Kate—" Jane started, but he shook his head to indicate he'd answer.

"I like them very much."

"Even girls?" she asked hopefully.

Putting down his fork, he pretended to contemplate that question. "Yes," he said with a decisive nod. "Every bit as much as boys. Why?"

Her gaze slid away from him for the first time that morning. "I don't think my daddy liked girls."

Considering the scar on Jane's neck, Sebastian could understand how she might've arrived at that conclusion. "But that's not because of you. You understand that, right? Some people don't like anybody."

She toyed with what was left of her meal. "*Sometimes* he was nice."

Her confusion broke his heart. "It'd be easier if the people who hurt others came with a warning sign on their foreheads, don't you think?"

She giggled. "Yeah."

He picked up his fork and went back to his meal, but she wasn't finished speaking. "He killed my uncle," she said.

Sebastian could tell that Jane was dying to put a stop to the conversation, but he was grateful she had enough faith in him to let him handle it. "That's what I hear."

"And he stabbed my mom." She touched her neck. "Right here."

A wave of protectiveness swept through him. "I've seen the scar. That's very sad."

"She almost died."

"I'm glad she didn't."

"Me, too. But…I don't think my aunt Wendy's glad."

There was a clatter behind him. Sebastian turned to see that Jane had dropped her spatula. "Sorry," she muttered.

"Maybe she's confused about what really happened," he said to Kate.

"That's what I think. That's what my grandma says, too."

"Kate, concentrate on eating so you won't be late for school," Jane said.

"I'm full." Setting her knife and fork on her plate, she got up to carry everything to the counter.

"Then get your teeth brushed," her mother said.

Kate started to leave but paused at the hallway entrance to address him one more time. "You'd never hurt anyone, would you?" she asked.

The bite he'd been about to take hovered in midair. *"Never."*

Doubling back, she gave him an unexpected hug. He didn't even have the chance to put down his fork and hug her back. "I like you," she whispered before her mother could shoo her out of the kitchen.

Clearly embarrassed, Jane laughed. "Sorry about that."

"Sorry for what?" he asked.

"The questions, the fascination, the sudden affection. I'm sure it was a bit overwhelming."

It wasn't overwhelming; it was endearing. Kate's behavior reminded Sebastian of how quick children were to love, how quick to forgive, how much they wanted to trust adults, how much he missed his own child. "I don't mind."

"You're definitely a novelty around here."

Sebastian thought he heard his phone ringing in the living room. He paused to listen when Kate hurried in with it. "It's—" she checked his caller ID "—Constance Sherwood," she said as she handed it to him.

He would've let it go to voice mail, but she'd just announced that a woman was trying to reach him at seven in the morning. It would look odd if he didn't answer. "Thanks," he said and hit the talk button. "Hello?"

"Is it true?" Constance demanded.

He was aware of Jane collecting her car keys and her purse as he answered. "Is what true?"

"I got another call from Malcolm last night."

The tension Sebastian was so familiar with returned. "What'd he say?"

"That you've been sleeping with his ex-girlfriend."

Why would Malcolm bother to call Constance about that? Just to cause trouble? What a vindictive bastard. "That's a lie. He said the same thing about Emily, remember? He's insecure, paranoid."

"So you haven't been with her."

Jane stood at the front door, waiting for Kate to zip her backpack. He looked up to see if she was listening and saw her watching him. "I just told you I haven't."

"Is everything okay?" Jane asked.

Apparently, she could sense the change in him. To keep Constance from realizing he wasn't alone, so the conversation wouldn't deteriorate into a senseless argument, he nodded instead of speaking. But the suspicion in her next question indicated that she'd heard Jane's voice. "Have you been with *anyone?*"

Memories of Jane in the shower filled his mind, from the thrill that'd gone through him when he first heard the door, to the sweet taste of her mouth, to the warmth and softness of her beautiful body. She hadn't been timid last night. She was beginning to lower her guard, to feel comfortable with him—to ask for more, take more, give more. He liked that. A lot.

"Sebastian?" Connie repeated.

"Don't ask if you don't want to hear the answer," he said.

"That's a yes! Were you cheating on me the whole time? Have you met someone? Is that why you won't come home?"

She still didn't understand what was driving him, how the murders had affected him. Maybe she never would. "I can't come home until I find Malcolm. You know that. It hasn't changed."

"But you've met someone else, haven't you?"

He waved goodbye to Kate as she and Jane left the condo. Then he strode over to the window so he could see them get into the car. "Maybe."

The silence that followed was more deafening than Constance's customary rapid-fire questions.

"I'm sorry," he added. "I—it's my fault we fell apart, Connie. I'm just in a different place right now, and I can't find my way back."

"You haven't even tried," she complained.

"That's not true."

"Yes, it is. Come home to me. Come today."

He pinched the bridge of his nose in frustration. *"No."*

"Who is it?" she demanded. "Who are you seeing?"

"No one I've mentioned before. I just met her."

"You can't give me a name? We were together for six years and you can't respect me and my feelings enough to give me a name?"

Did they *have* to do this? "I don't want to hurt you even more by talking about another woman."

"Just tell me where you met her."

He rubbed a hand over his face. "She works for The Last Stand, okay? It's a victims' charity here in Sacramento. She's helping me search for Malcolm."

"So that's where I went wrong. I should've flown out there and proved my devotion by dedicating my life to your investigation."

He wanted to hang up, to silence her with the simple push of a button. But they'd been together for a long time, and as he'd told her, he felt the breakup was more his fault than hers. The least he could do was make sure it ended well. "Stop the sarcasm, Connie. I never expected you to fly out here. I'm not holding it against you that you didn't. Jane's been through a lot. I've been through a lot. We have some common ground. That's all. Somehow we...fit. At least for now."

"I was *such* a fool," she said.

He winced at the sob in her voice. "You weren't a fool."

"Anyone who loves you is a fool!" she spat and disconnected.

Sebastian shoved his phone in his pocket. "Shit!" He had so much adrenaline charging through him that it was fifteen minutes before he could settle down enough to think. Then, trying to forget that he'd just hurt the woman who'd been waiting for him for a year, he logged on to his computer.

There was another e-mail waiting for him—from Malcolm.

What? You don't have anything to say? You can't even respond?

Sebastian *wanted* to respond. He wanted to tell him to set Latisha free, but he knew it wouldn't do any good. Sebastian was also tempted to tell Malcolm what a sick son of a bitch he was for doing what he'd done to Marcie. But that would only let Malcolm know how squarely he'd hit his target, and Sebastian refused to give him that satisfaction.

Forgoing all the accusations and recriminations that churned in his head, he wrote the one thing that really mattered.

You said it all. It's you or me.

"Glib asshole," Malcolm muttered.

"What is it?" Latisha asked.

He glanced over at the table, where she was eating

the chocolate he'd purchased when they'd gone grocery shopping this morning. Latisha seemed to believe what he'd told her about the murder of his family. He supposed it didn't hurt that he'd been a cop. That provided him with a certain amount of credibility. But he hadn't expected to find her sympathy so irresistible. He was growing more and more certain that he wanted to keep her forever. "The man who killed my wife and son," he said. "He's answering the e-mail I sent him before we went to the store. He's taunting me."

"Why would he do that?"

"Because he thinks he can get away with it."

She seemed to consider his response. "What will you do when you catch up with him?"

Kill him like he deserved. But he couldn't say that. Not to Latisha. He was still trying to reassure her that he wasn't guilty of her sister's murder. Her youth and naiveté worked in his favor, but she was brighter than a lot of girls her age. "Make sure he goes to prison."

"It's so sad that no one believes you, that you can't convince the other officers that he's alive. You shouldn't have to do this all alone."

He smiled to himself. "DNA is powerful evidence." Lord, didn't he know it. "And unfortunately the DNA evidence suggests Sebastian's dead."

"You'll get him."

"Damn right I will."

"Are we still going to watch the movie we rented?" she asked.

Now that he no longer had a relationship with Mary, he had nothing better to do. He was just getting up from his chair when he got a new message. Pausing to check what had come in, he was surprised to see an e-mail from Constance.

If he'd ever doubted that Mary had been working with Sebastian, this was proof. Constance had the same e-mail address as before; he recognized it from the various communications they'd had regarding Colton. But his address was new, something he'd created after moving to Sacramento. She could only have gotten it from Mary through Sebastian.

"Damn her," he muttered, thinking about Mary. He'd expected so much more from her.

He clicked on the message and scanned the contents.

He's not sleeping with Mary. He's with a woman named Jane, a victims' advocate from a charity there in Sacramento called The Last Stand. It sounds as if she's helping him find you. It sounds as if they're close.

Confused, he read those lines again. "What? Why the hell would she tell *me* that?"

"Tell you what?" Latisha asked.

"Nothing." He considered the possibilities, but it didn't take long to decide on the most likely scenario. Sebastian had dumped the proud Constance Sherwood for another woman, and she wanted revenge.

What an unlikely ally. He couldn't help laughing at this fortuitous turn of events.

"Wes? What about the movie?" Latisha asked.

"Be there in a minute," he told her. "Go ahead and start it without me." Settling back in his chair, he opened his Internet browser and did a search for The Last Stand.

In seconds he had a picture of the building that

housed the charity, their mission statement and what he'd been looking for all along—their address. Now he just needed to figure out what he was going to do with Latisha while he was gone.

Rocking back, he glanced around the kitchen and spotted the sack of groceries they'd purchased, still sitting on the counter. Latisha had put away the perishable items, but there were a few things in the sack—one of which was a bottle of rum.

"How's the movie?" he called out.

"Good," she replied. "You done? You coming?"

Letting his computer hibernate, he poured them each a glass of rum and Coke. He wished he'd thought to drop by the Red Room Motel off Stockton Boulevard on their way home. He'd met a dealer there who'd give him a good price on some speed. That'd be quicker to use, more fun. But he was all out.

The alcohol would have to do.

"Want a drink?" He carried the glasses into the living room, then went back for the bottles.

Latisha watched him. "What's all this?"

"Rum and Coke."

"I've never had rum and Coke. Gloria doesn't let us drink."

"It doesn't hurt if you only do it once in a while." He handed her a glass. "Come on, I'm in the mood to celebrate."

"What are we celebrating?" she asked.

"You," he said. Then he toasted their upcoming marriage, his love for her, their odd meeting, her willingness to trust him, her forgiveness, her beauty. Before long, she was so drunk she could hardly stand up.

* * *

"Latisha's alive!" Gloria screeched.

It was late afternoon, but Jane had just arrived at the office. Dropping her purse and her briefcase on the floor in the reception area, she gripped the phone tighter. She'd expected a far different greeting when she'd answered this call. "How do you know?"

"I just got an e-mail from her."

"You're sure it's her?"

"It came from her account. She's the only one who'd know the password. It *has* to be her."

Jane didn't see how it could be anyone else. Not unless Latisha had shared her password. "I guess so." She *hoped* so. "What did she say?"

"She say she fine. She don't want me to worry 'bout her. She say she comin' home in two weeks."

The oddity of the message pierced through Jane's elation. "Two weeks? Did she mention how or why?"

"No."

What was going on? Malcolm couldn't afford to let Latisha go. If they ever caught him—and they would—she'd be a witness for the prosecution. "Did she give you any clue about her location or surroundings?"

"No," Gloria said, but the lack of answers didn't seem to dampen her relief and excitement. She wanted to believe what she'd read, wanted to believe it so badly she wouldn't look any deeper. "Hallelujah! She alive! She'll be comin' home soon."

Only if they found her before Malcolm killed her. He couldn't have let Latisha go or there'd be no two-week delay. And if she'd managed to get free on her own, why would she send an e-mail? Why wouldn't she just come home?

Something was up. "Have you called Detective Willis?"

"Not yet. I wanted to tell you first. I'm starin' at her message right now. I can't hardly believe it."

"Gloria, I..." She'd been about to explain why this message might not be a good thing. It wasn't fair to get Gloria's hopes up and then have them dashed in the cruelest possible way, which to Jane's mind was a greater possibility than Malcolm releasing Latisha on a specific day. But she couldn't bring herself to spoil Gloria's happiness. Besides, she didn't know everything. Maybe she was wrong.

"What?" Gloria said when she didn't continue.

"I want you to know that we do care."

"I know you do," she said. "That's why I called you."

"We'll find her before those two weeks are up," Jane said. "Detective Willis and several other officers are canvassing my neighborhood. Surely, someone saw *something*." Sebastian had been at the complex all morning, too, talking to anyone he could, but she figured there wasn't any reason to explain who Sebastian was. "I'm going back in a few minutes to help. I had to open the office for the volunteers who do telephone soliciting around dinnertime."

"Will you let me know what the police find?" Gloria asked.

"I will."

Jane had just hung up and was picking up her purse and briefcase when Jonathan let himself in. "Good, you're here."

"You've been looking for me?"

"That security guard over at Cache Creek called this morning to say he's found several images of your man."

They'd already established that Malcolm frequented the casino, but Jane wanted to see him in action. "Can we view those images?"

"He burned us a DVD of the segments that contain Malcolm."

"Great! I'll head over there right away."

"I already got it for you." He took it from his coat pocket and held it up for her to see.

"How nice!" she said.

"I figured you were pretty busy, what with your guest and all."

She narrowed her eyes. "How'd you know I have a guest?"

"After I got the message, I tried to call you and Kate answered. She said you were in the Quick Stop, picking up a snack for her lunch."

"I'm assuming that wasn't all she said."

He grinned. "No. She was pretty excited to report that you'd had a man stay the night. She seemed quite taken with him."

They must've been on their way to school. "She didn't tell me you called," Jane said.

"I told her not to worry about it, that I'd contact you later. Then I went to get the DVD myself."

Jane wondered how long it would be before Kate mentioned Sebastian to the Burkes—or Wendy. "Have you seen it?"

"Not yet. I just got back and now I have to run off again."

"I appreciate the help." She tried to take the DVD, but he held it out of reach.

"Jane, I hope you know what you're doing with this Sebastian guy. I really don't want to see you get hurt." He looked—and sounded—more serious than he usually did.

Grabbing his arm, she finally got her hands on the DVD, which she promptly put in her purse. "I won't get hurt," she said, scoffing as if it was ridiculous to worry. But she knew there were no guarantees. Especially now. Whether she wanted to acknowledge it or not, she was falling in love with Sebastian.

And love had never been kind to her before.

Twenty-Two

There it was.

Malcolm drove past The Last Stand twice before turning in. It was only six o'clock in the evening, but dark came early in January, and he wasn't really worried that he'd be recognized—at least, not at first glance. He'd stopped by a secondhand store on the way and bought a wig, a pair of glasses and some women's clothing. Although he'd never used a disguise before, the image staring back at him whenever he looked in the rearview mirror seemed pretty damn convincing, certainly convincing enough to let him move around unnoticed, especially after dark. If he'd been a bigger man, it might not have worked so well, but this was one time when being only five foot nine was an advantage.

The reception area appeared to be closed for the night, but there was a light in one of the back offices. Did that mean someone was working late? Jane Burke, perhaps?

The possibility sent a tremor of excitement through him.

A single car sat in the lot, parked behind the building, by the rear exit.

The Chinese restaurant and the liquor store at the far end of the adjacent strip mall had moderate traffic. Malcolm drove around to the front and parked his van there so it wouldn't stand out. Then he waited for a man who'd just exited the liquor store to drive off—he saw no reason to invite scrutiny of his costume up close—and climbed out.

An obscure-sounding church and a few thousand square feet of empty retail space were sandwiched between the liquor store and The Last Stand. Wearing size ten high heels, which clicked confidently against the pavement as he walked, Malcolm passed them, along with a dry cleaner, as if he had a legitimate reason to be there. Then he ducked into the narrow alley between the end of the mall and the building that housed the charity and took off his shoes. How women maneuvered in such uncomfortable footwear, he had no idea.

Shoving a heel in each pocket of the heavy wool coat he'd bought to go over his dress, he hugged the cinder block wall as he slipped on his tennis shoes and moved around to the back. Once there, he stood in the shadow of the building, waiting to see if he could catch a glimpse of the occupant.

Movement in the hallway outside the office with the light on caught his attention. Someone was standing there, using a copier. Malcolm could see the distinctive glow each time the machine lid was lifted. But it wasn't a woman. This person was far too tall.

Disappointed, Malcolm cursed under his breath. He'd been entertaining visions of leaving Jane Burke bleeding on her desk. If he couldn't get to Mary, he'd take someone who meant even more to Sebastian. He liked the ruthlessness of giving the bastard an immediate and vicious response to his e-mail.

But he hadn't really expected it to be that easy. He had to do his homework, make plans. This was more of a reconnaissance mission than anything else. He'd known that from the beginning.

Carrying a stack of copies, the man went back into an office, and Malcolm took out his gun before creeping closer. The door was unlocked. He could tell without even touching it. The guy inside probably saw no reason for heightened security, not this early at night and not if he was only stopping by to make a few copies.

Would he come back into the hall right away?

No, Malcolm didn't think so. From the muted sounds drifting toward him, he could tell that the man was now on the phone.

With one gloved hand, Malcolm pulled the swinging door open far enough to squeeze inside. Maybe he wouldn't meet Jane in the next few minutes. But he'd meet her soon. Especially if he could learn a little more about her. Starting with her address...

"So he looks like his picture?" The voice of the man in the office came to him more clearly, since they were both in the building.

"He's put on some weight, but you can definitely tell it's him."

The second voice surprised Malcolm. Maybe this person wasn't alone, after all.

Leaning slightly to the right so he could see into the

room, he found the guy he'd watched in the hall standing behind a desk, collating copies. The second voice was coming from a speakerphone.

"When was he last there?" The punch of a stapler punctuated this question.

"Just after Christmas."

He plopped the document on a stack of others and stapled the next one. "Did he win anything that night?"

"No. From what I can tell he generally loses."

Afraid of giving his presence away, Malcolm stepped into the room closest to the office and pressed his back against the wall.

"Stands to reason," the man said. "A good gambler wouldn't have to kill his wife."

Were they talking about *him?* Was that Jane on the phone—or someone else?

"Sebastian says he isn't good at anything. That's why being a cop meant so much to him. He used the uniform to create some self-respect and to cover up his shortcomings."

Malcolm's hand tightened on his gun. Sebastian would say that. He'd always felt so damn superior.

"Sebastian told you that, huh?" the man said. "So he's still staying with you?"

"Jonathan, cut it out. I don't want to get into that."

He chuckled. "It's a simple question, Jane."

"He doesn't want to leave me here alone. He's afraid Malcolm will come back and somehow find out which condo is mine."

"Then I'm glad he's staying. Don't take any chances." The stapler sounds had stopped. "I'm finished here. I'll check in with you later."

"Thanks again for picking up that DVD from Cache Creek. It helps us get a feel for the kind of monster we're dealing with."

Monster? She had no idea. But she'd soon learn, Malcolm thought.

"It was nice of that security guard to provide it," the man said.

"I just hope they call us if he comes back."

"Did they say they would?"

"Sebastian hired another guy, one who's working security at night, to keep a lookout."

"Then let's hope that particular guard's there when Malcolm or Wesley or whoever the hell he is shows up."

"It's Malcolm Turner. Sebastian's right. He didn't die in that burning car."

"I'll take your word for it. Talk to you tomorrow," he said and that was the end of the call.

Anger simmered in Malcolm's chest as he stood in the empty office next door. He wasn't good at anything? He'd known Sebastian felt that way all along. Sebastian had always considered himself better than everyone else, had always done what he could to make Malcolm look bad, especially to Emily and Colton.

But Sebastian wasn't as smart as he thought. Maybe he'd paid the security personnel at Cache Creek to rat him out. But Sebastian would be dead long before Malcolm ever went back to that casino.

All Malcolm had to do was find out which condo belonged to Jane Burke, and she'd be dead, too.

The man Jane had called Jonathan turned off the light and passed right by on his way out. Malcolm heard him lock the door behind him, but he didn't mind getting shut in. He could throw the bolt from the inside whenever he was ready to leave.

Meanwhile, he had work to do.

Waiting until Jonathan had driven off, he turned the light back on and poked through the offices until he came across a name placard that read *Jane Burke*. Surely, somewhere, there'd be a Rolodex card, an envelope or a piece of paper with her home address on it.

But he didn't find the information he needed in her office. It was in the storage room. Apparently, she'd brought in several empty boxes from shipments she'd received before Christmas.

Thank God for recycling.

According to the labels, she lived in unit 53.

Jane stood in the middle of her living room, staring at the grainy image on TV. That was Malcolm Turner, the man guilty of murdering his wife and stepson, impersonating a police officer, kidnapping two teenage girls and ultimately stabbing one of them. Who knew what he'd done to Latisha—or what he might do if they didn't get to her in time. Jane had no faith whatsoever in the e-mail Latisha had sent. She wasn't sure what that was about, but she was confident it didn't reflect Malcolm's true plans.

How did Malcolm justify his actions? she wondered. How could he live with himself?

By avoiding responsibility for what he'd done. As long as he could blame others for provoking him, he wouldn't have to accept any of the blame. At least, that was how Oliver had done it.

"You're watching that *again?*"

Jane turned to see Sebastian behind her. For the past

forty-five minutes, he'd been helping Kate with her homework. Jane had tried to step in—she was always the one who helped, except when Kate was at her grandparents'—but Kate had been far more interested in Sebastian. "I want to know what he's thinking," she explained as Malcolm threw the dice at a craps table.

Sebastian's attention was fixed on Malcolm, too. "You wouldn't understand it, even if you could read his mind," he said. "Looking for sanity and reason in people like Oliver and Malcolm will only drive you crazy. They have a twisted view of the world and of themselves."

"All they can see is how it affects them," she agreed.

"We should know. We've had front-row seats." He grabbed his coat, which he'd tossed on the couch.

She felt her eyebrows go up. "You're leaving?"

"Some of your neighbors weren't home earlier. I'm hoping to catch them this evening."

She'd been more than a little disappointed that they hadn't located a single person who'd heard or seen anything that morning, not even in the units closer to the parking lot. Malcolm had entered the lot and broken Sebastian's window, then dumped a dead body in his backseat. Granted, that wouldn't take a lot of time, but it seemed bizarre that it could go unnoticed in such a public setting, on such a busy street. "Do you want some help?"

"No, you stay with Kate. She might have a few more questions on her math."

"I don't think she had any questions to begin with. Not really. She just wanted your attention."

His grin told her he already understood that. "She's a great kid."

Jane tried not to let the fact that he was so good with

Kate influence the way she felt about Sebastian, but Kate's adoration chipped away at her biggest objection to getting involved with him. "I'm proud of her."

As Sebastian left, her cell phone rang. Leaning over so she could retrieve it from the coffee table, she checked caller ID—and immediately recognized the number.

"Hello, Luther," she said.

"You called?"

"Yes. I wanted to make sure you'd heard the latest."

"That Latisha e-mailed Gloria?"

"Yes."

"Gloria told me."

"Okay." She'd expected his negative energy to be difficult to tolerate, but it wasn't as bad as she'd thought. Tonight Latisha's father seemed uncharacteristically subdued. "I'll talk to you later, then."

"He drives a van," he suddenly announced.

Jane brought her phone back to her ear. "What did you say? *Who* drives a van?"

"The man who took Latisha and Marcie. I been talkin' to the girls on the street. They tell me Officer Boss drives a white utility van."

"You don't happen to have a license number, do you?"

"Not yet, but everyone I know is keepin' an eye out."

"I appreciate the information. I'll call you if we find anything on this end."

He didn't answer right away. Assuming he wouldn't, she started to hang up again, but the sound of his voice made her hesitate. "Thanks for callin'," he said. Then he was gone.

Jane pursed her lips as she pressed the end button on her phone.

"What's wrong, Mommy?"

Preoccupied with Luther's phone call, she met her daughter's curious gaze. "That was a man from the case I'm working on. I thought I disliked him, but…"

"You don't?"

"Not anymore. I guess I never really did. I was just scared of him."

"Does he think you're nice, too?"

"I don't know if I'd go that far," she said with a laugh. "But maybe he's figuring out that I'm not as bad as he thought."

"Is he like Sebastian?" she asked.

No one was like Sebastian. "Not really."

Kate used her chewing gum to blow a bubble that popped in her face. "It's too bad Sebastian doesn't have kids," she said as she pushed her gum back into her mouth.

Sensing a setup, Jane cocked her head. "Why's that?"

"He'd be a perfect daddy."

Jane rolled her eyes at her daughter's attempt to be sly. "That's quite a hint, young lady."

Kate's smile stretched across her face. "If you married him, maybe he'd go with me to the Daddy Daughter Derby at LeAnn's house this spring."

Sobering, Jane took her child's hands and pulled her close. The Daddy Daughter Derby was a day of water-skiing and barbecuing sponsored by one of her friends, who was being raised by a single dad. "Hey, don't get your hopes up, okay? He lives in New York. He'll be going back there once this case is over."

The sparkle in Kate's eyes winked out, but she lifted her chin. "I figured it'd be something like that. I was just sayin'."

Jane smoothed her hair. "Your grandpa will take you."

"Yeah. That'll be fun," she said, but there wasn't any enthusiasm in her voice, and her shoulders slumped as she headed down the hall to finish her homework.

Dropping the remote, Jane sank onto the couch. All this time, she'd believed she was protecting her daughter by barring any potential love interest from entering her life. But maybe she wasn't protecting Kate so much as she was denying her the chance to have a complete family.

No matter what happened with Sebastian, maybe it was time to start dating. Even if she didn't deserve the happiness that could come from meeting a good man, Kate certainly did.

Something had changed. Latisha wasn't sure what it was, but she woke up feeling lost, disoriented. She didn't even know where she was....

Wait—she did know. She was in Wesley's bed, which wasn't so unusual. They'd spent a lot of time here in the past couple of days. He couldn't get enough of her. He was always telling her how beautiful she was, how much he wanted to be with her. It was flattering to think she'd made such an impact on an older man—a cop, no less.

So where was he? He'd been with her earlier, but now he was gone.

She tried to remember what had happened but couldn't. He'd turned off the movie, put on some music and brought out a pack of cards. Whenever she lost a hand, he made her have a shot. And she'd lost practically every one. But then what?

Had she gone to sleep or passed out? Maybe she'd passed out and he'd carried her to bed. She felt woozy.

Squinting, she shoved herself into a sitting position and tried to bring the window into focus. It was dark outside—nighttime. That felt strange in itself, as if part of life had passed her by. Last she knew, it'd been the middle of the afternoon.

"Wes?" she called.

The house remained completely silent.

Dizziness overwhelmed her, and she dropped onto the pillows. They'd drunk too much. Her head was still buzzing. Tempted to finish sleeping it off, she rolled onto her side, but a sense of unease kept her from drifting off again. That unease had to do with Marcie, with the fire in the barrel outside, with the blood spatter on Wesley's shoes....

But Latisha didn't want to think about those things. Wes had explained them—or most of them, anyway. She hadn't asked him about the barrel or the shoes, but if he said he let Marcie go, he did.

The alternative was too terrible to contemplate. She preferred to believe him. Then she could like Wes—the Wes she'd come to know in the past few days, anyway. He'd told her about the man who'd murdered his wife and kid. No wonder he acted out. Latisha knew all about people who acted out. Her father was one of them. Her mother hadn't been any better. The best person Latisha knew was Gloria, but that didn't make Gloria easy to live with. Stubborn and demanding, she gave Latisha little freedom. All she cared about was seeing Latisha graduate from college so she could "be somebody."

Gloria wouldn't be happy to learn that Latisha was now planning to skip college and get married. But even Gloria would be jealous of her ring. No one in their family had ever received one like it. Wes had also promised her a nice house and a family. She'd be a stay-at-home mom, giving her children the kind of care she'd always longed for. And she'd never suffer the poverty she'd known growing up. She'd be middle class. College couldn't bring her much more than that, could it?

She allowed her eyes to close, but opened them a moment later. If Wesley was gone, she could use his computer to see if Gloria had responded to her e-mail. He was so protective of his laptop, and of her, that he hadn't let her check her e-mail today. He kept saying, "Later." She got the impression he was threatened by Gloria's hold on her, that he might refuse until she'd given him the two weeks she'd promised, which meant this could be her only chance.

Dragging herself out of bed, she stumbled down the hall. "Wes?" she called, but she knew he wasn't home. He would've responded to her when she called out the first time. Since he'd quit chaining her to the floor, he was at her side every second. She just hoped that, wherever he'd gone, he hadn't taken his computer with him.

When she rounded the corner, she found it in its usual place and breathed out in relief. "Still here!" she said with a giggle and began to sing, "Here comes the bride...here comes the bride..."

She sat down and logged on, but it was difficult to see the screen clearly in her current condition. After blinking several times, she made out the list of messages in her in-box and was rewarded when she spotted what she'd been looking for.

"Ta da!" She clicked to open it.

I'm so glad you're okay, she read. Where are you?

Can you tell me? E-mail me, call me, do anything you can. The police are looking everywhere for you. So is a woman I contacted from a victims' charity. I'm getting anyone I can to help.

It sounded as if she was going to a lot of trouble. "I told her I'd see her in two weeks," Latisha mumbled and hit the instant-message button.

Gloria? You there?

An answer came almost immediately. Latisha? Is it u? Hey, her sister was online. What timing. Yeah.

I've been on this thing just about every minute since you wrote me. I've barely let myself sleep. Where are u?

Dont no.

Where is the man who kidnapped u?

Gone.

Can u get away?

Latisha frowned. Here was the tough part. How did she explain that what she'd thought about Wesley in the beginning was no longer true? How did she make Gloria understand that he wasn't as bad as he'd seemed? They'd been having so much fun lately....

I dont want to get way. He goin to marry me, G. He goin to buy me a big house and we're gonna have kids.

He treat me god. She was struggling to hit the right keys and was making mistakes, but communicating was more important than fixing everything so it read perfectly.

What r u talkin bout?

U shod see my ring.

He bought u a ring?

He luvs m. Tel Maecie we wrre wrong bout hum.

Her mistakes were getting worse. She was normally a good typist and a great speller, much better than Marcie or Gloria, but her fingers seemed to fumble all over the keyboard. He ben thru a lt. He feel bad he wasnt nic to us at feirst. At lest he lt Marcie go, rit?

What r u talkin bout?

She made more of an effort to type correctly. At least he let Marcie go.

That don't make sense, Latisha. He didn't let Marcie go.

Latisha straightened in her seat. She was beginning to sober up. Sure he did. She's not here anymore.

Marcie's dead. And that man killed her. U gotta get help before he do the same to u. U gotta get away!

The smell of smoke seemed to penetrate the house as if Wesley was out back doing the burning all over again. But Latisha knew that wasn't the case. She was still alone.

U lyin', she typed. Gloria just wanted to make sure she came home and finished school. Gloria wanted to keep them all together.

I'm not. He killed her, Latisha. Stabbed her to death. And dead is dead. Get out! Now!!! I can't lose both of u.

"'I can't lose both of you,'" she read aloud. It was those words, more than any of Gloria's accusations or exclamation points that finally convinced her. Gloria was tough. She didn't say anything sentimental. Not unless she'd been stripped of the pride that kept her going from day to day.

Jumping to her feet, Latisha tripped and almost fell into the table. The empty rum bottle was still on the counter. A package of sleeping pills lay next to it.

Had Wesley put them in her drink? If so, why?

Because he'd wanted to leave. That much was obvious. And he'd wanted her to be here when he returned. But where had he gone? And why had he lied? He'd said he wanted to marry her!

Images of the time they'd spent together in the bedroom came back to her, and she understood. He'd been using her. She made life more comfortable for him out here in this lonely house. He wouldn't let her go. He was lying about that as well as the future he'd promised her.

Her heart raced as she clutched at her aching chest. She'd believed him. She'd ignored the blood on his shoes and the burning he'd done out back because she didn't want to acknowledge that her sister was dead. It was so much better to think of her at home with Gloria, where she belonged. Gloria would take care of her. It was Gloria who'd always taken care of them both.

But now…Gloria wasn't here.

He'd kill her eventually, Latisha realized. Maybe not today or tomorrow. She was still of some use to him. She wasn't like Marcie. She'd let him control her, let him take what he wanted. But what if she ever defied him? What would happen then?

The answer was all too clear. Gloria was right. She had to get away.

How? Where could she go for help? They were in the middle of nowhere. It was pitch-black outside, which meant she could easily stumble into a ravine or a ditch. She couldn't think as clearly as she needed to, because of whatever he'd given her. And, more frightening than anything else, she had no idea when he'd be back.

Remembering the way he'd kicked Marcie in the face, she cringed. He wouldn't like it if he caught her trying to leave him….

Come morning, would he be burning clothes with *her* blood on them in that barrel outside?

Twenty-Three

It wasn't as easy to get inside a condo as it was a house. He needed to be cautious. Make a plan.

Malcolm sat at the bus stop across the street from where he'd dumped Marcie's body, wearing his female disguise. To cover his face, he'd wrapped a large scarf around his head the way some Russian immigrants did, and no one had looked at him twice. It was starting to rain, which helped; most people either stayed inside or sheltered beneath an umbrella. Only an old lady with no teeth, who kept her eyes closed and mumbled to herself, and two teenagers listening to iPods and purposely ignoring everything else around them, waited at the bus stop. When the bus arrived, the three of them got on, but no one seemed to notice that he didn't.

Getting to Jane was going to be tricky. Although her unit was on the ground floor, her complex faced a busy street. Late at night, traffic thinned considerably—he knew because that was when he'd dumped Marcie—

but because of it he didn't feel comfortable entering from the front.

If he went around back, there was less chance of being spotted, but more chance of standing out if someone did happen to see him. He'd already circled the complex in his van to get a sense of the layout. Each unit had a back door, with a porch and a small patch of fenced yard.

That would be his point of entry. He could easily scale the fence and go in when he was sure Sebastian wasn't there. According to The Last Stand Web site, some of the women who worked for the charity were experts in self-defense. They even offered courses. Jane could be one of them. There was no need to get in over his head. He'd take her on alone, kill her and wait for Sebastian to return. Then he'd get to witness Sebastian's reaction....

Malcolm studied the units on either side of number 53. With such close neighbors, a gun would be too loud. Only a quiet killing would give him the time he'd need to wait for Sebastian, which meant he'd have to use his knife again. Fortunately, such an intimate murder wasn't as hard as he'd thought it would be. All it took was enough hate.

"Excuse me. Do you know how much longer it'll be before the bus comes?"

He glanced up to see one of those freaky "green" types who biked to work in a suit. Tall and skinny, the guy wore biking gloves and had his bicycle with him. The gloves looked sporty—but his glasses were fogged up and he had a rubber band around one pant leg. Apparently, the guy was tired of getting wet or had left the office later than usual.

Malcolm had no clue about the bus schedule. Neither did he care. He couldn't talk, anyway. Maybe he was small enough to pull off dressing as a woman, but there was nothing feminine about his voice.

Shaking his head, he waved as if he didn't speak the language and shuffled off.

Once he'd turned the corner and was out of sight, he strode more briskly toward the van, which he'd parked on a nearby street. It was almost nine. He had to get back before Latisha woke up. She wasn't anything like her sister—thank God—but he couldn't leave her alone too long.

Imagining her sleeping in his bed, awaiting his return, he smiled. There was something to be said for hooking up with someone so young and naive. She didn't fight him the way his previous wives had; she gave him complete control.

Maybe kidnapping her had been the best move he'd ever made, he thought, and took off his costume while he was still in the van so he could stop at the grocery store and buy her some flowers.

It was *so* cold. When she'd first left the house, Latisha had embraced the damp, chilly weather. That and a surge of adrenaline had helped clear her mind of the cobwebs left from the alcohol and the pills. But now she wished she'd taken a blanket from the bedroom. She didn't have a coat. It had been bright and sunny the day she and Marcie had gone to buy doughnuts—and wound up in Wesley Boss's van. Because they hadn't planned on being away for longer than thirty minutes and had the car heater to take the edge off the sixty-degree weather, they hadn't thought they'd need coats. And Wesley had bought them clothes but no outerwear.

Now Latisha's hands and feet were so numb she couldn't feel them. And her wet clothes—the new ones she'd got at the mall—clung to her, making her legs feel heavier and heavier as the rain continued. She would've been okay if the cold was all she had to contend with, but she didn't feel well. She'd hoped the vomiting would get the drugs out of her system, but being sick made her even more light-headed.

Headlights appeared around a bend not far away. Latisha had been careful to stick to the road. It was her escape to the world outside the farmhouse where she'd been held hostage, her best chance of getting help. But it also presented the greatest risk of getting caught by Wesley when he came home.

Hurrying into the brush, she squatted down, out of sight, while waiting for the vehicle to pass. She'd checked under the mattress for his gun, but it was gone, which meant he'd taken it with him.

As the vehicle zipped by, she realized those headlights didn't belong to a van. It was some kind of car. She should've flagged down the driver and would have done so if she'd known....

Tears blurred her vision as she lurched back to the pavement. She hated feeling that he could come upon her at any moment. But she was afraid to leave the road for fear she'd end up lost or run into a vicious animal or even a loose dog. She'd been hoping to find another house, but she hadn't seen any lights.

Her shivering grew more violent as the minutes ticked by. Was she traveling toward town or farther into the country?

The thought that she might have to be out all night

tempted her to go back to the house and retrieve a blanket, or layer up with the rest of her clothes. Maybe she'd have a better chance of getting away if she didn't feel as if she might freeze to death....

But Gloria's message kept her moving forward: Marcie's dead. And that man killed her.

Wes was a murderer. But was it true that he used to be a cop? Was it true that his wife and son had been killed? That he was hunting the man who did it? If so, she felt sorry about the tragedy that had twisted him. But he was the one who'd ended her sister's life. Gloria said so, and Gloria was always right—wasn't she?

Suddenly, Latisha stopped. Gloria always *thought* she was right. But what if this was one instance where she was wrong? What if Wes had dropped Marcie off as he'd said, and someone else had killed her? In her attempt to get home, Marcie could've thumbed a ride with someone dangerous. She was probably frantic, not thinking straight. And there could be another explanation for that fire in the barrel and the blood on Wes's shoes. *I didn't even ask him about those things.* Maybe what she'd found wasn't really blood. She'd been jumping to con- clusions. She'd automatically thought the worst.

Sinking into the brush along the shoulder of the road, she curled up for warmth. Was she abandoning the man she loved? Or saving her life? She wasn't sure. She was too cold and sick to decide—and too cold and sick to care. She didn't think she had the strength to go any farther.

Another set of headlights appeared, these a little higher than those of the previous car. As the sound of the engine grew louder, Latisha knew before she ever saw the van that it was Wesley.

* * *

"Anything?" Jane asked. She'd just hung up after speaking to David. She'd called to let him know what Luther had told her.

Sebastian peeled off his coat and draped it on the back of a kitchen chair. "No."

She gave him a saucy look. "Well…I got a tip while you were gone."

Now that it was getting late, he was beginning to think about bed. And these days, whenever he thought about bed, he thought about Jane….

His gaze lingered on the opening of her robe, and he wondered if she'd let him slip his hand inside. "Who from?"

She placed her fingers under his chin, bringing his attention up to her eyes. "A pimp."

"You know a pimp?" he asked, arching an eyebrow at her.

"Latisha's dad. We seem to be friends now. At least, our relationship is improving."

He backed her against the counter, grinning as she glanced behind him to check that the coast was clear. He had a feeling they might end up in the bathroom again tonight. "Glad to hear you're winning him over," he said. "What'd he tell you?"

"Malcolm is driving a white van. Luther couldn't give me the license-plate number, but he's got everyone he knows keeping an eye out."

"And how would a pimp know what kind of vehicle Malcolm is driving?"

"Gambling isn't Malcolm's only vice."

Moving his lower body against hers, he bent his

head until their lips were a fraction of an inch apart. "Is Kate in bed?"

"That's your next question?"

"Were we talking about something else?"

She laughed, then their lips met—right before Kate spoke from the entrance to the kitchen. Jane stiffened, but Sebastian felt that scrambling away from each other would only imply that they were doing something wrong. Slipping an arm around her shoulders, he turned to face her daughter as if it wasn't any big deal that she'd caught them kissing.

"What did you say?" he asked Kate.

"Nothing," she mumbled with a furious blush and hurried back down the hall.

"I think she's on to us," he told Jane, keeping his voice light.

She pulled away from him, her expression more concerned than amused. "I think so, too."

Malcolm couldn't believe it. Latisha was gone.

He stood in the bedroom doorway, holding his stupid flowers and gaping at the bed where he'd left her. He'd never dreamed she'd wake up so soon. He'd given her only one sleeping pill, but with all the booze he hadn't thought she'd need more than that. She weighed maybe a hundred and twenty pounds soaking wet!

So what now? He wasn't sure what upset him more. The fact that he'd begun to trust her and she'd betrayed him, or the fear that she might remember where he lived. The safest approach would be to get out, leave and never come back.

Unless he could reclaim her. Was there any chance?

Tossing the flowers on the floor, he dashed back down the hall, checking each room he passed, including the closets. She wasn't anywhere in the house. What had she done? Struck out on her own—walking? If so, maybe he could find her.

It was then that he spotted his computer. Why hadn't he taken it with him? He'd been so eager to reach The Last Stand offices, so confident that Latisha would be unconscious for several hours, at least, that he hadn't even considered what she could do on the Internet.

Jiggling his mouse, he dissolved his screen saver. She'd left nothing open on his desktop, but a quick check of his browser history revealed that she'd logged into her e-mail account. That meant she'd probably communicated with someone.

Damn it! How had she been coherent enough to do that? She should've been completely stoned!

Sweat trickled from his temple. Should he grab his stuff and go? Forget her? Or should he try to find her? Most of Emily's money was gone. He didn't want to pay for a motel, not when he'd just paid his rent and this place was so perfect.

He'd go after her, he decided. He'd find her and bring her back. Then he'd kill her and burn her body in that barrel. She'd become too much of a liability; she was more like her sister than he'd thought. He liked female companionship in bed, but the situation had changed and the price was too high. Over the next few weeks, he had to be more agile, had to be able to come and go as he pleased—at least until he'd taken care of his most recent problems.

Grabbing his keys, he tore out of the house. He was

about to take care of one of them right now. If Latisha was on foot, she couldn't have gotten very far.

Latisha could hear Wesley calling her. He wasn't far away. He'd been driving up and down the road, stopping every few minutes to get out and stab through the brush with a flashlight. Once she saw the beam of his light pass right over where she was. She hadn't moved since she'd curled up, was beginning to believe she'd die if she didn't answer. The night sky swirled above her. She'd grown so dizzy she could no longer stand.

I think I'm falling in love with you, in love with you, in love with you... His voice seemed to echo in her head. *You'd like to be a mother, wouldn't you, wouldn't you? How do you like the ring, ring, ring?*

She liked the ring, all right. It represented everything she'd ever wanted.

"Latisha!"

He was drawing close again, sounding more and more frantic.

"Latisha? Where are you?"

"God help me." Her lips moved, but she couldn't even hear her own voice. Every time she opened her mouth, she heard Gloria yelling at her in her mind. *Don't you dare, Latisha! Keep your head down. Don't let him find you!*

"Are you trying to break my heart?" he yelled. "You know how I feel about you. I thought you loved me, too."

She squeezed her eyes shut. The weird thing was...part of her did love him. Was that possible? She hated him *and* she loved him. Afraid of him though she could sometimes be, she wanted to go back and finish the movie they'd been watching, crawl into bed, talk about their plans.

"Latisha? Baby, please. I know you gotta be out here somewhere. I brought you some flowers—but you broke my heart."

A tear slipped from her eyes. *Gloria! Help me!*

"You're gonna make yourself sick if you don't come in," he said.

She was already sick—and so cold.

"Let me take care of you. Let me get you warm and dry. I'll give you another massage. You liked that, didn't you?"

In truth, she'd never felt anything so wonderful in her life. Wesley had introduced her to a lot of enjoyable activities, including drinking. Gloria had been so strict about alcohol. What was the big deal about having some fun once in a while?

"Hello?" Wes cried. "Latisha? You gonna leave me out here in the cold all by myself?"

No. She couldn't continue to freeze. She was better off taking her chances with him, wasn't she? She'd die for sure if she didn't move.

Putting all the energy she had into sitting up, she concentrated on his voice and the beam of his light. He wasn't that far away, and he was coming closer. Should she call out to him? Or just wait?

Then she spotted another pair of headlights. They were coming around the bend, like the ones before, only this car seemed to be going a lot slower than the others.

Remembering her sister's bruised face, she clambered to her feet and stood there, swaying in the rain as she summoned the strength to walk. She'd do what Gloria told her. Gloria always had her best interests at heart. Maybe she and Marcie had resented their older sister for being so strict, but Gloria was loyal and fiercely protective. She was the one person in Latisha's life who could be trusted.

"I'm coming, Gloria," she muttered, and it was the thought of seeing her sister again that gave her the energy to put one foot in front of the other.

The car was drawing closer. She'd have to wave, yell—do something to attract the attention of the driver.

Suddenly, Wesley's flashlight swept over her. It moved on, but then jerked back—and landed squarely on her.

He'd found her.

"Latisha, no!" he yelled and began to run.

Don't fall. Don't fall. If she crumpled now, she'd lose her one chance to go home. A heap at the side of the road wasn't likely to get the attention of the person in that car.

Wes's footsteps pounded the earth. She could almost hear his labored breathing. But he'd snapped off his light. He didn't want to be seen by that car. He was hoping to get to her before she could get to whoever was coming toward them....

With one huge, final effort, she screamed, "No!" and stepped into the middle of the road. The oncoming car would either hit her—or stop.

When it began to slow, she thought she'd won. Help was only seconds away. Surely he'd back off now—run, hide.

Headlights blinded Latisha, tires squealed and the car began to hydroplane on the wet pavement. Flinching, Latisha threw up her hands to protect herself, although she knew that would do nothing.

The car didn't hit her.

Had it stopped?

Yes. It was less than a foot away, its hot engine causing steam to rise in the cold weather.

Bolstered by a fresh surge of adrenaline, she glanced at Wesley. He was a few feet away and had drawn his gun. The rain was pouring down but she could see him well enough to know he had the muzzle pointed right at her.

Would he kill her in front of this stranger?

A resounding blast told her he'd try. She didn't even have the energy to duck. She felt a burning sensation in her right arm and realized dimly that he wasn't giving up, wasn't afraid of whoever drove the car. He'd probably kill them, too. What would stop him?

Nothing.

The woman who shoved the gearshift into park and opened her door to poke her head out had to be at least seventy-five. It was an old lady with gray hair, and she couldn't be more than five feet tall. "I just about hit you!" she cried. "What the heck are you doing?"

And then she seemed to understand what the blast had been about. As she spotted Wesley and his gun, terror dawned on her wrinkled face.

Latisha hadn't saved herself. She was going to die— along with some white person's grandmother.

Twenty-Four

Malcolm used his sleeve to wipe the rain from his eyes. He could feel the beat of his heart all the way to his fingertips, but it was okay. He could still salvage this situation. All he had to do was shoot the old lady, hide her car in the barn and drag Latisha home. Maybe he'd keep her around for another night. Maybe he'd kill her slowly. He'd have the luxury of deciding once he got rid of the driver. He'd bury both bodies tomorrow, after he'd had a chance to sleep. There'd be no real hurry, not out here where there was no one to see what he was doing.

Turning his pistol on the old woman, he squeezed off another shot, but the car stood between them and acted as a barricade. She was too damned short. He adjusted, tried to fire again—but she was quicker than he expected and jumped back in the car.

The thought crossed his mind to shoot her through the windshield. He couldn't let her escape. But she didn't give him the chance. Gunning the engine, she yanked the transmission into drive and steered right for him.

She was trying to kill him!

Diving to avoid being hit, he landed hard. A rock bruised his hip and his knee, some thorny bush scratched his face and he lost his gun. As he patted the ground, searching frantically for it, he heard a thin voice yell, "Get in!"

A door slammed shut the same second he found the warm metal of his pistol. With his chest rising and falling as if he was in the middle of a marathon, he grabbed it and turned to fire. He was a good shot. He could still solve this.

But he was too late. The old lady's taillights glowed through the rain, but she was already half a mile down the road and racing away faster by the second.

Undeterred, he fired several shots. This couldn't be happening, he told himself. No way had he just allowed Latisha and a witness to escape!

But that was exactly what he'd done. Far as he could tell, he hadn't even hit the damn car.

After emptying his gun in the direction they'd gone, he sank to his knees. "Son of a bitch! I'm going to kill you for this. I'm going to kill you both!" he screamed. But when the rage receded, he knew there wasn't a thing he could do to either of them. They were gone. He had to go to the house, pack his belongings and get the hell out. Maybe Latisha wouldn't be able to lead the police to this place. But he was fairly certain the old lady could pinpoint exactly where she'd been accosted.

"What is it?" Sebastian murmured. Like Kate, he'd heard the phone ring. They both stood at Jane's bedroom door, listening to her talk to David.

"Latisha escaped," she told him.

"Is she okay?"

Brushing her hair out of her face, she sat up. She'd answered the phone automatically and hadn't really comprehended the first few words. But the meaning of what David had told her, what she'd just repeated to Sebastian, was beginning to sink in, and she could hardly believe it. Latisha was alive—*alive!* Thank God! "She's been shot, but the bullet passed through her arm and didn't cause any lasting damage."

"Does Gloria know?"

Jane repeated the question to David, a question she would already have asked if she'd been coherent. It was barely an hour before she had to get up, but with Sebastian in the living room, she'd spent another sleepless night. Although she hadn't been with him physically, she'd tossed and turned, thinking about him.

"She was pretty delirious when the doctors first saw her," David said. "An older lady brought her in—a Louise Stetzel."

"How did Mrs. Stetzel find her?"

"I'm still piecing that together, but I wanted to give you a heads-up. I thought you might like to call Gloria while I deal with the situation around here."

That was sweet of David. He understood how personally invested she'd become in this case. Maybe they'd been enemies six years ago, but he was now one of her favorite people. "Of course." Imagining Gloria's relief, Jane felt her eyes swim with tears. "I'll call her right away."

A click signaled that he was gone. After returning the phone to her nightstand, Jane focused on Sebastian and Kate.

"Who's Latisha?" Kate asked.

"Remember that person I told you about after the last time we got a call in the middle of the night?"

She came into the room. "The one who needed help?"

"Yeah."

Hope filled her innocent face. "She's okay now?"

"She's okay."

Kate walked around to give her a hug. "I knew you could do it, Mom!"

Jane laughed weakly. "I did my best, but I don't get the credit for this." It could easily have gone the other way; she was surprised it hadn't.

Sebastian stood by the door. He was wearing a pair of pajama bottoms and a T-shirt.

"Did you find out if Gloria knows?" he asked. He was relieved, too. She could hear it in his voice.

"I'm about to tell her." She nudged Kate, who'd plopped down beside her. "Will you run out to the kitchen and get my cell phone, sweetie? Gloria's number is in my address book."

Kate jumped up and, squeezing past Sebastian, hurried out of the room. She returned seconds later and handed Jane her cell. "Who's Gloria?" she asked.

"Latisha's sister," Jane explained.

"She's going to be happy, huh?"

"Very." Holding up a hand to forestall any more questions, she made the call.

Gloria answered on the third ring, sounding a bit disoriented. "Hello?"

"They've found Latisha," she announced. "Your sister's alive."

Silence, then muffled weeping came across the line.

"Thank the Lord." She cried some more before controlling her tears. "Where she at now?"

"Sutter Memorial Hospital. She's been shot in the arm, but the doctors have assured Detective Willis that she's fine."

"Do they have him? The man who did this? The man who killed Marcie?"

Jane's elation dimmed. "Not yet. At least, I don't think so. I don't have any of the details."

"Okay." She sniffed. "I'm headin' down there right now."

"Gloria, I'm..." Jane didn't know how to describe what she felt. Realizing, once again, how little power anyone had to overcome another person's evil intentions was frightening. It was humbling, too. Everything she'd learned in the past few months, all the bravado that swelled inside her when she talked about fighting back, had done nothing to bring this girl home. Yet, somehow, Latisha had survived. "Relieved and grateful," she finished.

"Me, too," Gloria said. "Will you be there, at the hospital?"

"Of course. I'll be over as soon as I shower."

"See you there."

As Jane hung up, she dashed a hand across her wet cheeks. Slightly embarrassed, she swallowed the lump in her throat and smiled at Sebastian. "Hearing she's okay feels so good."

His nod said he understood; Kate gave her another hug. She started to get out of bed—then remembered that there was another person she should contact. Once again searching her cell phone's address book, she called Luther.

He didn't pick up. Keeping one arm affectionately around Kate, she waited for the beep that would signal her to leave a message.

"Luther, it's Jane Burke." She allowed herself a watery smile. "Latisha's safe. I just…I didn't want you to worry about her anymore. So call me when you get a chance—or talk to Gloria if you prefer," she said and disconnected.

Folding his arms, Sebastian leaned against the doorjamb. "That was Latisha's father?"

Jane nodded while reaching for her robe.

"You didn't tell him where she is."

"I think I'll leave that up to Gloria. She might want to spend some time alone with her first." She addressed Kate. "Try to get some more sleep while I take a shower. I'll drop you off at school on our way to the hospital."

Her face fell. "Can't I go with you?"

Latisha's story wouldn't be pleasant, and Jane wasn't about to have her twelve-year-old in the room when she heard it. "Not today."

"Why not?" Kate whined. "It's Friday. We don't do a lot on Fridays. I could miss school." The oblique glance she cast over her shoulder told Jane that Sebastian was part of the attraction. Seeing her mother in a romantic relationship was exciting and new. Interrupting that kiss last night had ignited her daughter's imagination.

"You can't miss school," Jane said. "There's no need for that."

"One day's no big deal. I want to be with you guys. Please, Mom?"

Sebastian interceded. "How about if we take you ice-skating tonight instead?"

Brenda Novak

Jane watched her daughter struggle to rein in her reaction. She could tell that Kate wanted to continue pleading. On the other hand, she didn't want to make a bad impression on Sebastian. Finally she backed off and sent him a grateful smile. "That'd be fun."

The image of her late husband creeping down the hall with a knife suddenly appeared in Jane's mind. She was so used to protecting her daughter, so used to protecting herself. It wasn't easy to lower her guard. Not after what Oliver had done. Not even for Sebastian. Especially for Sebastian. She wasn't just tempted to sleep with him, to love him—she was tempted to trust him.

"Are you okay with that?" he asked.

Was she doing the right thing getting involved with him? Had she given herself enough time to heal? What would she do when Sebastian went back to New York? Forget him and move on?

She knew it wouldn't be that simple. But life was all about taking chances. Somehow she had to learn how to embrace normal risks again.

"Sure. It's a date," she said and went into the bathroom.

"Can she give us any indication of where she was kept?" Jane asked. She and Sebastian had bumped into David in the hall on their way to Latisha's hospital room. They were standing off to one side, speaking in hushed voices—partly in deference to the setting and partly to keep others from overhearing their conversation.

"No," David said. "She told me he pulled her and her sister over by putting a Kojak light on top of his van."

"We'd wondered about that," Sebastian said. He'd showered in Jane's second bathroom, but not until he'd made breakfast for Kate. By then, he didn't want to take the time to dry his hair, despite the cold weather. Still damp, it was curling over his ears and the back of his neck.

"I guess Marcie was driving their car," David went on. "Latisha admits the van didn't look like a public vehicle. And Wesley Boss, as she knows him, wasn't wearing a uniform. But when he explained that he was an undercover officer and flashed a badge, she thought that was the point—he wasn't supposed to look like a cop."

"Pulling someone over without the proper authority takes a lot of nerve," Jane said. "I'm afraid I would've believed him, too, and I have a lot more experience than they did."

David raised his eyebrows. "Let's hope you would've checked his badge a lot more closely."

"Maybe I would have, but we're talking about two young girls who were probably afraid they were going to be ticketed."

"That's exactly what they thought. They had a taillight out. They assumed that was the reason they'd been stopped."

"Is that why he chose them?"

"Could be. I think he was looking for the kind of target—targets in this case—who'd be unlikely to question his authority. It was a Saturday morning, not late at night. They were together." David shook his head. "They didn't see the danger."

"How'd he get them into the van without anyone noticing?" she asked.

David straightened his tie but the wrinkles in his shirt suggested these were the same clothes he'd worn yesterday. Had he even slept? She knew he'd gone home. He always made a point of it because of the kids. But he wasn't taking good care of himself. "They went willingly. He told Marcie there was a warrant for her arrest and asked her to step out of the car. When she did, he slapped handcuffs on her."

"He has balls the size of coconuts," Sebastian grumbled.

"No kidding," David agreed. "Anyway, he took Marcie to the van, then told Latisha she could ride to the station with him, that the car couldn't be driven because of that taillight."

"So she left the car and got in the van."

"Without an argument. Before she could figure out what was going on, he threw her in the back and cuffed her to the same metal bar he'd already cuffed her sister to. Next thing Latisha knew, they were at some old house in the country."

"Another house like the one in Ione?"

"This one's in Turlock."

Jane searched for the courage to ask her next question. "Did he rape them?"

"Apparently he didn't rape Marcie." She saw a pained expression on David's handsome face. "What happened with Latisha is less clear. She had a diamond ring on her finger when she arrived here. She claims he bought it for her, that he wanted to marry her."

"What?" The sudden change in Sebastian's voice showed how surprised he was. Jane was equally shocked.

"After a few weeks?" she said.

"He got her drunk, slept with her, promised her he'd always take care of her. Had to be pretty damned confusing for the poor kid."

"Did she know he killed her sister?"

"I don't think so. She said she believed him when he told her he'd let Marcie go." David frowned. "But…in the next instant, she burst into tears, saying she'd found Marcie's blood on his shoes."

"The poor thing." Jane felt Sebastian's hand at her back. She would've enjoyed the comfort his touch offered—except that she was afraid David might notice the subtle intimacy of it. She didn't want to be questioned about their involvement.

"What about Malcolm?" Sebastian asked. "Does anyone have any idea where he might be?"

"Mrs. Stetzel, the woman who brought her in, was driving out to her ranch when she came across Latisha. She said Latisha was in the middle of the road and there was a man with a gun, shooting at them both. Because it was dark and it all happened so fast, she didn't get a good look at him. But she knows the area and should be able to lead us to the exact spot. She's in a patrol car now, attempting to do just that. I'm on my way to meet them."

"So the old lady saved her," Sebastian said.

David chuckled. "Basically. I don't know how a seventy-three-year-old woman managed to get Latisha in the car and drive away without wrecking or being shot, but she did."

"An unlikely hero," Jane murmured.

"As unlikely as they get. But there's no question that she saved Latisha's life."

Would they finally catch Malcolm, thanks to a Good Samaritan? "What does Gloria have to say?"

"Not much," David replied. "She's been at Latisha's bedside since she got here, crying and listening. If she makes a comment, it's generally something encouraging like 'You'll get through this.'"

"Gloria's a strong woman. If anyone can help Latisha recover, it's her." Jane glanced toward the door she'd seen David walk out of just before they'd encountered him. "Is it okay if we go in?"

David gestured toward the room. "Go ahead. I'll call you when I reach the place where she escaped, let you know what I find."

Latisha was a very pretty young lady. She had a bandaged arm and a scrape on one cheek but, physically, she seemed in good shape, especially considering that Sebastian had never expected to see her alive.

Jane had gone into the room ahead of him. "You okay?" she murmured to Gloria and gave her a hug before turning to meet Latisha.

"This is Jane Burke, the woman I told you about," Gloria said to her sister.

Latisha's reaction seemed a bit skeptical. "Hello."

"I'm so glad you're safe." Jane looked as if she wanted to embrace Latisha, too. Wisely, she refrained, settling for a slight squeeze of the hand, but her apparent sincerity began to thaw Latisha's initial reaction.

"Thanks." She managed a slight smile.

"This is Sebastian Costas from New York." Jane seemed about to explain his presence, but she didn't get the chance. Latisha had gasped at the sound of his name.

"You're the one!"

Sebastian sent a questioning glance at her and then Gloria. He couldn't imagine what she was talking about. "The one who what?"

"Who killed Wesley's wife and son! He's been searching for you!"

Jane's eyes widened. *"What?"*

"He told me what you did."

Jane spoke before Sebastian could respond. "That's not true, Latisha," she said, her voice gentle. "Malcolm killed his own wife—for her money. He also killed a fourteen-year-old boy, mostly out of spite. That boy was Sebastian's son."

Sebastian curled his hands into fists. Malcolm had tried to blame Colton's murder on *him?*

"Who's Malcolm?" Latisha echoed in apparent confusion.

Careful to maintain enough distance to avoid frightening her, Sebastian moved a step closer. "Malcolm Turner is Wesley Boss's real name."

"No!" She shook her head. "He told me—"

"He told you lots of things, girl, and ain't none of 'em true," Gloria piped up. "That man's the devil."

Sebastian had to agree. If the devil had a face, it was that of Malcolm Turner. "I would *never* harm my own son."

"Then he killed Marcie," she announced, tears welling in her eyes.

Gloria patted her hand. "We already knew he did, honey. We'll miss her, but—" she fought to subdue her own emotions "—we'll get by, you and me. We still got each other. He didn't get you."

"Yet." Her eyes shifted beseechingly to Jane. "What if he comes after me? He's still out there…."

If only Sebastian had been able to catch Malcolm before the kidnappings… He wished to hell he'd been successful. He'd felt so close then, when he and Mary were communicating with him online.

A lot had changed.

"We're doing everything we can to put him behind bars," Jane said. "What you told the police should help. They're on their way to the place where Mrs. Stetzel found you."

"It's not far from his house," she said. "It can't be far from his house. I—I couldn't have walked more than a—a mile or so."

"We'll find him," Sebastian assured her. But Malcolm probably wasn't at the house where he'd kept Latisha. Not anymore. He wouldn't simply wait for the police to come and arrest him. Unless something had happened to stop him, he'd fled the minute Mrs. Stetzel's car drove out of sight.

When and where he might turn up was anyone's guess.

Twenty-Five

Malcolm tossed his bags on the spare bed in the cheap motel room he'd rented under a previous alias, put a *privacy* sign on the door, and used the security lock to bolt himself in. He had a lot to do, a lot to think about, but first he needed to regroup. He'd be more capable if he could sleep first.

Now that he'd gotten safely away from the house, however, the memory of that old lady driving off with Latisha was keeping him so agitated he had to turn on the television to distract himself.

He'd liked his little slave, damn it. He didn't want to lose her. But if she was going to be a bitch after all he'd done—the diamond ring and the proposal and the chocolate—to hell with her. He hadn't met a woman yet that he couldn't live without. Not Mary, not his first wife, who'd remarried before he'd met Emily, definitely not Emily and not his sexy little Latisha. What really bothered him was that Sebastian would consider Latisha's escape a victory.

So what, he told himself. Sebastian wouldn't be cele-brating for long.

One eye on the television, Malcolm booted up his laptop. He wasn't sure why he wanted to use his computer. He had no plans to e-mail anyone, no plans to use it for anything specific. He just had to keep his hands busy while he tried to figure out how to lure Sebastian away from where Jane Burke lived. An offer to meet wouldn't do it; Sebastian would expect a trap. So what would motivate him to go to a location of Malcolm's choosing? A location where Malcolm would have the privacy and control he needed to finally destroy the man he detested above all others—and do so without alerting the police?

Then it hit him. Sebastian had gone to Mary's house to save her. He'd also given Emily money or covered for her if he thought it might get her out of trouble or make her life easier. He was a fucking knight in shining armor, always trying to rescue the women around him.

Excitement coiled inside Malcolm. If Sebastian cared about Jane, and it appeared that he did, he'd do the same for her as he had for the other females in his life. That meant it would be stupid to kill her too soon. All he had to do was kidnap her and use her for bait.

But how would he get to her with Sebastian staying at her condo?

Simple—he'd take her from the office.

"There might be other people at the office," he said, thinking aloud, "like that man I saw there before."

But she'd be the only one getting into her *car.* Thanks to the early darkness of winter, he could wait in her backseat. She wouldn't even see him. Not until it was too late.

And once he had Jane, Sebastian would do anything he was told.

"I'm a damn genius," Malcolm said and shut down his computer. *Now* he could sleep.

David was still at the isolated ranch house in Turlock where Latisha had been imprisoned when Sebastian pulled into the driveway with Jane in his car. They couldn't go inside, since the forensics team hadn't finished gathering evidence, but Sebastian had wanted to come out here, anyway. He wanted to see where Malcolm had hidden for so long and to get a feel for how he'd lived.

Somehow, Sebastian had expected it to be nicer. He couldn't say he was *surprised* to discover that it wasn't. It just stood to reason that if a man was going to kill his wife for money, that money should put him in a better place. This old rambler wasn't even as nice as the house in Ione. It hadn't been updated in at least three decades, to the point that it looked and felt abandoned.

"David's coming out to get the lunch we brought," Jane informed him as she twisted around to get it out of the backseat.

Sebastian nodded and climbed out of the car. He wasn't in a talkative mood. He was relieved that Latisha was safe, but he had no idea when Mary would be able to return to regular life—or how much was left of his. New York was beginning to seem like a whole other world to which he no longer belonged.

The front door opened and David strode purposefully toward them. "Thanks for the meal," he said as Jane handed him the sack containing the hamburger and fries they'd picked up on the way.

"What're you finding?" she asked. "Anything that might help?"

"Actually, there's a lot here, so much it'll take a while to process. Hair fibers, blood on the carpet, mattresses where the girls probably slept, metal stakes in the floor where they were restrained, alcohol, sleeping pills."

"He didn't have time to clean up," Jane mused.

"He barely had time to pack an overnight bag."

Dark clouds rolled across the sun and the temperature plunged. She pulled her coat closed. "So...if we can find him, there should be more than enough evidence to convict him."

"Along with Latisha's testimony, I should think so."

Sebastian was staring at the house, wondering what Malcolm had been thinking whenever he approached the front door. This was no kind of trade, not for the life he'd once had. Malcolm had once owned a comfortable home, had a respectable job and parents and siblings who seemed like decent folks, a lovely wife, and the opportunity to make a real difference as a parent to a very good kid. *His* kid.

"What an idiot...."

Jane and David glanced his way. "Excuse me?" David said.

"After what he had in Jersey, he's willing to settle for *this* dump?"

"Used to be a dairy farm," David explained. "The original owner sold off the stock shortly after his wife died, when he got too old to run the place. It was paid for and he'd spent fifty years here, so he stayed until he died, five years ago. His kids inherited, of course, but they're spread out across the country. One's even in Japan, teaching English. No one wanted to move here. None of them could afford to bring the farm back. They've been trying to sell it ever since but in the current market it's not easy to sell something like this. I'm sure they rented it to Malcolm pretty cheap."

"Free wouldn't be cheap enough," Sebastian muttered.

"You have to admit it'd be perfect for someone who enjoys his privacy," Jane said.

Sebastian glowered at what he saw. "Or needed that privacy to commit unconscionable acts."

"There's that." David was eating his burger as if he hadn't seen a meal in a while—or didn't have the time to eat this one.

"Did you find his gun?" Sebastian asked.

"No," David replied between mouthfuls. "We haven't come across any weapons at all, unless you count kitchen knives."

It would've been good if he'd left his gun behind so they could match it with the ballistics on the bullet from Latisha's arm, but Malcolm wasn't that stupid. "What about his police uniform, his badge?"

"That's gone, too."

Of course Malcolm would take those things with him. They were the symbols of his power, the accoutrements of his fantasy.

"Any idea where he might've gone?" Jane asked.

"He could be staying with a friend or at a motel," David mused.

"That means he could be anywhere," Sebastian said.

"We found something that tells us he probably hasn't left the area."

Sebastian shoved his hands in his pockets. "What's that?"

David swallowed his last bite and smashed the sack. "Just a minute."

Jane sent Sebastian a curious glance. "What do you suppose it is?"

"You got me," he said.

Fortunately, they didn't have to wait long for the answer. David came back a couple of minutes later, wearing surgical gloves and holding a piece of paper. "I can't let you touch it, but you can see it," he told them and turned it so they could read what had been written with a black felt-tip marker.

I'm coming for you, Sebastian, it said. *Don't think I won't.*

Visions of Noah lying dead in the bed she'd shared with Oliver floated to Jane's consciousness as Sebastian drove them back to town. Would she someday find Sebastian in his own blood?

The thought made her stomach churn with acid. How could she protect him? How could she make sure nothing like that ever happened?

"You need to go home," she blurted.

He steered with one arm slung over the wheel. "You mean New York?"

"Yes."

"Malcolm won't hurt me, Jane."

"You don't know that. Noah was bigger and stronger than Oliver. And you should've seen what Oliver did to him…" Closing her eyes, she tried to wipe the revolting scene from her mind. "I'm sure he never dreamed

Oliver could overpower him. He thought I was crazy for even telling him to be careful."

"This is different." Although he was arguing with her, his tone indicated that he understood what she was feeling. "Malcolm isn't my brother so I'm not about to give him the benefit of the doubt. And I'm well aware that he's dangerous. No one has to convince me of that."

"He followed you from Mary's. He knows where the condo is."

"It's in your name."

"He could connect us."

"How?"

There wasn't anyone who knew her who also knew Malcolm, but she didn't like taking chances. Not with Sebastian's life. *I'm coming for you...* Those words were so ominous, so...purposeful. "He could be watching my condo. Maybe he's already seen us come home. Even if he hasn't, why couldn't he knock on a neighbor's door and ask a few questions? What if he stumbles on Bob walking his dog, for instance? Bob knows your name, knows you've been staying at my place."

Sebastian let his breath go in a long sigh, but didn't speak. Was she getting through to him? Unable to tell, she reached for his arm. "What do you say?"

"I can't leave you there alone, just in case he *has* associated the two of us." Lines appeared on his forehead. "But if he hasn't made the connection, I don't want to draw him to your place, either. I'm not sure what to do."

"Will you let *me* decide?"

"No. You'd put me on the first plane back east."

She said nothing.

"That's not the answer, Jane. This thing between Malcolm and me—it has to end sometime."

"It's the *way* it might end that bothers me." She'd lost enough. She couldn't stand losing the one man who made her feel hopeful again. There were moments when she thought about having another baby, and those moments made her think that maybe it wasn't too late to start over, to offer Kate more than she'd had, to build a better life, one less traumatized by the past.

"You trust David, don't you?" he said.

She scowled. He was changing tactics on her. "Of course I trust David. He's an excellent detective. But that's beside the point."

"Jane, if Malcolm really wants to kill me, running away won't solve the problem." He pulled into a drugstore.

"What are we doing?" she asked as he parked. "Why are we stopping here?"

"We need to buy something."

"Gum? Film? Shaving cream?"

He opened his door and got out. "A pregnancy test."

Jane's hand froze on the latch. She wasn't ready to discover whether or not they had other big decisions to make. It felt as if she still had the option of sending Sebastian away, of going on with her life as though this week had never occurred. But if she took a pregnancy test and that pregnancy test was positive…what would they do? How would they handle it? "I don't know if this is such a good idea."

"You can wait here if you'd like."

"Sebastian—"

"I'll be right back."

She remained in the car, trying to imagine how she'd

feel if she turned out to be pregnant. That was easy. She'd be scared. She was in her mid-forties. There were significant risks. And she'd never expected to have another child. But what if the test was negative?

Part of her would be disappointed; she couldn't deny that.

He held a small brown paper bag when he returned. He tossed it between them as he got in, and Jane eyed it as if it contained a snake. "Sebastian—"

"If you're not pregnant, we'll start using birth control," he said. "If you are, there'll be no need."

"You won't accept my advice and head back to New York no matter what it says. Why should I take it?" she countered.

"So I'll know whether to stop at my motel and get those condoms before I drive you home. It'll save you from having to deal with that Shield." Starting the car, he backed out of the parking space. "If we're going to deliver on our promise to take Kate ice-skating, we don't have much time."

He was worried about following through on a promise to her daughter? That was something she hadn't experienced in years—a pleasant something. "We just…we won't do it again," she said. "If we stay away from each other, we won't need birth control. And we won't need to know whether or not I'm pregnant. Not right away."

He gave her a look that told her he wasn't about to let her out of this. "I don't think staying away from each other is very realistic, do you?"

She rubbed her face. "Probably not," she sighed.

He drove across the street to the gas station. "There's the bathroom," he said and handed her the bag.

*   *   *

Butterflies swirled in Sebastian's stomach for the first time since he could remember. Was it really possible that in nine months he'd become a father again? So much had changed. He'd lost Emily and Colton and Constance and all the momentum he'd achieved with his work. He no longer had the money he once did. He couldn't believe he was even thinking about having another child, let alone pacing outside a gas-station restroom in California while the woman he'd been sleeping with took a pregnancy test.

"Jane?" he called when he couldn't wait anymore.

She didn't answer, so he tapped on the door. "Hey! What does it say?"

Again, no answer. Did that mean what he thought it might? Or was it just that she hadn't finished or couldn't hear him? "Jane?" he called again.

Finally, the little sign that read Occupied disappeared as she turned the lock. But she didn't come out. She opened the door a few inches and peered through the crack.

"What'd it say?"

Her chest rose as she took a deep breath. "It's negative."

"You're sure?"

She passed him the test strip. He didn't know what gray meant, but he didn't question it. He stared at it for a second; then he reached around to put it on the sink. "That's good, right?"

"I guess so. But despite everything, in a way, I'm disappointed."

He understood because in a way he was, too. Even with the risks involved. Regardless of what anyone watching from the gas pumps might think if they saw him, Sebastian stepped into the woman's restroom and closed the door so he could draw her into his arms and kiss her gently. "It's okay."

"I know. It's just...this isn't only about whether or not we're having a baby."

He tilted up her chin. "Then what's it about?"

"You."

"Me?"

"Yes." Her voice dropped. "I'm pretty sure I've fallen in love with you."

Laughing at the hopelessness in her words, he kissed the tip of her nose. "I'm sorry that upsets you."

"You live in New York!"

"You're the one who keeps trying to send me back!"

"I still want you to go, if it'll keep you safe."

Feelings he hadn't experienced since before Colton's death began to simmer inside Sebastian, chasing all the negative events into the background. He was suddenly stronger, more like himself, so much happier. "I'm not going back. I'm staying here, with you."

"But it's important that you go—at least until the police capture Malcolm."

"Trust me to take care of myself," he said. "Trust me to take care of you and Kate."

"It's *him* I don't trust," she argued.

"We'll come out of this. We'll be fine."

She laid her head on his shoulder. "How would you have reacted if there was a baby?" she asked. "Would it have scared you away?"

What kind of fickle asshole did she think he was? "Not at all. I'm forty-five, Jane, not twenty-five. I know what a baby means. I said I'd be happy, and that hasn't changed. I would've been okay with it, as long as you were."

"And how does the fact that there is no baby change the situation?" Her head came up. She was expecting him to tell her why he wasn't ready for a permanent relationship. He could tell. But that wasn't what he had to say.

Taking her face in his hands, he kissed her again. "It doesn't. I still want you."

"You're serious," she said, searching his face.

"Completely."

She smiled. Then she hugged him tighter and it was her turn to kiss him. She didn't ask any more questions. Apparently she was willing to let it go at that, and he was glad. He had no idea what he'd do about his job in New York, if he'd relocate or she would, if she'd mind that he'd spent all his money chasing Malcolm and would need time to rebuild. It was too soon to discuss any of the practical issues of how they'd be together. But they knew they wanted to be together. And for now, that was enough.

Jane could hardly believe that she'd found another man she cared about. Sometimes she'd look up to find Sebastian watching her with such tenderness that a warm tingle would go through her. This was what she'd been missing. This…contentment. She'd never really had it, certainly not with Oliver. He'd always been too selfish. Sebastian was different, mature, confident, willing to care for others. What she felt for him was so wonderful it frightened her—because she was afraid it wouldn't last. Good things seldom did. She had a bone-deep conviction that she wasn't meant to be so happy, didn't deserve it. And if she ever forgot that, she didn't have to go far to be reminded. She knew how Wendy would react to the news....

"Mom, you watching?" Kate called.

"You're doing great, honey!" Jane smiled and waved at her daughter, circling the ice with Sebastian. Although Jane had gone skating quite often in her early teens, it was Kate's first time. She seemed a bit shaky but she was enjoying herself...and enjoying all the attention Sebastian was lavishing on her.

Jane went to the restroom, which was why she'd gotten off the ice. She was on her way back to the rink when her cell phone rang. It'd been so long since she'd skated that she wasn't much steadier than Kate was, so she answered before stepping onto the ice.

Caller ID showed it was Skye. "Hello?"

"Jane? Hi!"

Leaning against the railing, Jane searched the crowd for Sebastian and Kate. "How are you?"

"Better. We've found the child we were looking for."

"That's wonderful news! How'd you do it?"

"A relative of the father, a cousin. They got into an argument, so the cousin finally came forward."

"What was the argument about?"

"Dishes," she said with a laugh. "They were living together, and it wasn't working out too well."

"Lucky for you. So are you coming home soon?"

"We're flying out tomorrow. I can't wait. I'm so homesick for my family I can't stand it."

"I know they'll be glad to see you."

"How's everything going?"

Kate took a spill, but it wasn't a hard fall and Sebastian helped her up. "At the office?" she asked.

"At home, too. It seems like forever since we've had a chance to talk."

Jane considered everything she had to tell. Where did she start? The case? No, she'd save that until Skye got home. She didn't want to focus on Malcolm; she was more interested in talking about the positive developments in her life. "I've met someone," she said.

"You have? Wow, this is a first. I haven't even been able to get you to go out on a date. Who is it?" The excitement in Skye's voice brought a smile to Jane's face.

"An investment banker from New York."

"Where'd you meet him?"

"At the office."

"He's a client?"

"More of a...volunteer."

"He sounds interesting."

"He's...*special.*"

"Special is good. It's better than I ever expected to hear from you. How long have you known him?" she asked.

"Only a week. But we've spent nearly every minute together."

"No kidding? Have you introduced him to Kate?"

Kate was the litmus test, and Skye knew it. "Yes. We're ice-skating right now."

"Damn, why does everything happen when I leave?" she complained with a laugh. "I'm looking forward to meeting him."

"When you're back."

"We'll be there on Monday. I doubt we'll be in the office much for the first few days, probably just long enough to go through our messages, but at least we'll get to say hello. I was thinking it might be smart to have a short meeting. Sheridan said she'd bring her baby so we could see him again, and we can get caught up and sort of plan out the week."

"I'll be there. What time?"

"How about four o'clock?"

"Four it is. I'll see you then. Have a safe—"

"Jane?" she cut in.

"Yeah?"

"It's *great* to hear you sound so happy."

"It's great to feel this happy," she said and hung up just as Sebastian and Kate came to a stop on the rink in front of her.

"Hey, you getting back on?" he asked.

"Of course."

They waited for her at the opening, each holding out a hand to help her onto the ice. "Who were you talking to, Mama?" Kate asked.

"Skye."

Sebastian steadied her as they started off. "She still out of town?"

"She's coming home tomorrow."

"Are you going to tell her you worked on your first case?" Kate asked.

"I will. I wish I could also tell her we have the bad guy behind bars, but..."

"You'll get to say that soon," Kate said.

Jane exchanged a glance with Sebastian. "You bet I will."

Twenty-Six

Malcolm spent most of Saturday and all morning Sunday studying The Last Stand's Web site. They had a feature that allowed someone interested in getting help to petition—anonymously—for information. The charity catered to abused women and children, for the most part, so he imagined this was a way to make a woman who didn't know how to escape her situation feel safe enough to ask about her options.

It was a really nice idea.

It might also be the perfect means to ensure that Jane would be at the office tomorrow afternoon. At least it was worth writing in to see who responded....

Clicking on the *I Have a Question* link, he waited for the form to come up, then began to type.

My husband gets very violent, especially when he drinks. He hits me—he broke my nose last week. Sometimes he even hits or kicks our children. I have to do something, for their sake. But if I get him in trouble, he'll kill me. He told me so when I went to his sister. I'm afraid he'll really go through with it! Is there any way I could make an appointment to see someone about getting help? My husband is out of town tomorrow. I could come in at six, if anyone will be available. I apologize for the inconvenience. I don't want to be a bother. I just don't know where else to turn.

He didn't make up a name to sign the message with. He figured it would be just as believable without one.

After he'd sent it, he watched some television, called his bookie to see if he could place another bet, was refused because he hadn't paid for the last few and began to pace. If he'd thought living alone in that ranch house was stifling, this was even worse. He felt so cooped up, so…limited.

His life was shit. Why was he putting up with that?

Cursing, he decided to head to Stockton Boulevard. It'd been a long time since he'd played at the "prostitute bribes undercover cop" fantasy. Maybe if he could find a black woman who was young and pretty, like Latisha, he'd be able to pretend it was her….

"Would you and Kate like to come to dinner?"

Switching her cell phone to the other ear, Jane hesitated at her mother-in-law's offer. She, Sebastian and Kate were at the kitchen table. They'd been playing board games for most of the weekend. She got the impression it was the first time Sebastian had forgotten about chasing Malcolm in a long, long while. She enjoyed seeing him relax, hearing him laugh. She'd prefer to spend the rest of their Sunday as they'd spent it so far—just the three of them—but she'd been busy lately, consumed by work, and her in-laws had been so good, helping with Kate whenever she needed them. She figured she could at least *ask* if Sebastian would like to go.

Covering the mouthpiece, she whispered to him. "Kate's grandma is inviting us over for dinner. Any chance you'd be interested?"

"Can she cook?" he teased.

"She's a *really* good cook!" Kate told him.

He winked. "Then I'm in. I never turn down a home-cooked meal."

Remembering the lasagna he'd paid her to make, Jane smiled and returned to her conversation. "We have someone visiting us who's hankering for some old-fashioned home cooking. Is it okay if we bring him along?"

"*Him?* It's a man?" Betty asked. "Who is it? That P.I. from work? Or one of the volunteers?"

Jane tried not to chuckle at the fluster behind those questions. "No. Someone else. His name is Sebastian Costas."

"You've never mentioned a Sebastian before. I'd remember that name. Costas—is he Greek?"

"You haven't heard of him because we just met last week. And, yes, I think his name's Greek."

"It is," Sebastian confirmed.

"What's Greek?" Kate asked.

Sebastian explained while Betty continued questioning Jane. "Is this a romantic interest? Because it kind of sounds that way. It sounds as if you've finally met someone."

Jane told herself she should've known she'd be grilled. Betty had been urging her to start dating for the past three years. But she wasn't making any commitments. She knew it was silly, superstitious, but she was afraid she might jinx her own happiness if she did. "Maybe."

"Then of course you can bring him! I've been praying you could—" She stopped. When she struggled to go on, Jane realized it was because she'd suddenly choked up.

"I'm going to be okay," she said gently. "Even if I spend the rest of my life alone, I'll be okay."

"I know, it's just…you've been through so much."

That reminder brought one other consideration to mind. "Will Wendy be coming tonight?"

"She might be. I always invite both of you. Someday she'll understand that it's useless to hold a grudge and she'll let our family be whole again—or as whole as it can be."

Jane appreciated the sentiment and the effort her in-laws made to close the rift. But did she really want to have dinner with Wendy? This had been such a good weekend….

"Grandma has a great big dog," Kate was telling Sebastian, her face as animated as Jane had ever seen it. "I want you to meet him. And Grandpa bought me a trampoline. I can do some tricks. You'll see."

With a sigh, Jane decided it didn't really matter whether Wendy was going to be at the Burkes' or not. "We'll be there," she said. "What time?"

The tension in the room was palpable. Sebastian had noticed it from the moment Jane's ex-sister-in-law trooped in with her boys. Wendy sat across from him now, wearing a stony expression as she picked at her food. Occasionally she looked up long enough to glower at Jane.

Jane sat stoically beside him, giving Wendy a brief but hopeful smile whenever their eyes met. Sebastian understood that she felt guilty for what she'd done. He thought she *should* feel guilty; she'd made a serious mistake. But it bothered him that Wendy continued to withhold her forgiveness when Jane was obviously so eager to receive it. She'd been paying penance for five years. What more could she do? She regretted her actions. Besides, she hadn't meant for anyone to be hurt, she wasn't the one who'd killed Noah, and she'd been going through an extremely difficult time when she'd gotten involved with him. How did Wendy know her husband wasn't equally to blame—or, for that matter, even *more* to blame?

Sebastian answered politely as the older Burkes asked him the usual questions—where he was from, what he did. They seemed intrigued by him, but all he could think about were the daggers Wendy was staring at Jane.

"So how did you meet?" Wendy asked, breaking her "I will ignore Jane and anything to do with her" rule, which she'd upheld to this point.

"We've been working on a case together," he said.

"What kind of case?"

"A kidnap case," Jane inserted, gazing down at her plate.

The clipped response told Sebastian Jane didn't want to elaborate. She was trying to protect Kate from hearing how bad the man they'd been chasing really was. And they couldn't discuss murder at the table. Not with this family, who'd had firsthand experience. But it was Kate who jumped in. "Don't worry, the girl's home safe," she piped up.

Sebastian smiled at the relief in her voice, but Wendy scarcely acknowledged her niece. "How does an investment banker get involved in a kidnap case?" she asked.

"I have a personal interest."

"The victim was your daughter?"

"Not exactly." He gave her a pointed look. "But close."

She seemed to take the hint that he wasn't prepared to discuss his connection to the case in front of the kids. So she waited until Kate and her sons had finished eating and dashed off to play video games in one of the back rooms before she brought it up again.

"I'm curious about your reason for coming all the way from New York," she said as they sat in the living room with an after-dinner drink.

Maurice and Betty tensed at her determination to unravel the mystery, but Sebastian conjured up a friendly expression and spoke before they could intercede. "The man Jane's been trying to find killed my son," he said bluntly.

Her eyes widened.

"So you're not the only one who's lost someone you love," he added.

His voice held no sympathy, nor did it conceal the irritation he was feeling. She rocked back in surprise and Jane's jaw dropped, but Sebastian took this in while keeping his eyes on Wendy. "Tragedy happens," he said. "It hits some people harder than others, but don't think for a minute that you're alone."

She dropped the thin veneer of politeness she'd

assumed so far. Seeing Jane with a man seemed to bring out the worst in her; he could tell she'd been dying to express her disapproval from the beginning, which was why he'd given her the opportunity. "Maybe that's true, but how do you feel about the man who killed your son?" she challenged, sending another glower at Jane.

Jane flushed crimson. "Sebastian, it's okay," she said. "Wendy has every right to feel the way she does."

"No, she doesn't." He took Jane's hand to show his support. "Jane didn't kill your husband, Ms. Burke. She was as much a victim as you were." With his free hand, he indicated her scar. "Don't you agree she's been punished enough?"

Grabbing her purse, Wendy jumped to her feet. "I don't know who you think you are!"

He kept his voice even but enunciated every word. "Then let me explain. I'm the new man in Jane's life. No one will mistreat her as long as I'm around. Although I'm sorry for your pain, that includes you."

She gaped at him as he turned to Betty and Maurice and bowed his head in farewell. "Dinner was excellent. Thank you so much for having us over." He tugged on Jane's arm. "Ready to go?"

She got to her feet. "I *am* sorry," she whispered. "I'd do anything to be able to take it back."

Wendy glared at her with such hatred, Jane quickly called Kate and they headed for the door.

"That was an interesting dinner," Jane said when they were in the car.

Sebastian was already beginning to regret what he'd done—or maybe it was just the way he'd done it that seemed wrong. He'd come across too strongly for someone so new to the situation, which probably hadn't endeared him to anyone. He hadn't been able to protect Emily and Colton, so he was overcompensating with Jane. But he couldn't allow Wendy to mistreat her. Now that he had a second chance to do a better job with the people he loved, he figured he'd rather err on the side of overstatement.

"She needed to hear it," he said.

Jane left it at that, but he guessed she might've said more if Kate hadn't been in the car. Why couldn't he have waited until the third or fourth meeting to plunge right into the heart of her family's problems? Why did he always have to try and fix everything?

Kate chattered all the way home about Horse, the dog at her grandma's (which was so big it looked like its namesake), the trampoline in the backyard (her "absolute *favorite* thing ever"), her male cousins (one of whom she called "mean" for teasing her about being a shrimp). She didn't seem to notice the strain between Sebastian and Jane. When they got home, she went to bed asking if Sebastian would be there when she got out of school the next day. She said she planned to make him a "gift" in her pottery class.

Sebastian wasn't sure if he'd be around. Jane meant a lot to him; he wanted to make their relationship work. But he was afraid their histories would always taint their actions in one way or another, make them over-react when they shouldn't or withdraw when they should persist. He wasn't positive they could overcome all that, wasn't positive Jane would be willing to work through the rough patches.

"You still mad at me?" he asked when they were finally alone in the living room.

She was just logging on to her computer. He'd been surfing the Internet on his, pulling up maps of Sacramento and motels where he thought Malcolm might go because they were cheap.

"No," she said. "It just…it surprised me, I guess. I'm not used to having anyone fight my battles."

"I think it surprised everyone."

"No kidding." Shaking her head, she began to laugh. "Wendy looked like she'd swallowed a golf ball."

"Maurice and Betty were struck speechless," he added with chagrin.

Jane's laughter subsided, but her smile lingered. "Will you always be so take-charge?"

He wished he could say no, but he knew himself too well. "Probably."

"That's what I thought."

Watching her carefully, he posed his next question. "Do you think it'll be a problem?"

She met his eyes. "Sometimes," she admitted. "But I'll let you know when you're stepping on my toes."

He smiled. Maybe he'd overreacted by assuming they couldn't make room for each other. "That's fair."

She started typing, and he signed on to his e-mail account. Mary had sent him a message telling him how much she wanted to come home. He wrote her a quick reply, asking her to be patient. He'd also received a message from the handwriting specialist. She confirmed that the directions to Cache Creek he'd found in Ione were indeed Malcolm's handwriting. It was a bit late for that information to help, but when he'd hired her, he hadn't known things would develop the way they did. Thanks to Latisha's brave escape, they had all the forensic evidence they'd need. The problem wasn't proving Malcolm was alive or even guilty; the problem was finding him so they could use the evidence they had to put him away.

Without leads, Sebastian had no idea how they'd do that. And yet…he wasn't as distraught as he would've been a week ago. Somehow, being with Jane took the edge off the emotions that had cut him so badly.

After returning the rest of his messages—a note from his mother and another one from his boss in New York—he sat with his computer open as if he was still working, but watched Jane instead. A frown creased her forehead, but she was so darn pretty he thought he could stare at her all day.

Glancing up, she caught him. "What is it?" she asked.

He wanted to tell her he'd just been thinking about how differently he'd begun to view everything since he'd met her, but those emotions were too new to put into words. "You were frowning. Something wrong?"

"Not really. I've just been checking an e-mail account connected to the Web site at work. Skye usually does it, but she asked me to see to it while she was gone. There's a message in here that concerns me, that's all."

"What kind of message?"

"It's from an abused woman. Sounds like she might be in serious trouble."

He closed his laptop. "She's asking for help?"

"Yeah. She wants to meet with someone tomorrow afternoon."

"Will you take the appointment?"

"Might as well," she said as he walked over to her. "It'll be right after the staff meeting. Skye, Ava and Sheridan will be there, but Sheridan'll have the baby and Skye and Ava have been gone so long they need a chance to see their families. I can do it. It shouldn't take long."

"I can stay here with Kate," he said.

Her frown dissolved into a grateful smile. "Thanks. Let me respond to her e-mail—then I'll be done, too."

He massaged her shoulders while she typed. "How long does it take Kate to fall asleep?" he asked as she sent it.

She twisted around to look up at him. "I don't know. Why?"

Jerking his head toward the hall, he grinned. "How'd you like to make up in the shower?"

She didn't answer with words. She stood and turned to face him, and her hands tugged his shirt from his pants as they kissed.

There weren't a lot of girls out tonight. It was too cold. And the ones Malcolm saw looked nothing like Latisha. Mostly, they were fat white girls with a few Asians and Mexicans thrown in. He couldn't even pretend they were like Latisha. Not once they opened their mouths, anyway. The profanity made them seem so…hardened. Odd that he hadn't ever noticed that before. Or cared.

Being reduced to searching for a look-alike made him feel like hurting somebody. But even with the sparse pickings, he wasn't worried that he'd be able to get a girl into the van. All it took was money.

He pulled to a stop at the corner of Stockton and 65th

Street and lowered his window. When he made eye contact with a Mexican hooker, she smiled and sauntered closer. "Hey, you lookin' for a date?" she said.

It couldn't be more than fifty degrees outside but her skirt came up as high as her ass and her blouse plunged down to her belly button. She wasn't wearing a bra, no doubt to show off the nipple piercings that could easily be seen through her thin shirt. She wasn't black, but her skin was almost the same golden color as Latisha's.

Would she do? He wasn't particularly excited about her, but he couldn't afford to be picky on a night like this....

"How much?" he asked.

"Depends on what you want."

"It's too cold to be standing on a street corner," he said.

She straightened, studied her long red fingernails and glanced at the vehicle behind him as if she had a dozen takers lined up. "You ain't gonna get *this* for free, but if you want oral sex the likes of which you ain't never seen, you've come to the right place."

He considered his options. She'd just offered him a blow job. Did that mean she wouldn't do it in the traditional way? Some of these girls tried to avoid it, or insisted on a condom, so they wouldn't pick up a disease. If that was the case with this one, he was more interested rather than less—because chances were good she'd kept herself clean. "Will you let me tie you up?"

"For the right price."

"How much?"

"A hundred bucks."

She was dreaming. She wasn't going to get a

hundred bucks out of anyone. This was Sacramento, not New York. But he didn't bother to argue. He didn't plan on paying, anyway.

Popping the locks, he reached across to open the door. "Climb in."

"Circle around," she said. "I gotta get my purse from inside."

"What do you need your purse for?"

She rolled her eyes. "I always provide the condom. That's the one rule I won't break, so take it or leave it, eh?"

He studied her. She wasn't like Latisha, wasn't half as sweet. He almost drove off and left her. He wasn't going to let a woman—least of all a gutter-grade whore—act as if she had even a hint of control. But none of the other girls he'd passed had dark skin. Since Latisha, he needed dark skin to get excited.

When he came around the corner again, she was waiting for him as promised, posing to make the most of her limited assets.

"You gonna be sorry," he mimicked when he drove up, but he said nothing loudly enough for her to hear. He just opened the door and she got in.

"You mind if I call you Latisha?" he asked.

She chomped her gum. "Say what?"

"Your name during our time together will be Latisha."

"Whatever gets you hard, baby. For the right price you can call me Mother Mary. So where we goin'?"

"You know of a hotel close by?"

Taking out her gum, she stuck it on a Styrofoam cup that'd been in his van for weeks. "You got a van. Can't we park behind a building for a few minutes?"

"It'll take a bit longer than that." Pulling out the bag

of meth he'd purchased on the way over, he tossed it in her lap.

A gleam of anticipation lit her eyes. "So this is gonna be a *party.*"

"All night long, baby. And the dope's free."

Twenty-Seven

On Monday, Jane made herself go to the office after driving Kate to school. So many things had piled up while she'd been focused on finding Latisha. There was mail that needed to be sorted, calls waiting to be returned, projects she was overseeing that the volunteers still had to finish, banking to do. Normally, she stayed on top of the clerical stuff, but last week she'd been too busy.

With Skye and Ava coming in this afternoon, she wanted to get caught up. They'd be more likely to let her take on her own cases if she was able to maintain her usual workflow until they could hire a part-timer to replace her.

She managed to get a few things done, but she was having trouble concentrating, moving at only half-speed. Every now and then, she'd find herself staring off into space, thinking about Sebastian and the way they'd made love last night. Had she ever been this happy? She couldn't have been. This relationship was so different from any of her others, so unexpected and yet...fulfilling. It could go bad; it could always go bad. But for now, it was perfect.

Thoughts of Wendy occasionally crept in. Jane wondered if Sebastian's words had made any difference—besides escalating her sister-in-law's hatred.

By the time the staff meeting came around, Jane was eager to see Skye, Ava and Sheridan but even more eager to see Sebastian. The day already seemed long. She preferred to be out looking for Malcolm, as David was doing, watching the casinos or calling his ex-wife and former friends to see if anyone had heard from him. She wanted to tell his family that he was alive, to enlist their support in the search. Although the DNA at the ranch house had yet to be analyzed, which would take a while, there was proof that he was still living, in the form of that handwriting expert's report—at least, enough proof that the authorities should listen.

Sebastian had sent her text messages throughout the day. He'd spent the morning calling every hotel and motel in town, asking for a Wesley Boss as well as a Malcolm Turner—but had found nothing. This afternoon, with David's permission, he was out interviewing people who lived in the general vicinity of the ranch house where Malcolm had kept the girls. Sebastian thought he might find someone who'd spoken to Malcolm or befriended him in some way, someone who might have let him move in. But for all they knew, Malcolm was sleeping in his van. Once again, he seemed to have disappeared from the face of the earth.

She heard someone unlock the back door. "Jane?"

It was Skye. She'd arrived before Ava and Sheridan. Excited to see the person who'd saved her life and then helped her through the darkest period of it, Jane went to the reception area to greet her. Most of the volunteers had already left for the day, but there were two in Sheridan's office, finishing up a big fundraising mailer. They poked their heads out to say hi, but when they went back to work, Jane and Skye stepped into the conference room for a few minutes alone.

"It's about time you came back," Jane said. "It's so great to see you."

"It's good to be here." After a tight hug, Skye held Jane at arm's length. "You look *fabulous.*"

"Stop it," Jane said, laughing. "It's only been a couple of weeks since you saw me. I look the same."

"No, you look better." She lowered her voice. "You must have your groove back."

"Hi, everyone." Ava peered into the conference room before Jane could respond. "Where's Sheridan?"

"She's not here yet," Jane told her.

"Darn. I can't wait to see the baby." She turned to speak to the volunteers who'd once again come out to the reception area to say hello, then did a double-take when she focused on Jane again. "Wow, you look great!"

Exasperated, Jane rolled her eyes. "That's crazy. I don't know what you guys are talking about."

Skye leaned close to Ava so the volunteers, who were already returning to work, wouldn't hear. "Don't let her fool you. She's got her groove back."

"That has to be it," Ava agreed as she took the chair next to Skye. "I heard about your new man."

They peppered her with questions until Sheridan arrived, and after that, the baby drew all the attention. Relieved to be out of the spotlight, Jane sat through the meeting, listening but adding little. She didn't tell them about her case, didn't mention wanting to take on more. She was reluctant to do anything that would make the meeting last longer. They'd be in tomorrow, and the day after that and the day after that—there'd be plenty of time to discuss everything that had gone on during their absences.

Although she loved seeing them all, she was glad when they left. One volunteer remained behind, a high-school boy named Rick who was trying to finish up the mailer, but he wasn't planning on staying much longer. Neither was she. She had just one more meeting; her domestic-abuse victim would be in shortly.

Then she could go home to Kate and Sebastian.

Sebastian had come to California to catch a killer—and found a second family. As he sat at the pizza parlor with Kate, listening to her talk about her day and her friends and how badly she wanted a dog, he could hardly believe that so much had changed, and so fast! For the past twelve months, he'd been consumed with the thirst for revenge. In fact, he'd feared that if he ever found Malcolm, he'd become a killer himself. He'd almost welcomed it.

But he didn't feel like that anymore. He'd do the right thing because that was the only way he could protect Jane and Kate from suffering more than they already had. If he didn't, he couldn't be part of their lives.

"Leonard asked me to go out with him today," Kate said, acting shocked that this boy could have so much audacity.

Sebastian hid a smile. He could see himself back in

seventh grade, thinking Kate was cute, maybe even working up the nerve to see if she might like him. He'd never been particularly shy. "Where did he want you to go?" he asked, taking the question literally on purpose.

She shook her head. "No, that just means...you know, that we'd be together."

He nodded. "Right. You'd go out together. But where?"

"Stop it!" she giggled. "You know, he'd be my *boyfriend.*"

"Oh! I see. So he won't be borrowing his folks' car and taking you to the movies or anything."

"No, silly."

"That's good, because he has to be at least thirteen before I'd ever let you ride with him." The words were out of his mouth before he realized how fatherly they sounded, but she didn't seem to mind.

"Thirteen?" she echoed.

"And only if he can grow a mustache by then."

She continued to laugh. "Boys can't grow a mustache at thirteen."

"Then you'd better tell him no."

"Really? You want me to say no?" She nibbled the crust of her second piece of pizza.

It was hard for him to imagine that any boy could be worthy of her, but he figured he was being overprotective again. "That'd be my initial reaction. But I don't know him," he said. "What do you think?"

"He's kinda cute."

"Okay. I guess you could say yes—" Sebastian pushed his plate away "—if he's willing to speak to me about his intentions."

She giggled again. "You're funny."

He sobered as she pushed her plate away, too. "And you're going to have a whole string of boys who'll want to go out with you. Unless you really want to say yes, I say, what's the rush?"

"There is another boy I'd rather go out with."

"Then give *him* a chance, okay?" He slid from the booth. "You ready to go?"

"I'm ready." She took a final sip of her soda.

"That stuff'll kill ya, you know."

"I know, I know. My mom tells me that all the time," she grumbled and started out ahead of him.

Sebastian caught a glimpse of himself in the glass as they walked toward the exit. Damn, he'd let his hair get long. "Hey, you don't know where I could get my hair trimmed while we wait for your mom, do you?"

She paused at the door. "Mom's a haircutter. She can do it. She does my hair."

"And it looks nice, but—" he checked his watch "—it's only six. She said her appointment would take about half an hour. In the meantime, I thought I might as well get cleaned up." He winked. "I want her to think I'm handsome, you know."

The blush that tinged Kate's cheeks nearly made Sebastian burst out laughing. Kate's personality was entirely different from Colton's, but she possessed the same innocent charm. "I bet she already thinks you're handsome," she confided.

He held the door for her. "So…will she say yes if I ask her to go out with me?"

Her head pumped energetically. "*I* think so."

"What about you? Would you mind if we…you know…got together?"

She stopped walking and gazed up at him. "Do you like me, too?"

Her lack of artifice brought a lump to his throat. That was all she asked of him? He could certainly give her that. "Oh, I like you, all right," he said. "As a matter of fact, I'm pretty sure I'm falling for you *and* your mom."

With an expression that showed her pleasure at his response, she slipped her hand in his, and Sebastian smiled as he opened the car door. Not only had he found a second family, he could feel something besides anger.

He was pretty sure it was hope.

Jane didn't know how long to wait. It was six-thirty and her appointment hadn't shown.

She checked the Web site e-mail account as well as her personal account, which was the one she'd used to send her reply. Other than a brief confirmation of the appointment, sent late last night, she'd received no further communication.

Maybe the woman's husband had returned from his trip early, or something else had interrupted her. Or was the poor thing just too scared? Jane didn't want to leave if her victim was battling traffic, still planning to come. But she also didn't have any way to confirm that and didn't want to waste any more time if she *wasn't* coming.

"I'll give you fifteen more minutes," she said aloud and gathered up the items she needed to put in her briefcase.

"You talking to me?" Rick tapped the inside wall of her office as he looked in through her door.

"No, I'm grumbling to myself," she said. "My last appointment's late."

"I saw someone pull in about ten minutes ago and circle the lot, but it was a guy."

"I'm definitely waiting for a woman."

"Okay, well, I'm out of here, and I'm taking the mailers with me. I know we've missed the post office for today, but I'll ask my mom to take them over while I'm in school tomorrow, if that's okay."

"That's fine, as long as she doesn't mind."

"She won't. She's been talking about coming down here to volunteer herself. She thinks more people should get involved."

"We'd be glad to have her." Jane moved around the desk. "Let me at least help you get the boxes into your car."

He waved her off. "Nah, I already did that. I just came in to say goodbye."

She returned to her seat. "Thanks, Rick. We really appreciate everything you do."

"No problem." He pointed at the clock. "You gonna wait any longer?"

It was now 6:35 p.m. "Another ten minutes," she said. If that e-mail hadn't sounded so desperate, Jane might've left. But she wanted to offer this poor woman every chance she could.

Standing in the alley, Malcolm breathed a sigh of relief as the beater Mustang turned into the street. He'd been afraid he'd given himself away. Hoping to figure out which car was Jane's, he'd cruised through the lot one too many times—and nearly ran over a tall, gangly kid who suddenly emerged from the building carrying what looked like a heavy box. Rather than act suspicious, Malcolm had stopped and smiled and gestured him across the blacktop, but he worried that the boy had somehow sensed that he wasn't supposed to be there and gone back inside to alert Jane.

Apparently, he hadn't done anything of the sort. He'd loaded his car and driven off. Now there was only one vehicle in the lot, and Malcolm had no trouble guessing who it belonged to. Jane had confirmed the meeting he'd requested when he posed as the unfortunate victim of spousal abuse. She had to be here, waiting for her appointment. He'd been watching the place since six. She wouldn't have left before that.

When the sound of the Mustang had faded away, he peered around the corner. The exterior lights had come on about the time he'd arrived. They were brighter and more plentiful than he'd expected; obviously, someone was worried about security. But the extra light wouldn't be a problem because Jane's car was parked in a shadowy spot, and he'd been lucky enough to find her alone. No one would see him get into her car. There was no one around. He'd keep one hand on the latch, and if she spotted him as she was climbing in, he'd be able to get to her before she could summon help.

With a quick glance in both directions, he stepped out of the alley and crossed the blacktop, whistling as if he owned the car parked there. He had two door stoppers and the rubber-ended wire he'd need in a paper bag; it would take maybe a minute to break in.

He was thirty seconds into it, had barely wedged the bigger of the two door stoppers between the door and the frame, when a car on the side road came to a squealing halt. Malcolm heard the whine of reverse. Then someone yelled at him. "Hey! What the hell you doin'?"

Although Malcolm couldn't really see the driver, he could tell from the voice that it was a man. He also got the impression of considerable size. But he didn't let that rattle him. He could sell anything if he remained calm.

Knowing he was too old to look like a typical car thief, he waved. "Locked myself out!"

The man's suspicion seemed to instantly dissolve. "You need me to call Triple A?"

At that moment, Malcolm tripped the unlock button he'd been fishing for inside the door. "No, I got it. Thanks, anyway!"

"You bet!" the guy said and took off.

Malcolm called him an asshole while he checked to see if all the yelling had brought Jane to the door. The inside lights were on. He would've been able to see her if it had. No one was looking out.

"Piece of cake," he muttered and climbed into her backseat. After dropping his tools on the floor so she wouldn't find them on the pavement, he locked all the doors except the closest one and crouched behind the passenger seat, where she'd be least likely to see him.

He felt conspicuous. But how many times had she come out of that building and gotten in her car to drive home? How many times had she popped the locks and hopped in without even considering the possibility that someone might be waiting for her?

Chances were she wouldn't even glance at the backseat. To her, this was a day like any other.

Only Malcolm knew that it would be her last.

Twenty-Eight

The woman wasn't going to show. Had something happened to her? Or had she simply chickened out? Jane knew that the people who most needed help were the last ones to follow through. There were a lot of reasons for that, many of which Jane understood. But she'd thought this woman had seemed ready to change her situation.

Frustrated that she'd wasted so much time waiting around for nothing, at 6:45 p.m. she grabbed her brief-case and turned off the light in her office. She'd just called Sebastian and Kate to tell them she was on her way. They'd saved her some pizza and wanted her to hurry so they could see a movie. She was still a little nervous about letting them spend a lot of time together. She was afraid the stability Sebastian offered would prove to be an illusion, as it had with Oliver. But he and Kate seemed to be getting along. Kate had sounded happy on the phone.

"You have to take some chances," she reminded herself. Sebastian wouldn't disappoint her. She'd never met anyone like him.

Her cell rang as she locked the building. She dug it out of her purse, saw that it was her mother-in-law and hit the talk button as she crossed the lot to her car. "Hello?"

"Jane?"

They hadn't spoken since Sebastian's uncomfortable confrontation with Wendy. Jane wasn't sure she wanted to have a conversation with her just yet. She had no idea how Betty might react to what had happened Sunday night and didn't want to deal with a negative response. "Yes?"

"How are you?"

Using the button on her key ring to unlock the car, she tossed her briefcase onto the passenger seat, but she was too nervous and preoccupied to climb in. She stood next to the car, her head bowed as she kicked a pebble from foot to foot. "I'm fine. You?"

"I'm good. I just…I wanted to talk to you. Do you have a minute?"

Not really. But Betty had never used this tone of voice with her. At least, not since Oliver was killed. "Of course. What is it?"

"I'm worried about you."

"Mom, don't be—"

"I can't help it," she interrupted. "I know I've been at you to start dating again. But that man you brought here last night… Are you sure he's the type you want to get involved with?"

Jane hadn't been sure about anything, but she immediately felt defensive of Sebastian. Maybe he'd interfered with something he should've left alone, but he'd done it to protect her. She believed that much. She also believed it was more than Oliver would've done. "I know he might not have given you the best impression. But he's a very nice person."

"You're *sure?* You haven't known him long. That's what surprised me—that he'd attack Wendy when he's not really part of your life."

He *was* part of her life. He just wasn't part of their family. That was the real difficulty for Betty, and Jane knew it. As much as she wanted Jane to be happy, she also didn't want Jane to be with someone who threatened the existing relationships. "He's...different from us," she explained. "If he has a problem with you, he makes it clear. He doesn't pretend."

"But...is that *polite?*"

Jane nearly chuckled. Oliver had been a serial killer, but he'd always been polite. "Maybe not. It's honest, though. I think I need *honest* more than I need *polite* at this stage of my life." Jane checked the time on her phone. If she didn't get moving, they'd miss the movie.

"So you like him."

There was some disappointment in that statement, but Jane took it at face value. She thought of Sebastian's confidence and no-nonsense approach to life and smiled as she got behind the wheel. "Yeah, I like him."

"A lot?"

Jane was fairly certain that what she felt was much stronger than "like," but it was premature to admit it. "Enough that I'd like you to give him a chance."

Betty hesitated but ultimately acquiesced. "If that's what you want, that's what we'll do."

Jane smiled. "Thanks, Mom."

"Be careful," she said, and Jane didn't ask her to explain. They both knew what was at stake.

"I will. I'll talk to you later, okay?"

When they hung up, Jane was still preoccupied by the conversation and by the cautious hope she was feeling. She made a move to set her phone on the console so she could start the car, but it was wrenched from her grasp—and a pair of strong hands cut off her breath before she could scream.

Where the hell was she?

Sebastian paced the living room of Jane's condo. She'd said she was leaving the office, but that was more than thirty minutes ago. It didn't take thirty minutes to drive to Howe Avenue. He might've thought her appointment had shown up at the last second, but if that was the case, why hadn't she called him?

With a curse, he dialed her cell again. He'd already tried half a dozen times to reach her. Every call went straight to voice mail.

This one was no different. "Damn it!" he said and threw his phone on the couch in frustration.

"What's wrong?"

Kate stood at the entrance of the hall, her expression worried. After pizza, Sebastian had encouraged her to get her homework done so they could go to the movie. She'd been in her room long enough that he'd assumed she was engrossed in her math.

"Nothing," he mumbled, but he was too upset to sit down. It felt as if he should be doing something with his hands. What, he had no idea, so he thrust them in his pockets.

"Where's Mom? Didn't she say she was on her way home?"

"She probably stopped off at the store." He spoke casually, but when his phone rang, he snatched it off the couch.

Unidentified appeared on caller ID.

He punched the talk button. "Hello?"

"I've got something you want," a man said.

Sebastian's chest constricted until he could hardly breathe. He recognized that voice. Although it had been a while, he'd talked to this person at least every weekend for several years. It was Malcolm Turner, Colton's stepfather and murderer, the man he'd spent an entire year searching for. "What is it?" he asked, but he was stalling, trying to come to grips with what might be going on. In his heart, he knew Malcolm was talking about Jane. He'd have to be an idiot not to know. He could tell by Malcolm's self-satisfaction.

"You can't guess? She's not very big. She's a half-pint, really, especially compared to you. But she sure is a handful. Oooeee, what a feisty thing. Pretty, too. I can see why you'd like her, although she doesn't seem like the snobbish type you used to date."

Nausea roiled in Sebastian's stomach. He knew what Malcolm was capable of doing and felt helpless to stop him. "I don't know what you're talking about."

"You don't? *Tsk, tsk.* I thought you might be skeptical. But, here, I'll make it easy."

Sebastian's grip tightened on the phone as he heard Malcolm encourage someone to speak. Then Jane's voice came through, her words a frantic rush. "Don't do it, Sebastian! Don't do *anything* he asks! Take care of Kate and stay away—"

The scream that cut off those words went through

Sebastian like a shard of glass. Swallowing hard, he glanced at Jane's daughter. She was still standing in the hall, watching him curiously. "Malcolm, don't you dare...."

"Don't dare what?" he taunted. "Don't *kill* her? I might've broken her jaw, but she's not dead. Yet. *You're* the one who'll decide her fate. Not me."

Somehow, he had to remove Malcolm's power. "You're punishing the wrong person," he said. "I don't care about her. Not like you think. There's no way to hurt me through her."

Sebastian had struggled to make that lie convincing, but his performance evoked a laugh. "Nice try. But I know better. You dropped Constance for her, didn't you?"

"No. Constance and I grew apart." Jane was proof of how far they'd drifted. But there was no denying that she made him whole in a way Constance never had.

"That's not what Constance told me," Malcolm said.

"You're lying. Constance might be angry, but she'd never contact you. She hates you, just like I do."

"Well, you know what they say about a woman scorned. I can forward you the e-mail, if you like."

It was true, then. Malcolm was taking as much pleasure in letting him know that Constance had betrayed him as he was in having the upper hand with Jane.

Closing his eyes, Sebastian kneaded his forehead. What could he do?

"Sebastian? Is everything okay?" Kate asked.

She was getting frightened. He spoke to her openly, so Malcolm wouldn't feel threatened by any whispering and harm Jane. "It's fine. Are you done with your homework?"

"Except a couple of really hard problems."

"Can you work on them a little longer?" he asked. "I'd help you but this is a very important business call."

"So it has nothing to do with my mom?"

He winced at the hope in her eyes. "No." Would he have to recant later? Would he have to tell her that her mother was dead?

Visions of Emily's lifeless body, of Colton's, stole his strength. *No...*

"Who's that?" Malcolm demanded.

"Can't you tell? It's a child."

"Whose child?"

Sebastian waited until Kate was back in her room. "Jane's," he breathed, his voice barely audible. "If you kill Jane, you'll make this child an orphan."

"If you care about Jane or her child, I suggest you do everything I say."

"What?" he asked.

"I'm offering you a trade—your life for hers."

"How?"

"Come to the farmhouse."

Sebastian preferred to keep Malcolm in town, if possible, where there'd be a better chance of escaping or getting help. "I don't know where that is."

"Then get a pen. I'll give you the address."

What should he do?

"You still there, tough guy?" Malcolm asked.

"I'm here," Sebastian said from between clenched teeth and pretended to write down the address he rattled off. "When can we meet?"

"Now."

"You're asking for trouble, Malcolm. The police

haven't even finished processing the house. They could be there for all you know."

"Crime-scene techs don't work this late, not when they've got most of it done. And the police are in no hurry because they can't even find the suspect. We'll be fine."

As usual, it was too easy for Malcolm. Sebastian wanted to tell him he'd go to prison or hell—preferably the latter. But Kate had come out of her room again, this time on the pretense of getting a glass of water. "She's your only leverage," he said.

"What are you talking about?"

"You know what I'm talking about."

He chuckled. "That's one hell of a way to make your point, Sebastian. *She's your only leverage.* That's all you've got to say?"

That was all he could say in front of Kate. "I'll make the trade. Just...see that you don't—" he glanced over at Kate, who was watching him as she sipped from a glass "—you know."

"I won't hurt her. Unless you call the police. Do that and she's dead."

Sebastian knew that unless they got very lucky, Malcolm would kill her regardless. "I'm on my way."

"Clock's ticking," he said. Then he was gone.

Jane was handcuffed to a rod in the back of a utility van that had no windows, other than those in the front. She could feel the tires thrumming against the pavement, could hear music playing on the radio. And once she'd managed to focus her blurry vision, she could see the back of the man who'd attacked her when she'd gotten into her car. It was Malcolm Turner.

She would've known him even if she hadn't carried his picture around with her every minute for a week. She hadn't found him; he'd found her.

After subduing her long enough to bind and gag her, he'd disappeared. But he'd returned almost immediately, this time with a white van he left idling beside her Camry while he dragged her from one vehicle to the other.

Jane vaguely remembered him using her cell phone to call Sebastian. Then a torrent of memories descended—what he'd said on the phone and how explosively he'd reacted when she'd tried to tell Sebastian not to listen. It hurt to move her jaw. The way her cheekbone throbbed made her wonder if he'd broken bones in her face. Her right eye was so swollen she couldn't completely open it.

Had she escaped Oliver only to die at the hands of the man who'd killed Marcie? If she was murdered today, what would happen to Kate? Would Wendy raise her?

God, no—please, no. She could imagine the many small ways Wendy might torture Kate for mistakes that had nothing to do with her. Wendy wouldn't do it intentionally, of course. She was basically a decent person, and had once been someone Jane admired very much. But the hurt and resentment that had festered since Noah's death would eventually manifest itself. Jane felt sure of it. Problem was, she didn't want Kate to live with the Burkes, either. They were too old to be raising children.

Kate needed her mother. Which meant Jane's only option was to get out of this alive. As frightened as she was, as unsure as she felt of her own ability to withstand this fresh onslaught of terror, she had to dig deep, think quick, act brave.

She looked at the tattoo on her hand. She saw no answers there, but she did see a reminder of who she was. She'd been through this before and survived it. She would survive again. For Kate's sake. For Sebastian. Finally, she had a chance at happiness. She wasn't going to let someone like Malcolm take that away.

"Hey, you coming around back there?" Malcolm hollered.

Jane hadn't expected him to speak to her. He'd seemed too absorbed in his thoughts and the music.

With a tortured sigh, she laid her throbbing head on her arms.

When she didn't answer, he turned around to see her. She could hear the difference in the volume of his voice. "How you feeling?"

"Like I've been beaten up by a loser with no conscience," she muttered.

"That's funny," he said. "You're a real comedian. But maybe you should show some respect and just be glad you weren't killed by that 'loser.' It's not too late for me to change my mind, you know."

She knew that very well. But if he hadn't killed her already, he was keeping her alive for a reason.

"What are you doing, Malcolm?" Her tone suggested he was nothing more than a recalcitrant child. She wasn't about to give him the pleasure of revealing how much he frightened her.

"You know what I'm doing. I'm using you to get to Sebastian. I'm tired of his bullshit. We're going to get this over with once and for all. And then I'll be free."

"Maybe you'll kill Sebastian. Maybe you'll kill me, too. But you won't be free. Your actions will be with you every day of your life. My partners at The Last Stand won't rest until they track you down and put you in jail. It will *never* be over."

"Don't try to scare me," he said. "I outsmarted the entire police department back in Jersey. I can certainly handle three broads running a two-bit charity. They wouldn't find me. No one will." He laughed triumphantly. "Sebastian wouldn't have been able to follow me to Sacramento if I hadn't been stupid enough to trust Mary. And I never would've gotten back at him if he hadn't been stupid enough to trust Constance. It's trust that gets you into trouble every damn time. If you don't trust anyone, you don't have anything to worry about."

"If you don't trust anyone, you don't really have a life," she told him. "You might go through the motions, but it doesn't mean anything." She groaned as if trying to get more comfortable, but she was really testing the handcuffs. Was there any way to slip her hands out?

No, they were so tight they were cutting into her wrists. The pole was solid, too. Even if she used all her strength, she wouldn't be able to bend or break it. She was trussed up like a turkey, completely powerless as they hurtled closer and closer to the fate Malcolm had planned for her. "Believe me, I know about trust," she added.

"You sound jaded."

"I've got good reason to be."

"Yeah, well, don't we all."

Where was her cell phone? Malcolm had taken it. He'd grabbed it from her right before plunging his fist into her face. Or maybe he'd hit her with something other than his fist? She hadn't actually seen a weapon, but it'd felt more like a baseball bat.

"What would make you forget about Sebastian?" she asked.

He laughed out loud. "Now you're trying to bargain with me?"

"You've already killed his son. Isn't that enough?"

"Colton was just like his father. He deserved it."

"Colton was a *child.*"

"Shut up! I don't want to talk to you anymore!"

She pushed against the back doors with her feet. Maybe he hadn't locked them properly. "You'd be smarter to toss me out on the side of the road and take off while you can."

"I'm not leaving until you're both dead."

Those words brought back the fear. His intentions were unmistakable. And no matter how hard she pressed on the doors, they wouldn't budge. There was no way to free herself, no way out. "You won't get away with it," she said. But with every passing mile, it looked more and more as if he would.

Sebastian had dropped Kate off at Jane's in-laws and was racing through the countryside in his Pontiac. The police still had possession of the Lexus. He was getting charged for both cars, but that was the least of his worries right now. He hadn't called the cops about what was going on, but it wasn't because Malcolm had warned him not to. He planned to text David once he reached the house. He had the message all typed out. He just needed to buy himself a little time first. He couldn't afford to have the police take control before he was ready, and he knew if he involved them they'd do exactly that. He was only a civilian. They'd tell him to stay out of the way. But he couldn't trust them to save Jane. David cared about her, but not as much as Sebastian did. This was between him and the man who'd already killed his son. He'd known it would come down to this eventually....

But that didn't mean he wasn't second-guessing himself with every passing minute. As he drove closer to the ranch, he also grew more inclined to call David before he got there. Was he overestimating his abilities?

He didn't think so, but maybe he was no longer capable of being objective. He kept recalling the moment he'd laid eyes on the cold body of his son. Colton and Emily had been killed before Sebastian had even realized they were facing a serious problem. He wouldn't let that happen again. Ever. Not to anyone he loved. He'd save Jane if he had to sacrifice his own life to do it. A cop could give her no more.

The gun he normally carried under his seat rested in his lap. He was willing to use it if he had to—but he knew a weapon was no guarantee. Malcolm would have a gun, too.

So how would he get Jane out of the house before all hell broke loose?

He'd try to outsmart the son of a bitch.

The ranch house came up on his right. Slowing to a crawl, he found the driveway and inched forward, eventually parking to the left of a white van. Except for a single porch light, the place was dark. Malcolm had made it impossible for Sebastian to see inside.

But Sebastian had chosen the perfect parking spot; Malcolm couldn't see him, either. He wasn't about to march up to the front door. If Malcolm could get off a clean shot, take him down that easily, he'd do it. Then there'd be no reason for him to keep Jane alive.

After sending David the text, he left his keys in the ignition so Jane could drive it if he was lucky enough to get her out of the house, and he went around to the trunk. There, he peeled off his coat and strapped on a bulletproof vest he'd bought over the Internet several months ago. He had a flashlight in the trunk, too, as well as a pair of infrared goggles and an army helmet to strap it to. Twelve months of preparation had come down to this.

Although the temperature felt like it was dropping fast, Sebastian put his coat in the trunk. He didn't want to wear anything that might restrict his movements. He had too much adrenaline pouring through him to be bothered by the cold, anyway. "This is it," he promised himself. "This is where it ends."

After stuffing ammunition in every pocket, he closed the trunk with a quiet click. Then he crouched with his gun at the ready and began working his way to the back of the house.

Twenty-Nine

Malcolm stood to the side of the living room window. He'd seen the car slow, then turn down the driveway, watched as the headlights drew closer. He'd been tempted to shoot at that vehicle. Maybe he could hit the driver before this went any further. But he knew he might just shatter the window and scare Sebastian off before he could get him in the house.

He had to bide his time, wait for the right moment.... But his nerves were stretching taut. The forensics team that had been processing the house was gone, as he'd expected. They wouldn't be coming back tonight because there was no reason to think he'd return, but there was plenty of proof that they'd been here. Fingerprint dust and Luminol covered everything. What it revealed made Malcolm anxious to be on his way. The bloodstains on the carpet going down the hall and into his bedroom were the perfect shape of his footprints. He could see them fluoresce in the darkness and hated Latisha for forcing him to allow so much evidence to fall into the hands of the authorities.

"So what?" He told himself to keep a cool head. He couldn't get back at everyone. He'd take care of Sebastian and Jane, the two people who really mattered. Then he'd get the hell out of town and disappear for good.

Jane groaned. Apparently, she realized that lover boy was here. Whether she truly believed it or not, Sebastian was about to meet his maker, and there wasn't a damn thing she could do about it. Malcolm had tied her to a chair—gagged her, too. When Sebastian didn't immediately show himself, he put a gun to her head. "You'd better hope he doesn't try anything funny."

As they waited, Malcolm could feel sweat matting Jane's hair. Maybe she acted tough, but she was scared. She had reason to be. If he could, Malcolm planned to blow her away right in front of Sebastian. Maybe he'd even rape her first, take from Sebastian what Sebastian had taken from him. There wasn't enough he could do to torture the man he hated above all others.

He imagined wounding Sebastian, then tying him up so he could have all kinds of fun with them both. Maybe he'd slit Jane's wrists and rape her while she bled out at Sebastian's feet.

Malcolm smiled at the thought of making her moan and writhe in pain while Sebastian looked on, helpless to stop him. "Relax, sweetheart." He smoothed her hair when she began to tremble. "This will all be over in a minute."

Where the hell was Sebastian? Leaving Jane a few feet away, Malcolm leaned against the cold window, trying to discern the shadows over by the cars. Before his breath fogged up the glass, he could see fairly well. But he couldn't make out the shape of a man. There was no sound, either. No movement.

"You're pissing me off, asshole," he sang out, and Jane whimpered. "You get it," he told her. "You know he's pushing my buttons, don't you? I'm going to punish you both for that."

Then he heard a bang loud enough to wake the dead. He jumped at the sudden noise, relaxing only when he figured out what had caused it. Sebastian had just kicked in the back door. He was in the house.

Taking a calming breath, he turned Jane's chair in the other direction and stood behind it, his gun to her temple. The show was about to begin.

Jane's heart pounded in her throat as she silently prayed. *Please don't let him be killed. Please don't let him be killed.* She didn't think she could take seeing Sebastian shot down—not after finding Noah, the only other man she'd ever really loved, lying dead. She'd asked Sebastian to stay away, *wanted* him to stay away, despite what it meant for her. But she knew that the man who'd approached that Ione house like a member of the local SWAT team wouldn't play it safe. If she had her bet, Sebastian hadn't even called the cops.

What did that mean?

It meant someone wouldn't walk away from this tonight. That someone could be Sebastian, or it could be her, or it could be both of them.

Only if they were extremely lucky would it be Malcolm.

Determined to make sure that Sebastian knew where the danger was, Jane began to grunt and moan as loudly as possible.

"Shut up!" Malcolm hissed and hit her with his pistol, once, twice, three times.

Pain ignited with each blow. She could feel blood rolling into her eyes, but she wouldn't stop. Malcolm wouldn't kill her. Not yet. She was Malcolm's insurance policy—and Sebastian's handicap.

Following the muted sounds from the living room, Sebastian found what he was looking for. But he didn't enter the room. He used the kitchen door as a shield against any bullets that might fly toward him.

With his infrared goggles, he could see Malcolm standing behind Jane, who was tied to a chair. He would've squeezed off a shot himself, but he couldn't shoot in that direction, because he couldn't risk hurting the wrong person.

"Let her go," he said.

Malcolm was so angry, Sebastian could hear him wheeze with each gulp of air. "The stupid bitch!" he was yelling. "I'm going to kill her. I'm going to kill you both, so help me God."

"You're going to need someone's help," Sebastian told him. "Because if she's dead—you are, too."

"She's not dead," he cried and lifted her head by the hair. "Say something!" he screamed at her.

Jane groaned and her eyelids fluttered open, but she seemed confused, dazed. And she was obviously bleeding. The sight of her injuries made every muscle in Sebastian's body tense. Malcolm had beaten her. Sebastian hadn't expected that. He'd expected Malcolm to care too much about getting to him to risk hurting her.

Malcolm was losing his edge, sacrificing reason to emotion. But that wasn't a good thing. It made him less predictable and far more dangerous.

What now? Sebastian needed Jane to be conscious, alert. He needed her to walk out under her own power and be able to drive the car. He wanted her as far away from this place as she could get.

"Jane? You okay?" he asked.

There was no response.

"Answer him!" Malcolm raised his gun as if he'd hit her again, but Sebastian growled a warning that stopped his downward thrust.

"You hit her one more time and I'll shoot you this instant. Do you understand me?"

"You don't know how to shoot," Malcolm said, but that went against all evidence to the contrary. Sebastian was no longer the trusting, law-abiding dad Malcolm had known a year ago. And there was enough uncertainty in Malcolm's voice to tell Sebastian he'd noticed the changes.

Getting down on one knee, Sebastian took careful aim. "Try me."

It was a bluff, but it worked. Malcolm didn't strike Jane. Lowering his gun, he shook her with the opposite hand.

"Hey, snap out of it. Sebastian's here. Tell him you're fine." He tore off her gag. "Tell him you want to go home."

"I wanna go home," she repeated dully, and Sebastian wished, more than anything, that he could make it possible.

"Untie her. She has nothing to do with this, Malcolm. This is between you and me."

"Throw down your gun and I will."

Sebastian couldn't do that. The second he did, he and Jane would both be at Malcolm's mercy. "I won't give up my gun."

"Sebastian, get out of here." Jane seemed to be regaining her faculties, but Sebastian ignored her. He couldn't afford the distraction. Not right now.

"Cut her loose and let her walk out," he told Malcolm.

"Are you kidding me? So she can help you? So she can call the police?"

Sebastian's finger began to sweat on the trigger. He wasn't getting out of this as quickly as he'd hoped. The police were probably on their way. Would they intervene before he could finish? Would the surprise cause Malcolm to fire? "This is your game, Officer Turner. What kind of play do you want to call?"

"That's it. She's dead." Malcolm spoke as if he was tired of fooling around, as if killing Jane was his only way out. So this time when he put the gun to her head, Sebastian feared he'd really pull the trigger.

In a panic, he raised his own weapon to get off a shot he hoped would save her life. It was her only chance. But the blast that nearly blew out his eardrums told him Malcolm had fired first.

The noise took Malcolm by complete surprise. He'd been about to pull the trigger when someone fired at him from the other doorway. Who the hell was it? Had Sebastian called the police? Malcolm had been so caught up in his standoff with Sebastian, he hadn't noticed any other movement, any other noise—but he hadn't been listening for it, either.

Scrambling to take cover before he could be fired on from both directions, he managed to roll behind the couch, which effectively shielded him from both doorways. Jane was the only one out in the open. She was tied to that chair and couldn't move, but Malcolm didn't care about her. He thought it would be the greatest irony in the world if Sebastian shot her himself. Then maybe he'd rot in jail while Malcolm took off for the Bahamas or some other tropical paradise.

Another shot rang out. This one sounded as if it lodged in a wall. A third followed. Sebastian cried out to whoever it was to stop, but if this was a cop, he didn't seem to realize that another person was at risk. He just kept firing.

Sebastian dashed in to save Jane—and took a bullet. Malcolm heard the shot and the resounding grunt. He'd been firing himself, had done so several times, but he didn't think he'd hit anything.

In an instant, Sebastian toppled the chair and threw himself on top of Jane, protecting her with his body. Now that he was so low to the ground, Malcolm couldn't hit him without standing up, and he knew the second he got up he'd be dead.

"Who are you and what do you want?" he cried out to the stranger.

"I want you," came the response.

"Luther? Luther, stop!" It was Jane. She seemed to recognize the man's voice, but Malcolm had never met a Luther. Who was this person and how had he found them? Why did he have a gun? He was quite obviously not the police.

And then it became clear.

"This one's for Latisha," the man yelled and fired again. "You will *never* touch my daughter, or any other man's daughter, again."

Malcolm became aware of Sebastian pulling Jane from the room. He wanted to stop them, but he couldn't lift his head without the risk of having it blown off. It seemed the stupid son of a bitch who'd pinned him down from the opposite doorway was determined to keep shooting. But just as that thought went through his mind, the bullets stopped.

"Take her and get out of here," Luther called in the ensuing silence, and it was only then that Malcolm realized his error. The bullet Sebastian had taken must've been his own because Luther hadn't been shooting toward Jane. He'd been shooting away from them, giving Sebastian the cover he needed to get her to safety.

And now Latisha's father was shooting to kill. There was nothing to stop him.

This was over. He had to get out, but how? The police were on their way. Even if he could make it to the door—and that seemed impossible—they'd be on top of him before he could get as far as the drive. And being captured would be worse than death. Then everyone he knew from before, his family, his neighbors, his friends on the force, they'd all know what he'd done.

The sirens were drawing close. Seconds later, he could hear the slam of car doors and the shouts of men he didn't recognize. He had to make a decision. Dropping his gun, he lifted his hands and stepped in front of Latisha's dad.

"Do it!" he yelled. "Do it now! I'm right here."

His actions took the man by surprise. Seemingly determined to give Malcolm exactly what he'd asked for, he aimed. But then he lowered his weapon. "Hell, no. You ain't worth it. I'd rather leave you to your own kind." Then he fired a final shot into the ceiling and ran out the back.

The stampede of feet told Malcolm the police were coming through the front door. Scrambling for his gun, he reclaimed it and raised it, pointing at the entrance to the room. If he couldn't get Latisha's dad to shoot him, he'd provoke the first officer. But that officer didn't fire. Instead he ducked behind the wall and yelled out, "Put down your weapon!"

"You're not taking me in. I won't go to prison," Malcolm said. Then he turned the gun on himself. Squeezing his eyes closed, he swallowed hard and told himself to pull the trigger. One shot, and his brains would splatter on the wall. It would all be over. It was the only way left to win.

But he couldn't do it. He didn't have the guts.

Sagging to his knees, he let the gun fall as tears began to streak his face. Sebastian had won.

Jane couldn't believe that Sebastian was safe. She saw the dent in the bulletproof vest he'd been wearing that showed where the bullet had gone. It had hit him hard enough to knock the wind out of him. He admitted that it hurt, said he'd have a bruise on his chest, but it hadn't seriously harmed him. He was fine and, although she felt as if her head was about to explode from the beating, Jane knew she'd be okay, too. Once again, she'd survived.

"Where's Kate?" she asked as Sebastian held her in the back of David's car. David was inside now, but he'd called an ambulance, was insisting that both of them get medical help. Afterward, they'd have to answer a lot of questions. But that could wait. The police had more important things to do right now.

"At the Burkes'."

"Does she know that I was in danger?"

"No. I didn't tell her."

"That's good." She closed her eyes until she felt Sebastian nudge her gently.

"Can you believe it's over?" he murmured.

She gazed at the car that held Malcolm. He wasn't looking at them. His head was bowed as if he knew he'd made the biggest mistake of his life.

"He's going to prison," she said.

"He was a cop who murdered three people. They have irrefutable proof. I think he'll get the death penalty."

"Where do you suppose they'll try him?"

"Here."

"But he killed two people in New Jersey. They have the death penalty there, too, don't they?"

"They do, but they haven't had an execution since 1976."

An officer crossed the lawn and strolled up, frowning over some notes he'd been taking on a clipboard. "When I got here, I heard two different kinds of gunshots. But you two were the only people I met coming out. Was there someone else inside the house, someone besides the two of you and Mr. Turner over there?"

Jane sat up despite the blazing pain in her head and looked around them. Where had Luther gone? He'd appeared and disappeared in a matter of minutes. Why hadn't he stayed?

And then she understood. There must be warrants out for his arrest. If he'd stayed, he would've ended up in jail himself, even though it was largely because of him that she and Sebastian had made it out alive. "No, I don't think so," she said. "But then, I'm a little confused. I—I was punched in the head. I heard shots. But I have no idea where they were coming from."

The officer turned to Sebastian. "What about you?"

Sebastian glanced at Jane, seemed to grasp what she was doing—and why she was doing it. "I fired a few shots. And Turner over there fired a bunch. He hit me with one. But that's it, far as I know."

The officer frowned. "I'll be damned," he muttered and walked away.

Jane smiled at Sebastian, then asked for his phone. He pulled it out of a pocket that was otherwise stuffed with ammunition and turned it on before handing it to her.

She wasn't sure she could remember Luther's number, but after three attempts, she reached him. "How did you know?" she asked without preamble.

"Know what?" he said.

"Where we were?"

"I came over to the office to see if I could fin' you. I wanted to tell you that our boy was roughin' up some hos earlier today, that he was back to his old tricks. I saw the van turn out of the drive and knew it was him. That was the same car my girls described to me. I tried to follow it but lost him. Took me a while, drivin' that damn highway, to find it again. But then I saw it sittin' there, plain as day in the driveway."

"You saved our lives."

"You did all you could for Latisha. I…appreciate that."

It was the kindest thing Lucifer—Luther—had ever said to her. "Wow," she murmured. "You've got me feeling all warm and fuzzy. Like maybe you don't hate skinny white bitches anymore."

His laugh was a deep rumble. "Don' let it go to your head."

She slipped her hand into Sebastian's. "The police were wondering about a third shooter," she told Luther.

"What'd you tell 'em?"

"That we don't know of a third shooter."

There was a slight pause. "That's probably the best," he said.

"We thought that might be the case. But they may not let it go. The evidence tells a different story, you know."

"That's okay. They'll never know it was me unless you give them my name."

That was probably true, as well. "How can I give them your name?" she said. "I didn't see you there. I was too confused to really understand everything that occurred. And Sebastian didn't see you, either."

"Then there's nothing to worry about."

She could tell he was about to hang up. "Luther?"

"Yeah?"

"Thanks," she said and smiled as she disconnected.

"You feeling okay?" Sebastian asked.

She snuggled closer to him with a contented sigh. "I'm doing better than I have in a long while."

"Because you're in love with me?" he teased.

"Because *you're* in love with *me*," she said and pecked him on the lips.

Epilogue

The Valentine's Day party Jane had suggested was a great idea. With Malcolm in custody, Sebastian felt like celebrating.

He stood at the periphery of the crowd that milled around the conference room and reception areas at The Last Stand. There were a lot of people he didn't know—people who volunteered for the charity, legal associates and so on—but there were a few he did. Jane's former in-laws. Kate. Jonathan, a private investigator he'd met at the office a few days ago, and his fiancée, Zoë. Sheridan and her husband, Cain. Mary, too, had come at his invitation. She'd bought herself a new dress and was smiling and chatting with everyone. Gloria and Latisha were in the corner talking to Skye. Even Luther had shown up. He didn't mingle. He folded his arms and leaned against the far wall, watching everyone, but he seemed pleased.

"Jane tells me you plan on staying in Sacramento."

Sebastian turned to see that Mary had made her way over to him. "That's right."

"For good?"

"I think so." Unless he could convince Jane and Kate to go back to New York with him. But he understood why they were reluctant to do so. He didn't want to take Kate from a school she liked, either. Maybe when she graduated in six years, they'd be ready for a change.

"What will you do about work?"

"I'm hoping to stay in the same field. I have some interviews this week." He actually wasn't too worried about finding employment. Lincoln Hawke Financial hadn't been happy to receive his resignation, but he'd been their top performer and they'd promised him a glowing recommendation. He was eager to get back to regular life, to try his hand in this new tougher market and to start earning money again so he could buy the house he wanted for Jane and Kate. If he found a buyer for his condo in New York, he'd be able to do that even sooner.

"Wow," Mary said, but it had nothing to do with his response.

He pulled his eyes away from Jane, who'd just smiled at him from where she was admiring Sheridan's baby. "What's wow?" he asked Mary.

Her grin was crooked. "I don't know if I've ever seen a man so in love with a woman."

"It's that obvious?" he said with a laugh.

"You can't take your eyes off her."

"No," he admitted. But part of that was simply his astonishment that he could feel whole again when he'd thought he never would.

"I hope to fall that hard some day," she said wistfully

and turned to thank someone who'd complimented her on her dress.

Sebastian was about to walk over to the makeshift bar, but he saw Jane approaching with one of the TLS partners he had yet to meet. "Sebastian, I'd like to introduce you to Ava and her husband, Luke."

He offered his hand to Ava and then to her husband, a tall man with a military haircut and blue-green eyes. "It's nice to meet you."

"It's nice to meet you, too," he said with a firm shake.

"You must be very proud of Jane," Ava added.

"I am. She's an excellent investigator."

"I've come to that realization myself," she said. "What a story."

"I wasn't the one who saved Latisha," Jane said.

Ava waved her words away. "No, but you did your best and handled it all so well. Gloria tells everyone who'll listen how amazing you were."

Sebastian lowered his voice. "You heard what went down at the ranch house."

"I did." Glancing over at Luther, she raised her glass to him in acknowledgment, and Jane offered him a conspiratorial smile.

"Another unlikely hero," she said.

Sebastian remembered her saying that about the old lady who'd saved Latisha's life, but the sentiment certainly held true. Malcolm would've killed them both if Luther hadn't arrived when he had. "As unlikely as they get." Repeating David's line from that earlier conversation, he put his arm around her.

"What'll happen to the woman who gave Jane's information to Malcolm?" Ava asked.

"Constance? I don't know, but she's going to be prosecuted. The police have a copy of her e-mail on Malcolm's computer."

"It's hard to believe she'd do that. Could she really have meant to cause so much harm?"

He thought of the woman he once planned to marry—and was glad he hadn't. "She let jealousy make her do something stupid and now she'll pay the price. And she's not the only one. Apparently, Malcolm paid some lab tech to help him establish the DNA match. The police are going after her, too."

"Did she help him come by the body he burned?" Ava asked.

"No, she claims he was going to steal a body from a cemetery. But he was afraid that would make it too obvious."

"So he killed a homeless man," Jane inserted.

"How do you know?" Luke asked.

"He confessed," Sebastian said. "He's hoping to avoid the death penalty, so he's doing everything he can to cooperate."

David joined them. "Hey, someone's asking for you," he told Jane.

"Who?"

David motioned toward the door.

When Jane turned, her eyes widened, and Sebastian felt his own surprise. It was Wendy. She stood just inside the entrance, dressed for the party.

"Why do you think she's here?" Jane asked Sebastian.

He'd dropped his arm when she turned but squeezed her hand. "I invited her. I called and apologized for upsetting her when we had dinner. Then I said it was time to let bygones be bygones and get on with the business of living and asked her if she was up to the challenge."

"And she said…"

"She hung up on me." He grinned. "But judging by her attire, I'd say she's changed her mind."

He could tell Jane was nervous. She crossed over to her sister-in-law, looking hesitant, unsure, but that seemed to melt away when Wendy gave her a hug.

Sebastian wanted to approach but didn't. They needed time to work everything out. He watched them step into a corner. He knew from their expressions that they were in earnest conversation and smiled to himself. This was a turning point. He was sure of it the minute tears began to streak down their faces and they embraced a second time.

Shoving his hands in his pockets, Sebastian took a deep breath. What he'd been through, what Jane and many others had been through, wasn't easy. But with forgiveness and hope and the sheer determination to persevere, there could be a rebirth.

Smiling again, he went to get a drink.

* * * * *